For my family.

HIT AND RUN

Andy Maslen

TYTON PRESS

Acknowledgements

Thank you to my many readers, some of whom are fans and a few, friends. I love getting emails from you, and I promise to answer them all personally for as long as I can.

I am lucky enough to count among my friends people willing and able to take a book in its infancy and help me nurture it through adolescence to adulthood. My first readers were Jo Maslen, Merryn Walters, Charles Kingsmill, Jane Kingsmill, and Katherine Wildman. Thank you all.

For their help and guidance on police matters, I want to thank Sean Memory and Ross Coombs. Any errors on procedure, equipment, or the law are entirely mine. I am also grateful for Gabriella Gowman at Greenfields Gunmakers in Salisbury, who walked me through the technical points of long gun design, use, and purchase.

You *can* judge a book by its cover. For the brilliant cover on this one, I thank my good friend Darren Bennett.

My editorial and production team are a superb group of talented and forgiving people. This book is better because of their help. They are my editor, Michelle Lowery; proofreader, Jessica Holland; and production managers, Jason Anderson and Marina Anderson.

As always, I reserve my biggest thanks for my wife, Jo, and my sons, Rory and Jacob, without whom I would be a much lesser man.

Andy Maslen
Salisbury, 2017

ALSO BY ANDY MASLEN

The Gabriel Wolfe series

Reversal of Fortune (short story)

Trigger Point
Blind Impact
Condor
First Casualty
Fury (coming soon)

"I'll never pause again, never stand still,
Till either death hath closed these eyes of mine
Or fortune given me measure of revenge."
William Shakespeare, Henry VI part 3

CHAPTER ONE
Hit and Run

6 MARCH 2009

THE BABY'S CRYING grew louder. It had taken on a frantic edge. Richard Drinkwater knew the translation off by heart.

Feed me! Feeed meee!

But he couldn't.

Not till he got her home, anyway.

He didn't have the equipment, as he liked to joke to his wife. But she'd gone back to work with the Metropolitan Police, leaving precisely measured-out bottles of her milk in the fridge each morning.

Now Lola was hungry and she wouldn't stop screaming.

The traffic was murder. It was rush hour. And there'd been an accident somewhere to the north of them. It would have been quicker to unbuckle Lola from the car seat and walk her home. The lights up ahead seemed stuck on red. Even when they did turn green, one car, at most, managed to squeeze through.

"Come on, Lola," he crooned. "Soon be home. Then you can fill up on Mummy Ultimate. Kristina will be there too, so you can snuggle up with her." Sometimes he thought his daughter loved her nanny more than either of her hard-working parents. Either her or the giant teddy bear they'd christened, for no reason they could fathom, Mister Jenkins. When squeezed, the bear emitted a random sequence of squeaks, bleats and catlike mewing sounds that seemed to amuse Lola.

The baby paused in her efforts to burst either her lungs or her father's eardrums. Drinkwater's shoulders dropped a little, and his stomach began to unclench. He checked the rear-view mirror, sitting up straight in his seat so he could catch sight of his three-month-old daughter. Her face was red and streaked with tears and snot. As he watched, she drew in a mighty breath and then let it out again in a scream so high-pitched it made him flinch. He caught a whisper of milky breath in his nostrils that made him smile despite the industrial noise issuing from his daughter's tiny mouth.

A car behind him sounded its horn. Twice. One of those twin-tone numbers precisely calibrated to emit the most horrible discord possible. He angled the mirror so he could see the make. Bastard! It was a Porsche. Some rich git working in a bank and earning more in a week than he did in a year. *Well, darling*, his mother's voice sounded deep inside his head, *perhaps you should have become a criminal barrister instead of all that human rights nonsense. Then you'd be earning a proper living instead of scraping along the bottom looking after your so-called clients.*

His own car was a silver 1974 Fiat Mirafiori he liked to claim to friends was a classic. He slammed it into first and lurched forward, closing the gap between him and the car in front, a big, shiny, royal-blue BMW.

Lola's screaming had settled into a steady, metallic screech now. In for five, hold for a beat, let it out in a shriek until her throat caught and she coughed, choking and wailing to silence. Repeat till Daddy had an aneurysm.

Then, a miracle. The traffic lights ahead turned green again, and instead of merely sitting there as they cycled through amber, red, red-and-amber, green, as had been happening for the last five minutes, the traffic moved off smoothly.

"Yes!" he shouted, slamming both open palms onto the steering wheel and bringing forth an even more desperate scream from the baby. "Oh, sorry, darling. But look, Daddy's on the move again. We'll soon be home, and everything will be all right."

As he approached the front of the queue, Lola screamed again. *Will we have to wait through another red?* he thought. *No. We're going.* He put his foot down and surged towards the traffic light, smiling as he began to catch the car in front. He craned his head to snatch another look at his baby daughter in the mirror.

The baby burbled out a couple of random sounds, "da ba". Then she smiled, a wide, gummy expression of pure joy.

His eyes popped wide open. "What, Lola? Did you say 'Dada'? Oh, my God, your first word. In a traffic jam too. Mummy's going to have a fit."

He accelerated across the box junction, heart full at the sound of his name on his daughter's lips.

The light was on amber now, but that was just a 'hurry up' signal in this part of London.

The lights changed to red just as Richard Drinkwater reached the white line indicating where stopped traffic should wait. Oblivious to anything but his daughter's renewed screams, he flew across the junction to a chorus of angry blasts of motorcycle and truck horns. He drove on for another mile or two, through gradually thinning traffic, until he reached Putney. Turning off the High Street, he heaved a sigh. The road was empty ahead and behind, as if somebody had barred anyone else from entering this little part of residential London.

Sticking the indicator on and singing to Lola, whose screams had subsided to a steady, muted keening, he turned into the street that led towards Oxford Road, and their house, and sped away from the junction.

Then it was his turn to scream.

Approaching on his side of the road was a car. It was being driven at speed. He swerved to avoid it.

But it was too little, too late.

The bang as the oncoming car smashed his offside rear wing with its own front end was loud enough to rattle windows in the houses on each side of the street. He, himself, heard nothing. His slewing, bouncing progress across the street was terminated by a cast-iron pillar box, manufactured during the reign of King George VI, and as solid now as it was then.

The Fiat hit the kerb and left the ground. Richard Drinkwater's last coherent thought was that Lola had stopped screaming. Then the top of the pillar box punched in the side window and met his head coming in the opposite direction at thirty miles per hour.

As people began to emerge from their houses and run towards the car, intent on rescue, Drinkwater's corpse was catapulted back against his seat, his skull smashed like an egg.

Detective Inspector Stella Cole was sitting at her desk on the Specialist Crime and Operations Division's Homicide and Major Crime Command floor at Paddington Green Police Station. She was joking with a colleague about a recent case they'd closed.

"No way, Jake," she said, laughing. "He's as sane as I am. If that brief tries to plead insanity, she's going to get My Lady Justice Miranda Jeffery's patent leather stiletto right up her Cambridge-educated arse."

The paunchy, balding detective sergeant perching on a desk beside her spread his hands wide, revealing an expansive belly that stretched his grey shirt tight.

"You say that, Stel, but you weren't there when we nicked him. I'm not saying he had his old mum's corpse in a rocking chair, but it wasn't far off." He raised his head and called across to another DS. "Oi, Frankie. Tell her. Wayne Stebbings's flat. It was in a right state, wasn't it?"

The female DS ambled over, hitching up her black polyester trousers, which had slipped down over her hips.

"He's right, boss," she said. "Stebbings had all these dildos and whatnot lined up on shelves."

The male DS, Jacob "Jake" Tanner, grinned. "Go on, Frankie. Tell her the best bit."

Frances "Frankie" O'Meara blushed. "There was one of those sex dolls, boss."

"What, a blow-up one, you mean?"

"No. Like a real woman. Jointed and everything, looked like a sort of shop-window dummy." The blush spread, deepening from a pale pink to a furious coral. "She ... it, well it was all done up in underwear, boss. Like a tart's, I mean. You know, stockings and suspenders, corset, the works."

"Unbelievable," Jake said. "And as for his porn stash, well, let's not even go there, because…"

Frankie shushed him, her eyes signalling a warning. "Shut up, Jake."

From the door leading to the rest of the station, Detective Chief Superintendent Adam Collier was signalling to Stella. His handsome face was stern, lips set in a straight line.

"Stella, could I have a word in private, please? My office?"

He turned on his heel and left.

"Wonder what that's all about," Jake said. "Is it true you're going to confess to being the phantom KitKat stealer?"

"Fuck off, Jake," Stella said, rising from her chair.

She reached DCS Collier's office three minutes later, knocked once, then entered, as was station protocol when summoned by a senior officer for a private chat. Usually it meant either a promotion board was coming up, or you were in the shit. But Stella hadn't heard of any vacancies for a DCI, and Collier hadn't called her "DI Cole" either, so a bollocking wasn't on the cards.

Collier was immaculate in his charcoal-grey suit. He always was. They called him "The Model" behind his back because he looked like he'd been recruited from an agency to promote a healthy and clean image of the force. His white shirt gleamed in the light from the fluorescent tube above his head, and the knot on his bright pink tie was a perfect equilateral triangle. He glanced up, found Stella's eyes and held her gaze. His smooth-shaven cheeks looked tight, and there were creases around his eyes that brought his upper lids down to darken their irises.

"Have a seat, Stella," he said in a soft voice.

"Thank you, sir," she said, frowning. "Everything okay? You heard my lot just nicked Wayne Stebbings for the Mannequin Murders?"

"Yes, yes I did. Excellent work. We can close Operation Palermo today. Really, very, I mean, yes, a great result." He looked down at his fingers. "Look, I'm afraid I have some bad news. Normally we'd have a family liaison officer here, and someone close to you, as well, but we go back, so…"

Stella's pulse suddenly began bumping in her throat, and a surge of adrenaline flushed through her body.

Oh, no. Please, God. Not Lola. Please not Lola.

"It's the worst, I'm afraid."

No. Anything but that. My house burnt down. I'm being kicked off the force.

"There was a fatal traffic accident. Richard–"

That's funny. Who turned the sound down? I can see your lips moving but I can't hear what you're saying. Why call me in about a FATACC anyway?

Stella sat very still in her chair watching as The Model's mouth opened and closed. She could hear surf roaring in her ears, waves crashing in over shingle, then *shushing* back out to sea again. Her hands gripped the hard, plastic arms until her knuckles turned the colour of bone. Slowly, oh so slowly, she let her head fall back on her neck until she was staring at the ceiling. One of the tiles had a crack in it that looked like a duck. Or maybe it was a rowing boat. Or Portugal. She drew in a deep breath. And groaned it out again. It wasn't a scream. Not as such. More like the sound of an animal in pain. Her mouth hung open, and she let the deep, wounded cry sail out from between her stretched lips.

Collier leapt to his feet and came round the desk to comfort her. He knelt in front of her and pulled her unresisting body towards him and hugged her tight. The moaning went on, even when her head flopped forward like a rag doll's, and she buried her still-open mouth in his shoulder. Frankie O'Meara appeared at the door.

"Sir?" she asked, green eyes open wide at the incongruous sight that greeted her.

"Can you help me up, please, DS O'Meara? I've just had to give Stella some bad news. The worst. And maybe take care of her? I've got an FLO coming up to talk to her but, you know, a friendly face…"

As his words tailed off, Frankie came forward. She prised Stella away from Collier and hugged her shaking body to her chest.

"Come on, Stella. Let's get you somewhere quiet where you can sit down. Then I'll run you home."

CHAPTER TWO
The Whole Truth

22 JULY 2009

INHABITING HER OWN body like a spirit, Stella sat on the hard, wooden bench outside the courtroom. Beside her, holding her hand in a soft grip, was her FLO, a plump, sweet-natured cockney WPC called Jaswinder Gill. It was 11.30 in the morning, and Stella's first pill of the day, washed down with a tooth mug full of white wine, was smearing her grief into something harder to get hold of and therefore less painful to bear. She'd not been able to attend any of the trial, but under Jaswinder's urging had agreed to come for the verdict.

A clerk emerged from the polished double doors.

He looked down at the two police officers.

"They're coming back."

"Come on, Stella," Jaswinder said. "Let's go."

Stella stood up, clutching Jaswinder's hand tighter.

"What if–?"

"We'll cross that bridge if we have to, OK?"

They pulled a door each and made their way to the seats reserved for friends and family of the victim. To Stella's right sat Jason Drinkwater, Richard's younger brother. His face was a mask of stone, scarred by childhood acne, betraying no emotion. He sat straight on the bench, staring ahead. As

Stella slid in next to him, he unclasped his hands from his lap and held one, palm uppermost, out to his side. Gratefully, she took it. Her parents were dead, both of cancer within a year of each other. Heavy smokers. Richard's parents sat on the other side of Jason. His father, Harry, offered her a small, tight-lipped smile, leaning around his wife. She, Annette, offered no sign that she'd even noticed Stella. Her lips were pressed together, accentuating the creases around them and the vivid pink of her lipstick.

Stella looked around the courtroom. The public benches were full. The usual mixture of pensioners who fancied somewhere warm to sit for the day, the trial junkies taking notes in grubby notebooks, and, she supposed, some ordinary citizens who simply wanted to see what happened when justice was enacted in their name. Also in attendance were a fair number of journalists, including a court artist, her bony hands twitching over the paper with coloured pastels.

The whole scene felt unreal. The barristers in their grey-white wigs and black gowns like crows; the judge in her red robe and longer version of the lawyers' wig. And there, in the dock, hateful, verminous, smiling – *Why?* – was the man who'd snuffed out her husband's life: Edwin Deacon. Cheap suit in shiny blue material. Blond hair cut short and greased into shape like a sixties barber's model. He was cleaning under his fingernails with one canine tooth and then inspecting his handiwork.

With a *huff*, a door opened against a damped closer, and the jury members trooped back in to take their seats. Stella watched closely to see whether any of them would look at her, or at Deacon. A young woman, third from the front, maybe twenty-three or twenty-four, looked at Stella from under a fringe of blonde hair. Her expression was impossible to read. A sad smile that could mean, 'we've brought you closure', or 'we've let you down'. When they were seated and the hubbub that accompanied any personnel change in court had subsided, aided by a sharp word from the judge, he turned to face the jury foreman. He spoke, in a crisp, upper-class voice.

"Have you reached a verdict upon which at least ten of you agree?"

The foreman cleared his throat, then he, too, looked at Stella.

"Yes, My Lord."

"What is your verdict? Please answer only guilty or not guilty."

The silence was total. Jaswinder squeezed Stella's hand. Jason's hand was sweating against her other palm. It tightened. *I wonder what he's going to say,* Stella thought. Then, *What will I tell Lola when she's old enough?*

The stocky foreman opened his mouth. He seemed to have moved into slow motion. Stella could see the jerks between the frames as the movie played out in front of her. She watched his chest inflating inside his suit jacket and shirt as he prepared to speak. Then, with an audible *click* inside her brain, reality snapped back into focus.

"Guilty."

Sighs and gasps hissed out around her. She could hear pens scratching at the reporters' notebooks and the oily scuffing of the sketch artist's pastels on the paper. Her mother-in-law was weeping, and a wisp of her perfume – Chanel No. 5 – curled away from her and enveloped Stella. The judge spoke again.

"Is that the verdict of you all or by majority?"

"Of us all, My Lord."

"Thank you all. You have discharged your duty, which, as I said at the beginning of this trial, is one of the most sacred duties a citizen can perform. It is right and proper that you should feel proud of your contribution."

The foreman smiled at the praise, turned and nodded to the others, and sat.

The judge looked down at Deacon, who looked, if anything, bored by the proceedings that were about to engulf him. Stella's focus was slipping again, and the judge's words were overlaid with a crackle of static. She closed her eyes, but that made the feeling of floating worse.

"Edwin James Deacon, you have ... guilty of causing death by careless driving. By your thoughtless actions, you ... on this family ... remorse ... three years ... and also banned from driving ..."

Stella was breathing fast, too fast, she knew. Her heart was stuttering in her chest. She heard Jaswinder from miles away asking her if she was OK. She nodded, but that made her head swim. Across the courtroom, she saw Deacon being led from the dock. As he stepped down, he looked directly at her. His face was clear and sharp against the darkening background. He smirked. Then his lips moved. What was he saying? It looked like, "You've been bad."

Then, mercifully, the curtains swung shut, and all was black.

The months that followed passed in a haze of tranquillisers and thin-stemmed glasses of white wine. During her waking hours, one thought more than any other circled around and around inside Stella's head: *three years.* Three! People got more than that for aggravated assault. With good behaviour, Deacon could be out in two. That wasn't fair. That wasn't justice.

Somehow, she knew she was going to get herself back to work. She was going to dig into the case files and she was going to find the evidence that would see Deacon retried for murder and put away properly. Just, not yet. A pill and a glass of the old Pinot Grigio first.

CHAPTER THREE
Sweet and Proper

3 NOVEMBER 2009

THE PHOTOGRAPHS SPREAD out on the table made for disturbing viewing. In contrast to the finely figured rosewood, which smelled of freshly applied beeswax polish, the images printed on the glossy photographic paper were raw, messy and grimy. The scene was the interior of what appeared to be a cheaply built council flat. A small box of a room, no more than ten feet square, steel-framed casement window on the back wall, cheap, functional aluminium fittings on the open door.

The lighting was over-bright: a flash aimed straight at the subject. It threw sharp-edged shadows of the few pieces of furniture onto the walls behind them. In the centre of the mud-coloured carpet lay a body. The body was female. It was dressed in a denim miniskirt, a white cap-sleeved T-shirt, through the thin, stained and ripped cotton of which could be seen a red bra, and that was all. The splayed legs revealed that she had no underwear on. The red knickers could be seen in the corner of the room, flung there, presumably, by her murderer. But the viewers' eyes weren't captured by the sexual aspects of the picture. That function was played by the wounds.

Both thighs had been slit open from groin to knee. The femoral arteries had been sliced into, and her heart had pumped virtually her entire blood supply out through the obscenely gaping wounds onto the carpet. A third wound had hardly bled at all. Presumably inflicted post-mortem, the slash across her throat had almost severed her head. It lay at a ninety-degree angle to her neck, connected by a thick chunk of muscle and connective tissue at the back of the throat.

Ignore the horror of the wounds, and what remained was a rather pretty young woman, of twenty or twenty-two. Soft, wavy, auburn hair framed a small, pointed face. The staring eyes were hazel and perfectly round, situated in perfect proportion above a small, upturned nose and a wide mouth.

"Not guilty by reason of insanity?" one of the people staring down at the photographs said.

"He had that clever bitch at 13 Lincoln's Inn Chambers defending him. The new QC. Marion Clarke," a second person said.

"She's the one who got the Hounslow Rapist off last year, isn't she?" The second speaker pushed the photos around on the polished rosewood, pursing his thin, pale-pink lips at each new angle of the horror.

"Yes. Fancies herself quite the psychologist. And she's a demon with expert witnesses," the first speaker said. "Had our shrink on the ropes in thirty seconds."

"We'll talk about Marion Clarke QC at another meeting," said a third speaker. "For now, what are we going to do about Nigel Golding? Did you see his face when they took him off to the loony bin? Smile as wide as you like. Evil little shit knows he'll be out on the streets in a year or so. 'Oh, *yes*, Madam Headshrinker,'" he adopted a singsong voice, "'I feel *so* much better now. The voices telling me to butcher my girlfriend have all gone *clean* away.'"

The third speaker brought the glossy eight-by-tens together into a pile and knocked them edge-on to the table, squaring them up into a neat stack before placing them to one side of his notebook. He looked up at the other two men.

"Call Mark Hollingsworth at SCO19. We'll need a team of his firearms chaps and an armed response vehicle."

The following day, at eight thirty in the morning, the Right Honourable Nigel Golding, Seventeenth Earl of Broome and Gresham, was being transferred to an armoured van from a holding cell beneath the Central

Criminal Court on Old Bailey, the street that had given the court its popular name.

He'd avoided prison, as do all offenders deemed not guilty by reason of insanity. In fairness to his lawyer, the insanity idea had been all his own. From the moment he'd been arrested, after being found drenched in blood and out of his head on crystal meth and high-grade Dutch skunk in his eighteen-and-a-half-million-pound penthouse apartment in Mayfair, he'd begun to play the role of a paranoid schizophrenic.

"They told me to do it!" he'd screamed at the arresting officers. "Uriel, Jegudiel, Barachiel: the archangels. They gave me orders. To stop him using the body of a human woman. She was Satan. I saw the red lights behind her eyes."

Then he'd sprung at the female detective, clawing at her face and earning himself a swift and brutal clout from her uniformed male colleague's extendible baton. The journey to Paddington Green Police Station had passed for him in a hazy nightmare of grinning clowns and talking Labrador puppies.

Throughout the booking procedure in the custody suite, the many interviews, the conversations with his solicitor, and his brief, Golding had maintained the shrieking persona he'd adopted: "Crazy Nige," as he'd mentally dubbed himself.

With time to kill awaiting his trial, bail having been denied, he refined and expanded his delusional narrative. The archangels were a masterstroke, he felt, but too commonplace. Waking at three one morning, he'd had a brainwave. Celebrities! Or, more specifically, a single celebrity. Rebecca Purefoy, the British actress as famous for her sex tapes and drunken selfies as her roles in a blockbuster female serial killer film.

"She told me!" he hissed at his lawyer, dotting her palely dusted cheeks with frothy little bubbles of saliva. "She wants to marry me. But she's under attack from Satan. He was using Francesca to get to Rebecca. 'Kill the vessel, kill the possessor,' that's what Becky told me. She loves me, you see. She always has. But she needs to be safe."

His performance in court was as flawless as his lawyer's complexion. Under her gentle questioning, and the rather more aggressive line of interrogation from the QC representing the Crown, he stuck to his script. At one point, he turned to the judge and began growling and gabbling in a low, guttural tone he'd seen used in a late-night rerun of *The Exorcist*.

He was smiling to himself as the private guards working for the prison security contractor escorted him up from the basement cells through a tunnel to the reasonably clean and reasonably fresh air at street level on Warwick Lane. He was looking forward to kicking back at some leafy sanatorium for the criminally insane. A bit of occupational therapy, group chest-beating with half a dozen losers with more tats than teeth, daily therapy sessions with some well-meaning cunt in a cheap suit and blood-coloured lipstick. And then, in the fullness of time, release. Or escape.

The Right Honourable Nigel had long known the true condition that infected his soul. He suspected his father and mother had too. Hence the strict military boarding school, isolated from the rest of the world by hundreds of square miles of bleak Scottish moorland. Hence the constant observation by an ex-British marine commando they had hired as his "valet." Hence their willingness to indulge him in solo rifle-hunting trips out onto the mountains. Where he could kill, butcher and consume whatever four-legged mammals he could bring down.

"I'm your basic, common-or-garden psychopath," he'd confided to a slaughtered stag one crisp autumn morning, as he'd squatted beside its gutted torso, munching contentedly on its heart and watching the steam rising from the pile of hot, stinking, silvery-purple guts beside him.

Outside, a waxy, yellow, November sun was shining. It warmed the skin but not the air, which was as crisp and still as it had been when he field-dressed the stag. Golding lifted his face to the crystalline blue sky and stretched his lips wide in a grin.

"Do you feel that?" he asked the guards. "Beautiful day, isn't it?" He pointed up with his cuffed hands.

"Shut up, you," the taller of the two men said in a low growl, yanking his prisoner's arms down again. "You should be going to Pentonville for what you done to that lass, or better yet, a fucking deep hole in the ground."

Golding shrugged as the other guard unlocked the rear doors of the white armoured van and thrust a hand in the small of his back so he stumbled as he climbed in, jarring his shin painfully against the raised steel lip of the passenger compartment.

Waiting inside was an armed police officer. Stocky, maybe five-feet-seven or -eight, shaved head, dark eyes, scowl. He wore the full tactical outfit of the Met's firearms squad. Black trousers with reinforced knees and thighs, black shirt under a heavyweight nylon windcheater. And even a Pro-Tec tactical helmet. On his right hip was a black nylon holster, protruding from which was the black plastic grip of a Glock 17 semi-automatic pistol.

"What's this?" Golding brayed in his drug-roughened upper-class drawl. "You've laid on a SWAT team just to get poor, mad little Nigel to hospital? How sweet of you. Now then, action man, shift along, would you?"

He sat down on the riveted steel bench next to the firearms officer and watched carefully as the two rent-a-cops took up positions on the facing bench. They glared at him. He smiled back. He was imagining what they'd look like with their heads in their laps.

With a rumble and a throaty clatter from its engine, the truck moved away from the rear entrance to the Central Criminal Court.

Golding nudged the firearms officer in the right bicep. "Is that real?" he asked, nodding towards the Glock.

The man stared at him for a second, face muscles slack, then returned to his eyes-front pose, placing his right palm ostentatiously on the butt of the pistol.

Golding looked across at the guards and rolled his eyes. He tutted. "I think guns killed the art of conversation, don't you?"

Then he smashed his left elbow into the armed cop's face, bringing forth a scream and two jets of blood from his nose. At the same time, he reached down and yanked the Glock free of the holster, the handcuffs forcing him to use a two-handed grip he was familiar with from TV. He delivered a blow with the barrel across the man's right temple. As he toppled off the bench, Golding stood, levelling the pistol at the two guards. Typical private sector:

they'd frozen. One had a dark patch spreading on the crotch of his navy uniform trousers.

"You!" he shouted at the man on the left. "What's the signal to stop the van?"

"It's a radio code."

"Well, give it, then. Or do you want me to shoot you in the face with this?" He gestured with the Glock. "And unlock these. Now!" he shouted, pushing his hands out at the guard.

The man shook his head violently from side to side and pulled his radio from his belt. He squinted down at it and pressed a button on the face. Some sort of emergency code generator. Seconds later, the truck screeched to a halt, throwing the two guards forward as the brakes bit. Golding had braced himself and stood above them, grinning down at the man fumbling with the handcuff keys.

"Stay there. If you move, you die."

Both men chose to obey. Not paid enough for heroics, was Golding's judgement.

Then the lock on the rear doors scraped, and a moment after that, the left-hand door swung open. As it did, Golding leaned back and kicked at it, doubling its speed, producing a sharp, wounded cry from the other side. As he jumped down, he saw a third uniformed guard sprawled on his back, hand clamped to his face, blood running freely through the clenching fingers.

With a laugh, Golding turned and sprinted away from the van.

He had run a total of ten feet before a shout stopped him.

"Armed police! Stop! Put the gun down! Armed police!"

He whirled round, Glock still in his hand, and pulled the trigger as he pointed it at one of the five black-clad firearms officers standing in a widely spaced semi-circle in the middle of the road.

The Glock clicked once, a sharp, metallic scrape. It was empty.

The Heckler & Koch MP5 carbines aimed at his head and chest by the police officers were not.

All five officers opened fire at once. The noise of the 9mm rounds exploding from the muzzles deafened Golding. But only for a moment. Then his auditory function shut down, along with all other vital signs, as the bullets found their target. With copper-jacketed rounds tearing into him, he spun and fell in a bloodied heap, the Glock still clenched in an outflung hand.

The disarmed SCO19 officer stepped down from the rear of the truck, a blood-splotched handkerchief clutched to his nose. He managed a grim smile. He picked up the Glock, extracted a magazine from his belt and slotted it home into the grip with a solid *click*. Then he holstered the pistol and went to join his colleagues, who were lowering their MP5s, moving the selector switches to safe, and slinging them over their backs.

"All right, Tom?" the sergeant commanding the armed response team asked.

"Tip top. One less on the to-do list, eh?"

The sergeant laughed. "Yeah. One down, all the rest to go."

Later, after swiping his ID card to check in his weapons at the armoury, the sergeant called a number on his phone. The name by the number simply said, P.

"Sergeant," the voice at the other end said, "how did it go today?"

"You'll see on the news, sir. But, basically, smooth as silk. He took the bait, and we got helmet-cam footage of him pointing Tom's Glock at us. Correct verbal warnings given and clearly audible. Couple of civilians took some phone footage, which we've had copied. Sir?"

"What is it, sergeant?"

"The suspensions. The investigation by Professional Standards and the IPCC. I don't want any of my lads charged with murder."

"Don't you worry about that. Leave it to me. The chairman of the IPCC is," he paused, "a friend."

"Thank you, sir."

"Check your account at midnight. I think you'll be happy. As will your wife. Where was it she wanted to go this year?"

"Florida, sir."

"Yes, well, I'd buy her a new bikini if I were you."

*

A pizza delivery driver looked up at the window of the four-storey house in London's Belgravia area as he sped northward along Eaton Place. He was a recent arrival from Afghanistan and not entirely legal. What had caught his eye was a trio of faces at a third-storey window, their complexions rendered an eerie pale blue by the screen they were staring at. Then an oncoming taxi parped its horn at him, and he corrected his line and carried on towards his next drop. Had he instead delivered the pizzas to number thirty-one, he would have been greeted by Sir Christopher De Bree QC, although not with any great degree of warmth. De Bree had taken silk ten years earlier and now, as a Queen's Counsel, was often to be found in this Crown Court or that one, and often the Old Bailey itself, prosecuting the most serious cases of murder, assault, terrorism, sexual violence and arson. He had lost his most recent case, which was why he now hosted six colleagues in his oak-panelled home office.

Between them, the five men and two women gathered round the computer monitor had seven bachelor's degrees, three PhDs, five law degrees, two knighthoods, and a baronetcy, and personal wealth of over seven hundred million pounds. Several would have been familiar to viewers of television news or consumers of online journalism. They would often be seen on the steps of the Central Criminal Court or the High Court, offering comments to the gathered media on the outcome of this case or that appeal.

As well as senior positions in the law, they shared something else.

They were members of the Executive Council of *Pro Patria Mori*.

"To die for one's country" might have been the English translation of the group's name, but none of its august members had any intention of doing so themselves. Or, at least, not until they had reached a good and well-remunerated old age. No. The people whose deaths for Britain they had in mind were criminals. Or, not precisely criminals. People who, it was quite obvious, were lawbreakers of the most serious and unrepentant kind, but for whom the law was an inadequate adversary. Either because they were wealthy or well-connected enough to afford clever lawyers, or because failings in the chain of evidence hampered a swift and efficient prosecution, or because of witness nobbling, or, simply, because the idiots who so often seemed to turn up on juries were incapable of seeing the evil standing meekly in the dock in front of them.

Their grumbles coalesced around a handful of problems, as they saw them. The parlous state of British justice. The enfeebling effect of the European Union, with its damnable Court of Justice. And the new breed of hand-wringing human rights lawyers. In response, the group of senior law makers, law enforcers and law testers had met in a club in London's St James's district the year before and decided to do something about it.

The result was Pro Patria Mori, or PPM as it quickly became known by its members. A club with very few rules, but the strictest penalties for breaking them. Rule number one: members to work for the good of Great Britain at all times, placing country above individual rights. Rule number two: justice is more important than the law and will be sought by members whenever and wherever their talents, connections and abilities allow. Rule number three: absolute secrecy. A handful of others had been agreed upon, including a solemn oath to support the police, but these three formed the group's credo.

Because the members enjoyed extremely senior positions within the British establishment, they had access to the kinds of resources that allowed them to suborn, cajole, bribe or blackmail such additional personnel as they needed from time to time. Civil servants with gambling problems, politicians with their hands in the till, police officers with larger houses and more expensive cars than their salaries should have made possible: all were under the magnifying glass – and thumb – of Pro Patria Mori.

The people enjoying the helmet-cam video in De Bree's home office that night were the group's founders. As Nigel Golding emerged from the back of the prison transport van, one of them inhaled sharply.

"There he is, the little shit," she said. "He wouldn't have got away with an insanity plea if I'd been hearing the case."

"No, Jan," the man beside her said. "You'd have been reaching for the black silk square, wouldn't you?"

"Shh, you two!" said a second man. "He's about to get the death penalty anyway."

Seven pairs of eyes focused on the screen as the firearms officers' cries of "Armed police!" blared from the PC's speakers.

They watched as Golding swung his gun arm up and pulled the trigger on the empty weapon.

Then the camera-bearing officer and his four colleagues opened fire.

"Yes!" someone hissed in the room, as blood and brain sprayed from the back of Golding's head. A dozen or more bullet wounds bloomed scarlet on the front of his blue-and-white-striped prison-issue shirt as he collapsed, twisting clockwise into an untidy pile of limbs, arms flung outward, the pistol still clutched in his right hand.

"Good riddance," the senior policeman said with a satisfied smile. "What's that, seven?"

"Eight, George. That teenaged rapist hanged himself in Wandsworth last month, remember?"

"Oh, yes. Silly me. Eight. Not bad for less than a year's operations, eh?"

As the footage snapped off, the members returned to the sitting room and reclined on dark-green leather sofas to drink De Bree's Taittinger champagne and eat lobster rolls, thoughtfully provided by their host, who had prosecuted in Crown vs. Golding, and lost. Then won.

CHAPTER FOUR
Back in Harness

6 MARCH 2010

"HELLO EVERYONE. MY name is Stella Cole. And I am," she sighed, willing herself to complete the litany, "addicted to tranquillisers. And Pinot Grigio."

The circle of twelve faces – some male, some female, some old, some young, some clear-skinned, some ragged with sores or sunken where teeth had fallen out – turned to Stella. Most managed a smile of some kind.

"Hi, Stella," they said in dreary unison.

"I haven't had a pill, or a drink, for two months, three weeks, four days and seven and a half hours."

The others clapped politely at this, the routine outlining of an addict's sobriety.

The group were sitting in a circle on grey plastic chairs with the kind of tubular steel legs designed to make stacking easy. The room was in the basement of a church – dusty parquet flooring, an upright piano shrouded in a faded red velvet curtain on one side, posters for mum-and-toddler music classes jostling for wall space with parish notices.

"That's brilliant, Stella," Clare, the youngish woman running the group, said with a smile as dishonest as her hair dye. In fact, she'd been at pains to point out to Stella when she'd attended her first meeting that she didn't so much see her role as to "run" the group as to "look after it".

"I'm like a shepherd. Or a shepherdess, I suppose," she'd said, then giggled. "If you're my sheep, I must be Bo Peep."

Stella had, briefly, considered punching this earnest, bespectacled woman with her sensible, one-inch heels and neat, blonde bob with half an inch of dark roots. Instead, she'd taken her plastic cup of scalding instant coffee to a chair as far as possible from Clare's.

Now, she felt she actually had something to share with the group.

"I've been to see our occupational health department and the FME, sorry, I mean force medical officer, and I've been signed off for return to duty. So, I'll be chasing the bad guys again starting next Monday."

Her news brought forth a smattering of applause.

"Well done, Stella," the doughy, heavily tattooed woman next to her said, turning in her chair. "Just keep coming here, won't you? I mean, the stress and everything. Don't want to fall off the wagon, do you?"

Stella smiled. "Don't worry, Sue. Job or no job, you won't get rid of me that easily. You'll still be seeing my ugly mug around here. Even if they do keep serving this shit coffee."

A few people laughed, and the meeting moved on.

*

Stella walked into the CID office. But why was the whole of the Murder Investigation Team laughing at her? It was her first day back on the job. She was a young widow. A recovering pill-head and alcoholic. Surely she deserved a little pity? A little compassion?

Then she looked down.

No trousers. Her feet stuck into scuffed black mules. And her knickers were on inside out. The label was showing. They were laughing so hard she couldn't hear herself think.

No. This is ridiculous. Wake up.

Stella groaned and rolled over in bed, flinging out an arm for Richard. It met only cold, smooth sheet. She turned the clock round and squinted at the green numerals: 3:15. Of course. When was it ever any other time? Ten milligrams of generic diazepam would fix this feeling. Or a snort of Smirnoff straight from the bottle under the bed. But they'd all gone down the toilet months ago.

She kicked the covers off and got out of bed. Wrapped her pale-pink-and-white kimono around her bony frame and wandered past Lola's room, then downstairs, flicking on the kettle on her way through the kitchen to the back door. While it was boiling the water, emitting strange growls and bumps, she lit a cigarette and stood on the deck, one arm round her stomach, the other held out to her side, the fag gripped between index and middle fingers. Her GP, a kind Jewish man with some sort of liver complaint that turned his skin a pale yellow, had almost begged her to give up smoking. But as she'd said, "Look, Doctor Samuels, I'm off the pills and the booze. Give me nicotine or give me death." He'd smiled at her dreadful misquote of Patrick Henry, but nodded his agreement. "Stella, after what you've been through, I suppose the occasional Marlboro Light isn't such a bad thing."

She stood now, shivering in the dark, the wooden planks rough under her bare feet, sniffing the tobacco smoke as it curled away from the end of her cigarette. Her grief counsellor had advised her that it was natural to feel anxious going back to work after any sort of prolonged absence, let alone one caused by such extreme circumstances as hers. But now, watching thin spears of pink rocket across the sky, she felt utterly calm. Not at peace. She doubted she would ever feel that again. But calm. No butterflies. No tremors or fluttering pulse. No tingling in the extremities. She was ready.

Except it was half past three.

No point even trying to sleep now, Stel. Best go for a run and compensate for the nicotine, she thought. Lola would be fine with Kristina, the live-in nanny, a sweet Polish girl built like a peasant with sturdy hips and a bosom that would have won her a job as a wet nurse a hundred years earlier.

She returned to her bedroom and pulled on sweat pants, sports bra, T-shirt, hoodie and her faithful Asics running shoes, and was out on Ulysses Road five minutes later.

As she ran down towards the park, feet flowing over the pavement in a familiar and comforting rhythm, she rehearsed her opening lines to Collier.

"Thanks for having me back, sir. I know you could have requested me transferred off Homicide. I won't let you down. I'm not over Richard's death, but I'm coping. Managing. I go to meetings. I have my support network. I'm taking care of myself. Now, what shit is there for me to deal with?"

Tyres screeched behind her, and she whirled round, heart pounding. A hatchback was tearing off in the opposite direction. Kids joyriding, probably. Or someone out putting their new toy through its paces.

"Fuck!" she said. Then louder. "Fuck!"

That was the one thing she hadn't dealt with. Not properly. Cars. She had a problem with them. She didn't like driving anymore. She hated it. Being a passenger was almost as bad. She'd sit there, sweating, palpitating. Feeling death was about to snatch her. In flames. Screaming. She'd had some therapy with a clinical psychologist paid for by the Police Federation. Cognitive Behavioural Therapy, it was called. Supposed to deal with what the young guy treating her had called "limiting beliefs". It had sort of worked. Enough for her to get a positive report to tag on her personnel file. She'd tackle it when it came up. She could always get Frankie or Jake or one of the others to do the driving. Or most of it, anyway.

Back home, she stripped off her soaking running clothes and threw them in the washing machine. She turned on the shower and, while it was running, lined up her gear on the dressing table. Warrant card. Notebook. Phone. Power pack. And her little helper.

*

Back in training, she'd been rubbish at the unarmed defence tactics course. But her superiors had said, even as a graduate on the fast track, she had to rotate through all the major roles, including firearms. That called for the ability to defend oneself and, if necessary, take down an assailant or a suspect who was resisting arrest, or attacking an officer or an officer's colleague.

Her UDT instructor, a bullet-headed, ex-army type everyone called Rocky, had taken her to one side after another session where she'd landed on her arse, this time with a split lip into the bargain.

"Listen, DS Cole," he said. "You're a woman, so you're not as strong as the men. I get that. But you're skinny too. And short. Some of those others, well, they're on the chunky side. DS Mills over there, she did aikido for team GB at the Olympics. You need a little helping hand. Give me thirty quid and see me here tonight. Six thirty sharp."

So, she'd fished two creased notes out of her purse, a twenty and a ten, handed them over, and returned to the classroom for the next theory session.

At half past six, she went back to the gym. All the physical education classes ended at six, and the place was dark. She pushed through the double doors and called out.

"Hello? Sarge?" Nobody called Sergeant Doug Stevens "Rocky" to his face. Not unless they wanted to end up flat on theirs. She flipped the light switches down, one after the other, and waited while the huge pendant lamps hummed into life before drenching the gym in cold, white light.

From behind her, a strong, hard hand clamped across her mouth, stifling her scream. She smelled aftershave and sweat. Her attacker wrenched her backwards until she was leaning against his chest. His right hand came round and into her eyeline. It was clenched around a dark cylinder.

Then the man released her, pushed her upright again and came round so she could see him.

"You're dead, DS Cole," he said. "Again. Look, I got something for you. A little helper."

He held out his right hand. Lying across the palm was a dark-brown leather tube about four inches long by maybe an inch in diameter. One end was closed with a circle of the same brown leather. The other had a narrow strap fixed over it with a brass press stud.

She took it from him. It was surprisingly heavy. She looked at him. He was grinning.

"What is it?" she asked.

"Let's call it a change purse. Undo the strap and take a look."

She flicked the press stud with her thumbnail and tipped the cylinder over towards her other palm. Out tumbled thirty one-pound coins; a couple rolled off her palm and clattered onto the gym's wooden floor.

"Sorry. I don't get it," she said, bending to pick up the errant coins.

"Don't you? Load it up again, and I'll show you what it's for." Stella dropped the coins back into the tube and clipped the strap over again. "Right. Come with me."

He led her over to a realistic male mannequin. It was a training aid they'd nicknamed "Marv" after a Hollywood film producer who'd gone apeshit on a plane. Some kind of legal high he'd popped in the First-Class lounge hadn't agreed with the free booze, and he'd attacked a stewardess.

"I don't want to hit him again, Sarge," she said. "It really hurts. In case you forgot, I'm not the one representing her country in ai-bloody-kido."

"Well, I do want you to hit him. But first, I want you to hold this."

He held out the roll of coins.

Insight dawned in Stella's brain.

She enclosed the leather cylinder in her palm, then wrapped her fingers and thumb around it. Opened them out again and played with the grip, just a little. Then she squeezed it tight. It felt good: not cold, exactly, just cool, and surprisingly soft. She looked at Rocky. He was grinning again, his eyes twinkling in the light from the overheads, the corners creased with what looked like genuine good humour.

She turned to face the mannequin, pulled her arm back in a short compression then struck out, straight and fast, as she'd been instructed, into Marv's throat. The soft silicone deformed as her knuckles connected, and the mannequin rocked back on its stand. She looked right at Stevens.

"I like it," she said, before whirling round and hammering her fist into the centre of Marv's face, feeling a satisfying click from inside the flesh, indicating that she'd broken his nose.

"Of course," Stevens said, "it's not exactly kosher for a detective to carry an offensive weapon, and any defence brief worth their salt would have a field day if their client claimed you'd thumped him with a home-made cosh. But I can't see the harm in a change purse, can you? I mean, what if you need some tampons from the machine in the ladies'?"

"Yeah, because that's all us girls ever do with our spare change, you sexist pig!" she said, but she was smiling. "Maybe it's called a change purse because it changes a person."

"I hope so, DS Cole. Those psychos out there make me look like a fucking new man, I tell you."

*

After standing under the hot water for twenty minutes, she went into the bedroom and stood in front of the mirror on the outside of the wardrobe door. *Jesus, Stel, where've your boobs gone? All this running is fine for your fitness, but you look like a boy.* Right. Pie and chips in the canteen every day until there was a bit more flesh on her bones. KitKats and Mars Bars, too. Full-fat lattes and kebabs after the pub. *Shit! The pub.*

Every addict would tell you, it was best to stay away from places that served alcohol. Especially those whose raison d'être was to sell as much of the stuff as possible. Restaurants? OK, at a pinch. Cocktail bars and pubs? No way, José. But that was where they did half their business. Mooching in mid-afternoon when the hardened boozers were nursing their sixth or seventh "lunchtime" pint and ready to offer a bit of information about some stolen laptops or who was into kiddie porn for the price of a few more. Or sitting around with your team at the end of the shift, swapping war stories or comparing notes. Well, it was orange and soda from now on, or J2O, or one of those other kids' drinks. The force was home to enough recovering alcoholics for this, at least, to be OK.

She got dressed. Functional, white Gap underwear, boot-cut jeans, white shirt, sky-blue knitted tank top, leather biker jacket, and a pair of low-heeled, leather ankle boots. She'd started out in CID wearing higher heels. But after catching one in a grating while chasing a suspect down an alley and going her length on the piss-soaked cobbles, she'd given up on that particular style of footwear, even if it did leave her, at five-three, the shortest member of the syndicate.

She loaded her jacket pockets with her gear, jamming her little helper well down into the right hip pocket, and went downstairs. She could hear little snuffles from Lola's room where her precious child slept within arm's length of her nanny, all paid for out of Richard's life insurance.

She dawdled over her breakfast of bacon, eggs, fried tomatoes, toast and marmalade – *start as we mean to go on, eh, Stel?* – but it was still only five when she loaded her mug, plate, knife and fork into the dishwasher. She wasn't due in until eight for her briefing with HR, then her return-to-work meeting with Collier.

She went into the spare bedroom. It had been her incident room. It contained a cheap desk from IKEA, a swivel chair and a filing cabinet in battleship-grey steel. One wall was covered with cork floor tiles, on which she'd pinned photographs, street plans and documents. No red woollen strings, though–that was strictly for TV super cops. She'd spent days on end in this little room, working her way through bottles of soft, fruity, seductive Pinot Grigio as she pored over witness statements and media reports. She'd accepted the verdict. She'd accepted Deacon's guilt. Her therapist had helped her to move past her blazing desire for vengeance. She was a police officer. A detective inspector. A bloody good one. And wasn't going to let Deacon destroy any more of her life. She would commemorate Richard's life by being the best bloody detective London had ever seen. But still, she analysed.

The questions hung over her like a cloud of biting flies. Why had he done it? Was he on his phone? Was he drunk? High? What was he doing on that quiet residential street in Putney when she knew for a fact his normal stamping ground was over in east London, Shoreditch way? Or was it more than just a FATACC? Was it a deliberate attack? A killing? Had somebody hired Deacon or somehow coerced him into doing what he'd done? She'd not been able – or allowed – to enter Paddington Green until signed off ready for duty by the FMO, so she'd not been able to look at any of the official files. She knew Collier would have a fit if he discovered what she was planning, so the whole thing needed to be handled off the books.

She wandered over to the collaged cork tiles and stretched out her right hand. She trailed her fingertips, with their bitten nails, over a photograph in the centre of the display. It showed Richard, her partner of seven years, holding their beautiful baby girl when she was two-and-a-half months.

"Oh, Lola," she moaned under her breath. "Why did he kill Daddy and not stop? How did he get away with it? Mummy's going to find out." She leaned closer and placed a soft kiss on the photo. "Then Mummy's going to see justice really done. And that means Mummy needs to be very clever."

CHAPTER FIVE

Light Duties

FINALLY! STELLA LEFT the house at seven thirty, black leather gauntlets in one hand, helmet slung over the wrist of the same arm. She'd checked on Lola, who was still asleep, with Kristina snoring gently in the single bed beside her. Good as gold, compared to the stories she's heard of babies driving their mothers half-mad with sleeplessness. She double-locked the door, then spent forty-five more seconds twisting the key against the stop and pulling on the brushed steel knob. Finally, muttering under her breath and biting her bottom lip, she turned away and went to the bike.

Ever since the hit and run, she'd not been able to even think of buying another car. But eventually, she'd realised that some form of personal transport was a necessity. Maybe for her eco-conscious girlfriends, public transport was good enough, but she valued her independence too much to stand around waiting for someone else to decide her needs mattered more than theirs.

She'd ridden bikes in her twenties. Hung out with guys who owned big Suzukis and Yamahas. Ended up buying herself a Harley-Davidson. Three months after the accident, and a newly car-phobic, thirty-two-year-old widow, she'd found herself hanging around outside a bike shop on Albert Embankment, staring through the window like a kid at a sweetshop. She might have stayed there all day had it not been for the hunky dude in a white T-shirt with a vintage Indian logo who wandered out and came to stand next to her. He swept his long, dark, but decidedly non-greasy hair away from his stubbled face.

"Pretty aren't they?" he said.

"I don't want pretty," she said, giving him a trademark glare that her pre-marriage girlfriends said used to burn guys in nightclubs who only wanted a dance.

He blushed. "No, sorry, I didn't mean because you're a, you know—"

"Chick?"

"No! A woman, I was going to say. They are though, aren't they? Pretty?"

Bless him. He was trying. And she did want a bike. And yes, they were pretty. Especially *that* one.

"Let's go inside. I want to have a closer look."

He led her inside, probably relieved this hard-core feminist hadn't castrated him on the spot.

The row of second-hand bikes started innocently enough with some small-wheeled scooters that she seriously reckoned she could outrun on foot. One had flower stickers applied to the helmet space under the seat. No thank you, very much. Running from right to left, the machinery began to gain weight and sex appeal, at least for Stella. A couple of two-fifties, a three-seven-five … moving up to five-hundreds, and then the serious stuff.

A Triumph Speedmaster, looking like some custom hot rod built in a garage. Matte-black, big, blocky, black-and-chrome twin-pot engine. Eight-sixty-five ccs. A Honda Fireblade, resplendent in white, orange and red Repsol racing livery. A whisper under a thousand ccs. A silver Suzuki Hayabusa sports bike. Thirteen-forty ccs.

She pointed at the Triumph.

"I like that one."

His brow crinkled. "It's a nice bike, but quite powerful for—"

Oops! Caught out again. "For?"

"A beginner rider. Have you got a bike licence? Cos you can ride a scooter on a standard driving licence."

She fixed him with a stare that had quieted football hooligans and drunks across half of London.

"One, I have a full bike licence. Two, my last ride was a Harley Sportster. Three, I want a test ride. Now. Please."

Clearly out of his depth with Stella, the salesman ran a hand over his silky mane and tried one final time.

"OK, great. You're the boss."

First, she bought new riding gear. Matte-black Bell open-face helmet, belted leather jacket – thick and protective but styled more like something you'd wear over trousers – black gloves and a pair of ankle boots.

After showing the guy her driving licence, including that precious symbol that indicated she was good for anything on two wheels, he had no option but to let her wheel the big black Triumph out of the shop.

"You bend it, you mend it," were his parting words, as she slung her right leg over the broad saddle. She nodded. Twenty minutes later, she was back inside the showroom, signing finance forms.

And now she was riding the Triumph back to work. She thumbed the ignition switch. The big engine coughed and then roared into life before settling into its familiar off-kilter idle.

She toed the gear selector down into first with a satisfying *clunk* that she felt through the boot sole, then eased out the clutch, lifted her feet onto the foot pegs as she crossed the pavement, and slipped out into the traffic.

Stella parked the bike in the underground car park beneath Paddington Green Police Station, enjoying the amplified blat of the exhaust as she passed the hard, sound-reflecting concrete walls. With the Triumph locked and levered onto the custom centre-stand she'd had fitted, Stella pushed through the door that led to the bare staircase up to the main floors.

After stowing her gear under her desk, on which someone had put a vase of daffodils, she went to the toilet to brush out her hair and apply a bit of lipstick.

At one minute to eight, she knocked on the door of Linda Heath, the occupational health manager, and went in. The woman behind the desk had cropped blonde hair and bright red lipstick. Her eyes popped wide as she looked up and saw Stella.

"Stella! Wow! You look great. Come in. Have a seat. Can I get you a coffee? Tea? Water?"

"It's fine, thanks, Linda. I had a coffee before I left the house."

Stella could feel about a million butterflies fighting to escape her stomach. Her palms were sweaty and she rubbed them on her jeans, hoping the woman who could help or hinder her re-entry into the Homicide Command wouldn't see the nervous gesture. *Fat chance!*

"Everything OK?" Linda asked, her brow creasing with concern. She had a buff cardboard A4 folder in front of her on the immaculate desk. Now she placed her palms flat on top of it. A waft of her perfume made its way across the desk: sweet, light and floral. *Girly.*

"I'm fine. Really. Just, you know, it's been a year and I'm a little–" *What? Freaked out? Fucked up?* "–you know…"

"Of course." The frown of concern morphed effortlessly into a compassionate smile, head tilted ten degrees to the left, mouth curved into a half-smile-half-pout that said, I understand, you lost everything and drank your way to the bottom, now I'm here to offer a lifeline to the top again. "Well, how are you feeling?" She opened the folder. Stella craned her neck to see what was written on the top sheet. It was a questionnaire of some sort.

"In general? Or about coming back to work?"

"Oh, in general. We were all so sad when Adam," she faltered, then regained her composure, "that is, Detective Chief Superintendent Collier, gave us the news about the accident."

"I'm okay. I still miss Richard. But I go to meetings and I see a counsellor every month, so," she shook her head, then shrugged, "on the road to recovery."

Heath's brow puckered for a second on "Richard", then she replastered her professional smile of concern onto her face. "That's good. You're so brave. Now," Linda's voice took on a brisk, no-nonsense tone, "I have to run through a little form with you, and then we can move on to discuss your new duties."

Stella frowned. *Good. Now we start.* "Wait. What? What do you mean, 'new duties'?"

"Let's do my little questionnaire first, and then all will be revealed," she said, in a theatrical, stagey voice presumably meant to reassure Stella.

"First of all, the basics, just so everyone can be sure I interviewed the right officer. You are Detective Inspector Stella Kathryn Cole."

"You know I am."

"Yes, but as I said, for the record."

"Yes."

"Hmm. You didn't take Richard's name when you got married?"

"Obviously not. Is that relevant?"

"No, no," Linda said brightly. "Very modern of you. Warrant number?"

Stella reeled off the letter and seven digits of her warrant number.

"Good! Well, at least we can be sure you are who you say you are. Let's get down to it, shall we?"

The next ten minutes passed as Stella answered a set of questions about her attitude to returning to work, stress levels, and basic physical fitness. Then Linda straightened in her chair.

"Now, question five. How would you rate your mood, on a scale of one to ten, where one is extremely low and ten is perfectly happy?"

Stella leaned back in her chair and folded her arms across her chest.

"I beg your pardon?" she said, heart bumping against her ribs. Then, as Linda drew a breath to repeat her question, continued. "How am I *feeling*? How the fuck do you *think* I'm feeling?"

"Stella, please," Linda said, placating now with a smile and the head cocked to one side. The other side, this time. "There's no need for bad language, is there? I'm only doing my job. We have to see how ready you are for a return to what, as I'm sure you don't need me to remind you, is a very stressful occupation. I mean, it's not as if you're a secretary, now is it?" Another smile. But was that a glint of steel behind those baby blues?

Stella breathed in deeply through her nose and let it out the same way, her eyes hard. She leaned forward and placed her elbows on the desk.

"Well, Linda, one year, four days and," she checked her watch, "fourteen hours ago, some evil little fucker," a pause to allow Linda to blink at the 'bad language', "called Edwin Deacon drove into my husband's car on our own safe little road, and killed him. His head was smashed in by a pillar box. So, on a scale of one to ten, where one is 'couldn't give a shit' and ten is 'mightily pissed off, angry and occasionally so fucking sad I can't stop crying', I'd say, ten."

Having delivered herself of this speech, she removed her elbows from the desk and slumped back in her chair. Linda smiled again. That infuriating expression, equal parts sympathy and professional patience.

"Oh, Stella, I do sympathise, really I do. I know you must be hurting terribly. If there's to be any justice in our world, evil people like that man will all meet sticky ends. But we do, still, have to compete this questionnaire, I'm afraid, and it will make both our lives easier if we could run through the rest of the questions without any more melodrama. You see, here's the thing." She pointed one beautifully shaped and red-varnished fingernail at Stella. "I have to write an evaluation for DCS Collier. And if you seem unfit to return to work, I could recommend a further period of rest. So, let's have a little bit less fucking-this and shitting-that and a bit more civility. Shall we? Now. Question six."

Struggling to comprehend the last few words uttered by the neatly dressed woman opposite her, Stella heard her next question as an indistinct mumble. She was asking about her sleep patterns.

"Eight hours. Every night," she answered. "Lola sleeps through, and the nanny's always there if she wakes, so lucky me."

She noticed that frown again. "Good," Linda said, after a pause. "Us girls must get our beauty sleep, mustn't we?"

Unconsciously, Stella reached up to twirl her ponytail through her fingers. She knew she needed a cut to restore her hair to its former sleekness. But booking appointments with hairdressers had slipped way down her list of priorities.

"It's 'we'," she said.

Heath smiled and crinkled her brow. "I'm sorry?"

"It's 'We girls', not 'Us girls'."

Two spots of pink blossomed high on Linda's pale, creamy cheeks. "Goodness me! A detective *and* a grammar expert. What other hidden skills do we have?"

"Sorry. Old habits. My Mum was a stickler for correct English."

As the questions came at her like bullets, Stella began daydreaming. Delegating the answers to that part of her brain trained to provide the right sort of information to officialdom, she thought back to her first murder.

A carpenter had been found in his workshop, face up on the floor with a one-inch chisel stabbed so deep into his right eye that only the worn handle remained visible. She'd turned away and vomited on the concrete floor of the converted garage, to the laughter of the other cops gathered round the gruesome scene. Bloodied but unbowed, she'd returned to the body, even going so far as to squat by the head and take photographs of the wound with her phone.

The wife and business partner both had solid alibis, and it was only after weeks of legwork that Stella had picked away at the wife's version of events to unravel the story. The two of them had been having an affair and had decided to get rid of the husband, pocket the life insurance and move to Portugal. As with so many cases nowadays, the key piece of evidence was data on the wife's mobile phone proving she couldn't have been at her book group on the day claimed. Not for the whole evening, anyway.

The older detectives had been adamant the murderer wouldn't be a woman. "They tend to go for poison, Stel," her DS at the time, a stocky East Londoner called Brian Gentry, had said. "No way a woman's going to have put a chisel through her old man's eye is there? Too bloody brutal."

The drinks had been on Brian the night they closed the case.

"Stella?"

"What?" Stella started out of her fantasy and refocused on Linda, who was eyeing her as if she'd wandered out of a lunatic asylum. "Are we done?"

"Yes. I just said. Do you have any questions for me before you go?"

"Just one. When do I get my reassignment to active duty form signed?"

Linda smiled. Stella felt the anger boiling up in her throat again. She held her temper. Just. "Let's not run before we can walk. I need to type up my report for Adam, I mean, Detective Chief Superintendent Collier. Won't be too long, though. I'm a fast typist."

"We're done, then?" Stella asked.

Linda nodded, already turning away from Stella to her monitor and tapping those glossy red nails on the keyboard.

Twenty minutes later, Stella was sitting opposite The Model in his immaculately tidy office. A large, blood-red, glazed pot stood in its matching oversized saucer on the carpet. Stretching from the surface of the compost almost to the ceiling was some kind of palm tree. Stella wasn't good with plants. Names of them or care of them. She'd had a spider plant at home, but after the accident she'd stopped watering it. For a while it clung on, turning paler and paler until its leaves lost their green and white stripes and became translucent. Then it bolted, throwing out dozens of babies on runners like a mobile. Finally, it turned brown, withered and died.

He looked up at her and smiled. His full lips parted, revealing the unnaturally white and even teeth that office gossip held had appeared during a Collier family summer holiday in Florida. As always, his hair was clean, shining, and parted with military precision on the left, the narrow white strip of scalp an even two millimetres in width all the way from hairline to crown.

He motioned for her to take a seat opposite him. Then he folded his large hands on the desk. She glanced down at the wide gold band on his wedding finger and a large gold signet ring topped with an oval of incised red stone on the middle finger of his right hand. Coarse black hairs curled on the backs of his knuckles. She wondered, as she often had before, why he didn't pluck them out; they were so at odds with the rest of his tailored appearance. He spoke.

"Welcome back, DI Cole. Stella. How are you feeling?"

"On a scale from one to ten, sir?"

He frowned. "I beg your pardon?"

"Sorry, sir. Just come from an interview with occie health. I don't think I ever realised how thorough they are."

"Linda? She's new. Has a doctorate in occupational psychology, and an MBA if you can believe it. Part of our professionalism drive to elevate operational standards. Don't worry. It's PBP now across most of the Met. Came in while you were, ah, away."

"PBP, Sir?"

"Professional Best Practice. It's a new one. You'll get used to it. Now, I expect you'll want to know about your new assignment, yes?"

Stella frowned. "New, sir? I thought I'd be back on my old duties."

Collier frowned. "The murder investigation teams are all operating with a full complement of detectives, Stella. I've taken a good, hard look at our orgchart, but they're all fully resourced. In any case, I'm not entirely convinced that's our best course of action for you right now."

"What do you mean, sir? You must have read my pre-return psych eval from the shrink at the hospital. I'm fine. I'm off the pills, and the booze as well. Going to meetings. The whole works."

Collier leaned back and stared at the ceiling before returning his cold gaze to Stella. "I did read it. And it's very encouraging. *Really* encouraging. You have made amazing progress. But—"

"But?"

"But I don't want you on the front line. Not yet. Give yourself time to reacclimatise to the job. It's not like going back to work as a librarian, after all."

"But I need it, sir. Please. There must be an MIT that needs me. Or what about another command? Special operations. Counter-terror. Sexual offences." *Now give me the bad news.*

"No, Stella. My mind's made up. I'm giving you an easy run in. There's a new cross-divisional administrative task force been set up. You're being temporarily reassigned there for a few months. Just until we can see how you've settled in. Light duties."

Stella barked out a short, sharp, bitter laugh. "Admin, sir. Really? You're putting me on the filing cabinet task force?"

Collier leant forward, fixing Stella with those dark eyes of his. "Yes, I am. Effective immediately. Report to Christine Flynn on the seventh floor. Corporate affairs. She's got the reins on this one. Now, if you'll forgive me, and it is good to have you back, believe me, but I have a meeting at the Home Office in forty-five minutes and I need a fresh shirt."

Stella stood. Swallowing hard, she looked down at Collier.

"Thank you. Sir."

CHAPTER SIX
Descent into Purgatory

FRANKIE O'MEARA MADE Stella a cup of the station's barely drinkable instant coffee – something to do with the water was the most commonly stated, and believed, explanation – and then leaned back against the counter, putting her lips to the rim of her mug and blowing.

"So, admin. Bummer. Thought we'd have you back with us, boss," she said.

Stella shrugged, before taking a cautious sip of her coffee and grimacing. "Me, too, Frankie. But The Model's got his mind made up, and you know what he's like."

Frankie stood straight and frowned at Stella. "I'm sorry, Stella. My mind's made up," she said, in a comically deep voice. "I have to consider what's best for the command."

They both laughed at the pinpoint accuracy of Frankie's impression of DCS Collier, only to choke back their laughter as the man himself popped his head round the partition between Homicide Command and the kitchen area.

"That's right, DS O'Meara," he said with a disarming smile. "I do. A word, please."

The immaculately groomed head disappeared and the two women glanced at each other, then snorted with more suppressed giggles. "Oh, shit, boss. I'm in for it now."

"Don't worry. Just do your 'sorry, sir' act and stick your chest out. You know he's got the hots for you."

"Guv! It was one drunken snog at a Christmas party. Two years ago!"

"I know. And look how it affected him. Must have been the pressure of your thirty-four Ds against that starched white shirt of his."

Frankie blushed a fetching shade of plum-red. "Got to go, boss. Pray for me." Then she winked and hurried off.

Stella blew on her coffee, took another sip, scowled, then carried the mug, which was decorated with the words, 'Not Now, I'm Doing Paperwork', along the corridor to the lifts. As she waited, she wondered why Frankie hadn't thought to ask about Lola. Perhaps tiny babies weren't her thing. Not all women had that maternal instinct.

She jabbed the call button and stood, looking at the digital number on the screen to the left of the doors as it flipped and shimmered downwards: 10 … 9 … a huge pause …

"Oh, come on, for fuck's sake," Stella groaned. "What are you doing up there, getting your old granny in with you?"

Finally, after what seemed like minutes, but was probably only ten or fifteen seconds, the lift was on the move again. Twenty seconds later, the control panel bleeped and the doors hissed apart. A group of detectives strode out, grim faced, one nodding at Stella before they wheeled left in lockstep and headed off towards SC&O Command's CID office.

Stella stepped into the lift and poked the button for the seventh floor.

"Hold the lift!" a male voice called.

She looked down, flustered, found the Open Doors button, and held her fingertip on its impressed surface until the voice's owner arrived and slid in beside her.

He was a bearded man in his early forties. More hair on his cheeks and chin than his scalp, which was shiny and pink from the forehead back to the crown of his head. He wore gold-rimmed, rectangular glasses on a thin, black, leather thong. His sizeable gut strained the thin, sea-green cotton of his shirt so that the spaces between the buttons gaped, revealing hairy ellipses of pallid skin.

"Well, well, well, if it isn't DI Cole. How're you keeping Stella?"

Stella turned to face him. She smiled a thin-lipped smile and stared at his piggy little eyes.

"Oh, you know, Pink, mustn't grumble. Just started work again today, actually."

"Listen, sorry about, you know. I mean, fucking awful way to go."

Stella maintained her stare. "You weren't at the funeral, were you?"

DI Howard "Pink" Floyd had the good grace to blush just slightly. "No. No, I wasn't. Thing was, Carol had tickets to see Celine Dion. I wanted to come, Stella, really, but those things are like fucking gold-dust. I did send flowers."

Stella looked up at the green dot-matrix display above their heads as the numbers worked their way to seven. *Why is the lift so bloody slow?*

"I know you did. Red roses. Very romantic."

"It was all they had," Floyd said.

"At the garage, you mean?" Stella closed her eyes. *Please let me get out, God. Please speed up this fucking lift.*

God evidently had other ideas. With a jerk that sent Stella sideways against Floyd's corpulent belly and a squeal of machinery from somewhere far above them, the lift came to a halt. The lights flickered, went out, then came on again.

"Bollocks!" Floyd said. "I've got a meeting in five minutes." He reached sideways and began jabbing his index finger at the button for the seventh floor. "Come on, come on," he urged the button. Then he screwed up his face into a snarl. "Well, fuck you, then!" he shouted and kicked the doors with the toe of his pale-grey, slip-on shoe.

Stella reached across and pressed the alarm button. "Relax, Pink," she said. "What's the matter, claustrophobia?"

"As a matter of fact, it is that," he said. "I've had hypnotherapy and everything for it."

"Take a few deep breaths then and try to stay calm. They'll have us out of here in no time."

Even though she would cheerfully kick the fat man's arse all the way down the stairs from the top floor to the basement, Stella also had a compassionate streak a mile wide. She didn't like to see people frightened, or in any kind of pain if she could stop it. Floyd was breathing steadily and deeply, though she noticed a film of sweat on his forehead and top lip. He'd closed his eyes too. Sweat patches had darkened under his arms, and she could smell the tang of his anxiety.

Then the speaker above the panel of buttons squawked into life.

"Hello? This is Orion Customer Response Desk. Who am I speaking to, please?"

To whom am I speaking? Idiot. "This is DI Stella Cole. Can you get this lift moving please?"

"Yeah, no worries, mate," the speaker squawked again. "There was a power outage in the master control unit. Just rebooting it now. Be about three minutes. You all right in there?"

"We're fine," Stella said, looking across at Floyd. His eyes were closed, and he was leaning against the wall and clutching the polished, stainless-steel rail that ran round the three enclosed sides of the lift. "Just get a move on, will you." She turned to Floyd, who had turned an unhealthy shade of pale green. "Hang in there, Pink. Help's on its way."

"I'm fine," he gasped. "Doing a lot better than that Lord Psychopath who got his last month."

"What do you mean?"

"Oh, come on, you must have heard. The Right-Fucking-Honourable Nigel Golding. Took a hit from the Cowboys and Indians Brigade trying to leg it from a prison transfer van. It was on the news, the web, Facebook, everywhere. What are you, a hermit or something?"

"Don't watch a lot of TV, to be honest."

"Well, you should have. You would have seen His Lordship take a few in the face. Bloody bastard. Got off easy if you ask me. Mind you–"

"Mind you, what?"

Floyd turned to Stella and leaned closer, beckoning her to lean in to hear what he had to say.

"It wasn't as much of a coincidence as you might think."

"What wasn't?" she asked, breathing shallowly to avoid inhaling any more of his flop sweat aroma.

"What d'you think? Him getting drilled like that."

"Like I said, Pink, I didn't see the story."

Floyd tapped the side of his nose, a typically comic-book response. "Look, I'm probably telling tales out of school, but let's just say he got what was coming to him. He might have got some clever Oxbridge-educated brief to get him off on an insanity defence, but there are people who see through all that flimflam. Powerful people, who can make sure justice gets done whatever those numpties on the jury bench say."

Stella was just about to ask him what he meant when the lights flickered again and the lift jolted into motion. Ten seconds later, the doors were opening on the seventh floor and, with a sigh and a shudder, DI Floyd squeezed through the opening doors like a cork leaving a bottle of cheap sparkling wine.

Frowning and shaking her head, Stella turned right out of the lift and walked the twenty metres along the green-painted corridor to her destination: an office door marked, "Christine Flynn, Corporate Affairs." As she knocked and reached down for the handle, she smiled quietly and nodded. *You did it. Stage One complete.*

Stella had never had cause to visit the seventh floor before. The haunt of Corporate Affairs and its bastard offspring – Communications, Public Relations and, *God help us, Stel!*, Marketing – it was the sort of place hardworking police officers tended to avoid if they could possibly help it.

Christine Flynn's office appeared to have been airlifted in from some other sort of organisation altogether. Whereas her operational colleagues of comparable rank enjoyed offices that reeked of officialdom, with photographs of their possessors shaking hands with the Queen or the current Prime Minister, a smooth-faced Old Etonian, Flynn's was an intensely personal space. The walls, for a start, were a shade of dusty blue that made Stella think of early summer days at the beach, misty skies not yet burnt clear by the sun. On those south coast expanses of pale-blue paint were hung paintings – or were they prints? – anyway, pictures of children picking daisies in meadows, flying kites on windy hillsides or, again, squatting on the sand, wavelets lapping at their feet as they built castles or dug little moats. A bundle of saffron-coloured sticks stood in a glass cube half-filled with an oily-looking liquid. They perfumed the office with vanilla.

The woman behind the empty desk was about forty. Auburn hair cut short. Minimal makeup. Her wide mouth was curved upwards into a smile so radiant Stella felt the heat of the woman's personality from across the room. She stood and walked round the corner of the desk, hand outstretched. Her long legs were encased in tailored trousers cut from some soft, dove-grey fabric that broke gently across the fronts of dark-green, snakeskin print shoes. All in all, a statement.

They shook hands, and Flynn gestured for Stella to take one of two low armchairs, upholstered in pale grey suede, opposite each other across a coffee table made from a single slab cut through a very large tree-trunk. Its rings of age were enhanced by some sort of staining process.

"DI Cole, welcome back. I know this will mean very little, but I am so sorry for your loss. Would you like some coffee? Or tea? I have chamomile, peppermint, ginger and–" she paused "–builder's, if you're like me and can't get on with all that hippy shit."

Stella's eyes popped wide open and she choked out a sudden laugh, caught out by the woman's earthy expression, the more so for its having been delivered in a cultured drawl from somewhere in the Home Counties. Maybe there were normal people in CA after all.

"Builder's. Please. And please call me Stella."

"Very well, then. Stella. And please call me Chris. Only my Mum and Dad call me Christine. Makes me feel ten years old."

The tea made and poured, Flynn spoke again. "I won't dress this up for you, Stella. You're a frontline detective, and a damn good one from what Adam tells me. So working in admin must feel like a prison sentence to you."

Stella took a sip of her tea, which was made from fresh leaves and so fragrant she could almost picture the hillsides of Sri Lanka where they had been picked. She shrugged and raised her eyebrows. "It wouldn't have been my first choice after a year of compassionate leave."

"No, I'm sure it wouldn't. However, this is a temporary posting, as I'm sure DCS Collier made clear. To give you some time to acclimatise."

"But what does it actually involve, this task force? I'm not going to be difficult, but me and meetings? Let's just say I have a low tolerance for boredom."

"The task force itself, which, by the way, the brass have decided in their wisdom to call Operation Streamline, is very much about meetings. But you personally won't be required to attend any." Flynn stopped again and frowned. She put her teacup down, dead-centre in its matching saucer. "It's records management we want you for."

Feeling some sort of show of disgust was called for, Stella clinked her own cup down, making sure to spill a little tea as she did so. "A filing clerk!" She let her voice rise upwards. "I'm a DI in the Met with eight years under my belt, and you're putting me in the fucking basement sorting out paperwork?" Her blue-green eyes flashed as she widened them, and she was gratified to see Flynn pull her head back under this mild assault.

"In a nutshell, yes. There are still files that haven't been digitised down there. The Evidence Room looks like something from the eighties. I want you to sort it out for me. By the time you're done, we should be ready for another psych eval. Then, all being well, you'll re-join your colleagues on an MIT and off you go, hunting down the bad guys. And girls, of course." Flynn risked a smile. She really was very attractive, Stella thought. *Good skin. Epic haircut: all angles and sharp edges. Must cost her a fortune.*

Enjoying her role, Stella reluctantly began to wind it down again. "It's not as if I have a choice, is it? When do you want me to start?"

"No time like the present. Why don't we finish these, then I can come down with you and introduce you to Reg."

Oh, shit! Reg the Veg. The most boring man in Paddington Green.

Police Constable Reggie Willing, the Exhibits Manager was well known in the station, if not well liked. Fifty-one years old, but acting many years older, cruising towards his thirty and a comfortable, pensioned-off life playing golf and tending his allotment. Ambition was to Reg as winning the Grand

National was to an old carthorse. Not. A. Thing. It said a lot that the powers that be had stuck him there when most other stations had a civilian running their exhibits rooms. He'd been shuffling about in the basement for as long as Stella had been working at Paddington Green nick. Now she'd be working alongside him. *Where, don't forget Stel, we want to be. Oh, yes. Sorry, Stel. My bad.*

CHAPTER SEVEN
Spring Cleaning

THE GENERAL PUBLIC have three basic ideas about the inside of a police station. Take the good, honest citizens, the ones who keep their noses clean and say "yes, officer, of course, officer, won't happen again, officer," when stopped for speeding, the ones who smile good naturedly at uniformed bobbies on the beat. They have a picture in their heads from the telly. Basically, the CID operations room. Lots of whiteboards and desks, and, if it's made by a particularly stylish director, some impossibly modern or, frankly, just plain impossible technology involving floor-to-ceiling glass panels with computer displays whizzing across them.

The same crowd, when called on to bail out their partied-out teenaged sons and daughters, or dodgy friends in the motor or jewellery trades, see more of the uniforms and fewer of the suits. Lots of foul, machine-made coffee and fouler tea. The faux politeness of overworked police officers who know your fence of a brother-in-law or car-stereo-boosting BFF is guilty as sin and why do they have to go through all this malarkey when banging them up now would save the taxpayer a shitload of money?

And the bad, dishonest citizens? The ones mugging, murdering and raping their way through life, or stealing other people's possessions and peace of mind, or generally acting like arseholes just because they can't say no to a final pint? Well, they know about the cells, with their smell of vomit, piss and disinfectant. The weeping and screaming from the sobering-up, the panicked and the mad. The barely concealed contempt from the custody sergeant and the bored routine of the fingerprint technicians and cheek swabbers.

But none of them know about all the background stuff that keeps a police station functioning as a building, a home for a massive public-sector organisation, and a machine for preventing, detecting and solving crime. Why would they? Sure, forensics is the new glamour job, with middle-class kids applying to study it at university. And maybe the odd computer tech gets a minor role in the latest cop drama, but basically, admin is admin the world over. Necessary, relentless and very, very boring.

Not to PC Reg "The Veg" Willing.

To The Veg, admin was about order. Precision. Tidiness. He'd spent twenty years on the beat. He'd pounded the pavements in the East End, breaking up fights between skinheads and gangs of Asian youths who'd decided enough was enough and had started carrying knives and baseball bats. He'd walked through the leafy avenues of Kew and Richmond, reassuring distressed, middle-class "ladies who lunch" that the police would do everything they could to recover their nicked Mercedes convertibles and BMW four-by-fours. Generally, that meant issuing a crime report number so the cashmere-clad ladies could visit a showroom in the fullness of time and replace the Merc or the Beemer. And he'd finished the active phase of his career as a foot soldier of the Metropolitan police, strolling through the shopping streets of the West End, giving tourists directions to Madame Tussauds, listening sympathetically to tales of bags snatched and wallets filched, and complacently accepting folded twenties and fifties from Arabs, Chinese and Russians who thought this was the way to treat police officers who were helpful.

But then came the breakthrough. The job Reg knew he had been born to do. Managing the records office and exhibits room at Paddington Green nick. After an interview at once laughably easy and the most stressful of Reg's entire life, he had been awarded the crown. His kingdom stretched over a floor the size of a city-centre supermarket, and the fact that it had no natural light or ventilation bothered him not. His remit covered all historical paper case files, the hundreds of thousands of exhibits from criminal cases, supplies – which sounds dull but in fact covers everything from toilet paper and pencils to tear-gas grenades and the paperwork from incoming shipments of new weapons for the station armoury – and personnel files, HR not having yet got round to digitising the records of the station's two thousand one hundred and seventeen employees, both civilian staff and police officers.

Reg was busy planning his next raised-bed planting scheme on a sheet of squared paper, tongue tip protruding from between his incisors, when the heavy door on its pneumatic closer hissed. He looked up. And smiled. Smiling was Reg's go-to facial expression. Partly because he was, at heart, a happy man. Partly because he had found, over the years, that it disarmed people, sometimes literally, and offered him time to think, a slow process at the best of times. Today, as he registered the two faces peering at him through the gloom, the smile widened into a genuine expression of good humour and welcome.

"Look out, Reg! Hide the weed!" he called out. "A DI *and* the head of Corporate Affairs. You'll be out on your ear!" Then he stepped out from behind his desk, manoeuvring his gut round the corner with a grace borne of weekends entering – and often winning – ballroom dancing competitions with his wife, and came forward to greet the two women. He brought himself into a comical approximation of an at-attention stance, held his pudgy hands wide and smiled again. "Ladies, to what do I owe this unexpected pleasure?"

Flynn sighed. "Reg, I think you know DI Cole," she said. "She's assigned here for a short adjustment period. A secondment."

"Yes, of course." Reg looked down, coughed to mask his embarrassment at being caught clowning inappropriately, then looked up again to give Stella a direct stare. "Sorry for your loss, DI Cole. Very sorry."

"It's OK, Reg. And there's no need to call me DI Cole. Stel's just fine."

Glancing at her watch, something in rose gold, Stella noticed, Flynn became all business.

"Well, I think I can leave you two to get acquainted. Reg, perhaps you could give DI – Stella – the tour and then show her what needs doing."

"*Naturellement!*" Reg said in a French accent so ludicrous it made Stella smile with genuine good humour. "Operation Sort This Effing Lot Out needs all the manpower – and womanpower – it can get."

Flynn left, and in the silence that followed the hissing of the automatic door closer, Stella could almost hear Reg's brain working. She broke the silence just as uncomfortable threatened to morph into downright painful.

"Going to show me around, then, Reg, or do I just set off with a ball of red string?"

"What?"

"You know, Theseus and the Minotaur. He unwound red wool so he could find his way out of the labyrinth again."

"Oh, yes, of course. No, you won't need anything like that. Just scream if you get lost and Sir Reginald of Recordsia will come galloping to the rescue."

He turned on his highly polished black heel and led her off into the bowels of the exhibits room. As they passed a desk cluttered with gardening magazines and a loose pile of various kinds of order forms, receipts and shipping notes, he pointed.

"That's where you'll find me if I'm not roaming my kingdom, Stel. Normally, I eat my lunch there; saves time compared to going out."

"What do you do for lunch?"

"Normally bring something from home that Karen makes me. Egg mayonnaise, that's my favourite. Now," he said, approaching a floor-to-ceiling steel mesh partition. "In there's your exhibits. Evidence, in other words, as you obviously know," he added as she opened her mouth to speak. "Everything that goes in or out gets signed for and countersigned by yours truly. And now by *yours* yours truly, as well." He winked. "There's enough illegal guns, Class A drugs, counterfeit cash and bloodstained clothing in there to start our own series of *CSI*. Mind you, we might need to work on the title a bit. CSI Paddington isn't very sexy, is it?"

Stella shrugged. The man's relentlessly cheery disposition and wisecracks were already wearing her down, and she'd spent less than ten minutes in his company. Next, he led her through to another room.

He pointed out dozens of rows of dented black steel filing cabinets. "Every original paper document from 1976 onwards is in them," he said. "Nowadays, they get scanned and entered into the system before shredding, but what with cuts and everything, there's a teensy weensy bit of a backlog. Plus, in the racking, you've got every bit of paperwork from all our current cases. Even after they're typed in, the originals have to go somewhere, so we get them all to log in and store."

"Who does the logging in?"

He shrugged. "I try to avoid it, get one of the assistants to do it. I'm not the world's most accurate typist." He dropped his voice to a murmur and looked theatrically up and down the empty room. "I suffer from FFS, you see."

"What's that, then? For Fuck's Sake?"

He shook his head, smiling. "Fat Finger Syndrome." He held out his hands palms upwards. His fingers looked like raw pork sausages. "Can't make them do what I want. For example, I'm always getting numbers round the wrong way, so thirty-four comes out as forty-three. Or 'witness'. Always comes out as 'wintess'."

More like witless in your case, Veg.

The following day, on her own in the exhibits room, Stella consulted the computerised listing of items logged under 'drug paraphernalia'. It took less than a minute to find what she was looking for. Halfway down the page was a reference number corresponding to a location on a rack and shelf. Nestling between bags of weed and assorted, brightly coloured pills was a white, cuboid cardboard box. It was about ten centimetres to a side and bore the logo of a medical devices company. The top had been slit through a shipping label that announced the contents:

BD Emerald 2ml Syringe with 23G X 1.25" Needle (100).

Inside the box were small plastic pouches, white on the back, clear on the front, each containing one slim syringe and a pre-fixed needle in a turquoise plastic sheath. Stella removed a single pouch. Then she went back to the computer and made a tiny correction to the record, adjusting the remaining quantity from "69" to "68".

CHAPTER EIGHT
Fight or Flight

BY THE END of her first week back on the job, Stella had learned three things. First, that the art of growing prize-winning vegetables was a lot more complicated than most people gave credit for. Second, that given the state of police record-keeping, it was a miracle any cases were successfully brought to a conclusion. And third, that she would cheerfully strangle Reggie Willing with her bare hands. His relentlessly upbeat outlook was no doubt a direct result of the full-fat pension heading his way, but it still grated.

Home at six p.m., she heaved the Triumph onto its centre-stand in her tiny, precious square of off-street parking, fitted the canary-yellow lock through the front brake disc, then headed inside to change, calling out "Hi, Kristina!" to the nanny, going to find her in the nursery and then giving her precious Lola a cuddle.

In the old, old days, Friday nights were special. She and Richard would have hugged, swapped news – his skirmishes with opposition lawyers, her dealings with arsey thugs – and opened a bottle of something cold from the fridge. If it was before Lola was born, they might have opened a second to drink with the Chinese food they had ordered. After she came along, they were both so tired it would be astonishing if they managed not to fall asleep in their microwaved ready-meals.

In the old days, after the accident, she would have still opened a couple of bottles of wine. Still have ordered the Chinese food. Then finished the evening by pouring a large vodka and sitting in front of the TV, staring at the inane, grinning presenters and their celebrity interviewees and wishing they were all dead.

But that was then. This was now. Stella Cole, clean and sober.

*

She couldn't remember exactly why she'd decided to get herself back together. But at some point in that year off, she'd gone to see Dr Samuels, who'd referred her to a specialist.

"Break the routine that makes drinking easy," her counsellor had told her. So she had. Every night, she'd go out running. A couple of miles at first, before she had to stop, doubled over and retching, before hobbling home, side pierced by a stitch, feet burning with blisters. Then, as she'd persevered, the mileage count grew. Five, six, seven ... into double figures sometimes. Along with her sobriety, she'd developed a taste, even an addiction, for running. The London streets disappeared under her feet as she racked up tens, then hundreds of miles.

After each run, she'd stand naked in front of the full-length mirror inside the wardrobe door, pink and sweating, and evaluate her physique. Her legs got stronger. The calves, quads and hamstrings took on the definition of a racehorse's muscles. Her stomach tautened and flattened. She couldn't stop. Not even if she wanted to.

The shoulders and arms needed some work though, she realised that. Stella had no time for gyms. Too many yummy mummies with their dinky designer shorts and crop tops. She Googled "home weightlifting for women" and skim-read the results until she found a set of exercises she could do with what the American blogger called, "your kitchen cupboard weight room".

After a few false starts, she settled on bags of sugar. Compact, good weight-to-volume ratio. Sets of ten bicep curls, lateral raises and overhead presses were easy, and she found herself powering through more and more reps, for more and more sets. She graduated to press-ups, ab crunches and pull-ups.

Soon, her deltoids, biceps and triceps had gained bulk and definition. Her stomach, never flabby, now looked as if six flat cobblestones had been laid just beneath the skin. She wasn't just fit. She was strong. Powerful. She could feel it. But what to do with all that extra power? She lay awake at night sometimes, burning with a desire to find the truth about the death of her husband. Would get up at two, three, four in the morning, put on her running clothes and pound the streets till dawn, swearing continuously under her breath and occasionally startling early-morning dog-walkers with the vehemence of her oaths.

She did some research, made a couple of calls, and tracked down Doug Stevens, the sergeant who'd given her the change purse all those years ago. He wasn't on the force any more. He'd taken his pension and set up a gym in the East End. He'd not gone for the easy naming options – "Sarge's" or "Rocky's" – instead calling his establishment TBL Fitness.

"It stands for Thin Blue Line," he'd explained, when she'd met him there for a personal assessment at seven forty-five, one rainy September morning. The gym wasn't huge, about the size of a school hall, but it was clean and painted white with a blonde wood floor polished to a satiny sheen. It smelled of soap, sweat, and something else – a tangy top note she recognised as adrenaline.

"It's cool, Rock– I mean, Sarge," she said.

He smiled. "It's OK, DI Cole. Most of my clients call me that. I never minded. I mean, pretty good role model for a fitness freak, wouldn't you say?"

She shrugged. "I guess, so. If I'm going to call you Rocky, you'd better drop the DI Cole stuff. Stel's fine. You remember Marv?" she said.

"How could I forget him? I seem to remember I taught you how to hit him properly, didn't I?"

She nodded. "That's why I'm here. I want you to teach me how to fight. Properly."

He folded his arms and narrowed his eyes. "And by properly, you mean?"

"Dirty. That's what I mean. Not what PACE says. Not what the Marquess of fucking Queensberry would say. I mean how you used to do it. You know–"

"You mean in the army."

"Yes, I mean in the army. If you wanted to put somebody down. For good."

He looked at her then. Hard. She returned the look. Maybe he detected a resilience in her unblinking gaze. Or maybe something else. Something determined.

"Maybe you should tell me why you want to learn how to fight."

"Self-defence. London's not getting any safer. I'm a single mother. I need to be able to protect myself." She did all but add, "Your Honour" at the end of this statement.

Stevens smiled. "And what instructor could resist that little speech?" he asked, with a grin.

"So you'll teach me, then?"

"Fine. I'll teach you how to fight, Stella. But there's something else you need to learn first."

"What's that?"

He whipped his right hand up, palm out, fingers stiff, and slapped her, hard across the face, knocking her sideways with the force of the blow.

"How to take it."

She rocked back on her heels, eyes wide with shock, tears starting from the inner corners. Her hand flew to the flaring red cheek where his blow had connected with a flat crack in the silent space of the gym. She sprang at him, right hand curled into a fist. He slid around the incoming punch with a lithe, twisting motion, caught her hand and pulled her over his outstretched foot so that she landed in a heap at his feet. Then he dropped to a crouch with his right knee pressing against the side of her neck, and stuck a pointing index finger into the soft place just under her jawbone.

"You're dead, Stel," he said. "Again. Come on, let's get you up."

He pulled her to her feet, and after she'd recovered a portion of her control and self-respect, they talked about a plan.

After that, they'd gone to work straight away. Stella told him she intended to keep up with her home weights and strength-building programme. She wanted him to focus completely on unarmed combat.

The gym had yet to open officially, so they had the whole space to themselves. Standing facing Stevens in the centre of a square of four scarlet crash mats, Stella felt, not happy exactly, but in control. As if she had rediscovered a sense of purpose. He was wearing pale-grey marl shorts and a black, sleeveless T-shirt with a regimental crest over the heart. She had on a plain, navy-blue T-shirt and matching baggy shorts with black Lycra cycling shorts underneath.

"The first thing you need to know," Stevens said, "is that fighting in real life is nothing like what you see on the telly. You know that from the job, but now you're learning to do it yourself. It's nasty, messy and very short. Thirty seconds, tops, and it's all over." Stella nodded. Watching him like a hawk in case he decided to throw out another surprise attack. *Fool me once, shame on you, fool me twice, shame on me.* "The second thing is, only idiots and amateurs punch the face. Why?"

"Like you said in training. It's a brick in a skin mask."

"Yes, I did. And yes, it is. You've got a centimetre of skin, fat and muscle, then a thick, bony container designed by Mother Nature to protect the brain. The weight of a human head is?"

"About five kilos," she said, almost adding, "Sarge" at the end.

"Yes. So, like I said, only an idiot's going to throw a punch with his bare hands at a human head. But they all do it. And they get broken fingers, blood poisoning from where a tooth breaks off in their knuckles and all the rest of it. Where are you going to hit them instead?"

"One, the throat. Two, the solar plexus. Three, the groin. Four, the kidneys."

"Not bad. You really did pay attention, didn't you? It's true, those are all good places. But there are other things you can do to a person's face that can really, really hurt them. Things you can go to prison for. But I'm assuming as this is all for self-defence, that won't present a problem for you?"

She shook her head, still watching his hands, keeping her weight on the balls of her feet. "Like I said. A woman alone."

"Good. Okay, I'm a rapist. I'm coming at you. I've got your wrists held tight." He took hold of her wrists and squeezed tightly enough that she couldn't pull them free. "Now what?"

"I don't know. Kick you? Knee you in the balls?"

"Both good options. But there's something they never expect, especially from a woman. A headbutt. You're close. He's taller than you so he's not expecting it, and his face is unprotected."

"But won't it hurt me?"

"Not if you do it properly. Let's break it down. First of all, pick your target. Go for the nose: it's well within range. It's mostly soft tissue and cartilage, and it's full of blood vessels and nerve endings. Even a glancing blow'll sting like crazy and bring enough tears to his eyes that he'll be blinded. Get a good one in, and he's going to bleed like fuck and possibly go down. *Then* you stick the boot in where it really hurts."

Stella fixed her gaze on Rocky's nose. It was a good nose. Straight, no breaks, despite his legendary career as a regimental boxing champion. "Okay, now what?" she asked.

"The backswing. Whoa! Not all the way back there!" Stella had taken her head back so far, her throat was exposed. "He could bite you, stab you, anything. Just enough to get some force behind it. Get some height, too, jump if you can. You're not very tall, so you need to put some extra effort into it."

This time, Stella pulled her head back a few degrees. "And now?"

"And now you hit him. You want to tuck your chin down so you use your forehead as the striking surface. The trick is to stop the forward motion of your head at the moment of impact. That way you transfer all the kinetic energy from your head to his. Keep going and you're basically trying to push him over."

"Blimey, Rocky! I never knew there was so much physics to butting someone," she said, before snapping her head forward.

Stevens was ready, and simply let go of her wrists and stepped back smartly to let her descending head pass harmlessly in front of his face.

"Not bad," he said. "Not bad at all. We'll make a street fighter of you yet."

After that first session, Stella had visited the gym twice a week, always after hours, or before, when nobody would be around to see this slightly-built yet muscular woman learning how to eye-gouge, fist-hammer and headbutt.

Rocky had finally signed her off one Monday night, ruefully rubbing the back of his head after Stella had dumped him on the mats for the tenth time in one session.

"Stella," he said as she shouldered her gym bag and swung the door open, "stay out of trouble, yeah?"

She smiled at him. And left. Clean, sober – and dangerous.

*

Inside the front door, she sighed as the silent house embraced her. With her first week back at work behind her, she wanted that run so badly it was a physical ache.

She called in on the nursery. Lola was sleeping, and Kristina was sitting in an armchair reading a novel. She didn't look up.

Ten minutes later, she was out on the street again, bike boots swapped for running shoes. As the burn in her lungs eased, to be replaced by a sweet sensation of oxygen being drawn in and used to burn blood sugar to produce energy for her muscles, she began to lose herself in the action of running itself. The outside world faded as her feet took her along one of her favourite routes. Along the residential streets, then a left turn down a narrow road that led to an industrial estate bordering the Regent's Canal.

Here, a person could forget they lived in a city of eight million people, where at any one time, half of them seemed to be preying on the other half. A blackbird was singing in a hawthorn bush as she swept past it, the song eerily like a nursery rhyme she used to sing to Lola. She kept running, focusing on her inner voice, the one that whispered to her throughout the day, the one that kept her calm. The one that repeated the same word, over and over again. *Justice. Justice. Justice.* It kept pace with her, repeating the two syllables in time with her feet as they briefly took turns to kiss the towpath.

Ahead, she noticed a movement. A white man in his early thirties was coming towards her. Five-nine or ten. Maybe ten stone. Slight, anyway. Small white dog by his side. What were they called? Scotty dogs, her Mum used to call them. Funny how you remembered things like that out of nowhere. The guy looked fine. Bland features, as if a police artist had created an e-fit called "Mr Average". Dog walkers weren't really high on Stella's list of "types". He was wearing a grey zip-up jacket and stonewashed jeans. Black shoes, bright-blue baseball cap with an orange-and-white New York Knicks logo embroidered on the front.

As she drew level with him, she stumbled. Then two things happened simultaneously. From somewhere in the distance, a high-pitched whistle sounded, and a woman's voice called out, "Angus! Come, Angus!" Stella looked down as the dog turned back the way it had come and scampered off. And the man in the cap turned and swung a fist out at her, landing a glancing blow on the side of the head. She stumbled, gasping in shock.

A knife appeared in his hand. A wicked-looking blade about six inches long with serrations along the top edge and a cross guard. He came towards her, fast, the knife held low in front of him.

Stella reacted. But not instinctively. Instinct was no help to her here. Instinct told her to run, to scream, to sink to her knees in blind terror. Instead, she reacted the way Rocky had taught her to react.

Fast.

Deadly.

And utterly without mercy.

She knocked his knife hand wide to his right, stepped inside his reach and butted him hard in the centre of his leering face. The impact broke his nose instantly, and she felt the hot splash of his blood on her forehead. As he staggered back, she kicked hard into his groin, drawing a high-pitched scream of agony from between his bloody lips. He stumbled, dropping the knife, and fell onto his back. Stella's hand darted down and grabbed it. His hands were held over his crotch as she stood over him, leaving his torso unprotected. She straddled him, right hand clamped tight around the hilt until her knuckles turned white.

"Don't," he pleaded.

Do, the little quiet voice in her head said.

She slammed the knife down into his chest.

She felt the serrations vibrate as they sawed their way in between two ribs before the point punctured his heart and he died, blood welling out around the blade and pumping from his half-open mouth in a smooth, unbroken flow.

"Excuse me, are you all right?"

Stella looked up into the concerned eyes of a woman in her late twenties.

Her brows were knitted together, and her mouth was pulled sideways as if she'd seen something troubling.

"What?"

"You must have fallen. Tripped or something. I was just coming along with my dog and you were on the ground. Did you hit your head?"

"No! I was attacked. Look."

She twisted round to point at the body then froze. No corpse. No crimson pool of blood. No hunting knife. The little white dog was there, nosing around a tuft of long grass before cocking his leg over it. The young woman placed one hand on Stella's shoulder and offered the other.

"Come on," she said, "let's get you up, there's a bench back there."

Despite the woman's concern that she must have banged her head, Stella insisted she was fine. She eventually persuaded the woman to take her dog and go by, promising she would take it easy and go home for a bath and a lie down.

Alone once more, Stella sat shaking on the bench. Cold clammy sweat broke out all over her body. She could feel panic gathering behind her like an oily black wave, primed to engulf her and send her screaming to the bottom. She stared at her left palm, willing there to be slash marks. Better bloody knife cuts than the alternative. The smooth pale skin was slick with moisture but otherwise unmarked. Her breathing was fast and shallow, and white stars were sparkling in her eyes. *No! Not now. I'm not having this.*

She stood. Grabbed the backrest of the bench as black curtains swung towards each other across her vision, then parted again. Squatting, she let her head droop between her knees and took a couple of long, slow breaths. Cautiously this time, she straightened her legs. No stars. No tunnel vision. She shook her head like a dog then trotted off, back along the towpath, towards home.

Later that same day, while Stella was sneezing amid the dust of the records of countless crimes, both solved and unsolved, two members of the legal establishment were having lunch. The restaurant hostess, a tall Slovenian blonde in a crisp white blouse, tailored black trousers and high-heeled black suede shoes that took her height to a towering six-feet-three, showed her two customers to a corner table.

"Thank you, Sabina," Charlie Howarth said, pulling out the beige upholstered chair facing the wall and sitting down.

His guest on this particular lunchtime was Adam Collier, who took the seat facing the room.

Moments later, burgundy leather-bound menus arrived, offered to each man by a male waiter with a sharp-pointed moustache and goatee and wearing nineteen-fifties-style circular tortoiseshell glasses that magnified his dark-lashed eyes. With a quick, sharp movement like a crow plucking at something it suspected might be good to eat, he snatched the thick, cream, linen napkin from the space in front of Collier and flourished it cleverly so that it came to rest across his lap. He repeated the act for Howarth, then smiled, stood to attention, eyes directed heavenwards, and began a recitation.

"Good afternoon, gentlemen. Today's specials. To start, we have *crevettes à l'ail*. The prawns were netted yesterday evening in Port-en-Bessin-Huppain and flown in this morning. The garlic is grown in our own kitchen garden in Buckinghamshire. For the main course, we have wild, line-caught turbot with samphire and braised heritage fennel, and also some very fine organic veal cutlets in a brandy and cream sauce with capers and Seville orange slices."

Leaving them to ponder their choices, he spun on his heel and was gone.

"Something to drink, Adam?" Howarth asked, peering at the wine menu, which had just been delivered by an equally attentive sommelier.

"Can't, I'm afraid," Collier said. "Meetings all afternoon including one with the Assistant Chief Commissioner.

"Pity. Well, fizzy water for you then, and I think I will have," he pulled his lower lip between thumb and forefinger, "a bottle of the '83 Margaux. You might have to help me out a little or I'll be asleep in front of His Honour Mr Justice Josephson."

Collier grunted.

Once the food had arrived and the wine and water had been poured, Collier spoke again, quietly so that only Howarth could hear him.

"I've stuck her in the basement. She's on our admin task force. I give her a week, two tops, before she freaks out from the boredom and either has another breakdown or quits in disgust."

"You seem very sure. What if she just sticks it out until she's passed fit for active duty?"

"Won't happen. My contact in occupational health is a supporter of our aims. We've agreed that DI Cole will stay down there until she leaves, rots away or dies."

"I hope you're right. I was talking to Leonard earlier this week, and he's mightily concerned that she's back in the frame. What if she starts poking her nose into things she shouldn't?"

Collier paused with a forkful of deep-red sirloin halfway to his open mouth. He put the fork down again. "There's nothing to poke into, is there? We got rid of a nosy human rights lawyer, Deacon took the fall for the hit and run, Leonard did his patriotic duty for the year, case closed."

"And you think the money will be enough to buy Deacon's silence? Permanently?"

Collier dabbed his lips with the napkin before settling it over his knees again.

"What, Eddie 'Looselips' Deacon? Not a chance. In fact, I've been thinking about him all this week. I don't think he's going to last till the end of his sentence. It's really not worth the trouble of letting him out and finding him a halfway house and a probation officer, and then monitoring him to make sure he doesn't start telling tales out of class about how he suddenly came into enough cash to buy a new BMW. Which is why he is going to find prison life becoming rather uncomfortable in the next day or two."

Howarth smiled. "How about that glass of Margaux now?"

CHAPTER NINE
Death in Custody

"DEACON!" THE FORTYISH prison officer called across the dining hall in HM Prison Bure. The prison squatted like a toad in the flat and unexciting countryside of the parish of Scottow in Norfolk. The locals didn't much care for having a prison on their doorstep – who would? – but the staff all drank in the village's two pubs and patronised the few little shops, so an uneasy peace reigned.

At the guard's yell, a head poked up from a knot of prisoners gathered round a table playing cards with a grimy, much-handled deck that emitted the cheesy, sweaty smell of old banknotes. His narrow, suspicious eyes flicked around trying to locate the shouter. Seeing who had summoned him, he stood and untangled his left leg from the bench seat, accidentally knocking his neighbour's card hand with his knee and earning a "Fuckin' 'ell, Deacon!" Then he made his way over to the officer, a burly man with a shock of coarse, ginger hair and a mess of adult acne across his cheeks.

"Mr Rooker, sir. You called?" Edwin Deacon said, his words smeared with false respect like cheap ketchup on a burger.

"You're being transferred. Get your things and be at the guardhouse in fifteen minutes."

Deacon's eyes lost their slitted look and widened. "What? Transferred? Why? Where?" he spread his hands wide, palms towards the prison officer. "I've been keeping my nose clean, haven't I?"

Rooker stared at him, then leaned in close. "You heard. Yes. No idea. Long Lartin. Yes, but I don't care."

"Long Lartin? You're having a laugh, Mr Rooker. That's Category A. I'm C. There must have been a mix-up."

Rooker glared at Deacon then lowered his voice to a half-growl, half-whisper. "Get your fucking things together, you little cunt, or there's going to be a mix-up between my baton and your thick skull."

Frowning, and with a sense of unease growing in the pit of his stomach at being ghosted like this – no warning, no time to inform family and friends – Deacon mooched back to his cell and gathered his possessions into a pile. There wasn't much to carry: a couple of paperback books; a washbag containing a small tube of toothpaste and a toothbrush, a razor and shaving foam, and a greasy black plastic comb, and a silver transistor radio with a cracked case. He formed the objects into a pile and made his way along the walkway, down the clanging steel steps, through the assembly hall and out into the yard. A few men were playing football, but the wind was driving sharp pellets of sleet almost horizontally across the yard, so the game was down to three a side.

Beside the guard house, a prisoner transport van was waiting. Operated by one of the proliferating private contractors who ran much of Britain's creaking prison infrastructure, it was painted a dark brown, with opaque Plexiglas windows lined on the outside with steel mesh. The engine was running.

A screw was waiting for him and pulled opened the rear door. He smiled as Deacon climbed in. "Have a nice trip," he said. "Hope you like your new home."

Four hours later, the van drew up at HMP Long Lartin's gatehouse. It was little more than an oversized phone booth with a chair and a control panel for the security barrier. Papers were checked, looks exchanged between driver and officer on duty, and then Edwin Deacon's descent into hell was almost complete.

As a Category A prison, Long Lartin housed men judged by the legal system to present the greatest risk to the public or to national security should they escape. Basically, murderers, rapists, the worst sex offenders, armed robbers, terrorists and major-league drug dealers. The population at Long Lartin regarded themselves as hard men, but as basically sound men. Men for whom prison was an acceptable and unavoidable risk of doing business. Or at the very least, a place where you did your time and didn't whine about it. One other thing: they didn't like paedophiles. And there were plenty of them on F Wing. Animals, beasts, bacons, wrong uns, nonces – the general prison population had plenty of words to describe them. And plenty of ways of dealing with them.

As a man convicted of causing death by careless driving, Edwin Deacon was surprised to find himself at Long Lartin at all. When the screw on duty pointed at the corridor that led to F Wing, Deacon's eyebrows shot up. And his mouth dropped open.

"That's for Rule 45ers, sir. That can't be right. They must have got the paperwork wrong or something. You can't put me with the nonces."

The screw just grinned. He leaned close to Deacon and placed his mouth against his left ear. "You're fucked, mate," he whispered.

Deacon had just finished unpacking his few possessions when he heard the scrape of his cell door opening. He whirled round. The doorway was filled by a barrel-chested prisoner whose biceps bulged so tightly against the sleeves of his pale-blue prison shirt, they threatened to split the seams. He was stone-faced, with dark, emotionless eyes like a shark's staring straight at Deacon. His shaved and shining scalp bore tattoos of lizards on both sides, crawling from the nape of his neck towards his rumpled forehead.

The man eased himself into the cell, to be followed by two more. They were well built, though not on the scale as their leader. Both had the same shaved skulls and the same cold, calculating look. The second man, taller than the other two, closed the door behind him. That's when Deacon noticed the table legs that slid down the inside of each man's right arm and into his fist.

"You're a nonce," the first man said, in a low growl, his accent from somewhere in the northeast, "which normally means we start with a welcoming committee, followed by the fines you have to pay. But given what you got sent down for, we decided to skip that bit."

Deacon stood, hands raised, palms outward, shaking, his mind racing to find the words that might save him.

"Look, there's been a mistake. I'm death by careless driving. I'm not a n–"

The table leg, which had been fashioned in the prison's woodwork shop, was not an elegant, lathe-turned affair. It was cut from square-profile stock and apart from six inches at the end where the man's beefy hands were wrapped around it, yet to be sanded. The crunch and snap as it connected with Deacon's right elbow were almost immediately drowned out by his scream. Two follow-up blows from the second and third men broke Deacon's knees. He collapsed forward onto his face, weeping and screaming. From that point, his life was forfeit. The three shaven-headed men took turns to smash their clubs down onto Deacon's back and head. When a pool of deep-plum-coloured blood welled suddenly from beneath his ruined face, they stepped back, looked at each other and nodded. Then they left.

*

In the basement, the next day, Reg the Veg was frowning and rootling about in the paperwork that threatened to engulf his desk.

"What's up, Reg?" Stella asked as she walked up to him between two rows of filing cabinets.

"Forgot my sandwiches, didn't I?"

"Didn't Karen pack your briefcase this morning, then?"

Reg's face puckered into a deeper frown. His trademark, I'm-mad-me grin had entirely disappeared. "Err, no. We had words this morning. Told me I could make my own lunch. I did, but I must have left it on the kitchen counter. You know, with the stress of it and everything."

"Tell you what, Reg. I was just about to go out and get something for myself. I'll buy you lunch. M&S sandwiches all right?"

His face brightened and he smiled. "That's very kind of you, Stel. I mean, you know, if it's not too much trouble."

Oh, no, Reg. It's no trouble at all. Not for me, anyway. "It's fine. Egg mayo, right? That's your favourite, isn't it?"

"You noticed, then? Great little detective you are, and no mistake. Yep. Good old egg mayo. Preferably no cress, but I'm not fussy. I can always pick it out."

"Okay. I'll get some crisps and a drink. What do you want?"

"Salt and vinegar and a Diet Coke please. I'll pay you when you get back."

"Don't be daft," she said, smiling. "I said, my treat."

She left then, checking the contents of her bag on the way out of the door.

In the local branch of Marks & Spencer, Stella mingled with the office workers buying their lunches, watching as outstretched hands hovered between the reduced-fat options and the salads or the New York-style deli specials and two-inch-thick, high-fat sandwiches that actually filled you up and tasted of something else besides virtuous self-denial.

"Excuse me," she said, squeezing an arm between a fat guy in an ill-fitting grey suit that strained across the shoulders and a pair of twenty-something girls teetering on six-inch heels and wearing that species of full, matte makeup that always reminded her of shop-window dummies. She snagged an organic egg-mayonnaise sandwich with watercress – *sorry, Reg* – and a pastrami on rye for herself.

After the almost surgical cleanliness of the supermarket, Stella's next stop felt more like the sort of place where she'd find what she was looking for: a drab convenience store lit by soul-destroying neon strip lights that gave even the fresh vegetables a deathly pallor. She headed towards the back of the shop where a couple of noisy chiller cabinets were squeezed between racks of toilet paper and disposable nappies. At the back of the left-hand chiller, sitting in a puddle of sticky, pink liquid, was a shrink-wrapped, black polystyrene tray containing a chicken quarter.

Her route back to the station took her past a small urban park, little more than a square of scrappy grass bordered by beds full of daffodils and a handful of birch trees. It was too early in the year for people to be eating their lunches outdoors, and the park was deserted apart from a handful of snaggle-toothed boozers at one end laughing and coughing in liquid gurgles as they swigged from cans in green, gold and black. *You got pretty close, Stel, don't forget that.* Stella shuddered.

She chose a bench as far away from the winos as possible. It backed onto a beech hedge, still rustling with the previous year's brittle brown leaves, which shielded her back. Ahead, she had a clear view of both entrances to the park. She took the pouch containing the hypodermic syringe from her bag and ripped open the top edge with her teeth. Holding the portion of shrink-wrapped chicken steady inside the carrier bag, she inserted the needle through the black plastic tray and into the blood. She tipped the tray a little and then withdrew the plunger, watching as the bloody juice fountained up inside the plastic body of the syringe against the green rubber stopper.

Out came the needle with a tiny high-pitched squeak against the polystyrene tray. Next, she pulled out Reg's sandwich. Finding a glued join in the outer, she pushed the needle between the two thin sheets of cardboard and into the soft, whitish-yellow filling of the sandwich. Using her thumb, she pushed the plunger down with a steady pressure, easing the needle out as she did, so that its payload wouldn't be concentrated in one spot. Finally, it was done. She squeezed the join in the cardboard between thumb and forefinger and pushed the sandwich packet back inside the bag. One of the winos had noticed her. He looked over and called out in a voice roughened by booze, fags, or just hard living.

"Hello, darlin'! Come over and have a swig if you like. It's Special Brew 2010 – a particularly good year!"

His friends cackled at this flight of wit, then turned back to their drinking. Stella wrinkled her nose, shook her head and left the park. On the way back to Paddington Green, she dropped the syringe, minus its needle, down a drain. The needle she placed inside an empty drink can she found resting on the top of an overflowing rubbish bin, crushing the can to trap the evidence at the bottom. The portion of chicken went into a second rubbish bin, a large commercial number in thick green plastic at the back of a fast food place. All that remained was lunch.

"Here you go," Stella said with a smile, handing over the carrier bag to Reg, who was staring intently at the monitor of his ageing Pentium III desktop computer when she arrived back in the basement at just after twelve thirty.

He barely looked up, acknowledging her gift with a perfunctory "Cheers, Stel," reaching out for the bag, which she hooked over his outstretched fingers.

"Enjoy!" she said, retreating to her own desk. It was a cheap, battered, plywood-and-steel construction with a dodgy screw-in foot on the front right corner that needed a folded wad of paper to keep it from rocking.

Even though she knew the raw chicken blood would take a while to work its mischief in Reg's digestive system, she couldn't help but keep an eye on him as he opened the packaging and took out the sandwich. He tutted as he saw the broad, flat leaves of the watercress. Over the next two-and-a-half minutes, he picked out every single leaf and stem and deposited them on the thin, cellophane film window. Content that he wouldn't be ingesting anything green, he took a huge bite, chewed it with his mouth open, then swallowed. Stella was mesmerised by the way his prominent Adam's apple bobbed in his throat. He caught her looking.

"What's the matter, Stel? Never seen a man eating before?" Then he blushed. "Shit! God, I'm so sorry. What an eejit. I was just, you know–"

"It's fine," she said, with a reassuring smile. *Given I've just fed you poison. Knock yourself out.*

After this, they ate their sandwiches, crunched their crisps and swigged their drinks in companionable silence, with just the whirring of the computers' cooling fans to break it.

The first intimations of disaster came about ninety minutes later. Stella had been keeping Reg under observation, flicking her gaze away from the spreadsheet she was updating to check on his skin colour, and look for any obvious signs of intestinal discomfort. Then, bingo!

He pulled a face, twisting his lips and frowning, while placing a hand carefully over his stomach. He belched loudly, then frowned.

"You all right, Reg?" she asked.

"Not sure. The old guts are sending up smoke signals, and I don't think it's to announce a party." His eyes widened, suddenly. "No, actually, gotta go, Stel, 'scuse me."

For a big man, Reg could move fast when he needed to. And he obviously needed to now. He skirted the corner of his desk, skimming it with his left hip, and was off down the canyons of filing cabinets, heading for the door to the corridor beyond and the toilets.

She screwed her eyes tight as she strained to hear any audible signs of distress, but only caught the bang of the door closing behind Reg.

Ten minutes passed. She nibbled the second half of her own sandwich while wondering just how rapidly Salmonella bacteria could multiply in the human gut and at what point their numbers would cause someone to feel the effects of their burgeoning population growth.

Just as she was worrying that she might have overdone it and Reg was dying on his knees in front of the toilet, he reappeared in the doorway of the exhibits room. His face was gleaming wetly in the light from the fluorescent tubes overhead. It was the colour of fresh putty. His mouth was hanging half-open, and he was clutching the door jamb as if it were the only thing between him and death. Which she reflected, perhaps it was.

"Oh, my God, Reg. What happened? Are you okay? You look like a fucking corpse."

"Not sure," he groaned. "Must have been the egg mayo. That'll teach me to get shop sandwiches. No offence."

"None taken."

"Oh, God!" he moaned before executing a smart about-turn and darting back to the security of the gents'.

The second time he appeared, Stella took charge.

"Give me your keys, Reg. I'm taking you home."

Until this point, she hadn't considered how she would remove Reg from the station. Now she found herself behind the wheel of his eight-year-old Honda CRV four-by-four, and she wasn't happy about it. Although compared to Reg, she was ecstatic. He was writhing now, clutching his stomach and moaning softly, his face smeared with sweat, while he gave off a sickroom odour that made her buzz the windows down on her side and his.

Somehow, she controlled her own feelings of incipient panic as she negotiated the three-mile drive to the semi-detached house he shared with the homely Karen, his wife of thirty-one years. Having got him in through the door and up the stairs to their bedroom, Stella beat a retreat, promising to call in the morning to see how he was getting on.

Forty minutes later, she was back in the exhibits room. On her own. Finally.

It was two fifteen. She pulled up HOLMES – the Home Office Large Enquiry System – and entered a search term.

"Richard Drinkwater + hit and run + 2009"

Moments later, she was staring at a home screen for the case that had turned her life upside down just thirteen months earlier.

Hit and run: 06/05/2009–CASE NO. F/PG/658832/67
File created by: P Evans

Ignoring the entries relating to the prosecution and conviction of Edwin James Deacon for causing death by careless driving, she clicked on the tab for evidence and then drilled down to the physical evidence window. She scanned the list of items recovered from the scene. Nothing much to go on. No fingerprints, obviously. No DNA, ditto. Not even any rubber from the road surface. Deacon hadn't even touched the brakes to scuff his tyres on the tarmac. She ground her teeth together as she imagined, once again, the movie projected in her head of Deacon, pissed or tweaking, barrelling into Richard's car and snuffing out the life of one of the only two people in the world who meant anything to Stella. Apart from glass fragments and bits of Richard's own car, the evidence list was empty.

CHAPTER TEN
Absence of Evidence

"NO, NO, NO, this isn't possible," she hissed into the empty air. "There has to be something. There has to be!"

Somehow, Stella had convinced herself that once she got Reg out of the way, the case would open up before her like the pages of a pop-up book. She'd pull them away from each other, and the fairy-tale castle with its turrets and flags would present itself with the evidence she needed to convict Deacon of murder stuck on its topmost tower. Her breathing came in short gasps as the castle crumbled, raining shards of stained glass on the handsome prince climbing up the outside and decapitating him.

Head in hands, she forced herself to stay calm and to follow the mantra she'd had drilled into her at Hendon and on numerous courses since – that it was a detective's job to think.

All evidence from a crime scene had to be logged against the case number. Standard procedure unless you wanted never to find anything ever again. That way the databases would all speak to each other, and you could find what you wanted. It might be a needle in the exhibits room haystack, but as long as you had the right case reference, you could find it in seconds. She had the right case number, but the database search was telling her there was nothing to find.

"Come on," she breathed, "give me something. I've waited so long for this."

She leaned back and stared at the ceiling, massaging the back of her neck. Then she frowned.

Somewhere in the primitive part of her brain, a buzzer had just gone off. A buzzer that said, *Hey! I just noticed something important and we should do something about it now.* Had Stella been a cavewoman, that "something important" would have been large, fierce and possessed of long, sharp teeth. Now it was a piece of information. Equally important, but unlikely to consume her for its dinner.

It was something Reg had said the other day. She couldn't retrieve the memory.

"For fuck's sake!" she moaned, rubbing her scrunched up eyes with her fingers.

Then she removed her fingers and opened her eyes. That was it. That was what Reg had said the other day. FFS. Not the expletive, but Fat Finger Syndrome. He switched numbers around when he was typing. That was why he tried to avoid it.

She leaned forward and stared at the screen again. She shook the mouse impatiently and when the screen glowed back into life, clicked back out to the case home screen.

There it was. The case number.

Hit and run: 06/05/2009–CASE NO. F/PG/658832/67
File created by: P Evans

Could it be this simple? Stella opened the search box and rekeyed the case number.

F/PG/568832/67

She held her breath. Said a quiet prayer. And hit Return.

The hour-glass icon rotated in a series of one-hundred-and-eighty-degree jerks.

Stella could hear her pulse roaring in her ears.

Then it stopped and the screen refreshed. Still no evidence.

"Come on, Reg, please tell me you fucked up your typing."

She tried again.

F/PG/658823/67

She held her breath, willing the screen to yield its secrets. After another agonising wait, the screen refreshed with the same depressing message.

"One more go. Please, be there. Please!" she almost shouted.

F/PG/658832/76

The hourglass went through its routine again. Stella stared so hard she thought she could feel the blood in her own eyeballs pulsing. The hourglass stopped tumbling.

And there it was: a single record logged against the non-existent case file. An evidence reference.

F/PG/658832/76-E/RW/1

The same case reference, then E for evidence, RW for Reggie Willing and 1 – indicating it was the first, and only, exhibit.

She clicked it.

ITEM: paint chip
CASE REF: F/PG/658832/76
EXHIBIT: 1
LOCATION: M71

Stella let out a slow, audible breath, somewhere between a groan and a gasp.

"Thank you, God," she said, staring at the reference and gripping the edges of the screen with white-knuckled fingers and thumbs. "And you, Reg. Sorry about the food poisoning."

She scribbled the reference onto a scrap of paper and left to find the shelf in the exhibits room where the paint chip had been misfiled.

Exhibit location M71 was at knee height. Stella squatted in front of the shelf, eyes flicking left and right, looking for the object she believed would lead her to justice for her husband.

There. Between a hammer and a pair of dirty, off-white knickers stiff with dark brown bloodstains. She plucked the transparent plastic bag from the shelf and held it up to her eyes. To a casual observer, she would have looked very strange. A woman, her face smudged with dirt, her clothes dusty, inspecting a transparent polythene sandwich bag with an open-mouthed expression of reverence as if it contained a priceless religious relic.

The observer, moving closer, would have frowned in puzzlement. Because the sandwich bag was empty.

No, not empty.

In the tip of the left-hand corner, winking in the light from the overhead neon tubes, was a tiny flake of glittering material. It might have been nail varnish, chipped from a rape victim's scrabbling finger. Or a fleck of plastic from an abducted child's favourite toy.

As Stella's eyes picked out the flake, her own expression changed. The lips compressed into a red line and her eyes narrowed. The forehead, smooth a minute ago, crinkled into lines as if scored with a thin blade. She turned and grabbed a magnifying glass from a nearby desk. No Sherlock Holmes number this, made of ebony and brass. It was rectangular, about the size of a paperback book, and made of pale, lard-coloured plastic. The handle had become grimy through much handling, narrow black furrows between the ridges.

The rear of the chip was dark grey primer. The glossy upper surface of the paint flake was a deep shade of purple, almost black, like the skin of an aubergine.

Earlier, Stella had pulled a pair of white nitrile gloves from a box in the storeroom. Now she took them from her jacket pocket and slipped them on. The rolled edges at her wrist reminded her of condoms.

She slit the red chain-of-custody tape with a penknife on her bike keyring and, holding her breath, tipped the bag so the jewel of paint fell noiselessly into her palm. She turned her face to one side and exhaled. The last thing she wanted to do now was cough or puff or sneeze the flake of paint onto the floor or under a shelving unit. Breathing shallowly through her open mouth, she held her palm up into the light and inspected the surface of the paint flake through the magnifier.

In the glare of the neon, its colour revealed itself as a gorgeous, rich purple, not as dark as it had first appeared. And it glittered as if impregnated with diamond dust.

"You're not from some crappy cut-and-shut job, are you?" she muttered. "Did Deacon nick you first?"

The paint fleck winked back at her.

Holding her breath again, Stella cupped her palm a little and tipped the flake back into the evidence bag and sealed it with the cut edges of the tape. Into her pocket it went, along with her keys. She picked up the folder and took it to the photocopier.

*

That night, in a twenty-three-million-pound townhouse facing a semi-circular park on the border between Knightsbridge and Chelsea, a man twitched as he slept. His name was Leonard Ramage. His full title, as listed in Who's Who and several other directories of establishment figures, was The Honourable Mr Justice Sir Leonard Ramage. He was dreaming. It was the same dream as always. And it ended the same as always.

Ramage started from sleep, his chest slicked with sweat.

"Fuck!" he said, reaching for a packet of cigarettes on his bedside table. He levered himself out of bed and walked to the floor-to-ceiling window, snapping the vintage gold Dunhill petrol lighter repeatedly until the flame jumped from the wick and he could draw in a lungful of smoke.

From the bed, a voice curled over towards him like the smoke now snaking away from the glowing tip of his cigarette.

"What's the matter, Judge?"

He spoke without turning. "Nothing. Go back to sleep."

"Do you want to make love again?"

"No. And I wish you wouldn't call it making love."

"Fine." The voice was petulant now. "Do you want to fuck me again? Is that better?"

"Yes. And no. In fact, I don't need you anymore today. Your money's there, on the dresser. Get your things on and go. I'll call you in two weeks. My wife's back from Paris in the morning, and she's staying here until her next trip."

"Fine. But I need a little extra this time."

Ramage turned from the window. "Why?"

The figure emerged from the shadows and came to stand facing Ramage, rubbing a hand over small, high breasts, the left sporting a small tattoo of a red rose dripping blood, and down over a flat belly. Her eyes were smudgy with dark grey makeup, and her glossy, blonde hair was tousled with sleep. "I've had a journalist from one of the posh papers sniffing around like a bitch in heat. She's been talking to all the girls on the high-end circuit. She seems to think there's some sort of conspiracy involving senior legal types. You know, Judge. Like you. Told me I could make myself a tidy little sum if I was to give her a few little titbits of information. All off the record, of course."

Ramage glared at the woman, who purported to be called Kiara. As well as the rose, she had a small butterfly tattooed under the angle of her jaw on the right. He pushed a fingertip against the hard plane of her sternum.

"Just what are you saying?"

The woman smiled. "Nothing. Just that a girl's got to live. And quite frankly, she's offered me a lot more than I get," she swept her hand around the bedroom, ending up with it pointing at the bed, "for doing this."

"So, you want me to pay you off, is that it?"

"I wouldn't put it quite like that. But the lady from the paper was quite persuasive."

Ramage exhaled through his nose. Then took another deep drag on the cigarette before blowing the lungful of smoke out towards the ceiling. "I haven't any more cash here than that." He pointed to the carefully stacked pile of banknotes on the dressing table. The money sat between an open-topped leather tray, divided into compartments for cufflinks, change and keys, and a trio of bottles of expensive aftershaves and colognes. "But I can get it easily enough. How much did she offer you?"

"Ten." She paused for a beat. "Grand."

Ramage doubted it was even a quarter of that ludicrous sum.

"I'll double it. But that buys your absolute and total discretion. For ever. Understood?"

"That's very generous of you, Judge. And, yes, of course. My lips are sealed. Except, you know, when you–"

"Shut up and get out! Now! And take your money. I'll call you tomorrow with a place to meet."

With the house to himself again, Ramage sat on the edge of the bed. He picked up his phone.

"Bit early isn't it, Leonard?" Howarth's voice was blurry with sleep and edged with irritation.

"I've got a problem. *We* have a problem."

Howarth's voice sharpened and his diction improved instantly.

"What sort of a problem, precisely? It must be serious if you're calling me at this ungodly hour."

"There's a journalist sniffing around. I'm not sure, but it sounds like she's heard something about PPM."

"And you know this, how?"

"And I know this because some grasping little tart just attempted to blackmail me. I've offered her double what she claimed the media bitch promised her."

"You're not going to pay her, surely? She'll only come back for more."

"Yes, thank you, Charlie. I have, actually, tried a few blackmail cases in my career. Of course, I'm not going to pay her."

"Then …?"

"Call Collier for me. I'm convening a subcommittee at six a.m. I want this dealt with permanently. Tomorrow."

At six that same morning, Adam Collier, Charlie Howarth and Leonard Ramage were sitting around Ramage's handmade walnut burl dining table. It had cost him more than a police constable made in a year, including overtime. His housekeeper kept the swirling copper surface buffed to a high shine with beeswax polish. They were eating flaky, buttery croissants and drinking freshly brewed coffee. And they were discussing a murder. A forthcoming murder.

"She can't really have anything, Leonard," Collier was saying. "The group's security is watertight. Airtight. Nobody would ever even hint at its existence. She's just fishing."

Ramage dabbed at his lips with a white damask napkin. "Maybe she is just fishing. But she's fishing for something in particular, and that concerns me, as it should you."

"Oh, it concerns me. As does your little friend's pathetic attempt at blackmail."

"Can we deal with that first ?" Howarth asked. "I have to be in court at ten and if I need to arrange anything I need to get it done as soon as possible."

"I'm going to meet her on an abandoned industrial estate a few miles from here. One of those derelict sites down by the river the developers are snapping up like dogs after butchers' scraps," Ramage said.

"That's perfect," Collier said. "I have someone in mind for the job. She's very capable, aced the sniper training course, shoots for the Met in competition. I gather the army tried to poach her when they found out how good she was."

"Loyal?" Ramage asked.

"One hundred percent. I vetted her myself. She's like a pit bull with guns instead of teeth. If I were to let her off the leash, I doubt there'd be a criminal left alive in the whole of the Met's jurisdiction."

"Excellent. I'll tell the tart to meet me at two this afternoon. I'll text you the exact location, and your attack dog can set up or whatever these people need to do."

"Shall we return to the subject of this journalist?" Howarth asked.

"By all means," Ramage said. "In fact, I have a plan for her. When I meet Kiara this afternoon, I'll get the name out of her first. So, Adam, better tell your pit bull to hold her fire until I give her a signal."

"Make it something obvious. We don't want her dead too early because you scratched your nose."

"I'll point straight up at the sky. How about that? Obvious enough?"

Collier smiled. "That should do it."

"Then what?" Howarth asked.

"Then we can do some sniffing of our own, can't we," Ramage said. "More coffee?"

CHAPTER ELEVEN
Kill #9

HER SHOOTING SKILLS had been developing since her father bought her that first, beautiful rifle when she was nine. Her total official kills amounted to two. The number of people she had dispatched unofficially was six. Each kill had given her an increasing amount of pleasure. Now she was making herself comfortable on the roof of a tower block overlooking a patch of disused ex-industrial land that stretched down to the Thames. A row of abandoned Portakabins stood with their backs to the river. Their windows were covered with perforated steel sheets, which were covered in graffiti, along with the rest of the tatty units.

Beneath her, she had spread a sheet of olive-green canvas. Beside her right elbow was her mobile phone. Next to the phone was a pair of Zeiss Conquest HD 15x56 binoculars. They'd proved their worth as spotting kit during early morning and twilight put-downs and had cost the thick end of fourteen hundred pounds, far more than she could ever have afforded; as PPM had paid, that didn't really matter. It was the piece of kit in front of her that she was focusing on.

The weapon wasn't a standard-issue police rifle. For its marksmen – and they had all been men until she joined – the Met had opted for a Heckler & Koch G3K semi-automatic rifle. She had tried out a variety of rifles during a trip to the US and had decided that the Accuracy International AT308 was a better weapon for her specialised role. Its folding stock made it more easily portable and less likely to attract unwanted attention, although her masters would see to it that she never found herself anywhere near the inside of a courtroom. Or not from the wrong side of the dock, at any rate.

When Adam Collier had introduced her to PPM and asked her about weapons, she had, without hesitation, told him she wanted the AT308 for her new duties. One had been procured, along with a telescopic sight, a suppressor and a bipod. Together with the .308 Winchester ammunition, the rifle spent its spare time in a black-painted, steel gun cabinet in her garage.

The rifle was mounted on its bipod now. She had leant on the bipod's legs to drive the spiked feet into the asphalt covering of the roof.

She checked her watch, a black-and-gold Casio G-Shock bristling with buttons, crowns, bezels and additional digital displays on the face. She loved the watch and thought it suited her wrist, which was muscular where other women her age had slight, bird-like bones.

13.58

She raised the binoculars to her eyes and watched the kill zone. Off to one side, she caught movement. A dark purple car hove into view and pulled up at the edge of the concrete apron in front of the Portakabins. Cars didn't interest her. This one was big and looked expensive, to judge from the chrome on display and the huge wheels. It was a beautiful colour. Like a glittering aubergine.

A man got out. Oldish. Maybe mid-sixties. He was in good condition. His skin was tanned and it looked genuine, rather than the orange glow of a salon. His silver hair was swept back from a high forehead. She put the binoculars down and switched her grip to the butt of her AT308, settled her right cheek against the black plastic pad on the stock and sighted through the scope. Every line and mole on his face was pin sharp. His eyes were dark brown with white crow's feet at the outer corners, slicing through the tan. Maybe he played sports all year round. Tennis probably, or golf. Tennis, she decided. She placed the junction of the Schmidt & Bender's cross hairs over his left eye.

"Pow!" she whispered. "You're dead."

He strolled to a position in the middle of the concrete apron, in front of the centre Portakabin. The door behind him was emblazoned with tags. The only one she could read said, "J-Mex"; it was done in black, white and a bright red that reminded her of the blood of the first deer she shot.

Three minutes passed. The man checked his watch and frowned. He looked around him and scanned the buildings beyond the kill zone. He looked straight at her position, but at that range – two hundred and fifty metres – he wouldn't be able to see anything beyond the general outline of the roof.

She switched back to the binoculars. Then she saw the target arrive in the kill zone. Her heart rate remained untroubled by the approaching action. She drew the bolt back to chamber the only round she knew she'd need, and pushed it forward again with a soft, muffled *click*.

A small red car, tiny in comparison to the man's, came round a corner between two larger industrial units. It pulled up with a jerk and the driver's door swung open.

"Target acquired," she whispered. She placed her binoculars by her right hip and snuggled her cheek against the AT380's stock again. "Target is a female. Slender build. Five foot six in her heels, which are, frankly, ridiculous. Why do tarts always dress like tarts? Black hair, looks like a wig, in a bun. Large gold hoop earrings. Tattoo of butterfly under angle of jaw on right side."

The man and the woman were talking now. Lots of hand gestures from the tart, although she was standing still, which made the shot easier. But less challenging.

*

At ground level, Ramage and the woman calling herself Kiara, though her real name was Lorna Hammond, were discussing how he could trust her to keep her side of the bargain.

"I told you, Judge," she said, hand held out for the padded envelope she believed contained twenty thousand pounds in cash, "I get the money, I clam up tighter than a nun's you-know-what."

"Yes, and I told you," Ramage said, still clutching the package of torn-up photocopier paper, "I need a gesture of good faith."

She smiled at him and fluttered her spidery false eyelashes at him. "It's a bit public for that, don't you think?"

He clamped his lips together in irritation for a second, then spoke.

"Her name."

"Sorry?"

"Give me her name?"

"Whose name?"

"Don't play dumb, you stupid little tart. The hack. The journalist. The nosy bitch who's been sniffing around my affairs."

"Oh, her. Why didn't you just say so? Money first." She held her hand out, and crooked her fingers, beckoning him.

He pushed the envelope towards her. As she closed her fingers around it, he gripped tighter.

"Name first," he said.

She rolled her eyes, which were a grey-green, like the sea in winter. "Fine. Vicky Riley. *The Guardian.* I think she said that's where she worked."

"You're sure?"

"Yes, I'm sure." She sounded impatient now. "I remember because my best friend at school was called Vicky. Now. Money, please."

Ramage released his grip on the envelope and took a step back. He watched as she ripped open the flap. Then took another step away from her. As her eyes flicked from the contents of the envelope to his, he smiled.

"What the fuck's this?" she asked, holding out a handful of plain, white scraps of paper.

"What? Do you think money grows on trees? Or falls from the sky?"

As Ramage uttered this last, rhetorical question of Kiara, he pointed upwards. And took a third step away from her.

She followed his pointing finger and stared up, exposing a long, pale neck.

The side of her head blew out with a sound like a bucket of water being thrown at a wall.

Blood, bone and brain matter sprayed out in a red, yellow and grey cone that reached the door of the Portakabin behind her.

The sound of the shot arrived a few milliseconds later. A dull "thump", it might have been a door slamming or a car reversing into a bollard.

She collapsed sideways, her knees buckling and twisting, and came to rest, a corpse now, rather than a person, facing the sky. A broad river of bright arterial blood fanned out from her broken skull and flowed towards the Thames.

A speck of something greyish-brown and glistening – like porridge he thought – landed on the sleeve of Ramage's suit jacket. He looked down and flicked it away with a fingernail.

A minute later, a plain grey transit van pulled up. Three black-clad men got out and approached Ramage, walking in step.

The lead man, shaved head, early forties, expressionless eyes, spoke: "Best you leave now, sir. We'll tidy up."

Ramage nodded, went back to his Bentley and drove off. He switched on the radio and began singing along to the music. It was *The Magic Flute*, on Radio Three. His favourite opera.

Wrapped in heavy-duty, welded steel chain secured with two fat brass padlocks, Lorna Hammond sank to the bottom of the Thames in a deep basin unaffected by the tides. Her little car exploded in a fireball ten minutes after that.

As the clean-up crew were brushing themselves off and climbing back into their van, a lone figure entered the kill zone carrying a black nylon bag. She nodded to them as she skirted the blazing car, feeling the heat warm her left cheek, and walked over to the Portakabin that had so recently formed the backdrop to her seventh unofficial kill.

The brass cartridge was already secured in a zipped pocket of her tactical vest. She smashed the lock on the door with a crowbar and entered. Judging the trajectory as the round had left the target's skull, and looking back at the hole in the door, she began her search at ground level. She scattered a loose pile of dusty junk mail spreading out from the rear of the door. At the pile's furthest edge, she saw that one of the envelopes had a neat round hole in its upper-left corner. She brushed the envelope to one side as her fingertips grazed the plywood floor.

"Hello, you," she said. Then, pulling the large blade from a penknife, she dug the bullet out of the flooring. The .308 calibre Winchester round was essentially in the same condition as it had been when it left the muzzle of her rifle. It was smeared with blood and striated from the lands and grooves of the barrel's rifling, but the copper jacket that ensured it would fly true over such long distances had maintained the shape and dimensions. It joined the brass in her pocket. Then she straightened and walked back to climb into the van, sniffing the smoke-filled air like a gun-dog.

CHAPTER TWELVE
Forensic Assistance

REG HAD BEEN signed off for two weeks with a confirmed case of Salmonella. Stella felt a pang of guilt when she took the call from Karen, but the feeling passed like a twinge from a sensitive tooth. A fortnight to do some serious digging around without Reg looking over her shoulder the whole time. Top of her list was the flake of paint.

She wandered down to the forensics office. Normally she avoided it – too many brainiacs sitting at computers showing each other coloured bar charts. Today, she actively wanted to be there. Just before she pushed through the door, she undid the scrunchie round her ponytail and shook out her hair. She'd put a spray of perfume – L'Eau D'Issey – down her cleavage that morning, happy to see that her boobs had come back. Now she undid that strategic second button, flicked the fabric apart with her thumb and forefinger, and went in.

As one, the six men and two women in the office looked up. *Like meerkats,* she thought, as sixteen eyes swivelled in her direction.

"Don't stop," she said with a cheery smile. But they hadn't. Clocking her as "that light-duties DI" from some inter-office memo or other, or maybe just from the station grapevine, they'd all returned to their computers, gas chromatographs, microscopes or surgical tools to resume whatever it was they'd been doing before this copper had interrupted them.

Stella made her way to a guy she'd worked with on a murder case a year before the accident. His name was Lucian Young. A black guy with a posh accent, a good six-two in height, an athlete's body and a neatly trimmed moustache and goatee. Station gossip held that he was an African prince. *Bollocks!* Stella knew he'd grown up in Oxford, the son of a university professor there. An expensive private education and a degree from his mother's university had seen to the accent. His friendly, optimistic outlook on life was all his own.

"Hey, Lucian," she said now, with a smile.

He looked up. "Oh, hello DI Cole. How are you?"

"I'm fine, all things considered. And please, call me Stella."

"Very well. Stella. I haven't seen you since the *Tool Box Murders*." He drew air quotes around the three-word phrase. It had been coined by the media for the crimes of a serial killer who'd despatched his victims with a selection of DIY tools, ranging from screwdrivers to a claw hammer, and then hacked the bodies up with a cordless power saw.

"No. That was some work you did on those bones, though. I think that's what got him convicted."

Lucian looked down, smiling, his hands resting lightly on his computer keyboard. He had long fingers with pale pink nails. *A pianist's hands*, Stella thought. "It was a team effort," he said. "Your interviews were legendary."

"Well, now we've inducted ourselves into the Paddington Green Hall of Fame, I wonder if you can do me a favour."

"If I can, I will. Ask away."

"How are you on car paints?"

"Identification, you mean?"

"Yes. Tying a flake of paint back to a make and model."

He spun his chair round so he was facing her. She'd sat on the corner of his desk and was now regretting the cheap move with the hair and the button. Lucian was far too nice to need that level of buttering up.

He frowned.

"I'm good. There are the usual databases, of course, and I did do some of my own work a few years back, building a samples file. You know, scanning and categorising paints from the major suppliers and cross-referencing them to the car makers. But you shouldn't get your hopes up too high. You know they all use the same paints, don't you?"

She nodded. "You could look for me though, couldn't you? If I had a flake for you to analyse?"

"Of course," he said, turning to his screen, long fingers poised over a keyboard. "What's the case reference?"

She tucked a stray strand of hair behind her ear.

"Oh, it's not from a live investigation. It's a cold case. I'm not really supposed to be working any cases, but, you know, I'm trying to stay sane down there and–"

He smiled. "Do you have it now?"

Stella pulled the plastic evidence bag from her jacket pocket and handed it to him. Their fingertips brushed as she handed it over and Stella jumped as a minute *crack* of static electricity discharged across the gap between them.

He grinned up at her. "Nylon carpets."

"No expense spared," she retorted.

He held the bag up to the light. "It's not a bad size for an identification. And I can give you one piece of good news already."

"What's that?" she asked, taking the opportunity to refasten her blouse button.

"It's not black. That knocks out twenty-five percent of the cars currently on Britain's roads. Nor silver, blue, grey, red or white. That takes out another seventy percent or so. What is it? A purple?"

"I think so. Sort of twinkly. Metallic. But a finer grain than in most metallics, wouldn't you say?"

"Let's get it under a microscope and then we'll be able to get a better look at it."

Stella stood. "You're sure you have time to do this now? I don't want to take you off a case."

"I was completing an online learning course in communications skills. Something the geniuses in HR believe makes us better employees. So, please, take me away."

She smiled as she remembered the bumptious woman who'd interviewed her on her first day back. "I think I preferred it when it was called personnel and they just dealt with hiring cleaners and receptionists. Come on. Let's do some science."

Science had been one of Stella's favourite subjects at Queen Mary's College in Maidenhead, where she'd grown up. She'd gained eleven GCSEs at the top grade of A*, including physics, chemistry and biology. She'd gone on to study psychology at A-level, along with English, Spanish and History. Then a first-class honours degree in psychology at the University of Bath, with a focus on abnormal psychology. While her friends had been boozing it up in the student bar or the city's pubs, Stella had been reading FBI reports on cannibalistic serial killers, wondering what made someone decide killing and eating people was a good idea.

She'd taught in secondary schools for a couple of years after graduating, but joining the police was always the plan. She'd seen herself as a top profiler, constructing detailed pictures of psychopaths and helping the front-line detectives bring them to justice. But within a year of joining the Metropolitan Police, that dream had been exposed as a callow fantasy.

A series of sexual attacks on poor women in the streets of East London had brought the media down in greedy flocks. The locations, not a million miles away from the Whitechapel locations of Jack the Ripper's kills, had produced, within days, the nickname, "Jack the Second". Initially confined to slashes across the buttocks, the attacks escalated when a street prostitute named Kacey Slater had been found dead in an alley off Mitre Square. Her throat had been cut and her tongue removed.

The senior investigating officer was a media hound of a detective superintendent known for his admiration of all things American. He had personally hired and signed off on the budget for a clinical psychologist to help develop a profile of the murderer. Her conclusions were that the police should be looking for a white, working-class male in his early- to mid-thirties. He would have low literacy and numeracy and possibly communications problems, a speech impediment of some kind, even a cleft palate. The report was long and detailed and the investigation was reinvigorated as, led by their enthusiastic SIO, the murder investigation team began tracking down local men who fitted the profile.

The end came while the detective superintendent was giving another press conference on the street outside his own station. He was promising that, despite the fact that two more murders had been committed with the same MO and nobody had been arrested for the crimes, the profile would yield a result. At the precise moment he began taking questions from the gathered reporters, a female Indian doctor named Gita Desai walked into Brick Lane Police Station, five miles away, and confessed. In cultured and perfectly modulated tones, she told a DS that she had committed the murders, and that she had been inhabited by the spirit of the goddess Kali.

After that, the young detective constable had sighed, packed up her dreams, and flushed them down the toilet. From that day, she concentrated on learning how to find, test and interpret evidence, conduct interviews, develop confidential informants and, generally become the best copper she could be. The hard work paid off. She passed her sergeant's exam the year after that and, on a fast-track programme, was promoted within six months. The rise to DI had taken another year, during which she'd earned a reputation as a no-nonsense detective who could booze it up with the boys when needed but was also sensitive enough with terrified victims or reluctant witnesses to draw them out to the point they would provide useful intelligence.

Useful intelligence was what she desperately needed now. She stood beside Lucian and watched as he mounted the chip of paint on a glass slide and pushed it under the stainless steel spring clips that held it still on the microscope's stage. His breathing was audible as he twirled the ridged plastic wheel on the side and adjusted the eyepiece – a soft whisper through his nostrils as he concentrated on bringing the tiny piece of paint into focus. Finally, he leaned away from the eyepiece and looked round at Stella.

"Want a look?" he asked. Then he scooted to one side on the wheeled chair so she could lean over the scope herself. As she did, his scent reached her nostrils: sandalwood, but soap, not aftershave. She had to make a tiny adjustment to the focus before the paint chip was pin-sharp. It looked like a shard of sheet metal under the intense magnification. Almost as though part of the bodywork of the car was lying twenty centimetres below her eye. It was beautiful in the harsh, white light from the LEDs shining down on its glossy surface. A deep violet colour with flecks of diamond embedded in its surface that reflected the light in six-armed stars.

She stared down the steel-and-brass tube, and the sounds of the forensics office faded to silence. The humming of centrifuges, the tap of fingernails on keyboards, the rattling of papers being spat from laser printers, the hubbub of any office where people are asking each other questions, discussing last night's TV or arguing over the significance of this email or that directive all disappeared as the razor-edged, irregular octagon of purple automotive paint seized control of Stella's mind.

You came from Deacon's car. You were there.

As she stared at the twinkling surface, registering the jagged edges and the layer of dark grey primer beneath the top coat, she found herself remembering her last moments with Richard. She'd been feeding Lola while he was stuffing some papers from the previous day into his briefcase. Lola's large blue eyes, fringed with impossibly long, up-curled lashes, were locked onto her own, and she could sense a deep connection that seemed to stretch back further than birth, further even than conception.

Stella jumped as Lucian laid a large, gentle hand on her shoulder.

"Are you all right?" he asked, his face troubled, brow scored with five parallel lines of concern.

"Yes, fine. Why? Do you want your toy back?"

"You've been there for ten minutes. I went off to get us coffees." He gestured to the desk next to the microscope where two mugs steamed with the station's infamous muddy brew.

"Jesus! Really? Okay, well, yes, you should have it back."

Stella took a sip of the coffee and perched on the edge of the desk. Lucian stood, arms folded, looking down at her. He spoke.

"It's actually a pearlescent paint, rather than a metallic. The crystals are ceramic, not metal. Normal metallics have coarser edges to the flakes of reflectant metal. They're rougher, too, so they don't reflect as much of the visible light back at the viewer. Plus, this colour is unusual. At first glance, I would say it's something high-end."

Something pinched at the muscles in Stella's chest. *High-end? On whatever piece-of-shit motor Deacon was driving? Pimped somehow?*

"That's great. What about makes, models?"

He smiled and put his hands out. "Not so fast! This is just a preliminary visual inspection. Just to get the gross physical characteristics. I've got a battery of tests I can do on it after this. Chemical, electrophosphorescence, conductance, laminar decomposition, then there's my trusty database."

Stella smiled, remembering why she liked the man, with his confusing mixture of upper-class manners and deep-brown skin that had thrown more than one police officer into a social tailspin before now.

"So, when, then?"

"It's always 'when', isn't it? You guys never give us time to do a thorough job."

"That's what I'm trying to do," Stella protested. "You tell me when, and I'll go away and leave you to do your *thorough job*."

"I'll need the rest of the day and maybe tomorrow as well. But–"

"But what?"

"Maybe I could share my findings over dinner? My place?"

Stella's eyes widened. "That's rather forward of you, Mr Young, don't you think?"

His eyebrows knitted together instantly. "Oh, I'm sorry. I just thought–"

She laughed then, a natural sound, full of warmth. "Just kidding. Yes, I'd like that. You can do the science bit for me. I'll even let you draw diagrams."

He smiled. "Tomorrow, about eight, then? Here," he scribbled down an address on a piece of paper, "this is me."

"Me" turned out to be a flat in a converted Docklands warehouse overlooking the Thames. The ride over took Stella thirty minutes, and as she reached Docklands, she wondered what had happened to all the original inhabitants when the developers moved in and built luxury flats right in front of the little cheek-by-jowl terraced houses that until then had at least had the benefit of a river view. Had they complained? Moved out? Or just suffered the arrival of the yuppies with working-class stoicism? And what did that make Lucian? He didn't seem like a yuppie – horrible, outdated term anyway.

She heeled out the kickstand and leant the Triumph over until the bent steel flange at the tip grated into the tarmac under the big bike's weight. She looked up and down the street; it was deserted. But it looked safe enough. Plenty of BMWs and Mercs parked outside their owners' homes. Still. You never knew. She bent to fix the chunky yellow lock over the front brake disc, threading the shackle through one of the holes and then plugging the key blank into the ignition, so the curly yellow plastic lanyard stretched tight between front wheel and handlebars. She'd only ever once driven off without undoing the disc-lock. A quarter-revolution before the half-kilo of forged steel hit the front forks, toppling the bike over and Stella to an ignominious tumble into the gutter.

Lucian opened the door dressed in faded Levi's, soft, brown, suede loafers – not Gucci, Stella was relieved to see – and a navy silk shirt that seemed to glisten in the soft light of the hallway.

"Hi, Stella. Come in. Can I take your jacket?"

She shrugged off the bike jacket and watched as he hung it on a brushed aluminium hook just inside the front door. It nestled between two other garments. A long, black, belted overcoat, made from some sort of fine wool-cashmere blend to judge from the softness as she let her fingers trail across it. And a tailored leather jacket, scuffed and battered but clearly not a chain-store item, judging from the cut and the way the distressed leather seemed to have been improved by its treatment. *You seem to be doing very well for yourself on a forensic tech's salary, Lucian.*

Stella wandered over to the huge window facing the river. Canary Wharf's towering bank and insurance buildings dominated the skyline. "You have a really nice place here."

"Thank you. I like it. Drink?"

"I brought this," she said, pulling from her messenger bag a wrapped bottle of elderflower fizz she'd bought at a supermarket on the way over.

"Ah. It's just I had a rather nice bottle of wine in the fridge."

"Alcoholic. Didn't the gossip reach forensics?"

He shook his head. "I never listen to gossip anyway. But that looks lovely. I'll put some ice and lime in it."

Sipping their drinks, they stood side by side at the window.

"I hope you don't mind my asking," Stella said, crunching an ice cube between her molars, "but how does a forensics guy afford a place like this. It's a good salary, but this is banker-land." *Please tell me you're not on the take, screwing up evidence that would put gangsters away.*

Lucian smiled. "Come and sit down, and I'll tell you."

He led her to a white leather sofa and she sat, sinking down into the *whuffing* embrace of its deeply padded cushions.

"What was it, lottery win? Inheritance? Bank robbery?" she asked, searching his face for a tell.

"Nothing so exciting, I'm afraid. When I was at university, two friends and I built a website that used spare computing power from its members' PCs to solve complex analytical problems. We sold it to an American software firm. The money wasn't enough to retire on, not that we would have wanted to, but we did well enough out of it to buy ourselves houses."

"You're a genius, is that what you're telling me?"

He laughed. "Not at all. We were in the right place at the right time. There was a lot of interest in crowd computing and we just had a different take on it. I won't bore you with the details, but it was an elegant solution to a particular problem. Now, you didn't come here to probe my finances, did you?"

"God, sorry, no. Old habits. Have you got something for me?"

"Yes, I have. I'll give you the summary, then we can eat, and if you have any questions, we can talk over dinner."

CHAPTER THIRTEEN
Viola del Diavolo

LUCIAN RETRIEVED A single sheet of paper from his briefcase and returned to the sofa.

"It's a very expensive paint. It's called," then he adopted a passable Italian accent, "*Viola del diavolo.*" Stella raised her glass to him in ironic appreciation. "It means *the devil's purple*, more or less. Pretty rare. Normally you'd find it on special-order Lamborghinis or Bugattis."

Could Deacon have nicked some banker's pride and joy and then headed across town to Putney to kill Richard in it? Really? A distant alarm bell began ringing inside Stella's head.

She frowned and shook her head to clear the thought.

"So, not a mass-market car paint then, or something you could order online? I mean, you wouldn't find it on a Ford or a VW?"

He shook his head. "Not a chance. The manufacturers keep a very tight grip on distribution. You can see why. If some squillionaire merchant banker finds his Bentley's the same shade of purple as some kid's pimped-out Fiesta, there'd be ructions for sure."

"Why did you say Bentley? I thought you said it was all Italian supercars?"

"Here's the thing. I called the UK distributor this afternoon. I spoke to a very nice young lady called Shelley. And Shelley told me that the only company in this country who's ordered any recently is Bentley."

"That's fantastic," Stella said. "It's so much better than I'd hoped for."

"Oh, there's more. I rang Bentley too. Laid it on a bit thick, said I was calling from the Metropolitan Police's international car smuggling division. They told me there were only five Bentleys they knew of painted in that colour. Apparently, they only offer it to, what did he call them, 'selected enthusiasts and collectors'?"

"You didn't get the registrations, did you?"

He shook his head. "I asked for a list, but he clammed up on me. Told me it was more than his job was worth to divulge information about customer cars without a warrant. I'm sorry."

She tucked her left leg under her right so she could turn to face him and put a hand on his knee. "No, no. What the hell are you apologising for? This is amazing. If we had that sort of breakthrough every day, we'd be laughing."

Lucian smiled. "In that case, you're welcome. Now, how about some dinner?"

Clearly, Lucian had found time to learn to cook as well as study forensic science and build crowd computing websites that netted him enough money for a Docklands apartment. He delivered two large, round, white plates to the table. They bore thick slabs of white fish, roasted until the salt-seasoned skin had turned brown and crisped up like a wafer-thin roof over the succulent white flesh beneath. Quivering dollops of a vivid green sauce. And herby roast potatoes cut into small cubes that rustled as they toppled from the serving spoon onto her plate.

Stella cut a chunk of the fish, scooped up some of the sauce and placed it into her mouth, which was already watering from the smell.

"Oh, my, God!" she said, eyes wide, once she had swallowed. "That is fucking awesome. What is it?"

He smiled. "Italian-roasted cod with *salsa verde*. That's a green sauce of basil, parsley, mint, Dijon mustard, olive oil, capers, anchovies, lemon juice, salt and pepper."

"Rich, good looking and a demon cook. And yet you're single. Apparently. No Mrs Young in evidence." She made a show of peering under the table.

"Not as far as I'm aware."

"What's the matter with you, then? Do you collect Star Wars memorabilia? Go trainspotting at the weekends? What?"

He smiled. "I'm gay."

"Well, that would explain it. No Mr Young either, though."

"No. I've had a couple of relationships, but I'm in the middle of a dry spell at the moment."

"So, do you get any grief at the station, then?"

"What about – being black or being queer?"

"Either."

"Honest answer? Not really. They all think we're boffins from another planet already. How about you? As a woman, I mean. Still a man's world, isn't it?"

"Allegedly. But I don't let it get to me. Anyone gives me any shit and I'll put them on the floor."

"Amen to that." He paused, and ate a mouthful of the food before speaking again. "Can I ask you a personal question?"

She shrugged. "Ask away."

"How are you coping? Being back, I mean. That was pretty rough, what happened to you."

"I'm fine." Then she shook her head, pursing her lips and frowning. "No. You've just been honest with me, so I owe you the same in return. I'm not fine. Not at all. I can function day to day. I get up, go to work, go home, see my baby, run for an hour or two, eat, sleep, then do it all again. But I miss him, Lucian. God I miss him." Tears rolled from the corners of her eyes and dropped into the remains of the green sauce smeared on her plate.

He got up from his chair and rounded the table to kneel by her side.

"DI Cole, do you need a hug?"

She sniffed and blew her nose on a tissue. "Forensic Officer Young, yes, I really do."

"Come and sit with me on the sofa, then. I'll give you a hug and you can tell me about what happened."

For the first time since the accident, Stella felt safe enough to open up about her grief. About the wild, mad-eyed shrieking in the early days when the neighbours had called the police, and she'd worried they'd send for Social Services and have Lola removed from her own mother's care, "for her own safety". About the sleepless nights and booze-soaked days. About the pills that had calmed her at first, then zombified her until her brain felt like it was a lump of mattress stuffing. And, finally, about the slow-burning desire for justice that had been banking up inside her ever since and now had reached an almost volcanic intensity.

When she finished speaking, her face squashed against his chest, his hand stroking her hair, he waited before speaking.

"But the law *did* work in your case, didn't it? I remember hearing about it. They got the guy. So, justice *was* served."

She pushed herself upright and turned to face him, her face reddened from crying, her eyes blazing.

"No! It was not. He got three years for causing death by careless driving. He's probably out by now for good bloody behaviour. And he looked at me as they took him down. He had that look like they all do. Smug little shits. It said, 'I've put one over on you'. He looked me right in the eye and mouthed it at me, or something like it. I know it was a put-up job, Lucian, I just know! He's a toe-rag. How could he afford a Bentley?"

Lucian looked down at his hands, which were clasped around one of hers, then back into her eyes.

"I'm not going to do anything that will put my career into reverse. But if you need any help on the forensics side again, off the record, come and ask."

*

Sitting at her desk in the exhibits room the next morning, Stella was adding information to a pocket-sized black notebook she'd carried around with her since starting work again. The faint-ruled page contained the intelligence she'd gathered so far, plus the questions she needed answers to. It wasn't a very long list:

Who was SIO?
Who was Deacon's defence brief? Jury members? Judge?
Paint chip: Viola del diavolo. Rare. Five Bentleys in UK. Investigate owners.
Orig. physical evidence misfiled on computer. Who had access?

She snapped a rubber band round the notebook's hard covers. Her bike jacket hung over the back of her rickety swivel chair; she stuffed the notebook into the inside pocket. The place was so quiet she was starting to miss Reg and his endless advice about vegetable growing, a subject Stella had signally failed to convince him she didn't care about.

The door opened and in walked Howard Floyd.

Stella looked up. Even though there were dozens of officers working at Paddington Green she'd rather see, she still smiled at him. A boring fat bastard was better than no bastard at all.

"Hi, Pink. You the exhibits officer for a case or something?"

Floyd strolled over to Stella's desk and sat on one corner. She couldn't help wrinkling her nose at the way the flesh of his buttocks sagged over the edge of the desk.

"Me? No. What do you think I am, some wet-behind-the-ears Hendon graduate?" Before Stella could frame a reply, he continued speaking. "I just heard something on the grapevine that you might find interesting."

He paused, clearly expecting her to prompt him in some way so he could drag out the moment of expectation. With nothing else to do, she went along with the script.

"Oh, yeah? What's that then? Doughnuts banned for the clinically obese? Compulsory wardrobe consultancy for the terminally slobby?"

He frowned and tucked his chin into the folds of fat at his collar.

"No. It's about Edwin Deacon."

Stella straightened in her chair and leaned forward, her fingers clenching into fists. "What about him?"

"Took a one-way trip to the infirmary at Long Lartin last night, didn't he? Seems he got misclassified in the middle of being transferred from HMP Bure. Get this. To a fucking paedo! A kiddy fiddler. A—"

"Yes! I get it, Pink. A Rule 45."

"Yeah. And it seems a few of the gorillas up there took a dislike to him on his first day. Beat him senseless with baseball bats they made in the carpentry workshop. They wheeled him into the infirmary, but he had some kind of brain bleed and flatlined." Floyd picked up a sheet of paper from the desk and turned it over in his hand. "Seems there is justice in this world after all, eh, Stel? Like I said to you the other day, there are people out there who are making things happen the way they ought to, instead of the way those muppets on juries figure it should."

Something about his I've-got-a-secret demeanour – all winks and nose-tapping – made Stella start listening to his story more closely.

"Sorry Pink, Howard, I mean. What do you mean, 'people who're making things happen'? What kind of people?"

He stood up, reddening and ran a hand over the shining scalp at the front of his head. "It's nothing, Stel. I just meant those guys at Long Lartin did you a favour. Did us all a favour, given what a little scumbag Deacon was. I've arrested him myself at least twice. Look, I have to go. I've got a shitload of witnesses to contact about a murder-suicide in some mansion flats over Maida Vale way. Later, okay? Maybe grab a coffee or something?"

"Yes, okay. That would be good."

Once Pink had left, Stella leaned forward and rested her head in her hands so the palms squashed her cheeks in. Her mind was full of conflicting thoughts and emotions. The bastard was dead. Good! But now she'd never be able to question him about what actually happened that day. Why he'd killed Richard. Whether it really was careless – or even dangerous – driving, or whether there was more to it. The files were still there, though.

Then she sat up straight, and smacked herself hard on the forehead. A horrible realisation was dawning in Stella's brain. Normally she'd think of it as a hunch. Only that sounded too much like a good thing. The look Deacon had given her as he was being led off to start his pathetic three-year sentence. It wasn't just the smirk of the affectless killer. It was smugness. He was grinning because he'd got one over on a cop.

"Fuck!" she said. "You told me. You didn't say, 'You've been bad,' did you? You said, 'You've been had.'" She slammed her fists down on the desk, making a plastic pot of chewed biros rattle and spill its contents. "It never was you, was it? Death-by-careless, death-by-dangerous, you didn't give a flying fuck one way or the other, did you?"

She reclined in the chair and let her head hang over the back. She stared at the ceiling and listened to a little, quiet voice inside her head.

Go back to the evidence, Stel, it said. *It all starts with the evidence.*

CHAPTER FOURTEEN
A Bad Day

AMID THE MOLECULAR gastronomy and playroom antics of London's more adventurous chefs, Vivre Pour Manger in Soho's Goslett Yard stood out for its utter lack of pretension. It was neither fashionable in its location nor experimental in its cuisine. It catered to a demanding, and loyal clientele who wanted traditional French *haute cuisine*, didn't mind what they paid for it, and would have been horrified at the idea that their beloved restaurant had resorted to anything so vulgar as advertising.

They came for the privacy. They came for the discreet but efficient service. But, above all, they came for the food, which a famous critic had dismissed in the pages of *The Times* with the phrase, "unadventurous food for people whose pockets are deeper than their thirst for new experience". Inside, soft, burgundy-coloured velvet curtains hung against the white brickwork to soften the acoustics of the room.

The two men eating at a dimly lit corner table were munching escargots served on stainless steel plates, the snails drenched in miniature baths of liquid, garlic-infused butter. The silver-haired man with his back to the wall was straight-backed, his deep-brown eyes gleaming healthily from a tanned complexion. He was a High Court judge, and very definitely of the old school. A man who, before the policymakers banned it, would have taken great pride, and pleasure, in being known by the populace as "a hanging judge". What was left to him now? No flogging. No birching. No stocks, stake or pillory.

Even "life means life" – or a "whole life order" as the less poetic legal code had it – was a rarely available privilege these days. Sometimes it seemed to him that every multiple murderer and paedophile could be relied upon to start bleating about their "rights" within seconds of grasping the polished wooden rail of the dock before him.

Opposite him sat a younger man. Dark-brown hair cut short and parted on the left. Startling cobalt-blue eyes that contrasted sharply both with his dark hair and the swarthy complexion. His cheeks were heavily shadowed with stubble. His hands were flat and square with immensely thick, blunt-ended fingers. He looked as though a circus strongman lurked inside the soft grey, wool and cashmere suit instead of its rightful owner.

In a way, he *was* a circus strongman. The ring he performed in was the courtroom. His feats of strength were verbal, rather than physical. And his stage rig, rather than a leopard-skin leotard knotted over one shoulder, was a sweeping black legal gown – smooth, starched, white lawyer's bands at his throat – and an off-white wig that he'd found in a chest in his grandfather's attic as a boy. Only up-and-comers purchased new wigs. Serious lawyers, from serious legal families, inherited theirs, or else had the sorts of connections that could procure a suitably distressed item that gave its wearer the appearance of having been practising law since the times of Oliver Cromwell.

The lawyer was speaking now.

"Did you hear about Stella Cole?"

The judge dabbed a slick of grease from his lips with a thick, white napkin. "Stella who?"

"Cole. Detective Inspector Stella Cole, Judge. It was her husband–"

"Oh, that Stella Cole," the judge interrupted. He steadied another cream-and-caramel-striped snail shell with his left thumb and forefinger. With a tiny, bone-handled fork he picked the delicious curl of dark-brown meat from its interior. "Forgive me, Charlie. One meets so many people." The judge let his remark hang between them like smoke.

"She's back at work. I spoke to Adam. I gather she's been put on light duties. They've bumped her down to administration. With any luck, she'll have a breakdown caused by acute boredom and get pensioned off the force."

The judge grimaced. "I wish it hadn't come to this, Charlie."

"Come to what?"

"PPM going after civilians, even troublesome lawyers and their families. Look at us. We're discussing how to force a detective inspector – a good one if my sources are correct – out of her job in the Met. We were never supposed to be about that, were we?"

Howarth paused, his fork halfway to his mouth.

"Not at the beginning, no. Of course not. But things change, you know that. Drinkwater was going to expose us. Either he or some journalist he'd enlisted for his crusade. Just remember why you got into this in the first place."

Ramage swallowed his last snail. He glanced up at the ceiling. He was remembering.

*

It had been 2007. July. A case at the Old Bailey. A sexual predator called Peter Moxey had raped and then murdered two women within a week of each other. He'd assaulted a third the following week, but somehow the woman had survived the attack. She was in a coma for two weeks then – miraculously, the doctors said at the time – she recovered. The police had their witness, plus physical evidence. Moxey had no alibi. It was, or should have been, an open and shut case.

Throughout the proceedings, Ramage had watched as Moxey had stood in the dock, winking at his friends in the public gallery as they arrived. He was smart, though. Never spoke unless spoken to. Maintained a head-down, eyes-lowered pose that Ramage could tell impressed at least two jurors.

As the evidence piled up against him, Moxey appeared to lose a little of the swagger that he had carried with him into the dock. But then, the star witness, the third woman he'd raped, faltered in the witness box under cross-examination. In seconds, under some respectful but clever questioning from the defence counsel, the Crown's case fell apart. It appeared that the police had coached the witness.

Despite his own clear belief that the man was guilty, and the unassailable weight of evidence, Ramage was forced to halt proceedings. He consulted with counsels for prosecution and defence in his chambers, then returned to the courtroom and announced, in a disgusted tone, that owing to certain legal complication he would decline to go into, he had no option but to dismiss the case and free the prisoner.

Two weeks later, a nineteen-year-old woman, home from university for the long summer holidays, was raped in Hyde Park. She went to the police and gave a perfect description of the man who had attacked her. It was Peter Moxey. Every scar and tattoo, every speech mannerism, every physical characteristic described as clearly as if he'd been standing in the rape suite with her. She returned home to her parents' house in East London while the police geared up to find and arrest Moxey.

They did find him. And they did arrest him, though not before he'd given one uniformed officer a broken nose, and a second a five-inch laceration to his face. And this time, the trial ended with a guilty verdict. But it was too late for his final victim. Leanne Wray took an overdose of antidepressants and tranquillisers in her bedroom the night after the trial finished. Her parents found her body the following morning.

*

Frankie O'Meara appeared at the entrance to the exhibits room. She signalled to Stella, beckoning her over.

"Hi Frankie. What brings you down to the Epic Pits of Doom?"

Frankie smiled, her eyes focusing on the floor. She brushed at a stray hair at her neck.

"I was wondering if you fancied coming round to mine for a pizza after work tonight. I thought you might like some company."

She touched her fingertips to the notch between her collarbones as she said this, and Stella observed the flush of red spreading out from the notch into the soft skin of her throat.

"I can't, Frankie. Sorry. I left Kristina alone with Lola the other night."

Frankie's smile slid from her face to be replaced by a look of concern, or was it sadness? Stella found it hard to tell these days, even though they'd been friends for years. Frankie's mouth was turned down at the corners, though. Definitely sadness.

"Well, how about I come to yours then and we order in?"

"I'd like that. It's been ages since you've been to mine. You can see how much Lola's changed."

Frankie's eyes were hooded by their shimmery green lids, but Stella couldn't help but notice the way her plump lower lip was trembling. Ever so slightly.

"Shall I come round about seven thirty? I'm guessing you guys keep office hours down here."

Sure," Stella said brightly. "That would be great. We can download a movie to watch, too. A real girls' night."

Stella's doorbell chimed at seven twenty-eight that evening. She bent to the cot and stroked Lola's cheek, smiling at her sleeping daughter's pudgy face, then walked down the hall to open the front door.

Frankie stood there clutching a bottle wrapped in crinkly, pink tissue paper. She stuck her arm out as if she was holding a fizzing stick of dynamite.

"Here, it's apple and pomegranate. Sparkling."

"Top woman," Stella said. "Come in. Let's order, I'm starving."

With the pizzas ordered – American Hot for Stella, Giardiniera for Frankie – the two women sat facing each other at the scrubbed pine kitchen table, sipping the sweet, bubbly drink.

"Stel," Frankie said, holding the glass tumbler between her outstretched fingertips, "is everything okay? With you, I mean?"

Stella shrugged. "Obviously, being a widowed single mum isn't all it's cracked up to be, and the job is driving me round the twist, but, you know, I manage. I miss Richard so much, but at least I've still got Lola to remind me of him. They've got the same smile."

Frankie gulped some of her drink down, then coughed.

"Sorry, bubbles went down the wrong way."

"Muppet! Listen, I want to talk to you about Edwin Deacon."

"Why? He was killed up at Long Lartin. Everyone was talking about it. Aren't you, you know, relieved? Pleased, I mean? He got what was coming to him."

"That's just it, Frankie. I don't think he did."

"But there's not much more anyone can do to him, is there? I mean, once you've topped somebody, that's basically it."

"That's not what I mean."

"Sorry, maybe I'm being thick here, but I'm not getting you."

"I don't think it was him at all. I think he was put up to it. Not the FATACC itself, just being charged and sentenced for it."

Frankie frowned and she tapped the table in front of her.

"Why? Who'd do that? It would have to be somebody with a ton of clout. Deacon was scum, we all agreed on that, but he wouldn't just roll over unless it was someone he feared."

"Maybe he didn't have to fear them. Maybe he was paid to do it."

"But why? Why would anyone pay Deacon to take the fall for a hit and run? If it was … sorry to say this, boss," she stuttered, "I mean, Stel, but if it was someone who actually planned it, why not just keep driving?"

"Because there'd be evidence left behind, wouldn't there? Cop's husband, it stands to reason there'd be heat on securing a conviction. So they put Deacon up to clear the case quickly. Before I could find out who really did it."

"OK, just for the sake of argument, we go with it. How do you know it wasn't Deacon in the first place?"

Stella finished her drink. "Here's why. One, he more or less admitted it to me." She waved away Frankie's protest with outspread fingers. "Not literally, but he spoke to me from the dock. He mimed it: 'You've been had.' Two, I found the physical evidence. It was misfiled, but I found it anyway. It was a paint chip. Off a Bentley."

"But how could Deacon afford a Bentley? No, he must've nicked it."

"It's possible. But there are only five in that particular colour. I'm going to get onto Bentley HQ and get the owners' names. Then, if none of them had their cars nicked last year, we'll know, won't we?"

Their conversation was interrupted by the doorbell. Stella collected the pizzas, tipped the young delivery guy three pounds and brought the food back to the table. The rest of the evening was the sort of back-and-forth cops go through when they're trying to get an angle on a case. All the what-ifs. All the yes-buts. All the, if-we-can-justs. It got to ten, and Frankie announced she had to leave.

The two women embraced awkwardly in the narrow hallway, and then Stella closed her front door and went back to the kitchen. She cleared away the boxes and the discarded crusts, washed up the glasses and put the empty bottle in the recycling box, then went up to take a look at Lola before turning in.

The baby was sleeping, emitting little snuffles through her upturned nose. Gently, she lifted Lola out of her cot and, cradling her against her chest, took her from the nursery and into her own bedroom.

Stella sat on the bed with her daughter, rocking gently and humming a snatch of an old lullaby her own mother had sung to her.

A voice from the other side of the double bed startled her. She clutched Lola tighter, causing her to emit a little mew of protest. The fitted wardrobe that filled the side of the room that had been Richard's had a central sliding door faced with a mirror. Stella looked into it now.

She could see herself holding Lola. Then she, the other Stella in the mirror, spoke.

"Did you hear what I just said?"

Stella's heart rate accelerated so fast she thought for a moment she might faint. Tiny stars were sparking in the outer edges of her vision.

"Who, I mean, why are you talking?"

"I'm you," the reflection said. "The real you. The you that knows what's going on. You were going to have to face it sooner or later. Your DS knows. Frankie's a clever girl. She'll go far."

"Face what?"

"It's Lola. She died that day as well."

*

Stella Cole's breathing is fast, and shallow. It's playing havoc with the gas balance in her bloodstream. Her neural circuits are having trouble adjusting too. She holds her baby tighter. The baby emits another bleat of protest.

"Don't say that! Lola's right here, on my lap. On *your* lap, for God's sake. Look!" Stella's voice has taken on a strident tone. Defensive. She can hear it, and she doesn't like it.

Her heart feels jumpy, and it seems to miss one beat in four.

Her mouth suddenly becomes very dry. It tastes of metal.

She holds Lola out in front of her, her palms gripping her under her armpits, and watches as the reflection does the same.

"Look," she says to her reflection.

The reflected woman holds up a baby. She turns it to face Stella.

As she does, Stella experiences a visceral jolt of fear.

What has happened to Lola's baby-pink skin? It is golden brown, the colour of toffee. Now she looks closer, it isn't skin at all, but fur.

Her breathing is coming in ragged gasps.

"Look down," the reflection says, not unkindly.

Stella looks down at her daughter.

"Wake up Lola," she whispers, urgently. "Wake up for Mummy, please."

Then she shudders, and her breathing stills.

Lola's eyes are glossy, translucent, amber discs, with big, black pupils. Slightly domed and comically oversized in that furry face. Her beautiful button nose has been transformed into a black triangle, stitched on somehow. And her ears stick out on each side of her head, pink-lined in silk, and furry like the rest of her fat little bear's body.

Stella grips Lola tighter, and the little bear emits one final, plaintive squeak from the sound box sewn into her belly.

Stella shakes her head, then finds she can't stop. "No," she whispers. "No," louder this time, a normal speaking volume.

Her hands are clasped together so tightly around the soft toy, the fingers are bloodless. "No, no, no, no … what have you done to my beautiful baby girl? Kristina!"

Stella shrieks this last word. Then again, even louder. Nobody comes. There is nobody *to* come.

*

Stella woke up the next morning with no recollection of having undressed, washed or got into bed. She swung her legs over, and as her bare toes sank into the sheepskin rug by the side of the bed, it hit her. Hit her hard. Like a punch.

Lola.

Is.

Dead.

She sat there for two hours, maybe three, looking at the way her toes dug into the long white hairs of the sheepskin. Pulling them out and then burying them again, wondering what to do next. Inside she felt empty. Hollowed out.

Perhaps a drink would help.

Or a tranquilliser.

But she realised.

She wanted neither.

Didn't have them in the house anymore, so would be pointless looking.

"Well, if you don't want a drink or a pill, Stel, what do you want?" The voice in her head was her own, but it sounded like a separate person. Like the woman from the mirror.

Stella rubbed her palm over her face, scrubbing hard.

"What I want is to find the man who murdered my husband and my daughter."

"Oh, really? Why? What would you do? Paint me a picture, Stella."

Stella looked at the ceiling and then closed her eyes. A scene took shape. He'd be tied to a chair. Naked. Shaking from fear. Probably had to be a deserted warehouse somewhere out East. Rotherhithe, maybe, in one of the old abandoned tobacco docks. Puddles on the concrete floor, dim sunlight coming through fly-blown windows, cracked and stained with age and frosted with grime. There'd be bits of old machinery lying around, ropes and pulleys, lengths of chain. The air would smell bad, of decay and stagnant water.

Was he a crackhead, skinny and pockmarked with running sores around his mouth and nose?

Or a drinker, maybe even a golf club type in soft, custard-yellow cashmere sweater and a pleading, Home-Counties accent?

Or a hard-faced ex-con with tattoos on his cheeks and over his neck, leering at her with broken teeth and dead eyes?

It didn't matter. He was the one who'd been behind the wheel that day. Now he was hers.

A chisel would be a start. But only a start. She'd take his fingers off, one by one. That would need a block of wood or a work table of some kind. Make it secateurs. Or loppers. Bolt cutters. The ones with the nice long handles. More frightening to look at and contemplate as the crescent jaws opened and Stella gently cradled his ring finger in between the heavy steel blades.

He'd break. Of course, he would. Weeping, sobbing, pleading to be let go. But, no. This was justice being played out.

At the crunching sound as his finger dropped to the floor and as the bright red blood spurted, he'd piss himself and begin screaming in earnest. If he passed out, she'd bring a bucket of cold water from a tap outside. To wake him up. To bring him back. He had to come back. Otherwise, where was the pleasure in killing him?

Stella had met plenty of brutal women in her career. Gang members who'd use their stiletto heels on a fallen opponent like daggers, stamping down on soft, pale flesh. Beaten women who'd snapped finally and battered their Neanderthal husbands to death with cast-iron skillets, fire irons, even a car's bottle jack on one memorable Sunday afternoon.

Oh, yes. Women could be every bit as bloodily brutal as men. Stella Cole intended to see to it.

Sometime in the night, part of her had died. The part that was loving. The part that was fully human. The part that believed in law and order. What remained felt distant, detached from reality somehow. It was as if she was a pilot inside a human body, operating controls to make it do what she wanted. A ghost in the machine.

Acting on muscle memory and instinct, she dressed herself and went to work.

She smiled at people as she signed in, cracked a joke for the benefit of one of the civilian assistants as she arrived in the exhibits room and set about her work, as if reorganising the filing system of the Metropolitan Police was the culmination of a career in law enforcement.

Except the work she was doing had nothing to do with filing, very little to do with the Met, and absolutely nothing at all to do with the law.

What it did have to do with was an ancient concept that the law was partly intended to replace.

Stella Cole no longer wanted justice.

She wanted vengeance.

"First things first, Stel," the voice in her head said. "The autopsy report. We should see it for ourselves. Just to be sure. Maybe it was a nightmare, and we got it wrong."

It seemed unlikely. But Stella knew she had to be certain. She stood and crossed the room to where a civilian assistant wearing all black – long skirt, long-sleeved T-shirt, Dr. Martens boots – was typing numbers into a spreadsheet.

"Hi," Stella said, with a smile. "Can you tell me your login for the central server please? It's because I need to log in with it."

During her degree studies, Stella had read of a psychology experiment where a researcher went to the head of a long photocopier queue in a university and uttered a scripted line: "Can I go in front please? I need to use the photocopier." The question worked half the time. Then, the researcher added the phrase, "because I need to make some copies". Even though the justification for queue-jumping was nonsensical – why else would you need to use a photocopier? – the proportion of people who let her in front jumped from seventy to eighty-five percent. It seemed giving a reason, any reason at all, made people do what you wanted. Stella had used the trick many times since, when interviewing suspects or gaining entry to residences without a warrant, and it worked just as well now.

The assistant looked up from her spreadsheet and smiled.

"Sure. It's TheaMJackson and my password is Gandalf." She blushed. "I like Tolkien."

Back at her own desk, Stella logged in to the central server for the whole station then clicked her way through to the database of medical and forensic files. She brought up the page for autopsies and clicked on the Search icon. And then she typed two words.

Lola Drinkwater.

There it was. Irrefutable proof that Lola was dead and Stella had been driven out of her mind by grief. Heart bumping painfully in her chest, breath coming in short gasps, Stella read the report, forcing herself not to skim it or to skip ahead. The first line startled her with its brutal simplicity:

Cause of death: thermal burns.

She read on, dry-eyed, the background burble of the exhibits room gradually fading to silence, as the pathologist detailed the tissue damage, both external and internal that had occurred, as she put it, *ante-*, *peri-* and *post-mortem*. Before, while, and after she died.

Stella wiped her hand across her forehead. It was clammy to the touch. Her stomach had tightened to a hard, painful knot. Her teeth, and the muscles of her jaws that were clenching them against each other, were aching.

Reaching out with a trembling hand, she clicked the mouse to close the file. She logged out. She stood, walked out of the exhibits room to the ladies' toilets. Entered a stall. And vomited into the commode. She flushed, then she sat for a while, focusing her energy on not screaming.

When she emerged, she had decided what she was going to do.

First, she would track down her family's real killer.

Then she would look him in the eye as she inflicted intense pain upon him. The kind that came from being burnt alive, for example.

Finally, she would kill him.

Which meant she would need equipment.

The preliminaries could be handled using the sorts of items one could purchase quite legally in kitchen shops and DIY sheds. They could wait until the weekend.

But there was one item that would be better procured at work.

CHAPTER FIFTEEN
Suffer the Little Children

ALTHOUGH SHE'D NEVER participated in one of the Met's long-term undercover operations, Stella was friendly with plenty of coppers who had. The aim was usually to infiltrate a pressure group and gather intelligence, though the odd crossover outfit distributing leaflets in shopping centres during the day and bombing research labs at night might also be a target. The trouble was, the animal rights people, the greens, the anarchists were getting smart and running the kind of background checks on willing new converts that wouldn't look amiss inside the shadowier organs of government.

The old, "just call me John" routine didn't work anymore. You had to have a full ID workup, from birth certificate on to driving licence and passport. And the method of doing it was now taught in the force. Anyone who'd read some of the old sixties spy books would know of it, but that didn't mean it didn't work. Plus, being the cops, you found that the wheels of state ground rather faster than they would for some freelance assassin.

Before she went any further with her hardware, Stella wanted something else badly. Something she felt she could use to stay hidden.

The morning after reading Lola's autopsy report, she spent thirty minutes Googling country churches in Hertfordshire. Then she took her bike out, heading for the M1 motorway. After an hour's ride north, she took the slip road at Junction 10 and made her way into the countryside.

The first five churches she visited had plenty of graves, but none that would serve her purpose. Flashing along a lane lined with hawthorn hedges and enjoying the sensation of the Triumph's weight shifting beneath her as she negotiated the alternating left- and right-hand bends, she made her way to a long, strung-out village called Offley, not far from Luton Airport

Leaving her bike parked under a walnut tree at the edge of the single-track road leading through the village, she made her way to the church: St Mary Magdalene. It was secluded, with a large graveyard. The tower of the church was red brick and appeared to be much newer than the flint and exposed wooden beams that comprised most of the rest of the building. One end featured a curious, blank-walled stone box with crenellations and four small turrets at the corners, as if a child had built a castle for her knights and forgotten the windows.

Stella hadn't come for the architecture, however, but for the graves. One grave in particular. She hadn't found it yet, and she didn't know who'd be buried beneath the sod, but she'd know it when she saw it.

In a corner of the churchyard, birds were singing in a tumbledown apple tree that had partially collapsed under the weight of its own branches. Poking around among the mottled and lichen-speckled gravestones, Stella felt the hairs on the back of her neck erecting. Something flickered on the very edge of her peripheral vision, and she whirled away from the tall, grey stone she'd been inspecting. But there was nothing to see. *Just graveyard jitters, Stel. Let's keep looking, shall we?* The sun had come out from behind a cloud and its warmth penetrated Stella's bike jacket, heating her back and bringing a light sweat to her brow and top lip.

After twenty minutes, she still hadn't found the child's grave. She was sitting on an old tree stump, drinking from a metallic purple water bottle she'd packed in her daysack and closing her eyes against the sun, when a light cough made her look up with a jerk.

"Beautiful day, isn't it?" The speaker was a slim young man in a tweed jacket and jeans, with a cleric's black shirt and dog collar. He extended his hand. "I'm sorry I startled you. My name's Luke, appropriately enough. Luke Terry. I'm the vicar here at St Mary Magdalene."

Stella took the vicar's hand reflexively and shook it, noting his dry palm and strong grip. No bookworm, this priest; must be one of those muscular Christians she kept reading about.

"It's my name too," she said. "Mary, I mean, not Luke."

He smiled. "Are you here doing genealogical research? We get quite a few people here now that tracing family trees has become so popular, what with the shows on TV and so forth."

She shook her head and reeled off the speech she'd prepared, just in case. "I'm a researcher for a production company, well, a location scout, really. We're making a film where a character loses a child in infancy and we need a gravestone. I don't suppose you have any, um, you know–"

"It's OK," the vicar said, "you can say it. Dead children here? They're with our Lord now, and I'm sure He will ensure their ears aren't burning. As a matter of fact, there are one or two of the poor little souls buried here. Come with me, I'll show you." He stuck his hands in his pockets, rucking up the jacket at the back, and strode off.

Stella walked behind the vicar, admiring the curve of his backside in the jeans as he took her between two rows of stones towards the corner with the apple tree. He stopped and pointed at a low, square stone in polished black granite, the inscription carved with sharp edges and picked out in gold paint.

"Here's one of our little guests," he said. "She died just a few years ago. Meningitis. Terrible thing. We saw her at Messy Church the previous Sunday, and she was gone by teatime the following Tuesday."

Already dismissing this gravestone as not fit for purpose, Stella felt a show of emotion of some kind was called for, and knelt in front of the grave marker to read out the few words carved there.

"Tallulah Harriet Foster, 18 July 2004 to 6 September 2005. Taken from us too soon. Safe with Jesus." She stood, brushing a few crumbs of mud from her knees. "Poor baby."

Then, as if hit by a storm, Stella's knees buckled and she collapsed to the ground. "Oh, my poor baby," she cried out. "You were taken too soon. Much, much too soon." Sobbing, she leant forward to cradle the hard granite in her arms, resting her cheek against the cool stone.

For a while, she stayed there, until her sobs subsided into a soundless heaving before stopping altogether. She looked round. Luke was standing there, watching her. He held a folded white cotton handkerchief in his outstretched right hand.

"Here," he said, his voice low and reassuring. "Take this."

She took the handkerchief, wiped her eyes and blew her nose.

Getting to her feet she offered it back to him but he shook his head.

"Keep it."

"I'm sorry. What must you think of me? I don't normally go around bursting into tears at the graves of strangers."

Instead of speaking, Luke took a step towards her and drew her right arm through his own. Then he did speak.

"Why don't you come and have a cup of tea with me inside? There's nobody about, so we won't be disturbed."

Stella allowed herself to be led by this quiet, confident man into the cool interior of the church. She looked around at the wall hangings, the windows, the plaques set into the floor and the flowers at the altar.

"It's very beautiful."

"Thank you, but the true beauty of a church isn't visible in its decor or the monuments to the great and the good. It's present in the love that people share with each other and with God. Now, here we are, the vestry. Or, as my wife likes to call it, *Luke's lair*. He put air quotes around the name, though Stella thought it barely warranted the emphasis.

The little room was painted in a nondescript shade of institutional pale green. It had a simple clothes rack with some embroidered green, white and gold robes hanging from it. A desk and chair with a second chair for a visitor occupied one corner. And, on a small table beside two armchairs, a kettle, mugs, teapot and jars containing coffee granules and teabags.

Five minutes later, they were sitting opposite each other in the padded chairs, sipping some fairly awful instant coffee.

Noting her wince, Luke smiled. "I know. Hardly organic fair trade Kenyan estate-roasted, is it? So, let me ask you something, Mary. Have you lost someone yourself recently? A child?"

She was about to deny it, but the fleeting sense of having been observed in the churchyard when she arrived, coupled with the evidence of her obvious distress, made her change her mind. She nodded.

"My daughter. A year ago. She was five months old. It was a hit and run driver. Didn't stop."

"I am sorry for your loss, truly, I am. Our daughter is only a year old, and I try not to worry when she's not with me, but it's hard. Did they ever catch the person who did it? The police, I mean. Prosecute someone?"

Stella took another sip of the coffee.

"No. Not really."

"Not really?"

"We're still looking at the case."

Luke frowned. "We?"

"They, I mean. I said we because, you know, I'm helping them. Pushing them. Keeping them focused. You know how it is. Look, I don't want to take up any more of your time. Didn't you say you had two children buried here?"

Luke put his mug down on the table.

"Yes, I did. If you're sure you're OK?"

"Yes. Thank you. I'm fine."

The grave was knee-high. A weathered golden-grey stone of some kind with an angel carved in relief at the top. No metallic paint this time, just plain letters carved into its smooth, flat front.

Jennifer Amy Stadden
b. 5 January 1978
d. 20 April 1980

"Suffer the little children to come unto me."

"Car crash," Luke said.

"Pardon?"

"Jennifer died in a car crash. Her mother had been drinking. It was before my time, but my predecessor knew the family and spent some time bringing me up to speed, as they say, with all the stories of the parish."

"Would you mind if I took a photo, for our director?"

"Be my guest," Luke said, spreading his hands wide. "As I said, where Jennifer's gone, no harm can ever come to her again."

Stella tapped her phone's screen a few times, making sure that the dates were properly in focus.

"Thank you. Luke," she said. "For the coffee and, you know…"

"I hope you find peace," he said. "God bless." Then with a soft, sad smile, he turned and walked back to the church.

Stella was back at Paddington Green ninety minutes later, calling the official police liaison at the General Register Office, the government department that deals with issuing copies of birth, marriage and death certificates. She explained what she wanted and read out the details of her soon-to-be alter ego, Jennifer Amy Stadden.

The woman at the other end told her it would take a few days to order up and print the birth certificate and did she, Stella, know that she'd have to contact the Passport Office direct for the passport and the Department of Transport for the driving licence? Stella confirmed that she did.

With the documentation for her new identity now being assembled, Stella refocused on the next, and most difficult, phase of her campaign.

CHAPTER SIXTEEN
Armoury Tour

THE FOLLOWING DAY, Stella took up a position in the ground-level car park at the rear of the station at 10.30 a.m. From her vantage point sitting on a low wall, she could see the rear door of the armoury. She lit a cigarette and waited. Ten minutes passed. Then another ten. She consulted her watch. Ten to eleven. She'd give it another ten minutes then leave it till after lunch. The nice-looking assistant armourer, an ex-soldier called Nick Probert, had told her that his boss, Danny Hutchings, usually took a cigarette break sometime around ten forty-five. "Regular as clockwork," he'd said after they'd been chatting in the canteen a week or so earlier. "Likes to beat the crowd."

Now she perched on the wall, watching the steel reinforced door for any sign of movement. Finally, it swung outward and Hutchings emerged. He looked left and right, then saw Stella and strolled over.

"Hi. I'm Danny. Haven't seen you on smokers' corner before," he said, by way of greeting, his accent from somewhere in south Wales.

Stella offered him one of her Marlboros. He took the proffered cigarette and, as she clicked her lighter for him, steadied her hand with his own before drawing in a lungful of smoke then releasing it upwards in a long plume.

"God, that tastes good," he said. "Thanks."

Stella lit another cigarette for herself. "I'm Stella. Cole. I'm a DI on the Murder Squad, but I've been on compassionate leave for a year."

He looked into her eyes, brow furrowing. "You the one who lost her family in that FATACC?"

She nodded, hissing out smoke between her teeth. "That's me."

"I'm sorry. You'd just left when I took up my post. Everybody was talking about it. They got the guy though, didn't they?"

She wrinkled her nose, deciding in a flash not to reveal what she now knew. "They did. A little toerag called Edwin Deacon. But it was only death by careless driving. It should have been death-by-dangerous, at the very least."

"That's not right, that isn't. I mean, just because the bastard was behind the wheel. If he'd used a handgun or something, well, that's game over right there." He blushed. "Oh, God, sorry. That was gold medal insensitive."

She offered a small smile. "Don't worry, Danny. People have said worse. Anyway, it's a long story, and we've only just met. How about you? How did you get here?" Hutchings smiled and pushed up his left shirtsleeve to reveal a tattoo: a laurel wreath surrounding Saint George and the dragon, with a crown and plume at the top.

"What's that? A regimental crest?" Stella asked.

"Royal Regiment of Fusiliers. I was a sergeant. Bloody loved it too, I did. Iraq, Afghanistan, Belfast, Germany, Kosovo. I went all over. But after the financial crisis, the army had to make another round of cuts, and suddenly I got my papers. Redundancy, just like I was some bloody metal basher in a factory somewhere." He took another long drag on his cigarette. "Didn't fancy private work like a lot of the boys go into, so I applied to the Met. This job came up, and I walked it. Don't get to shoot any of them. The guns, I mean, except for test-firing and a bit of training from time to time. But I'd rather work with weapons than anything else, so it could be worse, you know? Even if I do have an audit every six weeks. Just a glorified storeman at that time, I can tell you."

"Do you know what they've got me doing?" Stella asked, moving an inch or two closer.

"What's that?"

"Filing. I'm on the admin task force. I'd sooner be counting bullets for you than scanning in old witness statements."

He smiled at this. "Any time you fancy a tour, just let me know."

She checked her watch, though there was nobody in the exhibits room to monitor her comings and goings. "How about now?"

He looked over his shoulder at the steel door to the armoury, then back at Stella, smiling broadly. He winked. "Why not? Come on."

She pushed off from the wall and followed him in.

Inside, she watched as he waggled his laminated plastic ID at a control panel to the left of the access door that led to the inner area of the armoury.

"Okay, so this is the sign-in/sign-out area, where you lot come and pick up and return your weapons. You ever draw a weapon on duty, Stella?"

"I did a firearms rotation, but nowadays I let SCO19 do all the shooting."

"Probably very wise. Anyway, you come here and swipe your ID. That registers on our system what you've taken out. You always have to get it countersigned by two armourers, so me plus one of my assistants. Then, at the end of the shift or whenever you're finished with it, you hand it back, swipe your ID again and then it's on the computer that we have it, not you."

Hutchings pointed at a large steel box mounted on a wooden table. The box had a steel pipe about two inches in diameter protruding from the top at a forty-five-degree angle. "Any idea what that is?"

She shrugged. *It's the clearing box. I just told you I did a forearms rotation. Weren't you listening?* "None. Surprise me."

"Clearing box. Full of sand. You stick the barrel of your Glock or whatever into the pipe, then work the slide twice to ensure there are no rounds left in the chamber after you've dropped out the mag."

"Does anyone ever forget?"

He laughed, a warm sound that reminded her of Richard for a split second.

"Had a new DS just a couple of weeks ago. Forgot to clear his weapon and had his finger over the trigger. Fucking idiot discharged a Glock 17 in here. Everybody hit the deck while a nine-mil hollow point goes ricocheting off the floor."

"Loud?"

"Loud? You've been on the range, right?" Stella nodded. "They're loud out there, okay? So, imagine it in a room this size with no acoustic deadening furniture or fabrics. Bloody deafening, it was."

Stella laughed and was gratified to see Hutchings smiling back.

"So where are all the guns, then?" she asked, looking around the functional room with its desk and antiquated desktop computer.

"Come on, I'll show you."

He led her through a fire door and flicked on a row of light switches. The room was huge: maybe thirty metres by twenty. It was racked out with steel shelving and wall-mounted frames. The smell was a mixture of gun oil and burnt propellant, a harsh aroma that prickled the back of Stella's nose and made her frown. Everywhere she discerned the dull metallic gleam of black, dark-grey and blued weapons. The Glocks, she knew, had plastic frames and other parts, but they still shone like steel in the light from the overhead lamps.

"On the shelves, you've got your Glock 17s. I've got a rolling contract with Glock to supply these."

"Why a rolling contract?"

"It sounds a bit funny, OK, but they're only guaranteed for five years. After that, they say if we fire one and there's a problem, it jams or something, or there's a misfire, they won't cover it under warranty."

"Warranty?"

"I know, right? Just like your family hatchback. But that's the way it is. So I order them in batches of twenty five, usually, and decommission them at the five-year mark."

Stella motioned to a nearby pistol. "Can I?"

Hutchings nodded. "Seeing you're with me, that's not a problem. Don't point it at me, though, will you?"

She winked at him. "Well don't say anything to upset me then, Danny, eh?"

She hefted the pistol. It was heavier than she remembered it. She adjusted her grip and weighed it in her hand. Then turned away from Hutchings and held the pistol out in front of her in a one-handed grip.

"Shoot one like that and you'll almost certainly miss, and probably break your wrist into the bargain," he said. "Here, let me show you." He came up behind her and reached round to take both her hands and place them on the grip. "Right hand on the butt. Left hand cupped round it to support and guide."

"You better keep your right hand off my butt, Danny, or I bloody well *will* shoot you."

He released her and she turned to face him again. "You said if Deacon had used a gun, it would've been game over. But it's got a lot harder to put your hands on one these days, hasn't it? I mean despite what they show on the telly?"

"Well, as you know," Danny said, his voice dropping into an instructor's measured cadences, "since 1997, when Parliament passed the latest Firearms Act, the only people legally allowed to own handguns are the military and the police. Villains own them illegally, of course, but to be honest, it's not the guns that are the problem – it's the ammunition. It's why they make their own and end up blowing their own hands off, silly fuckers."

Stella grinned. "Yeah well, makes it harder for them to point another one at someone, doesn't it? So, what other weaponry do you have to show me?"

He smiled. "Come with me and I'll show you."

At the rear of the room was a long steel rack of assault rifles and shotguns.

"Those," Hutchings said, pointing at one end of the rack, "are Heckler & Koch MP5 carbines. Basically, infantry weapons, only with shorter barrels for urban work. The ones next to those are Remington 870 shotguns. Twelve gauge magnums. That means they're specced to take a higher propellant load."

Spotting a skeletal, matte-black rifle in the far corner, Stella pointed. "What the fuck's that for? It's taller than I am."

He grinned. "It's Czech. A CZ 550 bolt action rifle. Fires a round called a .600 Nitro Overkill. It's for shooting big game."

"Fuck off! I mean, I know we have some nasty villains, but I'd hardly say they need something that looks like a cannon to put them down."

"No, seriously. It's an elephant gun. Because of London zoo, right? Anything bigger than a monkey ever gets loose from there, we get a call from the zoo director or their head of security and a firearms team is despatched with that beauty over there to take it out. Can't have elephants stampeding down Oxford Street or a rhino overturning a bus. Bad for London's image. The Mayor'd probably have the Commissioner fired."

"What's that frame with it?"

"Bipod. You need that to stabilise it. Pull the trigger just holding the rifle and you'd put you and anyone behind you into the middle of next week."

They were standing directly in front of the elephant gun now. Stella reached out and ran her fingertips along the smooth steel of the barrel. She turned to Hutchings.

"Bullets?"

"What?"

"Where are all the bullets?"

"Oh. Well, for a start, we call them rounds. And they're back there."

He pointed at another door.

"How many *rounds* do you have back there then, Danny?"

"Oh, about half a million, give or take. Nine-mil, seven-point-six-two, five-point-five-six. The Overkills. Then we've got Hatton rounds for the shotguns, and some–"

Stella interrupted his paean to ammunition. "Hatton rounds?"

"You know when you go into a flat and one of the firearms team shoots the hinges off the door?"

"Yes."

"Those are Hatton rounds. They're lead powder and wax. At six-inch range, they're powerful enough to blow off a lock or a deadbolt or do in the hinges, but then that's it. No lead slug or shot travelling into the room and potentially injuring or killing anyone, or ricocheting back and injuring one of ours."

"Basically, then, you have enough kit here to take out every villain in London."

He grinned again. "Something like that. But only for people with a nice shiny ID on a lanyard."

"Oh, well," Stella said, then sighed theatrically. "I suppose I'd better start dealing with *my* villains with somebody else's weapons, then."

"I'm afraid so," he said with a smile. "I mean, obviously, I'd love to kit you out with a loadout and a few sacks of ammo, but you know what they say, rules is rules."

Smiling back, Stella made her play, the move she'd planned the previous night.

"You don't fancy a drink after work, do you? I'm usually ready to strangle somebody, so it would be good to unwind with a friendly face."

He nodded. "That would be great. But—"

"You heard about that too, right? I wasn't going to suggest the pub, actually. I was going to suggest maybe you could come to mine."

He frowned. "I'd love to, Stella. But me and the wife, well, we're going through a rough patch at the moment, so that probably wouldn't be such a good idea."

She touched his right shoulder then withdrew her hand again. "That's okay, but I'd still love that drink. Even if it is just lime and soda. I guess I could risk the pub if you swear to keep me on the straight and narrow."

"Don't worry, I'm a policeman," he said. They both laughed and agreed to meet at the rear of the station at six that evening.

Back in the exhibits room, Stella opened her notebook. It was time to start answering her list of questions. The easiest one was the identity of the senior investigating officer. She realised she'd never seen the case records before. In the days immediately following the accident – No! She corrected herself. Not the accident. The murder. In those early days, she had been almost comatose with grief. Then, on leave that began on compassionate grounds and metamorphosed into sickness, she had no access to the Police National Computer and its systems. She logged into HOLMES and began clicking and scrolling through the menus until she found the case number. Working through half a dozen drop-down menus covering every aspect of the case, from exhibits to media, witnesses to victims, she clicked through to police personnel and then the SIO tab.

SIO: DCS Adam Collier.

She wasn't really surprised. Adam was her boss and would have naturally wanted to be involved. She added his name to the page of questions in her notebook. Then she leaned back in her chair and closed her eyes.

A voice whispered in her ear. "He'd have had access to the evidence as well."

"I know that. But Reg misfiled it, didn't he?"

"Did he?"

"You know he did. Him and his bloody Fat Finger Syndrome."

"Which you are the only detective at Paddington Green ever to discover."

"What do you mean?"

"Maybe someone else misfiled it."

Then the voice disappeared abruptly, leaving Stella with the eerie sensation of having gone deaf in one ear. Just as she was about to start searching for more answers, her phone rang. It was Christine Flynn.

"Stella, I'm sorry to interrupt your work but there's a meeting starting in ten minutes that I'd like you to attend. Sort of a progress update on Operation Streamline. Could you make your way to the conference room on the fifth floor, please? No need to prepare anything, just fill everybody in on what you've been up to. Thanks." Then she rang off.

"Perfect!" Stella said as she replaced her phone. "An Operation Streamline progress update meeting on the conference room on the fifth floor. How really, very exciting."

She logged out of HOLMES and kicked back from the desk, toppling the ancient swivel chair. She righted it with a violent yank and marched off to the lifts.

The meeting took the rest of the afternoon. At 5.45pm, Stella scooted off to the ladies' toilets on the ground floor. She nodded to a couple of uniformed PCs chatting at the sinks and moved down to the end of the row.

She placed her battered, conker-brown leather messenger bag on the countertop to the left of the sink and took out a hairbrush. Remembered her mum brushing her hair out when she'd been in a long-hair phase at thirteen, a hundred strokes every night, lulling Stella into a trance as she chatted about her day at the council offices, working in the transport department. *No time for a hundred now, Stel, just enough to get a bit of a shine into it.* She watched the woman in the mirror performing this mundane action, and wondered if it were really her. She seemed so calm. Face unlined, blue-green eyes clear and bright. Dark-brown hair beginning to straighten and shine before she pulled it back into a ponytail and rewound the black scrunchie around it. She leaned closer and peered into the woman's pupils. Yes. There she was, just visible in the distance. A thin woman screaming: her head thrown back, tendons taut in the neck, hands tearing at that shining brown hair. *Hello, you.*

Next, the lippy. *Not too much. Don't want to look like I made a special effort. Just enough to take the death pallor out of them.*

She put the cosmetics away and looked down. Plucked at the top of her white blouse. Undid another button. Then did it up again.

"Is he worth it, ma'am?"

Stella turned round. It was one of the female PCs. Freckled complexion, frizzy ginger hair scraped back from her face. The woman was smiling and her friend, skinny with coffee-coloured skin, was, too.

"Definitely," Stella answered.

"Well, it never hurts, does it? Bit of boob, eh, Maria?"

"She's right, ma'am," the other WPC agreed. "Two buttons'll do it."

Stella rolled her eyes. "Yeah. We could have brains the size of planets and bank balances to match, but it's 'tits out for the lads' and they're happy."

The three women laughed, rank and duty forgotten for a moment or two.

*

The King's Head was quiet. Stella and Hutchings took their drinks to a corner table under a window constructed from the bottoms of wine bottles, which let multi-coloured light in, staining their table top with patches of green and red. In a corner, a lone gambler was playing a fruit machine. Its bleeps and whistles, mini-tunes and bells competed with some brewery-approved, early-evening jazz-funk issuing from ceiling-mounted speakers.

"Rough patch, then?" Stella asked, taking a sip of her lime and soda.

Hutchings put his pint down. "You don't go in for small talk, do you?"

"Life's too short, Danny. If you want to talk about your IKEA dining suite, I'm probably not your girl."

He ran a hand over his face. "Fair play. Yeah. I've been a bit of a naughty boy. Playing away from home. Tasha found out 'cos of my phone. Threatened to chuck me out."

"Your phone? What was it, sexting?" He took another pull on his beer, looking down. "Oh, Jesus! What are you, fifteen?"

He grinned. "Can't help it, can I? If I see a good-looking woman, I just got to let her know. Not my fault if they come on to me, is it?"

"Would you let *me* know?"

"Sorry? What do you mean?"

"Would you," she poked him gently in the chest, "let me know," she let her fingertip drift across and onto his arm, "if you thought I was good looking?"

"Yes. Of course. But, you know, you being widowed and everything."

"I'm a widow, Danny, not a nun. I won't faint if you pay me a compliment."

He looked her up and down then, not furtively, taking his time. She noticed the way his smooth glance stuttered over her cleavage before returning to her face. *Thanks, girls.*

"You're fit, Stella. No mistake."

"There. That wasn't too difficult, was it?"

After leaving the pub, Stella suggested a stroll along a stretch of towpath on the Regent's Canal that ran between two streets near the pub. It was time to strike. She threaded her arm through his and leaned in towards him.

"I like you, Danny," she said. "I feel I can talk to you. It's nice. Uncomplicated."

He turned to face her as they wandered on. "I like you too."

"Come for dinner. Tonight. Tell Tasha you've pulled a double shift."

He wrinkled his nose. "I don't know, Stella. I mean, like I said before, me and the missus, well, it's not going so well right now."

"So maybe giving her some space would be the smart thing to do. Come on, Danny. Like I said before, life's too short. I fancy you, and I think you feel the same way about me. A bit of pasta and maybe snuggle up in front of the TV, see what happens. It's not the end of the world, is it?"

He grinned and squeezed her arm between his bicep and chest. "Not even close."

CHAPTER SEVENTEEN
How to Vanish a Pistol

STELLA STOOD AT the hob, stirring the pasta sauce. She wasn't dressed for cooking. Beneath the butcher-striped apron, she'd put together an outfit she felt sure would have Danny right where she wanted him: tight black T-shirt with a scooped neck, orange suede mini-skirt and black tights, and black stilettos. Perfume on the pulse points behind her ears, on the insides of her wrists and a quick mist down the front of the T-shirt for good measure.

The recipe was one she and Richard had come up with together. Shallots, diced finely and softened in butter and olive oil, with lots of fresh garlic mashed into a paste with sea salt flakes; fresh tomatoes, diced; a tin of baby clams – fresh were better, but she didn't have any; a sprinkle of dried chilli flakes, and cracked black pepper; and, to finish it off, stir it through the spaghetti and fling some chiffonaded curly parsley over it for that 'pro-chef' look. The only wobble came when she added the glassful of white wine to the sauce.

Everyone said you had to ditch every last drop of alcohol from your house if you were an alcoholic. But Stella believed you couldn't prepare certain dishes without a splash of wine, especially not strategic meals like this one. She steeled herself as she twisted off the screw top. Looked across to the dresser with the wine glasses. Then shook her head violently. *No! Not tonight. Not ever. Not until Richard and Lola are avenged.*

Hutchings came up behind her and encircled her waist with his right arm.

The left held a glass of chardonnay. He put his lips against her right ear.

"Smells fantastic."

She smiled, without looking round. "Me, or the clams?"

"Both. When's it ready? I'm starving."

"You have to be patient. You can't rush it. Couple more minutes for the spaghetti, then we're good. Make yourself useful and lay the table. The cutlery's over there." She pointed with a free hand to a drawer under the worktop.

They sat opposite each other at Stella's scrubbed pine kitchen table to eat.

"Penny for them?" Danny was looking at her, smiling.

"What? Oh God, sorry, Danny. Miles away." She looked at his plate. Empty. Her own too. *That's odd. When did that happen?* "I haven't got anything for pudding, I'm afraid. There might be some ice cream in the freezer, I think. Haven't looked for a while."

"I wasn't really thinking of ice cream." He winked, a sleazy expression that he managed to pull off. "Remember what you said earlier?"

"Oh, that. Pour yourself some more wine, and then why don't we adjourn to the sofa?"

She could feel his hand on her breast. He wasn't a bad kisser either. She reached for his lap and gave him an encouraging squeeze and was rewarded with a sudden inhalation. *Now let's think. How am I going to get what I need out of him?* He was panting heavily now. *Let's take him to bed. Maybe the Mata Hari option could be the way forward.*

"Come on, you," she whispered. "How about trying out my new bed?"

He tried to manoeuvre himself on top of her, but Stella slapped his arm away. "Oh, no you don't, soldier," she said in what she hoped was a commanding tone of voice. "On your back. Now!"

He grinned up at her, eyes half-closed from the wine, which she'd taken care to keep topping up through the evening. "Yes, ma'am," he said. Then he complied, arms folded behind his head, watching as she straddled him. She'd kept her T-shirt on, the better to tease him. Now she crossed her arms in front of her, gripped the hem and drew it up and over her head in a single, flowing movement.

"What's that?" Danny asked, craning up to look at her left shoulder. "Got a tattoo, have you?"

"It's Mimi the Mongoose," she answered, following his gaze.

"Like you, is she?"

She nodded. "Snake killer."

He nodded, smiled and reached for her breasts, and after allowing him a quick squeeze, she pushed his hands away. "Wait," she said, then reached round to unclip her bra, a black lace push-up from La Perla, holding the cups over her breasts before shucking it off. Danny's eyes widened.

"They're lovely, they are," he managed to gasp out as she leaned forward.

The sex was perfunctory. He seemed happy enough, and Stella did a little moaning and groaning to keep his pride intact.

Later, lying awake and smoking, she shifted her weight left and right, nudging him with her elbow until he stirred. As she felt him wake, she resumed her staring at the ceiling, sighing deeply from time to time just to make sure he got the message.

"What's the matter?" he asked, raising himself on one elbow.

"Just thinking about how I'm ever going to get out of the filing bloody task force. I swear I'm going insane in there."

"Working for Reg the Veg, aren't you?"

She sat up and groaned, before putting her head in her hands. "Yes. I am. And it's really not helping."

"I wish I had you on my team. I'm stuffed at the moment."

"Why, what's the problem?"

"I'm down an assistant armourer. You know you can't sign out a weapon without two countersignatures?" She nodded. "I've got to decommission a bunch of Glocks and collect a replacement consignment. It's an offsite job and–"

"And you can't get away while you're a man down."

"It's a woman, actually, but yes. That's basically it."

She turned to him and planted a kiss on his lips, then pulled back a little. "You don't have to be a woman down, you know. I could help you out. Reg's still off, so I'm basically managing the exhibits room on my own. The brass want me out, I'm sure of it, so I can pretty much please myself what I do."

"Really?"

"Yes, I told you. Look, tell me about the, what did you call it, decommissioning?"

Hutchings lay back on the pillow and held his left arm out, cupping his hand and beckoning her down.

"Come here."

She curled herself against him and lay a flat palm on his chest. *Right then, sunshine, spill.* "I'm all ears," is what she said aloud.

"A weapon's out of warranty, okay? I have to put it beyond use. If it's one or two at a time, I do it myself if I'm not too busy. Remove the firing pin, maybe crush the muzzle in a vice, a few other things. You have to be sure because you don't want an ex-police weapon turning up in a crime. Very bad for the image of the force."

"Oh, I imagine the PR team would not be best pleased. Why can't you do that for the pistols?"

"There's twenty-five of them. And like I said, I'm short-staffed. Got my hands full issuing and receiving operational weapons, maintaining them, paperwork. You know."

"Oh, I know all about paperwork, believe me."

"Well, I have a shitload of it. So, when I can't decommission them myself, I use this outside company. Frame Security, they're called, on this industrial estate near Heathrow. They've got crushers, furnaces, lathes, the works. They can turn a Glock into a cube of metal and plastic in five minutes. It's all receipted and documented, just like the chain of custody on an exhibit."

"And the new ones?"

"Come in from Austria on a cargo flight to Heathrow, don't they? I sign for them, load them into the van and hey ho, away we go, back to the station. Book them all in, check them over, test-fire them, photograph and register the striations on the slugs and we're done."

Stella got out of bed and walked to the window, giving Hutchings a good look, then came back and sat facing him. *That's right, Danny, keep your eyes on my tits. It'll be easier to agree with what I'm going to ask you next.*

"Let me go."

"Pardon?"

"Let me go and do the drop at Frame Security for you. Then I can pick up the new lot and have them back for you to test-fire."

"I wish I could, Stel. Jesus, it wouldn't half make my life easier. Plus, I think Tasha's really going to chuck me out this time, and I'm trying to find a flat, so it's full on. But the regulations—"

Stella leaned towards him and draped herself around his neck "Please, Danny. Apart from this, my life's a fucking wasteland of boredom. Give a girl a bit of excitement." Then she reached between his legs. "I mean another bit of excitement."

He groaned. "Okay, fine. Come and see me tomorrow at nine."

Stella pushed him back down. And smiled. Her plan to liberate a pistol from the armoury had just taken on a much more satisfactory dimension. Now, the weapon within her grasp wasn't just a pistol – it was an untraceable pistol.

After being buzzed in by Danny Hutchings, Stella pushed her way through the security door into the armoury at 8.59 the following morning. Nick Probert, the assistant armourer she'd quizzed about Danny, was working on a G36 assault rifle. He had it stripped on a steel workbench and was working on the rear end of the barrel with a file no bigger than a pencil that rasped with a metallic buzz on each stroke.

"DI Cole, welcome," Hutchings said.

"Happy to help, Sergeant Hutchings," she replied, keeping her face steady and resisting the temptation to wink.

The assistant armourer glanced up, then returned to the G36's barrel.

"If you'd like to come this way, I can show you the Glocks due for decommissioning."

The pistols were lined up on a workbench in two rows of eight and one of nine. Stella ran her eyes over them: twenty-five black-and-charcoal semi-automatics. Each one perfectly capable of sending a person into the next world, but now no longer viable because, like a three-year-and-a-day-old hatchback, they were out of warranty. The arrangement made the ninth pistol in the top row look like something that needed to be tidied away. She reached for it and picked it up. Next to her she sensed the assistant armourer stiffen.

"Relax," she said, with a smile. "You've cleared them, haven't you?"

"Yes, ma'am," he said. "But, you're not really authorised. Not officially, like."

"It's fine, Nick," this was Hutchings, who'd joined them at the bench. "DI Cole's on the admin task force, and she's got time on her hands, so we're grateful for her help. Unless you'd rather do the round trip to Heathrow?"

"No, Sarge."

"Well, then. We just need to type up the despatch note and you can be on your way, DI Cole."

Stella put the pistol back down on the bench with a *thunk*.

"Despatch note?" She tried to keep her voice light: intrigued, rather than worried.

"Every time we send off a batch of weapons, we issue a document saying what make, model and quantity we're releasing. It gets countersigned at Frame's and they add a receipt, then everyone has a copy and there's no possibility of any of the Met's weapons ending up in the wrong hands."

Because we wouldn't want that, would we, Lola? "Oh, no, of course," Stella said. "Look, why don't you give me an old one for reference and a blank and let me do it for you? I bet I'm a faster typist than you."

Hutchings frowned. "Better leave that to me. I'd get shot if there was a mix-up. Not that I'm suggesting you'd get it wrong, but it's on me if there's a cockup."

"No, of course, sure," Stella said, shrugging. "Just trying to be helpful. Thought you might keep me on as a clerk and not send me back to the basement."

Hutchings and his assistant laughed at this.

Stella and Nick began loading the Glocks into black nylon holdalls with sturdy, two-inch-wide, webbing handles. Hutchings pulled a thinly upholstered swivel chair up to a desk supporting an ageing tower PC and began typing, pursing his lips as his two index fingers poked and prodded at the beige keys.

Five minutes later he was done. "There," he said, with an air of triumph, as if he'd completed a doctoral dissertation instead of a single-sheet, weapon decommissioning form.

Then the door from the corridor slammed back on its hinges and a quartet of black-clad SCO19 officers burst in, kitted out in tactical gear from their Pro-Tec ballistic helmets to bullet-proof vests and down to paramilitary-style, black ankle boots.

The squad leader, a stocky man made even bulkier by his gear, marched up to the desk.

"We're moving on a terrorist group in a flat in Kilburn. I need Glocks times four, G36s ditto and a Remington 870. Ammunition: Hatton rounds, a dozen, spare mag per man for the Glocks, same for the G36s. Better give me half a dozen flash-bangs and tear gas."

Stella was forgotten as Hutchings and his assistant moved off, gathering weapons and ammunition in economical, practised movements, skirting round each other among the narrow racked-out lanes that ran through the armoury.

The armoury echoed with the sound of slides being racked and bolts being worked to clear breeches, then magazines being slotted home into pistol butts and rifle receivers and slapped on their undersides to ensure they were latched. Stella backed away from the front desk, slid down onto the swivel chair in front of the computer and shuffled the mouse back and forth across its peeling, black nylon mat.

The screen woke up, displaying a grey-and-red form template. Hutchings had left the despatch note open. She scanned up and down the form fields looking for one in particular. There it was.

QTY. 25

Stella worked fast, not daring to look round, holding her breath.

Mouse click.

Backspace.

Keystroke.

File-save-close.

She hit Print and moved away from the PC to stand by the printer, which ratcheted into life with a series of buzzes, clicks and whirrs and a faint smell of ozone. As soon as the revised version of the despatch note slid into the tray she whisked it out, folded it into four and stuffed it into her trouser pocket.

She looked over her shoulder, breathing hard. The firearms officers were swiping their ID cards over an electronic reader, which bleeped as each set of weapons was registered as signed out to the officer who matched the ID in the central database. Then they each signed a firearms issuance form, and Hutchings and his assistant countersigned. She resumed her former position, standing out of the way at the end of a shelving rack, waiting for the activity to die down.

As quickly as they'd burst in to the armoury, the four men were gone, their boots thumping as they ran back down the corridor to their armed response vehicles: at Paddington Green, silver BMW 5 Series in full pursuit tune.

Hutchings took the sheaf of signed and countersigned weapons issuance forms and filed them in a black steel cabinet.

"Bit of excitement for you, there, DI Cole. Now you can see why being short-staffed in here makes my life difficult. Let me just print that despatch note for you and you can be on your way."

"No need. I did it while you were equipping the commandos," she said, with a smile. Look." She fished the folded paper out of her pocket and flourished it in the air. She pointed behind her at the bench. "All ah need's mah six-shooters and ah reck'n ah'll be on mah way, pardner."

Her comedy Annie Oakley accent did the trick.

"Jesus, is that how you get the bad guys to break, because it certainly worked on me. Here, let me get you the invoice and collection note for the new Glocks."

With the paperwork dealt with, Hutchings seemed happy enough to help her and Nick load the Glocks into the holdalls, five to a bag, five bags in total. Leaving his number two in charge, Hutchings helped Stella lug the heavy, clanking bags down to the rear of the station and over to a dirty and battered white Ford transit van.

"No armoured car?" Stella asked as Hutchings unlocked the rear doors and swung them open to reveal a plain loadspace lined with unvarnished plywood, sharp-splintered gashes gouged into its floor.

"Ha! No. No markings at all, if you notice. Thinking is, it's better to go under the radar. This looks like any old builder's van, doesn't it? Practically invisible." He handed her a sheet of A4 with two addresses typed on it in capitals, one for Frame Security, the other for the cargo terminal at Heathrow. The latter had flight details below it. "When you get to Frame's, there's a guard on the gate. Show your warrant card and the despatch note and say you've got a D61 order from the Paddington Green armourer. The guys on the gate all know me, but if there's a relief or they're doing a security audit, they might have tightened up. When you're in, ask for Maurice. He's the manager."

"What about Heathrow?"

"They unload the cargo, and it has to go through customs just like your bags when you come back from holiday or whatever. You give your invoice for the Glocks to the clerk and then wait in the receiving dock and basically sign for them when they come through. Then straight back here, please. They're a grand a pop, even with our discount, so I'll feel a lot happier when they're booked in."

The traffic out of London on the A4, and then the M4 motorway, was slow. Driving an unmarked car with no lights or siren made Stella realise, once again, just how shit most of the general public were at driving. Behind the wheel, her heart was pounding and her palms were clammy, but even in this heightened state of anxiety, she was still sharper and more observant than ninety-nine percent of the fuckwits on the road around her. Between Paddington Green and Hammersmith, where she planned to join the westbound A4 and out to the M4 motorway, she counted five near-misses, one involving a family of tourists in a rented estate car almost killing a young woman pushing a baby in a stroller. She screamed, "No! Lola!", then she was past them. She glanced fearfully in the rear-view mirror: the young mum was on the pavement, and the tourists were receding down the Cromwell Road.

It took an hour to reach the front gates of Frame Security. It occupied one whole end of a space signposted "Europa Business Park" down a concreted access road split and cracked with thick-stemmed weeds growing up through the gaps. On her way through what she couldn't help thinking of as an industrial estate, despite what the developers had named it, she passed units housing a car customiser, an outfit selling reconditioned tyres, a builders' merchant, a paint wholesaler and, bizarrely, an evangelical church – "The Devil Makes Work For Idle Hands: Come Inside And Get Busy!!"

Frame Security itself was kitted out like a fortress. Coils of glinting razor wire topped a nine-foot, spike-topped steel fence. A white-and-red plastic sign on the double gates announced "OUR GUARD DOGS BITE!" above a photo of a clearly very pissed-off German Shepherd showing yellow incisors and canines.

Stella switched off the rattly diesel engine and stepped out of the cab, easing a knot of tension in her right hip with a clenched fist that she pushed into the flesh there, over the bone. Immediately, the sound of dogs barking raised the hackles on her neck. It was a primitive response eased not even slightly as two monstrous beasts careered round the corner of a building and raced towards the gates before skidding to a stop, their slavering muzzles poking through the rough grey steel bars. Their barking continued until a tall security guard in thick navy trousers and matching uniform jacket strode over to greet her. He was wearing Ray-Ban Aviators with mirrored lenses despite the lack of sunshine. The effect, though clichéd, was disturbing. Stella decided to take control of the situation before rent-a-cop could go into whatever act he had planned.

"I'm Detective Inspector Cole, from Paddington Green Police Station," she stated, in the official voice she'd been taught at Hendon. "I'm here with a D61 from the armourer. Please get those dogs under control, then remove your sunglasses and let me through."

CHAPTER EIGHTEEN
Concealed Carry

THE SECURITY GUARD smiled. "Sorry, yes, of course," he said, whipping the glasses from his face and squinting. "Light sensitive. My eyes, I mean." Stella looked up into his eyes. They were rimmed with a deep pink: the lids looked inflamed. His mouth was wide and when he smiled, as he did now, she saw he had plenty of laughter lines etched into the tanned skin.

He looked down at the dogs and issued a command.

"Quiet!"

They whined once, then tucked their tails between their legs. He pointed back towards the main office building, a two-storey affair in sand-coloured brick with red-brick strips below each set of barred windows.

"Away."

The animals, meek as lambs now, slunk away, casting what Stella was sure were remorseful glances over their shoulders. The guard punched a code into the control box on the gatepost, and the doors clanked inwards on hydraulic pistons.

"You can put them on again," Stella said, walking up to him.

"What?"

"Your shades. I'm sorry. I didn't realise you needed them. Your dogs are just a bit full on, you know?"

He replaced the sunglasses. "Yeah, they're pretty impressive, aren't they? I trained them myself. The company likes us to do that so we work with animals who totally trust us."

"Trust? That's a funny word. I'd have thought that was fear they were showing."

He shook his head. "Not really. They were just embarrassed they'd been caught out in a mistake. They wouldn't normally react quite as bad as that. Maybe they smelled something on you. You got cats at home?"

"Nope. No pets."

"They can pick up on a person's fear. You know, through the sweat, if you're nervous."

Me, nervous? Now why would you say that? "Maybe that's it. The sign did make me a little edgy, to be honest."

"There's no need. Once they know I approve, they're like puppies really. Look, I'll show you." Before Stella could protest, he whistled – a sharp rising and falling tone – and the two dogs came scampering back towards them, rumps and shoulders dipping like seesaws as they ran. They arrived in a few seconds, but this time their jaws were hanging open and their long, pink tongues were lolling from their mouths.

"Gem, Skipper, sit," he said.

The dogs sat immediately, their tails sweeping the tarmac behind them.

"Paw."

The dogs lifted their right forepaws off the ground, heads cocked to one side. "Take Skipper's," he said to Stella. "He's nearest to you."

Stella extended a hand, ready to snatch it back if the dog's head moved a millimetre towards her. But nothing happened. It waited, paw trembling slightly. She took it and, not knowing what else to do, gave it a little shake before letting go. The pads under its foot were rough, like sandpaper. It replaced its paw on the ground. Stella straightened.

"Okay, so you've won Crufts, and I'm not nervous any more. As I was saying–"

"You've come from Danny Hutchings with a consignment for decommissioning. It's all right, me and Danny go back a long way. He and I served together, if you can believe that. Iraq. He went into the police; I went into the rent-a-cop business." Stella felt her cheeks flushing. "Don't worry, we call it that too. The management like to talk about 'security solutions' but that's just for investors and the press."

"Do you want the paperwork?" she asked. "He told me to ask for Maurice."

He held out his hand. "Please. If you don't mind me asking, how come you're doing a D61? I mean that's pretty low-grade work for a detective inspector, isn't it?"

Stella smiled as she handed over the despatch note, registering a small scar on the guard's chin, just to the right of a cleft darkened with grey stubble.

"We're investigating a possible gun-running operation. Albanians. Kosovans. Turks. Kazakhs. You name it, they're in on it. I'm familiarising myself with all the possible supply routes."

He scanned the front of the sheet.

"That's all in order, twenty-four Glock 17s for decommissioning, cleared and checked." He pulled a biro from his breast pocket and added his signature to the form. "You won't find anything wrong here, DI Cole. Place prob'ly has better security than your nick." Then he stood back and pointed to a loading bay. "Park up over there with your doors against the ramp. You don't actually need to see Maurice; the warehouse boys'll unload the weapons for you. Then you collect a receipt and another signature on your despatch note, they make a copy, give you the original, and you're done."

Stella climbed back into the transit, started the engine and moments later was standing by as a couple of brown-overalled storemen unloaded four holdalls from the back of the van. They placed them on the concrete floor of the loading bay, unzipped them and pulled out the Glocks one by one and laid them out.

In four neat rows of six.

One man – beautiful olive skin, maroon turban, black moustache and beard – came over with a sheet of computer-printed stationery. He pulled a biro from his breast pocket and added the make, model and quantity of weapons in three blank boxes, the date and his signature, then handed it back to Stella. She held the despatch note out to him, wordlessly. He seemed a man more inclined to silence than his garrulous friend on the gate. He signed across the bottom, then spoke.

"Be back in a minute, yeah?"

She watched his back as he stuck the sheet of paper under the lid of a photocopier, then grabbed the original and the copy and brought the former back to her. "Yours," he said. As she took it, she heard a high-pitched, metallic shrieking.

"What's that?" she asked.

"Grinder, innit? We're doing some assault rifles. Shame really, pretty nice weapons. They'll be in school furniture or a motorway bridge a month or two from now."

With that bizarre image in her head, Stella thanked him and turned on her heel to leave.

The ex-soldier on the gate saluted with a grin as she passed, his mirrored lenses obscuring what she felt sure were eyes crinkled in amusement, and she waved in return, smiling as she left for Heathrow and the cargo terminal.

She looked over and down, into the footwell of the passenger seat. There, almost invisible, was the fifth black holdall.

At Heathrow's cargo terminal, the digital display in the waiting area informed her that the plane bringing in the new Glocks had been delayed by thirty minutes. The room was furnished with hard plastic chairs in a shade of industrial grey that would never have passed the design committee for the passenger terminals. Low tables scattered with magazines bearing such titles as *Airfreight*, *Cargo* and *Freight Forwarding* dotted the room. Thinking that working for Reg the Veg might actually be more interesting than reading one of these, she wandered over to a pair of vending machines against a wall.

She returned to a seat by a table and winced as she burnt her mouth on the coffee. Her tongue, now roughened by the scalding liquid, couldn't tell her what it tasted like, which may have been a blessing. A KitKat eased the pain as she sat there, sucking the chocolate from the wafers and checking emails on her phone. One jumped out at her. It was from The Model.

> Stella. Would love to catch up when you have a moment. Looked for you in the exhibits room this morning, but couldn't find you. My office, five thirty this evening please. Adam.

Shit! What does he want? Well, she'd just have to play it calmly. Reg had been taken ill a few days earlier, and she'd been running the exhibits room. He'd shown her the ropes, so no major issues, and she'd just really needed a change of routine. That would do. It would have to. *Wouldn't it, Lola? Mummy's getting closer now. Little by little.*

Around her was the low buzz of conversation, and the beeping of electronic signatures being given as couriers came to collect shipments, mostly dressed in the branded uniforms of the big companies. Red and yellow for DHL, navy and purple for FedEx and Pullman brown for UPS. She noted a few drivers from local firms – no uniforms – and a handful of bike messengers in scuffed and scraped leathers. One rider had fashioned running repairs on his jacket with silver duct tape.

Finally, her name was called. A young guy with thick-rimmed glasses and a wispy black beard took a few details and had her sign in a box through a scratched screen protector on his silicon-clad tablet. Then he pointed to a gap at the end of the counter. "Yours is just coming out. Do you need a hand loading them?"

Stella turned to her right. A uniformed Heathrow cargo terminal employee was bringing out five cardboard cartons stacked on a bright-red hydraulic pallet lifter. Each carton was about a metre long, forty centimetres wide and thirty centimetres deep, and sealed along the top seam by a length of silver duct tape, just like the stuff holding the biker's leathers together. Despatch notes were affixed to the sides inside clear plastic envelopes. No other printing, though. *What did you think, Stel? They were going to bang bloody great Glock logos on the sides? Why not go the whole hog and put, "Contains handguns – please steal"?* She grinned, despite her nervousness.

"No, thanks. I'm fine. Can I borrow the trolley?"

"Sure," he said, with a smile. "Just bring it back when you've finished. You can leave it at the edge of the loading bay by the door."

Then he was dealing with another courier, and Stella had clearly disappeared from his mind. She took the handle of the pallet lifter from the storeman and tugged the clanking contraption around until she could pull, rather than push it.

"Here you go," an incoming UPS guy said, holding the door open for her.

She thanked him and dragged the load out into the loading bay and over to the transit van. The boxes were heavy, but not impossible, to lift, more unwieldy than anything else. She was glad of her weights work, though, as she hefted them into the back of the van.

Having arranged them in a flat rectangle, she took a moment to get her breath back, sitting on the nearest carton with her feet dangling over the edge of the loadspace. She reached for her cigarettes but then frowned as she saw a No Smoking sign on the wall next to a couple of fire extinguishers. She wondered whether the sign had been placed there with ironic intent.

This was a big moment, and she felt butterflies flittering in her stomach as she contemplated the firepower all around her. But she had a problem. One she hadn't considered until the cartons had been delivered to her. The guns were all stashed away behind duct-taped, and probably glued, cardboard cartons that appeared to be almost bullet-proof themselves judging by the weight of them. Then she thought of the biker. The solution presented itself in a flash.

Twenty minutes later, she pulled up outside a rundown hardware store on a dreary parade of shops in Hounslow. Planes roared overhead about every ninety seconds, so close to the ground she felt she could reach up and run her fingertips along their gleaming silver and white undersides. She could certainly smell the stink of them, the burnt aviation fuel raining down on her as a cloud of invisible particles that would probably give her lung cancer or asthma if she stayed for very long.

She pushed the door and entered the shop, looking over her shoulder. The thought of leaving twenty-five grand's worth of brand-new and virtually untraceable semi-automatic pistols in an unmarked transit van had brought her out in a sweat. Now she wished the van was emblazoned with as much fluorescent yellow-and-blue Battenburg livery as would fit on its sides. Even a "no tools left in van" sign would be better than nothing.

A few minutes later, she was walking back to the van with a flimsy red-and-white-striped carrier bag dangling from her left hand. She fished out her keys and swung herself up into the cab.

"Now to find somewhere quiet, Lola," she said. "Mummy's got some makey-do to be getting on with."

She found the perfect spot after swiping around on Google maps on her phone. She identified a little river called the Crane, and she could see a road that ran alongside it, with what appeared to be an access spur running almost down to the water's edge. She slammed the van into gear and found the access road after a few more minutes' driving. It must have been something the council had built for workers sent to clear the river: a single-track road bordered with rosebay willow herbs. She drove down to the end and turned round in the circle of concrete thoughtfully built just before the riverbank. Through the windscreen, she had a clear view of the track coming down from the main road. The rear doors faced the river, which was choked with reeds taller than she was, which wasn't saying much, admittedly, but they provided a thick screen from any prying eyes on the far bank. Grabbing the holdall from the passenger footwell, she got out and walked round to unlock the rear doors.

In the back of the van, Stella pulled one of the cartons closer. She took a box-cutter from the carrier bag and slid it under the edge of the duct tape holding the top flaps closed. A few minutes of careful sawing of the blade back and forth and she was able to lift the tape away from the cardboard. The flaps were glued as well as taped, as she'd suspected, and she eased her fingers under the flaps to break the seal with a series of sharp cracks. Then she was in.

Each pistol was individually packaged in a charcoal-grey, blow-moulded, plastic carrying case. From appearances, a member of the public might expect the cases to contain socket sets or some kind of cordless power tool. She lifted one case out by the handle, placed it on the lid of a second carton and unsnapped the catches.

A whiff of gun oil curled into her nostrils.

Snug in a shaped cut-out in the grey foam "egg box" padding was a brand-new Glock 17.

Unfired.

Unchecked.

Unregistered.

She could shoot whoever she wanted to with it, and nobody would be any the wiser about the murder weapon. As far as the entire world, bar some technicians in an Austrian factory, was concerned, this pistol didn't even exist.

Next to it, in another tailored compartment cut into the foam, was a spare box magazine. A small plastic ziplock bag containing a pale grey cleaning cloth, a tiny bottle of gun oil, and a black-bristled bottle brush completed the hardware.

From the nylon holdall by her side, Stella withdrew the Glock she'd brought from Paddington Green for decommissioning and then saved from the grinder and the furnace. One of twenty-five on the original paperwork but now, essentially, a gun with no documented existence.

Its overall condition was immaculate. The underside of the barrel was marred by a few tiny scratches, and she found a minute nick on the rear of the grip, but other than these imperfections it looked box-fresh. Silently, Stella thanked the engineers and designers at Glock for their dedication. The firm's much-vaunted quest for the perfect handgun had resulted in their products being manufactured from incredibly tough polymers that resisted damage better than most metals. Only the essential working parts like the barrel were still made from steel. She rubbed it down with the cleaning cloth and a little gun oil and then switched it for the new gun, which she placed into the holdall.

A few squirts of superglue and a length of new duct tape and the evidence of Stella's tampering with the carton vanished.

"Who's got a clever mummy, Lola?" she asked the empty air. Then she drove back to the station, stopping briefly at her house to leave the newly anonymous Glock in a kitchen drawer.

*

Back at Paddington Green, having phoned ahead, Stella was met at the rear door of the armoury by Hutchings and Nick Probert.

"Everything go okay?" Hutchings asked. "You were gone a lot longer than I expected."

Stella nodded. "Uh-huh. Your friend at Frame's a bit of a talker. Had me learning to shake hands with the Hound of the Baskervilles. Then the plane was delayed. Spent an hour reading magazines about freight handling. I tell you, there are some sad, sad people out there doing jobs you would never, in a million years, want to do. So, what do we do with this lot now?"

"First I book them in. Then we take them down to the range and test fire them. We photograph the slugs for the striations and log them on the database, then they just go on the racking until they're needed."

"Or five years goes by and they get turned into garden tools."

Hutchings laughed. "They tell you that at Frame's did they?"

"I like to learn, what can I say? Listen, I haven't been as good as I should have been at keeping up with my firearms training. Why don't you let me help with the test firing?" She looked around. Nick was inside the van, scanning barcodes on the shipping labels with his phone. She held her breath.

Hutchings grinned. "Why not? We can see how good your shooting is, can't we?"

As they were unloading the Glocks from the cartons, Stella positioned herself with her back to the two men. Then she picked up a screwdriver and nicked the corner of the case containing the rogue pistol.

When all the weapons were unpacked and booked into the computer, and the cartons stamped flat and piled in a corner, Hutchings turned to Stella.

"We'll do them in batches. Grab two cases and follow me down to the range."

She walked over to the bench and casually selected the marked case, along with a second, then followed Hutchings out of the room.

At the firing range, they laid the six plastic cases in front of them along the plain wooden bench that ran the width of the room. The range was five metres wide by twenty long, with a low ceiling striped with neon tubes. At the far end, a set of black-and-white, paper "aggressor" targets stood waiting in frames, pointing weapons back towards the shooters' bench. Hutchings spoke.

"We fire a handful of rounds from each pistol. Then I give the command, 'stop firing'. We place our weapon down on the bench. Then we walk down to the end and retrieve the slugs from the ballistic foam behind the targets. You log the serial number of each weapon on the computer, photograph the round using the rig over there," he pointed at a plinth-mounted, digital SLR pointing down towards a polished steel platen, "then log that with the same serial number to match it to the weapon. Hit 'save' and you're onto the next weapon. Clear?"

"As mud," Stella said.

Even with the black ear-defenders clamped over her head, the noise of the three Glocks firing unsuppressed in the concrete range was brutally loud. Stella enjoyed the way the weapon fitted into her hand, and the recoil that jolted her wrists as each 9mm round exploded out of the muzzle with a huge bang and tore a hole in the

(hit and run driver)

aggressor snarling at her from the target. The sharp tang of burnt propellant and the hot brass smell of the spent cartridges tinkling round her boots made her smile.

"Stop firing!" Hutchings yelled. The guns fell silent.

Stella pulled her ear defenders off and laid them on the bench in front of her.

"Enjoy that, did you, DI Cole?"

"Loved it!" she answered. She really had.

They walked the length of the range and, using penknives, or in Nick's case an impressive-looking hunting knife he produced from a sheath at his belt, dug the bullets out of the dense black foam that backed the targets.

Stella dawdled on the way back so she was last to reach the computer. Once the other two had logged their weapons, photographed the spent slugs and returned to the shooters' bench to begin loading their second set of weapons, Stella approached the computer terminal.

She typed in the serial number stamped onto the right-hand side of the barrel.

MP151977UK

The form field turned red and an error message popped up on the screen.

WEAPON ALREADY REGISTERED

Her cheeks burned and her stomach flipped. *How could you be so stupid?* She looked over her shoulder, but Hutchings and his assistant were chatting as they thumbed rounds into the Glocks' magazines.

She cleared the field and tried again.

1MP151977UK

The computer accepted this bogus serial number without a qualm. *Thank Christ for free-text form fields.*

She took the spent round to the camera, photographed it, then returned to the terminal. Under magnification, the striations where the six grooves cut into the inside of the barrel had marked the copper jacket of the bullet were as clear and defined as the furrows on a ploughed field.

Stella logged them against the same serial number, hit 'save' and moved back to continue the test firing.

After a day out to Hounslow and Heathrow, the rogue pistol was safely back among hundreds of its fellows, bearing a brand-new-but-fake serial number that should ensure it was never tracked back to its original consignment. She inhaled deeply and let the breath out in a sigh.

Her watch said twenty past five.

She tapped Hutchings on the shoulder.

"I have to go," she said. "Appointment with Collier. I think he wants to check I've been getting on with my filing like a good girl. Can we keep today quiet? I don't want it to get out I've been off having fun. He might banish me to the admin task force for ever."

Hutchings winked. "My lips, as they say, are sealed."

Then she left, to the sound of Hutchings and his assistant unloading a second pair of Glocks into the targets.

CHAPTER NINETEEN
A Friend

STELLA SAT FACING Collier at 5.30 p.m. For once, he looked less than perfectly groomed. He had a black bead of congealed blood on his chin where it appeared he had shaved too hurriedly. She noticed a second nick on his neck, close enough to his collar to have left a red smear on the folded white edge of the otherwise pristine, herringbone-patterned cotton.

He looked up from a sheet of paper he was apparently reading with great interest, frowning as he scanned its contents. He turned it over and moved it to one side. To Stella, the whole act looked contrived, as if he might have grabbed a random folder from his in-tray and started reading at the same moment as he barked, "Come!" before she entered.

"Ah, Stella," he said. "Thanks for coming in to see me." Like I had a choice, she didn't say. "I wanted to see how you've been doing."

What, since you dumped me where you thought I'd go crazy inside of two weeks, you mean? "Thank you, sir. For your concern, I mean."

"Come on, Stella, you can drop the "sir" business. Why so formal?"

Because yesterday I discovered you were the SIO when Richard and Lola were killed, and I'm starting to wonder whether that fuckup with the evidence was more than just Reg the Veg and his sausagey fingers and actually something to do with you. "Sorry. Adam. I'm doing okay, I guess. I mean, it's not detective work. But you were right. I was away for a long time, and I went through," she hesitated, calculating the precise number of seconds she should wait before continuing, "some fairly major avoidance activities, didn't I?"

"How's that side of things? Are you still on an even keel? Still attending AA meetings?"

She nodded, and parcelled out a little smile for him. An 'I'm doing my best for you, Adam' kind of smile. "Every other day. The only surprise is I haven't met any other coppers, you know?"

He nodded and gave his 'I understand' smile: downturned lips that still appeared to look as if he found something humorous, and his trademark crinkle-eyed stare. "Just so long as you're okay."

"I'm fine, really." *Although I'm a little closer to finding the person who murdered my family. And I have at least one new way of dealing with them.* "Was there anything else, sir – sorry, Adam?"

He shook his head and Stella pushed her chair back, getting ready to leave. He drew in a quick breath, loudly enough for Stella to stop, mid-movement. "Actually, there was one more thing," he said. "You've been spending time with Danny Hutchings, I understand." He stared at her, eyes bland, no more crinkles.

She felt a wriggle of doubt twirling in her stomach, and shrugged to cover her discomfort.

"You know, just trying to be helpful. Filing's not all it's cut out to be, and I will admit I get bored. He said he needed some help, and I volunteered."

Collier maintained his stare. Then offered the briefest of smiles.

"I think, all things considered, it would be better for you to keep to the exhibits room. Can't have you distracting our armourer, can we? Not while his marriage is, what shall we say, precarious? No, you keep on with your task force duties. If Danny needs help counting bullets or signing out weapons, he can come to me, yes?"

Stella nodded, striving to maintain a neutral face, even while her guts were jumping around like Paddington tarts on low-grade crack. "Absolutely. Sorry if, you know, I acted outside my remit. It won't happen again, Adam. I promise. Just looking forward to the day I can start working cases again."

He leaned back and favoured her with a warmer smile this time.

"I understand, Stella. Nobody wants to see you back hunting down bad guys more than me, you know that."

*

At eight o'clock that same evening, a mobile phone vibrated in its owner's pocket. The club had strict rules on phone conversations being conducted in its restaurant, so the Crown Prosecution Service official to whom it belonged excused herself from the table and walked through the crowded dining room to the marble-floored hallway between the restaurant and the members' lounge.

"Hello," she said, having gained the safety of the hall. "What is it?"

The voice at the other end of the line was male. Elderly. Its tone was papery, as if the lungs and larynx producing it had a struggle to force enough air between the lips. Yet she heard the authority there.

"I hear there's a member of the fourth estate sniffing around."

"Yes. A *Guardian* journalist, apparently. We're tracking her down, sir."

"You'd better. And when you do, you should find a way to steer her into safer investigative territory."

"Absolutely, sir." Despite herself, she began chewing and biting at her lower lip, tearing little slivers of skin away until she felt one pull at the soft flesh beneath and draw blood. She sucked her lower lip into her mouth, tasting the salty, copper tang of her own blood in her mouth. "We've managed before; we will this time too."

"Just see to it that you do."

The line went dead.

*

Eight miles away, in a terraced house in West London originally built to house brewery workers, and now worth more than ten thousand of them would have earned in a year, a freelance journalist named Vicky Riley was sipping from a glass of South African Chenin Blanc. In front of her on her desk was a battered black laptop. On its screen were notes relating to a story she'd been researching, on and off, for three years.

The document title visible at the top of the screen was Star_Chamber_2010_VR_1. In the main working area of the screen was a bulleted list of short phrases, sentences and questions:

Extra-judicial killings in Britain exposed by Vicky Riley.

Is there a conspiracy inside the UK legal establishment?

Ultra-conservative agenda – pledged to combat human rights law.

State-sanctioned death squads?

Collusion between CPS and police?

Richard Drinkwater/Edwin Deacon. What links their deaths?

Her mobile lay beside her laptop, and behind the glass of white wine, which was beaded with condensation. Beneath the phone was a slim, white envelope with a single word written across the front: "Stella".

She took a large gulp of the wine and picked up the phone, dialled a number and then waited. The phone at the other end rang eleven times. Just as she was getting ready to hang up, it was answered.

"Who is this?"

"Is that DI Stella Cole?"

"I repeat, who is this? You've got three seconds, then I'm hanging up."

Riley inhaled and spoke on the outbreath. "My name is Vicky Riley. I was a friend of your husband's."

She waited. The silence was filled with sounds. Her heartbeat, loud in her ears, like the surf rushing in and out through the coiled corridors inside a seashell. Clicks and whistles on the line as cell towers between Hammersmith and Stella Cole's house in Kilburn swapped the packets of ones and zeroes that constituted the call. And the steady breathing at the other end of the line, as she listened to her friend's widow deciding what to do next.

"What kind of friend?"

"The good kind. The kind he trusted with important information. The kind that was devastated when he was murdered."

"Richard wasn't murdered. It was a death-by-careless. Equivalent to manslaughter."

"I believe he was murdered. I'm a journalist. He confided in me. He said he suspected people were out to get him. Can we meet, please?"

"Who do you write for? What people? Why?"

"I'm freelance. I've pitched a story to *The Guardian*. About a conspiracy. High up in the law. I need to meet you. I really do. I'll come to you, or you can come here, to my house, I mean. Or a café, or the middle of Trafalgar Square, anywhere. You tell me when and where, and I promise I'll be there. There's stuff you need to hear. Stuff from Richard."

Another long pause: Riley waited it out. Slid the tip of her right index finger around on her laptop's trackpad.

"I'll come to you. Address?"

"It's thirty-one Overstone Road in Hammersmith. The postcode's–"

"Don't need it. What time?"

"Can you come now?"

"Give me half an hour."

*

Stella hung up. Put her phone down on the desk in her office. Closed her eyes. "Friend". It was such a simple word. Lola would have gone on to have friends. She would have had best friends. Then fallen out of love with them and hated them. Come home weeping onto Stella's shoulder about the betrayal. Then they would have made up. *But this lady says she was a friend of Daddy's, Lola. Sometimes grownups say "friend" and it's not a good thing. Let's go and find out.*

It had started to drizzle. Stella thumbed the bike's self-starter and gave the right grip a slight twist. Recently, it hadn't been catching on a closed throttle. As the Triumph's engine fired and settled into its comforting off-kilter idle, Stella looked up. Dark grey clouds were pressing down on the city, pregnant with rain. She kicked the bike into first and pulled away.

*

The two women faced each other on Riley's doorstep, Riley standing back from the threshold in tight, faded jeans and a white shirt, Stella in bike gear, holding her helmet in her left hand, shaking out her ponytail.

Stella took the journalist in at a glance. She was Richard's type. He'd always sworn he didn't have a 'type'. "*You're* my type!" was his stock answer whenever she teased him about ogling other women. But here was another representative. Dirty blonde hair. Streaks of brown amongst the sand rather than an even expanse of pale yellow tresses. Tall. Long legs. Why were men so predictable?

"Stella, I mean, can I call you that?" Riley looked down then back at Stella, scratching her scalp through the long hair Stella had already clocked. "Come in, please, it looks horrible out there."

She moved aside to let Stella come in, realised they'd end up squashed together in the narrow hall and turned to lead Stella down to the kitchen.

Pert little arse too. You're definitely his type. "You said you were a friend of my husband?" Stella asked. *Emphasise the possessive pronoun. Just to remind you who's who in this situation. I'm the one who gets to call him Richard, for now.*

Riley looked back over her shoulder as she reached the kitchen.

"Yes. I interviewed him a few times for stories I was working on. I specialise in miscarriages of justice. Police brutality, corruption, things like that."

"Which is supposed to endear you to me, is it?"

"Oh, God, I'm sorry! I didn't–, I mean I know most police officers are honest, and do their best, but you know, the bad apples…"

"How good a friend were you? To Richard?"

"We used to keep in touch about his cases and my stories. We'd buy each other lunch once a month. Didn't he mention me?"

"No. Funnily enough, he didn't. He never mentioned you once."

Riley's eyes widened and her hand went to her mouth for a second.

"You don't think we were–?"

"You were what?"

"Oh, God! You think we were having an affair, don't you? Look, we were friends, that's all. There was never anything between us. I wouldn't have minded, if he'd been single. I mean, he was a good-looking man. But he wasn't. Single, I mean." Her fingers were raking through her hair now. "I'm not a slut who sleeps with people to get stories, and I don't go after other women's husbands, either. Plus, he spent half the time talking about you, anyway. I'm sorry if you thought–"

Stella felt the steel clamp squeezing her chest loosen, then vanish. She inhaled deeply.

"Look, Vicky. It's me who should be apologising, not you. I was always a little jealous. Women naturally took to Richard and I used to feel insecure. No chance of that now, though, is there?"

"Why don't we sit down? I have a lot to tell you. I've got some wine on the go." Riley pointed at the opened bottle. "Do you want a glass?"

"No, thanks. But a coffee would be good. Milk, no sugar."

Riley made the coffee; ground, Stella noted, not instant, another tick in the credits side of the ledger she was keeping. She checked out the kitchen. It was a habit she couldn't break, assessing every room she sat in as a potential crime scene. The place was a mess. Plates and mugs piled up by the sink, even though there was a dishwasher tucked under the kitchen counter. Papers strewn over the table. A pair of deck shoes by the back door, and a pair of wellington boots, tumbled over as if drunk.

"Here you are," Riley said, finally, pushing a mug of steaming coffee across to Stella.

Stella took a sip, letting the smell of the really very good coffee drift into her nostrils. "Mmm. Good."

"Costa Rican. Fair trade, organic."

"And harvested by disabled lesbians, no doubt."

There was a pause, then both women laughed. The sound was loud in the little kitchen, and it broke whatever lingering tension lay between them. Riley spoke first, dabbing her eyes with a tissue.

"I'm sorry about Richard. And Lola. Really, I am. He gave me something and told me to give it to you if anything ever happened to him."

CHAPTER TWENTY
From Beyond

RILEY HANDED STELLA the envelope.

"He said to wait at least a year. To make sure you and Lola were OK. I don't think he ever imagined they'd go after Lola as well."

Stella took the envelope. Her fingers were shaking as she ran her thumbnail under the glued flap. "Who are 'they'? What are you talking about?"

"Read it. Then I'll answer your questions."

Stella's pulse was throbbing in her throat as if something was trying to push its way out. Her stomach was tight and the anxiety was making her crave a drink, or a pill.

Her thumb and forefinger were pinched round the edge of the sheet of paper inside the envelope so tightly the nails had turned white. She pulled it out, smoothed it flat on the table then held it up to read. The top edge fluttered.

My Darling Stella,

I am so sorry. You're reading this, and that means I am dead. By now, I hope the dust has settled and you and Lola are doing OK.

You've met Vicky. She is a friend, and someone I hope you will work with, as I have. She and I have been investigating a series of cases where people found not guilty, freed on appeal, or given noncustodial sentences, have turned up dead a few weeks later.

There is something going on in the legal system. A conspiracy, a secret society, a star chamber – we're not exactly sure what. They are acting as a parallel justice organisation, as judge, jury and executioner.

I can see you now. You're frowning and pulling your head back like you always do when you think something's bullshit. Talk to Vicky. She'll show you the evidence we've collected.

But be careful, my darling. These are dangerous people. They got to me. You have to keep Lola safe. And yourself. But you're the tough one. I know you can do it. Bring them down, Stella. Arrest them and get them in the dock. Expose them all.

I love you. I always will.

Richard

Stella folded the letter and pushed it back into the envelope. Looked across at Riley, who was crying silently, tears running down her cheeks, leaving greyish trails where her mascara had run. She pushed her palms against her own eyes and screwed them around, wiping away the wetness.

"He didn't know about Lola. It would have killed him," Stella said. Then she laughed, a cracked bark of a noise. "Poor Richard. They killed you before you could expose them, and they took our baby as well. I'm going to get them, darling. I'm going to get them all."

Then she sniffed and shook her head, blew her nose on a tissue and stared straight at Riley.

"I want to know everything you and Richard found out, dug up, suspected or just wondered about. Starting with, who, or what, we're looking for?"

Riley took a sip of her wine. "Since Richard was killed – murdered – I mean, I've developed a contact in the police force. He won't give me his name. I call him Deep Throat."

"What? After that old sex film?"

Riley shook her head. "After the mole in Watergate. When Nixon was bugging his opponents?"

Stella shook her head. "American politics isn't my thing, I'm afraid."

"It doesn't matter. Deep Throat told me he works in SCO19. That's—"

"Firearms, yes, I know. I'm a police officer."

Riley blushed. "Sorry, force of habit. He told me he overheard colleagues in the locker room talking about a job they'd done. It wasn't official police business. One of them said, 'We gave him PPM's message,' and the other one said, 'Die for your country'. Then they both laughed, apparently."

"What does PPM mean?" Stella asked.

"It's very interesting. If you Google 'die for your country' you get a poem by Wilfred Owen. He was—"

"First World War poet. We did him at school. I may not know my contemporary American history, but I'm not completely thick, you know."

Riley acknowledged her mistake with a nod. "My mistake. Again. The last line of the poem is 'Pro patria mori'. It's Latin. It means to die for your country."

"PPM," Stella said. "It's the name. Of this parallel justice outfit. Pro Patria Mori."

Riley nodded and sipped her wine. "That's where we got to, as well."

"And they're educated, or some of them are, anyway. I wouldn't expect a bunch of vigilante coppers to go around naming themselves in Latin." *Although I know a man at Paddington Green who's hinted twice that they exist.*

"Exactly! Richard thought it had to involve people right through the legal system. Police, lawyers, judges, even. Politicians too. In the Home Office, maybe. It's massive, Stella. And if we can break the story, it could be the biggest thing in British legal history since the Birmingham Six. Bigger."

Stella slurped the last of her coffee. "Okay, first, calm down. Second, this isn't just a *story*. If you're right, this is institutional corruption that includes fucking death squads on British soil. That's a bit bigger than fitting up suspected IRA terrorists. These people are murderers, Vicky. Dangerous people. With guns. You need to be careful. A Pulitzer Prize won't do you much good if you're tucked up all cosy in the footings for a new office block."

"I resent that. I'm not in this for glory. You're not the only one who cares about justice, you know."

Stella shrugged. "Sorry. I've never been the best of friends with your lot."

"Anyway. I know I need to be careful. That's why I contacted you. You're on the inside. You might even be able to find out who Deep Throat is. We have to keep going with this."

"Oh, I agree." *Because I need to find the people who killed my husband and my baby girl. I have plans for them.* "Just, you know, don't expose yourself to unnecessary risk, that's all."

They spent another three hours going over every angle, and every lead, thin as they were, that Riley had on her laptop and in her files. At the end of the evening, Stella turned to the journalist.

"I have to go. I'm too tired to do any more on this now. Keep in touch, OK? We can meet again, whenever you like. And if you get anything new, you call me. Immediately."

She left, then, and was back at her own desk in her spare room forty minutes later, with a fresh pot of coffee by her elbow. On an index card she printed the words, PRO PATRIA MORI. Beneath them, she wrote, 'high-level legal conspiracy'. Then she pinned it onto the wall in the centre of her display of documents and leaned back in her chair.

"I'm coming for you," she whispered.

*

Stella sat, thinking hard. The exhibits room had been busy all morning, with exhibits officers on various cases and operations coming and going, dropping sealed evidence bags off, collecting others, asking for help tracking down this bloody shirt or that bag of skunk. But now, mid-afternoon on the day after her conversation with Vicky Riley, it was quiet enough. She was doodling on her pad and scanning down the list of points and questions she'd written earlier.

She added three more questions.

Who murdered Richard and Lola?
Why?
PPM connection?

"Fuck this!" she shouted into the empty room. "Come back Reg, I need you here. I've got stuff I need to do."

Reg had called that morning, telling her he was still in pain and on medication, but would hopefully be back at work the following Monday. She decided to get back to the desk research into Edwin Deacon's case. That at least she could do from the exhibits room. Jiggling the mouse on the ancient computer, she murmured to it.

"Come on you antiquated piece of crap. Boot up for Mummy."

She waited for what seemed an eternity until finally the clockwork guts of the machine cranked it into flickering life. A few clicks later, she was staring at the main search screen for HOLMES. The case number was etched into her brain, and in a half-second of blurred fingertips she entered it. Up came the main screen for the case. She clicked on the one labelled 'court case' and then 'personnel'.

Defence barrister: Maurice Anstey

Prosecution barrister: Louise Stannah QC

Judge: Hon. Mr Justice Sir Leonard Ramage REPLACED Hon. Mr Justice Julian Frizzell-Gorman

Stella noted the three names, wondering why the original trial judge had been replaced, then cross-referenced them to a Metropolitan Police database of law firms and their members, plus all County Court and Crown Court judges. More notes followed the names into her phone: phone numbers, email addresses, physical addresses of their chambers.

Her finger was poised over the screen of her phone, ready to dial the number given for Anstey, when she realised she had no plausible reason to be ringing him. Or either of the others. Maybe Riley would be a better option. Journalists could always invent a cover story. She decided to hold off calling them till she'd discussed it with Riley.

Next stop, the purple Bentley. A list of owners was the prize, but now she had an identifiable vehicle she could at least get going on the CCTV. Her old street was free of cameras; it was far too quiet for any of that. But Putney High Street ought to be solid for coverage from Putney Bridge all the way through the shops and up to Tibbet's Corner, where drivers could choose from Wimbledon, Roehampton or the A3 towards Richmond and the southwestern suburbs of London beyond that.

She consulted another database on the PC, then picked up the desk phone and punched in a number. A woman answered.

"Wandsworth Police Station. Traffic."

"Hi. DI Cole here, Paddington Green nick. I need to review CCTV footage from Putney High Street for April ninth, 2009."

"Sorry, DI Cole. Not our cameras. It's the council you need to speak to."

"Which department, Highways?"

"Should be, yes, unless they've rebranded themselves."

Another search, another number. Stella dialled again. This time, having escaped the litany of automated options – everything from complaining about noisy neighbours to reporting fly tipping – she was through to a real human being. She repeated her credentials, and her request, breathing slowly to keep herself calm, despite her urge to yell and scream.

"Yeah," the man drawled after a wait of what was only three seconds but felt to Stella like three hours. "Not our department anymore. The council outsourced CCTV to a private firm eighteen months ago. Outfit called Urban Oversight PLC. You'll have to call them, I'm afraid."

"Okay. You don't have a number, I suppose?"

"No, we do. Hold on." Stella heard the heavy *clack* of inexpert fingers on a keyboard. "Here we are. Urban Oversight." He read out the number.

Stella thanked him, hung up, and dialled the number.

"That's over a year ago," the CCTV manager at the firm said when she finally reached the right person. "It's probably been deleted. Hang on, I'll have to check the archive. Could be it's been backed up at one of our data centres; we recently leased another ten thousand square feet in Sweden, just outside the Arctic Circle, if you can believe that." Stella could believe it, she told the man, while silently wishing him to shut the fuck up and tell her what she wanted to know. "I'm just going to put you on hold for a minute," he said.

The phone ticked and beeped twice and then went silent: no Vivaldi to soothe the jangling nerves or wind up the caller to breaking point depending on their state of mind. Just an eerie, echoing silence during which Stella began to wonder if she'd been cut off. Then the line clicked again.

"Hello? DI Cole? Sorry. To keep you waiting, I mean. You're in luck. Everything's there. When do you want to come over?"

Five minutes ago, that's when. "It'll have to be next week. Listen, can you put a flag on the footage so nobody deletes it by accident?"

"No problem. Not that anyone would, anyway. It's a new DAP from our CIO."

"A what from your what?"

"A digital archive protocol. From our Chief Information Officer."

"Thanks. Okay, I've got it. There's a DAP."

"That's right. Can't go breaking the DAPs can we?"

Stella sucked air through her teeth. "More than our job's worth. Listen, thanks. I should have said that before. To whom am I speaking, please?"

"Dave Locke."

"Thanks, Dave. I'll call you as soon as I can to fix an appointment. You've been most helpful."

"Always happy to help oil the wheels of justice, DI Cole."

The call over, Stella leaned back in the chair and stared at the ceiling. Something was hovering just beyond her conscious mind. In the old days, the good old days, she'd have parked it then mulled it over while sinking a bottle of Pinot Grigio in the pub. Now, religiously sober, she couldn't access her subconscious the way she used to. She tried slapping her forehead, but all she managed to do was give herself a headache. Maybe this was another item to add to the list of things she needed to discuss with Riley.

She picked up the phone again and called Lucian. She spoke as soon as he picked up.

"Do you still have the name and number of the guy you spoke to at Bentley?"

"I'm fine thanks, Stella. How are you?"

"Sorry. Hi Lucian, how are you? Are you fine? Good. So, I have a question for you. Do you still have the name and number of the guy you spoke to at Bentley?"

He laughed. "Yes, I do." She heard a *clonk*, then a muffled rustle. She pictured Lucian putting the handset down on his desk and sifting through bits of paper. "Here we go. Robin Brooke. Got a pen for the number?"

The phone number noted down, Stella spoke again.

"I want to talk to you about some more stuff. Are you free tonight?"

He laughed. "Sadly, yes. Do you want to come round?"

"Yes. I'll bring food, try to return the favour."

"I can come to you if it's easier."

"No!" She paused, slowed her breathing. "No, it's fine. Let me come to you. Steak all right?"

CHAPTER TWENTY-ONE
Paint

STELLA DIALLED THE number Lucian had given her.

"Bentley Public Relations. Robin Brooke's phone."

The voice was pleasant, light, female and very, very posh. Stella immediately felt at a disadvantage. She tried to elevate the tone of her own voice to match the cut-glass accent at the other end of the line.

"Yes, hello. This is Detective Inspector Stella Cole from the Metropolitan Police. Is Mister Brooke available, please?"

The woman sounded more amused than anxious, which further unsettled Stella.

"Goodness me! Has our Robin been a naughty boy and broken the speed limit in Mayfair, officer?"

"Haha!" *Oh, God, fake laugh. Come on, Stella, step up.* "No, madam. That would be a matter for my colleagues in Traffic."

"I'm glad to hear it. I'd hate to think how much taxpayers' money it would cost to send a detective inspector after a speeding motorist. Anyway, I see him across the office. Hold on a sec, would you? Robin?" Her voice increased in volume, but retained the easy, confident tone that had put Stella off her stride. "There's a policewoman on the line for you." She made "policewoman" sound like "sewage worker". Stella took a deep breath and let it out again. "Something about a speeding ticket." Her voice returned to its previous conversational pitch. "He's just coming, officer."

"Name?"

"I beg your pardon?"

"Your name, madam. For my notes. We like to keep quite detailed records of everyone we speak to."

"Oh, err, of course. Well, it's Miranda fforde. With two small f's."

"Thank you, madam. You've been most helpful."

"Here's Robin," she said, quieter now.

A young man's voice. Not so upper class, but still cultured, and with a hint of a drawl that spoke of privilege and breeding, if not necessarily education.

"Robin Brooke. How may I help you, officer?"

"Well, sir, for a start, it's 'Detective Inspector'. My title, I mean. But pleasantries aside, I believe you spoke to a colleague of mine recently. About some paint?"

"Oh, yes. One of those forensics chaps. Wanted to know about a special colour. It's called–"

"*Viola del diavolo*, yes, sir. I need a list of the customers who ordered that particular colour for their Bentleys."

He'd stonewalled Lucian, but Lucian was a tech. Now he was talking to a DI, would he have the nerve to brazen it out a second time?

"As I explained to your colleague, Detective Inspector, that information is confidential. Enthusiasts of the Bentley marque are private people, and they like us to help them keep it that way. I'm afraid that unless you can produce a warrant, my hands are tied and my lips are sealed."

Jesus! Was he making fun of her? *I'd like to tie your hands, believe me, son, I would. I'd have you screaming for mercy in seconds. Then we'd see how sealed your lips really were.* And what was all this shit about warrants? Sometimes it was like every member of the public was an amateur lawyer. That or a forensics specialist, always bleating on about latent prints and DNA. She took a deep breath.

"Which, of course, I am happy to go away and get from a judge. But I'm investigating a double murder, and you may not be aware of this, sir, but a day's delay, even an hour's delay, can help a criminal escape justice." Brooke tried to speak, but Stella cut him off and continued. "So, I'm thinking, I *could* get a warrant, as I say. And I could call a press conference when we finish our call and tell the media our prime suspect was driving a customised purple Bentley when he killed a man and his baby daughter. Of course, I can't be sure what that would do for your public image, or that of your privacy-loving customers. But I'm just a simple policewoman, not a public relations expert like you or the fragrant Miranda fforde with two small f's."

She waited. One, two, three …

"Fine. I need to go and talk to someone. Can I call you back?"

"Of course, and thank you for being so understanding. I'll give you five minutes. Then I'll call my press officer."

No. That won't be necessary. I'll call you in five. Or less."

"Fewer."

"Pardon?"

"It's 'fewer'. You'll call me back in five minutes or fewer. Less is for stuff you can't count, like patience. Fewer is for things you can, like minutes."

Three minutes later, her phone rang. She watched it and counted. No voicemail on these old things: they rang for ever or until the caller got bored and hung up. An exhibits room assistant passing her desk looked over. Stella smiled at her.

"Making someone sweat," she said.

The assistant, a plump, pretty girl in her early twenties with heavy-framed glasses, a shiny black nose ring and long blond hair, smiled back and walked away.

Stella let the phone ring eleven times before she lifted the handset from the cradle and placed it against her ear.

"DI Cole?" a man asked. It was Brooke.

"Yes, Robin. What do you have for me?"

"Five names. As requested. And five mobile numbers. I thought you'd want those, too. I can text them to you if you want, or email them?"

"That's really very thoughtful of you. Saves me a little bit of unnecessary legwork."

"You said it was a murder. A man and a baby. Well, that isn't right. I don't care who did it or what car they were driving. They should be caught. Just—"

"Keep your name out of it? No problem. Just read them out to me. No need for an email trail, is there? We'll just imagine I found it all out on the Internet."

The first name on the list made her eyes widen. Stella didn't follow sport. She'd snuggle next to Richard and watch England football games or the Olympics, the Wimbledon finals maybe, but more to keep him company than anything else. But you'd have to be a hermit or in a coma not to know who Barney Riordan was. Twenty-two, signed the previous year by Fulham for eight million pounds. Though he wasn't as good-looking as Beckham, he'd clearly snagged himself a capable agent. Londoners couldn't catch a bus or walk past a poster site without seeing his brooding face staring down at them from above a rack of steely abs and a pair of snowy-white boxers. He endorsed anything that moved, it seemed, and was rumoured to be making triple his salary in fees from brands delighted to have him shilling for their breakfast cereals, aftershaves, cars and, of course, underwear.

Well, well, this was going to make stage two a lot more fun. "Hey, Daisy!" she called out to the girl with the glasses, who was tapping away at a computer on a nearby desk. "Guess who yours truly is going to be interviewing next week?"

The girl turned round and frowned, looked upwards with her chin cupped in her right hand. She stayed that way for several seconds.

"The Chief Constable of South Yorkshire Police," she said finally.

"What? Did you actually think that one out logically or something? No! Barney Riordan."

Daisy's eyes widened and her mouth dropped open.

"Really? Rear of the Year Riordan?"

"Yes, if that's what you call him."

"Have you *seen* his bum? God, I'd give him one."

Having scored what she felt was a definite hit with her coup, Stella returned to the list of names and numbers.

The second and third names meant nothing to her. Arthur Godsby and Asha Singh.

The fourth name, again, meant nothing. Mark Easton. As she took in the fifth name her eyes widened.

Sir Leonard Ramage.

The judge in Deacon's trial. The judge who'd somehow muscled in on it instead of old Frizzell-Gorman.

*

As Stella rode east to meet Lucian that night, she opted for a more or less straight-line route that took her along the Strand, down Fleet Street, across Ludgate Circus and past St Paul's Cathedral on her left. The traffic slowed, then stopped altogether as she approached Old Bailey. She looked up to her left as she passed the Old Bailey itself, or the Central Criminal Court, to give it its official name. She'd given evidence there many times. She'd been attacked with brutal sarcasm by defence barristers earning ten times what she did – or more. And she'd waited with crying, shaking victims of crime while the juries deliberated.

Sometimes she'd punched the air when the defendant got sent down, hugged and skipped with jubilant families of murder victims, went out to celebrate with her colleagues later. Other times, she'd sat, stunned, on one of the hard wooden benches in the corridors reeking of fear-sweat, floor polish and wig powder, her hand aching in the clutch of a rape victim, watching her grinning attacker walk past after another collection of twelve bleeding hearts had got it wrong.

On top of the greyish Portland stone tower and lead-covered dome stood the gilded statue of Lady Justice. No blindfold necessary; her "maidenly form" was supposed to guarantee objectivity, according to the brochures Stella had read in the endless hours hanging about waiting to be called to give her evidence. In her left hand, the scales, representing the weighing of evidence. In her right, a sword, held aloft and ready to deliver punishment to the guilty. So why did she fail to do what was right in case after case? Why could organised crime groups buy their way out of prison, or even court itself? Why did perfectly good evidence get thrown out just because some expert witness got nervous and fluffed her lines? And why did the guilty go unpunished? If there were any justice in the world, those murderers, rapists and child molesters would all be sent away for ever, or put down like the animals they were.

A blaring car horn broke Stella's trance. She refocused on the road ahead. The traffic had eased up, and the van she'd been stuck behind was thirty feet away. But she didn't pull away after it. Instead she signalled left and pulled over to the kerb, allowing the taxi behind her to overtake with an angry parp from its horn.

She unclipped her helmet and pulled it off, placing it on the tank between her knees. Then she looked up again. At the statue. Lady Justice. What had she just thought? If there were any justice in the world? She'd heard that phrase recently. More than once. As she stared up into the darkening sky, the last rays of the sun glinting off Justice's five-pointed coronet, one of the two voices came to her. It was the guy at Urban Oversight. Something about oiling the wheels of justice. But who was the other, earlier voice?

"Come on, Stella, think!" she snapped, causing a passer-by, a young, bearded guy in a dark, tight-fitting suit, to turn round.

It was a female voice. Light, friendly but with an edge to it. The occupational health manager. Linda. She'd used the same phrase. "If there were any justice in this world, evil people like that man would all meet sticky ends."

But so what? It wasn't exactly a rarity, was it? People said it all the time. It was a cliché. She closed her eyes and tried to quieten the environmental noise from the cars, vans, buses and taxis, the cycling commuters yelling at the cars, people yammering into their phones, and the relentless, subsonic thrum that was London being London. What had Linda Heath said? Exactly? *Be a detective, Stella. Think! Like you were taught.*

Stella recalled her own frazzled state, felt her pulse kicking up and the knot of nervous tension tighten in her stomach. *Good. Let it come. Remember how it felt, as well as what you heard. Which was …*

"If there's to be any justice in our world, evil people like that man will all meet sticky ends."

Her eyes snapped wide open. Three differences. The tense at the beginning first. Not, "If there were", which would render the sentiment just one of wishful thinking, but "If there's to be", as if something real were coming. Then the word before "world". Not "the" but "our". And last, a second tense change from her initial recollection. "Not "would all", again, more wishful thinking, but "will all" – as if justice was going to be served.

*

Half an hour later, Stella bumped the Triumph over the kerb outside Lucian's apartment block, parked in the lee of the building and killed the engine. She looked up and down the long street. Nobody about, just like last time. No through traffic, since it ran parallel to a fast-moving dual carriageway. She leant the bike onto its kickstand and fitted the lock to the brake disc. The centre-stand was more secure, but she loved the look of the big black bike as it leaned over. Cooler by miles. Like something that film star with the shock of dark hair and sky-high cheekbones would ride. Anton Brinks, that was his name. Richard used to tease her about him. "Ste-lla and An-ton, sit-ting in a tree. Kay-eye-ess-ess-eye-en-gee." She'd punch him and he'd laugh. Lola would look up at her parents from the baby bouncer and gurgle contentedly.

She shook her head to dispel the image and pressed the buzzer on the brushed steel intercom. Lucian's voice came through, with less of the distorted squawking these things normally offered. More up-market apartments, better audio, it stood to reason.

"Hello? Stella?"

"Yeah, it's me."

"OK, come up."

The latch rattled loudly, and she pushed her way in.

Outside Lucian's door, her finger poised over the stainless-steel button to ring the bell, she felt her stomach fluttering. Which was odd. She frowned, hesitating. *He's gay, Stella. So, it can't be sex. Well what, then? I don't know, do I? I'm as much in the dark as you are. Press the bloody doorbell.*

She stabbed at the button, and a few moments later Lucian opened the door. She looked him up and down. Another beautiful, casual outfit: navy-blue chinos, a soft, white, cotton shirt with mother of pearl press studs and yellow suede loafers on bare feet. God, this boy could dress.

Lucian grinned, revealing even, white teeth. "Are you checking me out, DI Cole?"

"A cat can look at a king, can't she?"

He looked over his shoulder as he hung her jacket up. "I'm a king now, am I? Not a queen?"

She smiled. "King of forensics. In my book, anyway. I brought steaks, rocket, parmesan and a nice bottle of red."

"I thought you didn't drink."

"I don't. It's for you. Though I might have a little sniff."

They moved through to the kitchen, and as Stella prepared the food, Lucian poured some elderflower fizz for Stella.

"You remembered," she said.

He opened the wine and poured himself a glass, offering it to Stella. She bent her nose to the rim of the thin-stemmed glass and inhaled.

"Oh, God, that smells good," she breathed, as the deep aroma of blackcurrant and the volatile top note of alcohol swirled into her brain. "Here, take it back."

She arranged two piles of rocket leaves on plates, dressed them with extra-virgin olive oil and balsamic vinegar plus sea salt and cracked black pepper. Then, while she waited for the griddle pan to heat up, she spoke.

"Lucian, I'm getting into something that's so heavy I don't really know how to deal with it."

"What is it? You've gone all serious on me."

She frowned and pulled on her ponytail. "I want to tell you. I need to tell someone. But I need to know I can trust you."

He smiled, then took a sip of his wine. "Mmm. That really is an excellent Côtes du Rhône. And of course, you can trust me. Why, do you want to test me? Is that it?"

"Yes. Only, I don't quite know what to ask you."

"Ask me anything. You know I'll be frank with you. I told you I was gay, didn't I?"

She nodded, and sipped her own drink, though she barely noticed its off-sweet, flowery taste. Would Pro Patria Mori accept gay people into its world of vigilante justice? It seemed unlikely. But maybe that was it. Maybe there was the killer question. She inhaled, catching the floral scent of the elderflowers this time.

"I belong to a secret legal organisation called Pro Patria Mori. We are dedicated to exacting justice when the police and the courts fail. We are absolutely blind to race, religion and sexuality. All we care about is justice. I've been tasked with offering you trial membership."

She closed her mouth and pressed her lips together as tight as she could. Her heart was thumping and the whisper of anxiety in her stomach had turned into a hurricane. She felt sick, and the smell of hot steel from the griddle on the gas hob wasn't helping.

Lucian's face was a mask of horror. His eyebrows had shot up towards his hairline, furrowing his high forehead with five or six parallel ridges of skin. His mouth had dropped open and his eyes were wide.

He put the wine glass down on the counter.

Then he came towards her until he was less than a foot away.

"Stella Cole. Are you insane? I mean, have you lost your fucking mind? You joined some kind of professional lynch mob, some vigilante outfit, and you're seriously asking me to join it? Hello? Do the words Ku Klux Klan mean anything to you? Did you miss the part where I was black?"

Stella surprised him by stepping forward and hugging him, trapping his arms inside her embrace.

"Oh, Jesus, Lucian. Thank God. I love you. I'm so sorry."

She released him then, and stepped back, swiping tears from her cheeks with the back of her hand.

Lucian's expression had changed. The forehead was smooth, but now the brows were creased and drawn together. His lips were pursed.

"What the fuck just happened?" he asked, finally.

"There *is* a secret vigilante gang. I'm sure of it. But I'm not a member. I think they might have been involved in Richard and Lola's murder. I need friends, Lucian, I really do, but I had to be sure you weren't one of them."

"Look, let's get those steaks cooked and sit down. Then you'd better tell me what's going on. Because either you've lost it big time, or there is something rotten in the state of Denmark."

She nodded, blew her nose on a piece of kitchen paper, rewashed her hands and turned to the food.

Five minutes later, they were sitting at the table, facing each other, drinks refilled. She'd sliced the steaks into diagonal strips, charred on the outside, deep rose-pink within, and laid them on the rocket leaves, then scattered translucent shavings of Parmesan over the top.

Through a mouthful of steak, Lucian mumbled a question.

"Pro Patria Mori, is that what you called them?"

"That's right. It means—"

"To die for one's country," they said together.

Stella laughed. This was going to be all right. She spoke next.

"Here's what I know. When Richard and Lola were killed – murdered, actually – someone tampered with the evidence, well, they tinkered with the computer records. Some third-rate toerag took the fall for it, and he wound up dead at Long Lartin a few days ago. Someone recategorised him from Cat C to Cat A, and he was beaten to death in a cell with the Rule 45ers."

Lucian frowned. "Sorry, I'm not familiar with that one. Prison lingo's not really my department."

"Paedophiles, sex offenders. The nonces, yes?"

"Okay, yes. What else?"

"This one's a bit vague, but there's a woman in occie health, Linda Heath. Do you know her?"

Lucian nodded. "Blonde crop, pouty lips, bustles around giving out forms and acting like she's head girl or something."

"That's her. She said something about justice. The syntax was off. Really weird, like she was sending me a message or something."

"Off, how? Oh, and this steak is fantastic, by the way."

"Thanks. It's one of the few things I can make. So, on my first day back at work, I'm having my interview with her and at one point, she's commiserating with me about Richard and Lola. She says, or she *should* say, 'If there were any justice in the world'. But what she *actually* says is, 'If there's *to be* any justice in *our* world'. You hear the difference, don't you?"

"Not difficult, even without your helpful emphasis. One's just a thing people say, the other sounds like, I don't know, a mission statement or something. Like more of a slogan."

Stella smiled, and jabbed her fork towards him, making the morsel of beef and its frill of rocket leaves flick fragrant drips of oil and the dark balsamic vinegar onto the white tablecloth.

"Sorry about that. But yes! Exactly. Like it was a mantra. I think she's a member of PPM. That's what I'm calling them."

"Can I just play devil's advocate, only to test this out?"

"That's what I was hoping for. Just in case I've lost my marbles, seeing conspiracies where there are only cock-ups."

"Exhibits do get misfiled from time to time. Prisoners do get miscategorised. That's bureaucracy for you. Maybe the head girl is just rubbish with English idiom. It does happen."

"Yes, I know all of that. But there's more. I'm saving the best till last. You know Pink in CID?"

Lucian grunted. "Who doesn't? You know I said nobody gives me grief for being black and gay? He's one of the ones who does."

"He's an arsehole. And he's a stupid arsehole who can't keep his mouth shut. I think he's either a member or else he's heard something. Twice, he's pretty much come out and told me that they exist."

"Okay, and the best bit?"

"Richard wrote to me and told me PPM exists."

Lucian took a bigger sip of wine this time. "Wrote to you when? How?"

"From beyond the grave. Literally. I met this journalist he'd been working with. Or cooperating with, or whatever. He gave her a letter that she was to give to me a year after he died. *If* he died, I mean. And he did, didn't he? She, this journalist, showed me her notes. They'd been working on it for a while before he died."

Lucian put his knife and fork down together with a clink. Drained his glass, then refilled it. He gulped half of it down then looked across at Stella.

"Shit!" he whispered.

"Shit, indeed," she replied.

CHAPTER TWENTY-TWO
Shopping Trip

COLLIER PICKED UP the sheet of paper and turned it over. It was a record of logins used to access a particular file in the medical and forensics database. He'd received it a day earlier and was still pondering what to do. He recognised the usernames as belonging to the original team who'd worked the crime scene. Except one:

Drinkwater, L, autopsy report accessed by: TheaMJackson

Collier had no idea who Thea Jackson was or where in the station she worked. But whoever she was, she had no business accessing autopsy reports. Especially not this one.

He picked up his phone and called Linda Heath.

"Linda, it's Adam. I need to speak to someone. Thea Jackson, her name is. Middle initial, M. Can you go into the HR database for me?"

"Hold on," she said.

While he waited, listening to the distant clicking of Heath's fingernails on her keyboard, Collier sat immobile. He was focusing on his breathing, trying to ease a tightness in his chest as though someone had strapped a wide rubber band around his ribs.

"Here we are," she said with a brightness to her voice Collier always associated with force bureaucrats "Thea Jackson, police staff, works in the exhibits room. I can give you her extension if you like?"

"No need. Thanks, Linda."

A ten-minute fast-walk through the station took Collier to a place he had last visited four years earlier. At his level, evidence was largely a matter of memos and meetings, rather than weapons, clothes, fibres or body fluids.

Arriving in the exhibits room, he could only see one person there, a young woman dressed like a vampire in an all-black outfit that made Collier wonder whether the station's dress code for civilian employees – business casual – had ever been announced down here. He wandered over, hands in pockets, smile in place.

"Hi," he said.

She looked up. Dark purple lips curved into a smile that drew deep dimples into her cheeks.

"Hi. Can I help you?"

"I'm looking for Thea Jackson."

The smile broadened. The dimples deepened.

"Oh, well you're in luck. I am she. And you are?"

"I'm doing some research into our forensics database. Checking user statistics for the brass upstairs. Just for background, have you logged in to the autopsy folder recently?"

She shrugged.

"Nope. Not me, boss. Not guilty." Then she winked. "Of course, they all say that, don't they?"

"I see. It's just there was a record of your login. You are TheaMJackson, password Gandalf, aren't you?"

She nodded, the smile fleeing from her face now.

"Yes. But I really haven't used it for that." She drew in a sharp breath and put her index finger – black nail varnish – to the tip of her nose. "But I did give it to the detective who's working down here. Stella. Do you know her?"

He shook his head. Then thanked her, turned on his heel and retreated to his office.

*

The weekend arrived. And that meant a very special shopping expedition. Shrugging a teal-and-charcoal nylon rucksack over her jacket, Stella left the house at nine on Saturday morning. She rode fast, enjoying the weave and swerve as she shot past slow-moving cars and vans, and was climbing off the Triumph at a DIY store twenty minutes later. From the rucksack, she pulled out a black baseball cap, which she tugged down over her eyes. She tucked her hair up under the cap at the back. Then she put on a pair of tortoiseshell-framed sunglasses with comically oversized round lenses. She seemed to remember they'd been fashionable for a while.

She kept her head down as she entered the store and grabbed a wheeled orange plastic basket with a telescopic handle. As she dropped items into the basket, she wondered whether any of the other customers were planning an extended torture session. Or was it just her? Most seemed to be either happy young newly-weds buying wallpaper or tins of paint; middle-aged guys humming and hawing over electric lawnmowers; or older couples arguing in subdued but irritable voices about whether zinnias or geraniums were better for the front garden.

At the till, the young guy listlessly zapping her purchases with the laser gun had seven facial piercings including enormous white plastic rings inside his earlobes. She was surprised that the store's manager hadn't asked him to remove them. Then she looked down at the sleeves of tattoos on both arms – Japanese koi – and guessed that it was a seller's market.

"Arts and crafts?" he asked, with a smile.

Nice eyes, she thought. Brown. Shame about all the metalwork. She followed his gaze.

In front of her were a claw hammer, a pair of pliers, bolt cutters, three metres of blue polypropylene rope, a bundle of ten-inch, black plastic cable ties, a needle-pointed awl and a blowtorch.

"Something like that," she replied as she punched in the PIN for her credit card.

Her next stop was an independent kitchen shop. "Jeffers & Tanton" the British racing green sign said. Stella wandered between two racks of insanely expensive saucepans, enamelled in rainbow colours. She was looking for the knives. Up a ramp carpeted with the same bristly stuff they use for doormats was the cash desk. Behind it and off to one side were three glass-fronted cabinets. Each one was full of knives. Each one was locked with a small chromed cylinder in the centre of the right-hand door.

She stood in front of the cabinet not obscured by the cash desk. It looked like something a serial killer would have in his front room. The blades within ranged from heavy cleavers down to delicate little paring knives. One set caught her eye. The handles were made of a black wood. She wondered if it was ebony. Or was that one of those banned substances now, like tortoiseshell or ivory? The handles were inlaid with swirling silver motifs that made Stella think of dragons.

"Do you need any help there?" a friendly, female voice asked.

Stella turned. The woman who'd asked the question was a short, matronly sort, with a black and gold apron embroidered with the shop's name over her own clothes. She had purple-framed glasses perched on the end of her nose, prevented from falling to the ground by a string of matching plastic beads.

"I'd like to take a look at the knives, please. The inlaid ones."

The woman smiled conspiratorially. "Those are I.O. Shen. German weight and handle but Japanese steel and blade angle. Lots of chefs like them. Which ones caught your eye?"

Stella pointed to two knives, one a cleaver, the other a more conventional-looking, round-bellied blade.

"Those two."

The woman picked up a key from a scarlet ceramic dish behind the till, holding it between purple-varnished nails, and twisted it in the chromed lock. She slid the glass door aside and lifted the cleaver from its mount in the display. Then she handed it to Stella.

Stella curled her fingers round the inlaid handle. Now she had it in her grasp, she could see that the design chased into the handle wasn't a dragon but an abstract swirl. She could feel the silvery steel, cold against her palm and fingers. The cleaver was heavy. She turned it so that light from one of the halogen downlighters caught the razor-sharp blade.

"You could joint anything with that," the saleswoman said.

"Hmm?"

"I said you could use that to joint anything. It'll go straight through the thickest part and out the other side without stopping."

Stella put it down on top of a butcher's block in pale pine positioned to the right of the display case.

"Can I try the other one now, please?"

The saleswoman handed her the more conventional cook's knife.

"This is the Maoui Deba. It was actually designed by a chef, Karim Maoui. It has a beautiful balance, don't you think?"

Stella held the knife as she would to chop an onion. Then she flipped it so the blade was uppermost with the ball of her thumb pushed up against its thick rear edge. Spun it back again. Then she changed her grip again.

The saleswoman took a step back, a flash of anxiety visible in her face.

Stella was holding the big knife point downwards, her hand tight around the handle, whitening her knuckles. She rested the point on the sleek, varnished timber of the butcher's block. She looked down. Blood was welling up around the tip of the knife. Given that it was embedded in a man's eye that was only to be expected. She loosened her grip a little and twirled the point. The surface of the eyeball gave a little, then tore. The knife slid down to the back of the socket with a soft *pop*. She leaned on it and heard the distant crunch of thin bone. The knife sliced down into his brain. He was dead.

She looked round at the saleswoman, who was blinking rapidly, and smiled.

"I'll take them both. Can you wrap them for me?"

*

The following Monday morning, Stella arrived in the exhibits room to be greeted by a smiling Reggie Willing. Food poisoning seemed to have done him good. He looked about twenty pounds slimmer and was wearing a new suit and a wide smile.

"Well, well, well, if it isn't my favourite new recruit. How are you, Stel?" he asked, coming round the edge of his desk, arms wide, as if her to hug her.

She stepped back.

"Fine, Reg. How are you?"

He stood, arms still spread, and smiled.

"Funniest thing, Stel. Once I'd stopped rushing to the toilet every five minutes, which, I can tell you, was not fun, I don't know, I just found some sort of inner peace. I lay in bed while Karen looked after me. Woman's a saint. A real saint. Couldn't do enough for me. Got my strength back, little by little. But look at me!"

At this point, Reg executed a clumsy pirouette like a hippo in a tutu.

"You lost weight then, Reg?"

"Two stones, near enough. Karen had to go out and buy me new clothes. My old ones were that big they kept falling off me. Couldn't come to work with my trousers round my ankles, could I?" he said, winking.

Pushing away the image of a debagged Reg the Veg, Stella answered him with a straight face. "Glad to have you back, Reg. Anyway, listen, now you *are* back, I hope you don't mind but I've got some Operation Streamline meetings to go to this week. Might need to be away for a day or two."

"As you wish, dear lady, as you wish. You're not exactly a career administrator, are you?"

With that, he spun on his heel and marched off towards some distant corner of the exhibits room, the sound of his footsteps bouncing off the hard surfaces of the floor and ceilings.

Right, Stel, time to get going. Let's call Mr Riordan.

"Hello? Who's this?" The voice at the other end was friendly enough, with a Mancunian twang.

"Is that Barney Riordan?"

"Yeah. Who wants to know?"

"Detective Inspector Stella Cole, Metropolitan Police, Mister Riordan. I'd like to talk to you about your car."

"Oh, no! Some bastard hasn't nicked it, have they?"

"No, sir. But I would like to come and see you. Just a few questions. Would you be free tomorrow?"

"Can't, can I? Training in the morning. Then meetings with my sponsors all afternoon."

"It won't take very long, sir. No more than half an hour." *Unless I think you killed my baby and her daddy, in which case I'll make it last as long as you can draw breath.*

"I could fit you in right after training, I suppose. Get a shower first then meet at our ground."

"What time?"

"Twelve thirty all right? It's Craven Cottage, yeah?"

Stella told him the time was fine and that she knew her way to the ground – *which isn't a million miles from our old house* – thanked him and ended the call.

She rang the other four numbers, but they all went to voicemail. She left a short, polite message each time, asking the owners to call her back.

She started as someone tapped her on the shoulder. She spun round in her chair, then smiled.

"Jesus, Daisy! Don't creep up on me like that."

"Is it true? Did I just hear you arranging to meet Barney Riordan?"

The girl's heavily made-up eyes were wide with a mixture of delight and curiosity.

"You might have? Why, want to tag along, do you?"

"Oh, God, I'd probably wet my knickers!"

Stella decided to break another rule. Why not? It wasn't as if she'd had a spotless record since coming back to work.

"You can, if you want to. Be my number two. Normally, I'd have a DS with me, but I'm a bit *persona non grata* upstairs."

"A bit what?"

"An unwelcome person in a country. Like suspected terrorists or those mad religious fuckers who want to come over here and encourage people to bomb abortion clinics." The girl's eyes widened further, if that were possible. Stella smiled. "Which I'm not, obviously. But I am a bit short-handed. So, if you *did* want to come with me–" Stella let the sentence hang between them like a thread of cigarette smoke.

Daisy nodded. Fast. Then poked her glasses higher on the bridge of her nose.

"Yes," she said. "Yes, please. But, like, what should I wear? Am I on active duty? I'm only police staff here, you do know that, don't you?"

"Slow down. First, you work for the Met, like me. Like every copper in this station. Second, something simple and quiet. Black, maybe, or navy. Third, you do what I say, okay? No simpering or asking for his autograph. And definitely no selfies."

Daisy nodded, again. "Yes. I can do that. I have my interview suit at home. I can get Mum to press it for me."

"Good. We'll leave here tomorrow at eleven. And one last thing?"

"Yes?"

Stella felt sure Daisy would have agreed to sign over every penny she had in her bank account, and possibly her soul, for the chance to meet Riordan. *Be a shame if I have to kill, then.*

"Lose the nose ring."

*

Stella arrived in the armoury as a posse of stone-faced, black-clad firearms officers were clearing their weapons into the sandbox and signing them back in with Hutchings and Nick Probert. She waited, keeping well out of the way until the last of them had disappeared, then approached the counter.

"Hey, Danny!" she called over, at the armourer's back.

He turned. Saw Stella, and smiled. Came back to the grille.

"Hi," he said, smiling. "Thought we'd lost you. Haven't seen much of you since the fun and games with those new Glocks."

"I know, and I'm sorry. Been a bit preoccupied with Operation Neat and Bloody Tidy, to be honest, much though it pains me to say it. I thought you might want to come round tonight."

Hutchings grinned. It was a very attractive grin. Not smug, just a bit boyish, as if he truly believed everyone and everything in the world were conspiring to make his life as full of pleasure as possible.

"I'd love that. Same as last time? About eight?"

"Perfect. Do you like Chinese?"

Another smile. "Chinese, Indian, whatever. If I'm sharing it with you, it's fine."

She left him there, arguing with Nick about the best way to store magazines – empty or full – and took a detour on her way back to the basement.

Walking into the hubbub of the CID office gave her a sudden rush of adrenaline. She could feel it in the pit of her stomach. All around her, detectives were scanning computer screens, on the phone, standing at whiteboards presenting new findings, huddled in twos, threes and fours discussing cases. She had to remind herself that light duties had always been part of her plan. She inhaled, savouring the smell of coffee, marker pens, sweat, coffee and the raw tang of excitement.

She threaded her way through to Frankie O'Meara's desk, having spotted her coming back from the kitchen with a mug of tea.

"Boss! Hi, how are you?" Frankie said, once Stella had arrived at her desk, its surface free of even a post-it note. Frankie was obsessive about keeping her workspace clear and filed every single piece of paper the moment she'd read it. "I thought we'd never see you again."

Stella smiled. "I'm good. You know, slowly going mad working with Reg the Veg, but it's okay. They'll have to recall me to the team at some point or I'll be going postal down there myself."

"I feel your pain, boss. Is there anything I can do for you? I mean," she dropped her voice to a murmur, "The Model told us all you're kind of easing your way back in, and he'd prefer us not to burden you with operational detail." Frankie rolled her eyes as she mimicked Collier's measured cadences.

"There is something, Frankie. Do you want to come out the back for a fag break?"

Frankie looked puzzled. "I don't smoke, you know that."

"I know. Now, do you fancy coming down for a fag break or not?"

*

Paddington Green had a central courtyard enclosed on all four sides by administrative offices, the armoury, the custody suite and a block of holding cells, and the front of the station. The latter housed the reception area where members of the public were permitted, coming in to report lost dogs, snatched bags and suspicious characters milling around outside public buildings, who almost always turned out to be students, foreign tourists or winos congregating by a warm air vent.

The courtyard, with its nooks and crannies, also served as a discreet venue for the station's smokers to light up away from the disapproving eyes of their more health-conscious colleagues and those senior officers who felt smoking showed a lack of self-discipline. Not to mention the hated pen-pushers who'd banned smoking in the first place, forcing anyone who needed a nicotine fix to skulk around like a criminal.

Stella led Frankie to an unoccupied corner, nodding on the way to a couple of plainclothes officers she knew from an operation she'd worked on before the accident. The murder. Before the murder. He'd murdered them. *I'll make him pay, baby. Don't worry.*

Frankie was talking, but her voiced sounded muffled. It didn't matter. What did matter was the small child playing in the centre of the courtyard. She couldn't be more than eighteen months old, in a little flowery dress and pale pink sandals. Must belong to a witness or maybe a relative, or a guest of the custody sergeant. As Stella watched, the little girl retrieved a cigarette butt from a patch pocket on the right side of her dress and placed it between her lips. She took a lighter from the same pocket, thumbed the wheel and touched the flame to the blackened end of the butt, cupping her other hand around the flame.

Stella tried to run to her. To snatch the burning cigarette from between her fingers and grind it under foot. But she couldn't get moving. Her knees were locked together and she knew if she tried to run, she'd simply collapse. The little girl screamed as the cigarette flared with orange flame. The flame blew backwards into her face and within seconds her hair was blazing. The dress caught fire next, roaring as the flames were fanned by a sudden breeze. The screams intensified and Stella watched helplessly, wordlessly, tears streaming from her eyes as the little girl's skin peeled off in the heat before she toppled sideways and lay still.

Then she disappeared.

Stella lurched sideways, colliding with Frankie's right hip.

"Oh, God, no!" she wailed. "Lola!"

Frankie was leaning over her, an expression of concern creasing the normally smooth skin of her forehead.

"Boss? Stella? Are you all right?"

Stella got to her feet, brushing dirt from her jeans.

"I'm fine. Did you, did you see the little girl? In the flowery dress?"

Frankie frowned. "Where?"

Stella turned her head, knowing there'd be nothing but the scrubby patch of scuffed dirt and grass.

"Nothing. It's nothing. Just felt a bit faint. I missed lunch, that's all."

"You were staring over there. Your mouth was working, but you weren't making a sound. Did you not hear me talking to you?"

A voice in Stella's head was muttering the same two words over and over again, "run now, run now, run now". But she wouldn't. Couldn't. *Oh God, for a Valium now. Just half a one would do it.* A little round pill to quell those fucking sparrow-sized butterflies fluttering and panicking to be let out of her stomach. She fought down the fear, forcing herself to slow her breathing, and lighting a cigarette to buy a little time.

"Like I said. Just felt a bit woozy for a moment. Must be the thought of that fag." Stella took a drag and aimed for a smile, but she could tell it wasn't convincing from Frankie's doubtful expression.

"I'm going to let that go. For now. But you need to come out with me. Soon. For a proper conversation. You can let me in, you know. If you're having problems coping. I won't tell The Model. Or Miss Bitchy-Face from occie health."

"You know her too, do you?" Stella asked, knowing exactly who Frankie meant.

"Everyone does. We call her Eva Braun. She's like Collier's loyal little sheepdog. Always pestering us about this training or that evaluation centre. I think she imagines all the lowlifes on our patch just put their shit on hold while we go off to get lectured about appropriate professional standards and best practice. I'd like to give her a slap, boss, I really would."

Stella gave a wry smile. If what she suspected about Linda Heath was true, Eva Braun was just about on the money. And a slap would be only the beginning.

"Frankie, do you ever wonder whether we're truly the good guys?"

"What do you mean?"

CHAPTER TWENTY-THREE
Square Eyes

STELLA PAUSED. SHE was as sure as a body could be that Frankie O'Meara wasn't the sort of cop – the sort of woman – who would join a vigilante group inside the police force. Just as she had been about Lucian.

"I mean, what if there were people inside the force who were doing bad things?"

"Well, duh! No offence, seeing as you're my DI and everything, but bent coppers in the Met aren't exactly news."

"I know that, but I'm not talking about vice shaking down pimps or porn barons, or even cops on the take from gangsters. I mean seriously bad people on our side of the line going out and—" *Well, what are you waiting for? Go on, say it. Out loud.*

"What, boss?"

Stella inhaled deeply and rushed out a sentence before her lips clamped tight around the opening word. "Killing people they think are guilty no matter what the courts say."

Frankie paused for a second, then laughed.

"Really? I mean, it's a lovely idea, given what we see happening month in, month out, but come on, boss. This is London, not Hollywood."

Something about Stella's unsmiling expression must have spooked Frankie, because the DS suddenly became still and watchful. The same way Stella knew she'd be if they were on a stakeout or about to burst into a suspect's scuzzy tenth-floor flat with a psychotic dog barking on the other side of the cheap painted door.

"You're serious, aren't you? What's going on, boss?"

Stella pulled on her pony tail, letting the thick hank of hair slide through her closed fingers. She looked around. No smokers within twenty yards. She lowered her voice anyway.

"There's a group inside the legal system. Right here in town. They call themselves Pro Patria Mori. And they're offing people they believe deserve it. And for whatever reason, I think because he was onto them, they killed Richard. Lola, too, just because she happened to be in the car with him."

"Shitty death, boss! And you've got evidence?" She bit her lip. "Sorry, I mean, of course you've got evidence."

Stella shook her head. "No, nothing that would stand up in court, anyway. But I've met this journalist who's been digging around. She and Richard were working on it together. You know how we were talking about it the other night at mine?" Frankie nodded. "They got further. And now I know the motive."

"Couldn't it all be just, you know, journalistic speculation? Some nosy reporter looking to get a prize for investigative journalism. Or something."

"Honestly? Yes, it could, just. But it isn't, Frankie. I know it. I *feel* it. They got my family, and I want to get them."

Frankie straightened her back, and looked Stella in the eye.

"What can I do to help?"

"Right now? Nothing. But you know Lucian, from Forensics?" Frankie nodded. "I told him last night. He's one of the good guys. I need to form some kind of plan to bring them down, then I'll let you know."

Frankie smiled. But it was a grim smile. Her eyes were deadly serious. "Just let me know."

*

Now that Reg was back, Stella felt she had more leeway to pursue her real project. He seemed blissfully unconcerned with her comings and goings and just nodded complacently whenever she said she would be gone for a few minutes, or hours. After lunch, she announced she was "popping out". He didn't even look up from his phone.

Earlier, she'd called the CCTV guy at Urban Oversight, Dave Locke. He'd been happy for her to come round the same afternoon and review the tapes for Putney High Street from the sixth of May. She got the sense he didn't have a lot of excitement in his life, so helping a DI from the Met was probably the high point of his week, if not his year.

The company's offices were in a building in the shadow, literally, of the Gherkin, the phallic glass-and-steel tower on St Mary Axe in the City of London. The reception area was dominated by a sculpture of Janus, the Roman god with two faces, one looking backward and one forward.

After explaining who she was to the receptionist, a pale, severe young woman with tawny hair scraped back into a bun at the back of her head, she was given a visitor ID on a scarlet lanyard then told, not asked, to take a seat. Stella watched as the receptionist placed a call to Dave Locke. Botox, for sure, she thought, as the unsmiling, unlined, unmoving face spoke into the handset of the desk phone.

Five minutes later, a tall, smiling man in a well-cut, charcoal-grey suit, white shirt and solid red tie strode across the open area of floor to greet her, his hand outstretched. His grey hair was cut extremely short and it stood up all over his scalp, which showed, pinkly, through the silvery bristles.

"DI Cole? I'm Dave Locke," he said in an accent from somewhere up North. Yorkshire, she guessed. "It's a pleasure to meet you. Please, come this way. Derek will buzz you through."

Derek turned out to be a black security guard manning the pivoting glass security gates that formed a barrier between the reception area and the corridor leading to the lifts. Stella glanced at him, appraising him with a cop's practised eye. He stood six foot five in his boat-like black shoes and tipped the scales at two-fifty to three hundred pounds. A giant, anyway. He smiled as Stella approached the gate, and she noticed what she took to be Lupus scars on both cheeks, lumps and bumps of keloid scar tissue on his otherwise smooth brown skin. Then he placed an ID, held delicately between thumb and forefinger, onto the glass scanner screen set flush with the stainless-steel post supporting the gate.

She stepped through and thanked him, then followed Locke to a bank of lifts.

"I'm on the fifth floor. Won't take long," he said.

Members of the public all start to act guilty after a few minutes in the company of a detective. Stella had been told that in week one of her basic training. "Use it to your advantage," the sixtyish instructor had advised the class of hopefuls. "They're primed to tell you the truth, and as everyone has something to hide, they'll be as nervous as a bridegroom on his wedding night that you're going to sniff it on them." Locke fitted the stereotype. He was fiddling with his own ID badge, looking at the floor indicator beside the lift door, scratching the back of his neck and generally behaving like he'd stowed his wife's corpse under the patio.

"Do you get many requests from the police?" she asked him as the bell pinged and the doors hissed open.

"Now and then, yes. Depends, though, doesn't it?"

"On what?"

"Where the crime they're investigating was committed. Urban Oversight only has the contract for the London Borough of Putney, so it could just as easily be one of our competitors."

They stood in silence for a few seconds as the lift hummed them up to the CCTV department.

"Ever been asked to testify?" she asked.

He turned to her, as the lift doors opened at the fifth floor. He was actually blushing.

"Me? No!" he said. "Why would they do that?"

"I don't know. Expert witness? Explain to the jury how CCTV cameras work, maybe?"

"No." He shook his head. "I just manage the archive. Nothing as exciting as appearing in court. Purely admin, that's me."

I know the feeling, Stella thought.

Inside the CCTV department, Locke led Stella to a small meeting room, maybe eight feet square. It was furnished with a round, blond wood table and four hard chairs. A computer monitor was placed centrally on the table, with a wireless mouse and keyboard positioned in front. A printer sat on a separate table, tangled cables snaking from its rear to a grubby grey plastic conduit screwed to the skirting board. A whiteboard screwed to the wall bore the words, "stakeholder engagement" in scrappy green capitals. Stella had no idea what it meant.

"This is connected to our central server," Locke said, pointing at the monitor. "I cued up the footage from midnight through to midnight on the day you asked for – a complete twenty-four-hour period. All the cameras from Putney Bridge up to Tibbet's Corner on the A3. I warn you, there's a ton of them."

"Usual controls?"

"Pretty much. You can fast forward up to thirty-two-times normal. Slow down to half-speed and freeze-frame. Use the mouse and the on-screen control panel. You can print whatever you need using that icon there."

Then he left.

"Right then," she said to the four walls. "Let's find this fucker."

As a trainee detective, and then a lowly detective constable, Stella had spent many hours "reviewing the tapes" as it was still called, even though most cameras now had digital feeds. As a DI, she would never normally sit in front of a monitor staring at the world's most boring reality TV show, but this wasn't normal. If Collier knew what she was doing, he'd throw a fit. Investigating anything when she was officially on light duties would be a *problematic situation*, as he'd probably call it. Investigating the unlawful killing of her own family, without a warrant or reasonable grounds? It would need a longer, more pungent phrase. One that began with "What the–" and ended with "–were you thinking of?"

She shrugged. *What's the worst that could happen? If I get fired, I'll carry on anyway.*

For two hours, she sat watching traffic zipping along at four times normal speed. She'd decided on a plan. Watch the entire 24-hour period from the camera at the southern end of Putney Bridge. Find the purple Bentley. Track it from that time stamp until it turned off towards her house. Her and Richard's house. Her and Richard's and Lola's house. Her eyes were stinging in the artificially cooled air, and when she squeezed them shut the corneas burned from the lack of blinking. The room smelled of stale coffee and the sharp solvent of dry-wipe markers.

She jerked forward. A dark-coloured saloon was driving towards the camera. It was getting closer. Then it slowed to let a bus move ahead of it, into the inside lane. The monstrous red double-decker obscured all but a narrow sliver of dark purple flank.

Stella's breathing quickened and she leaned forward, willing the bus to move forward and reveal the number plate of the saloon. This was him.

"No!" she shouted.

The bottom half of the screen had degenerated into a flickering mass of disjointed pixels. Where there had been cars, motorbikes and pedestrians, now there were strobing diagonals of grey, black and white squares. It looked like snakeskin.

As if taunting her, a strip of purple roof cruised past the camera. It might have been a Bentley. It might have been a Ford. Or a Toyota. It was impossible to tell.

"Fuck you!" she shouted.

She switched to the next camera along. Waited, holding her breath. A knock at the door broke her concentration. Stella whipped round in her chair as it opened and a young man – black goatee, dark hair gelled into spikes – poked his head through the gap.

"What?" she barked.

He flinched. "Is everything all right?" he asked. "Only, you know, I heard you shouting."

"No. It's not all right. Your stupid security camera just fucked up my investigation. I mean, what's the point of privatising CCTV to some fucking profit-making outfit like you lot if you can't even give us a decent picture? It's not your gran's old telly, you know. We're not supposed to roll our eyes and bash the top with a fist. This is the twenty-first century, or hadn't you heard?"

The young man blanched. His eyes widened in shock, as if he'd been looking for a quiet drink and walked into a bar fight. "I'm sorry," he stuttered. "I'm just an intern. I can find someone if you want me to."

He looked close to tears. His breathing was coming in short gasps and his voice was quavering like a kid reciting a difficult poem at a school talent contest.

Stella shook her head. "No, it's fine. Don't be sorry. That was out of order. Just forget it, OK?"

He withdrew his head, clearly grateful to have escaped without having his face chewed off.

Stella turned back to the screen. She'd not paused the video so had to rewind back to the original time stamp. The next camera on Putney High Street, which was mounted on a post outside a fried chicken joint, failed to pick up the purple saloon. Yawning, she watched the images flick by, first at thirty-two times, then sixteen, eight, four, double speed, then real-time. No sign of it.

"Shit!" she muttered.

She Alt-tabbed through the open programs until she came to a web browser. Even though she knew what she was going to find, she called up a street plan of Putney. There it was. Between the two cameras was a side street. Not just any side street, either. Putney Bridge Road. It led to the northern end of Oxford Road. Bastard must have turned in there and then waited for Richard to come in from the other end. Must have known his routine. Must have followed him, gathering intelligence. Which meant he – and his poisonous friends – would have known that Richard always brought Lola home from nursery on a Wednesday. So, she was just collateral damage. Yes, that was what they would have called her. Her jaws were grinding together, producing a low grating deep in her inner ears. She detected a high-pitched hum, too, and as she stared at the web of yellow streets on the screen, she felt blood in her mouth. She'd bitten the inside of her cheek. Its coppery taste brought her back to the present.

She returned to the CCTV footage. But she knew she wouldn't find anything. He wouldn't have returned to Putney High Street. He'd have taken a circuitous route back to whichever rock he'd scuttled out from under, one with few or no cameras. Back streets and rat runs. That's what she would do.

After three hours working her way up the hill out of Putney and to the semi-rural landscape at the top, she groaned, arched her back and dug her fingers into the knotted muscles at the base of her neck. The intern she'd frightened had returned now and then with unasked for cups of tea and coffee, but now she was hungry and wanted, more than anything else, a proper drink.

"No!" she growled at the silent screen in front of her, which had begun to hum. "Not letting you off this easily."

She went back to the second camera's feed, cued it up from the beginning and watched. Her eyes were smarting in the dry air but every blink felt like a betrayal and she tried to ignore the pain.

The time stamp in the corner of the screen flickered as she wound laboriously through the feed.

17.55.

Nothing.

18.00.

Nothing

18.05.

Wait!

There it was. The fat-bodied purple Bentley cruising up Putney High Street. She must have blinked or yawned or just dropped into a microsleep the first time.

Heart racing, palms sweating, finger trembling on the mouse, Stella slowed the playback to half-speed. As the car approached the camera, she hit Pause.

Stella looked down at the screen.

The image was blurred, though not badly. The driver was clearly male, but something was casting a deep black shadow over the car's interior, and she couldn't make out his features. The car was a saloon, like Riordan's. The screen didn't pixellate like the previous time, but she could still only get a glimpse of the registration plate. It began with an R. She rubbed her eyes, which were smarting from staring so hard at the screen.

Opening them again, she ran through the rest of the footage, but the car made no further appearances.

*

While she waited for Danny to arrive, Stella sat motionless at her kitchen table. Her eyes were focused on a point roughly a million miles beyond the Welsh dresser with its display of plates, glasses and old champagne bottles. She was thinking. Reviewing what she'd discovered. Testing the evidence.

Five men own cars painted the same shade as the one that killed Richard and Lola.

The plate starts with an R. So it could be Ramage or Riordan

OK, that could be interesting. Rich blokes often go for personalised plates. But it could be a regular number issued by the DVLA. Or it could be a first name. Ralph, or Robert or Ramjesh.

Ramage was the trial judge who sent Deacon away for three years.

So?

So he's connected to the case.

But you couldn't see if it was him driving, could you? Could have been anyone behind the wheel. Godsby, Easton, Singh or Riordan. You're jumping to conclusions.

Yes, but...

The doorbell rang, twice, and the jaunty little jingle made her jump and dispelled her fantasy. For the moment.

Danny looked good in a scuffed, brown leather jacket, denim shirt, and indigo jeans, washed just enough to bring out paler patterns where his house or car keys sat in his front pocket, and over his knees. He'd obviously washed his hair; it was standing up in spikes here and there as if he'd run his fingers through it instead of using a comb. He held one hand behind his back. The other held a supermarket carrier bag that clinked as it knocked against his thigh.

He stepped through the door, leaned towards her, fast, and pecked her on the cheek. He smelled good. Some woody, spicy aftershave. And clean skin.

"Hi," he said. Then he stepped back as she turned and led him, wordlessly, to the kitchen. "That was, all right, wasn't it? I was just being friendly. After last time, I mean. I don't know what you've heard about me but I don't really do one-night stands."

"No. Yes. It's fine. You just took me by surprise, that's all." Her pulse was racing. This wasn't part of the plan.

"I hope these don't tip you over the edge, then," he said with a smile, producing a bunch of yellow roses from behind his back like a stage magician.

She smiled. "I think I'll cope. They're lovely, Danny. I'll be honest, it's been a long time since a man bought me flowers. I'll get a vase."

While Stella busied herself snipping the ends of the stems and arranging the roses in a tall, heavy-bottomed glass vase, Danny pulled a bottle from the carrier bag.

"I got you this. Sicilian lemonade. It's supposed to be artisanal," he paused, "whatever the fuck that means."

Stella laughed. It was almost genuine. The ghost had nearly merged with the machine, and she felt barely conscious of looking out through her own eyes.

"What do you fancy, then? To eat, before you say anything smart."

"Thai would be good. Anywhere round here do delivery?"

Forty-five minutes later, they were sitting at Stella's kitchen table eating green chicken curry, sea bass in a garlicky sauce, and steamed coconut rice. Stella was drinking the lemonade, which tasted like regular lemonade only with a fiery extra kick of ginger. Danny had put four bottles of Czech lager in her fridge and was currently on his second.

"How's it going with Tasha?" Stella asked between mouthfuls of the curry.

He pulled a face, twisting his mouth sideways as if he'd bitten on something hard and hit a filling.

"Honestly? Not good. She's got our bedroom, and I'm sleeping downstairs."

"You think you'll patch it up?"

"Probably not. We were only nineteen when we got married. Used to go out with each other at school. She stuck with me through the army, moving around, living on base, but I think whatever we had, we haven't got any more."

"Sorry."

"Don't be. I'm not exactly a choirboy, am I?" He grinned at her then, that boyish expression that had probably got him out of all kinds of scrapes in his life, from footballs kicked through neighbours' windows to improperly polished boots.

"What about work?"

"Same old, same old. Keeping the Cowboys and Indians happy with their toys, you know how it is."

"You ever hear any of them talking about what they do with all those toys?"

He shrugged.

"A little. Not much. They're all grim and grit on the way out and sort of high on adrenaline when they come back. If someone's discharged their weapon, it's like, 'Yeah! Saw action today!' and then, 'Shit! Now the paperwork begins.' So, they're mostly just in and out." He took a mouthful of the fish. "Why do you ask"?

"Nothing. Just always wondered whether I should have gone down that route."

He shook his head. "It's not as glamorous as they like to make out. Mostly it's sitting around waiting for shit to go down. In the army, we used to call it 'standing by to stand by'. You know, like we say, 'hurry up and wait'. That and a lot of practice on the range and safety briefings."

"So, just for the sake of argument, supposing you wanted to make a movie."

"OK."

"A movie where there was like a rogue set of firearms officers who set up a death squad."

His eyes narrowed. "In London, do you mean, or in America?"

She looked up at the ceiling and made a show of deciding. "Let's say London. Why should the Yanks get all the fun? Could they use the weapons from the armoury, or would they need to get, I don't know, untraceable ones?"

CHAPTER TWENTY-FOUR
Ammunition. Lots.

DANNY PUT HIS fork down. Stared at her long and hard. "No armourer worth his badge would let weapons get signed out for anything like that. Never."

"But how would you know? If they came with the right paperwork, signed by a commander, you'd issue the weapons on the requisition form, wouldn't you?"

"I suppose so. But all our weapons are logged, and we photograph the striations. You remember, you helped. So, it wouldn't exactly be hard to find the weapon and trace it back to the police. Not very smart."

She pursed her lips. "I guess not. Although if the commander was running the death squad, they could just steer the investigation in the wrong direction, couldn't they? Lose the ballistics report or corrupt it somehow?"

He finished his food and placed his knife and fork together, dead centre, running north-south across the smeared plate.

"What's going on, Stel? Why are you asking about death squads?"

"Just making conversation," she said, brightly. "Another beer?"

"Sure. Let me help you clear up."

As they cleared the table, Stella kept probing.

"You have to admit, though, there are times when putting some of those fuckers we're hunting under the ground would be satisfying. A lot cheaper than dragging them through the courts only to see them let off by a bunch of idiots in the jury box."

"You really think that?" Danny was frowning now. He'd stopped helping and was standing with his hands on the table, leaning towards her.

"No, of course not! But I mean, you never took people to court in the army, did you? Not the enemy. Kill or be killed, wasn't it?"

"Listen. I served my country, OK? I did what had to be done. Yes, it was us or them. But there are still rules. It's called the Law of War. Like, you can't deliberately kill civilians. Or prisoners. Or use torture, despite what sometimes happens. And anyway, this isn't war. It's policing. You swear to uphold the law, not take it into your own hands."

Stella held her hands up in mock-surrender.

"No, you're right. Sorry. I've just been going mad down in the basement and started fantasising about shooting Reg the Veg and it sort of spiralled from there."

"Well, now you mention it, if we're talking about offing people at Paddington Green, I've got my own list. Maybe you and me should start our own private death squad."

He laughed.

Stella laughed too.

Later, after the sex, Stella lay awake, listening to Danny's breathing. Long, steady inhalations and exhalations. No snoring. No snuffling. No talking in his sleep. Not even a twitch. She prodded him on the shoulder, just above a tattoo of a bulldog standing on its hind legs and holding a flag of St George, the red cross on the white ground fluttering realistically. He didn't move. She whispered his name close to his exposed left ear. Nothing. But then, after four lagers and a couple of large whiskies, one of which had a crumbled sleeping pill in it, that was only to be expected.

She checked the clock radio on her side of the bed. One thirty a.m.

She lay on her belly and slid her legs out wide to the right, letting their weight pull her torso out from under the duvet until she was kneeling at the side of the bed. She dressed, making no noise, and twirled an elastic band around her hair to fasten it into her usual ponytail. Danny's leather jacket hung on the back of a simple wooden chair next to her vintage, white-painted dressing table. She'd noticed the way the right-hand pocket bulged and decided that was where he'd have his work keys. Two long, silent strides took her to the chair. Keeping her gaze fixed on his sleeping form, she reached down sideways and poked the fingers of her left hand into the pocket. They closed around cold, metal keys. *Right first time! Have a gold detective's sticker.*

Danny's ID card was next. She found his wallet in an inside pocket and slid out the scuffed rectangle of white plastic. *Should have been a dip, Stel!*

With keys and card clamped in her hand, she stole to the door, took one quick final look at Danny and then stepped through. She made her way downstairs, where she pulled on her bike boots and grabbed her helmet, and was out through the door moments later.

With the keys and ID card zipped into the inside pocket of her jacket, she rode fast through the night-time streets. London is never quiet, but the traffic was mostly taxis and commercial stuff. Easy enough to wind through and around, filtering down the outside of the queues at traffic lights. She reached Paddington Green just before two.

Keeping to the shadows to avoid the station's CCTV cameras, she swiped Danny's ID at the staff entrance – so any Professional Standards snoops would only see his details on the access records – and was inside. She headed towards the armoury, running on her toes and looking left and right at every turn in the corridor. Nobody was about. Anyone on duty would either be out on patrol or in the CID Office. Budget cuts meant civilian police staff were kept to an absolute minimum overnight, and she reached the reinforced door to the armoury without seeing another soul.

Now for the only tricky bit of the whole operation.

Rules and regulations stipulated that the armoury, as a 'mission-critical' function of the station, was to be permanently staffed, 24/7, three hundred sixty-five days of the year. After all, it wasn't as if armed robbers said, "We can't do the job on Monday – it's a bank holiday."

She paused at a turn in the corridor just before it opened out into a small rectangle of space that accommodated the lifts from the other floors, and the door to the armoury itself. Peering round the corner, she could see the two assistant armourers wandering back and forth beyond the barred window.

She withdrew her head, backed up a few feet and then slammed her elbow into a fire alarm's glass window.

The effect was textbook. As the electronic klaxons hooted, the door to the armoury opened, and the two men came out. The second one through turned and locked it before they walked at a smart clip, past the lift doors to the stairwell at the far end of the corridor. Stella ran to the door, checked the make of the lock, and selected the only key that matched it.

She knew she had to be fast. Emergency services would probably have a link to the armoury's fire alarm. There could even be a lockdown.

Inside, she jogged past the racks of long and short weapons, the pistols, rifles, shotguns, submachine guns and all the rest, and headed straight for the shelves of ammunition. With the klaxon blaring and her heart racing, she stood in front of the shelf she'd earmarked on her previous visit. She was staring at hundreds of boxes of 9mm ammunition. Shelf-edge labels divided the ammunition into 'FMJ' and 'HP'. Full metal jacket and hollow point. She lifted down two boxes marked HP, rearranged the remaining boxes so that the gap moved to the very back of the shelf, stuffed them into her rucksack and moved away. She'd heard Danny talking about six-weekly audits. "Like a stocktake," he'd said. The audit was supposed to ensure that the equipment listed on the computer matched what was actually present on the shelves. But that was somebody else's problem. As she was leaving, a second shelf-edge label caught her eye.

HATTON ROUNDS

Danny had said they were what the tactical entry teams used to blow the hinges and locks off doors they wanted to get through. Stella reckoned she could bluff or charm her way into Ramage's house, but what if he had a panic room? Or just barricaded himself in somewhere before she could deal with him properly? She grabbed a box, did another camouflage job, and was on her way.

The following morning, she made Danny breakfast: bacon and eggs, toast and coffee, and more or less shoved him out the door at seven fifteen.

Back inside, she climbed the stairs, went into her bedroom and closed the curtains. She fished her rucksack out from under the chair where Danny's jacket had so recently hung and dumped its contents onto the bed. The three boxes of ammunition were heavy enough to make the mattress bounce a little before they settled into the soft embrace of the duvet.

Next came the Glock, which she'd placed in a shoe box at the bottom of her wardrobe. It smelled of gun oil and the metallic, industrial stink of the armoury: burnt propellant, steel, brass and sweat. She dropped the magazine from the butt into her left palm and placed it, and the pistol, side by side on the bed.

She slit the tape securing the lid on one of the boxes of 9mm ammunition. The hollow point rounds inside were almost comical in their physical insignificance. She'd taken multivitamins that were almost as large. She rolled it on her palm: a slim brass cylinder no longer than the top joint of her little finger, tipped with a snub-nosed cone of copper-covered lead. Except that the bullet wasn't completely covered, was it?

The copper sheath ended in a sunken pit of pale, silvery-grey lead, like the pupil of an eye. Danny, and firearms instructors before him, had explained all about that innocent-looking lead eye. How, on impact, the copper sheath would split along four precisely cut grooves and splay outwards like the petals of a flower. And how the lead, freed from its jacket, would flatten and deform as its kinetic energy searched for a way out. Hollow points were supposed to be beneficial because they didn't pass through the target's body, so they couldn't injure a member of the public. And to that extent, they worked. They weren't so beneficial to the target, however, bouncing around and travelling a random path through muscle, bone, blood vessels and organ tissue, creating a monstrous wound cavity as they slewed to a stop. *Shouldn't carry a shooter, then, should you?* Stella thought.

She picked up the round and pointed it at her own eye, rolling it between her thumb and forefinger. She let her mouth fall open a little and stroked the bullet along her lower lip. Then across her top lip. She pressed them together then. "You'll do," she whispered.

From the kitchen, she fetched a tea towel and a pair of thin latex gloves she used when she was chopping chillis. Back in her bedroom, she put the gloves on and used the towel to clean the rounds she'd handled.

Using her thumb, she pushed a round home into the magazine against the resistance of the spring. She worked another sixteen rounds into the rectangular plastic box, then slotted it home into the butt and pushed it all the way in until it latched with a double click.

The plastic grip felt cool in her hand as she picked up the pistol.

Curling her right index finger around the outside of the trigger guard, as she'd been taught, she extended her arm and sighted along the barrel, aiming at a print of a tiger, shown in profile, that hung above her bed.

Keeping both eyes open, as she'd been taught, she aligned the front and rear sights on the tiger's left eye.

Then she uncurled her index finger from the guard, brought it inside, and, not as she'd been taught, rested it on the trigger. The instructor's words came back to her, synchronised with her breathing. "If you're touching the trigger, it's because you're going to shoot," he'd said.

No, she wasn't going to shoot. Not yet, anyway.

She dropped the magazine out again and thumbed every single one of the seventeen rounds back out and onto the duvet. She remembered the end of the argument between Danny and his assistant, about storing magazines. Empty was best long-term, Danny had said, because storing it full meant the spring could settle slightly and fail to push a new round cleanly into the chamber, causing a misfire. Stella wasn't planning on storing the Glock long-term. She had plans to use it as soon as she was able. But she didn't want anything to impede her operation, so out they came.

Next, she turned to the white cardboard box of Hatton rounds. It was labelled with several lines of crude black capitals. The only set that interested Stella read:

CLUCAS: HATTON ROUNDS (DOOR BREACHING) FIVE (5)

She opened the flap with her thumbnail and tipped the shells out onto the bed. They were much bigger than the hollow points, but just as unremarkable.

Translucent plastic cylinders, flat at the top and set into a brass base. She could see the powder and lead projectile through the translucent plastic casing.

"What are they for, Mummy?"

Stella dropped the shotgun shells and spun round on the bed, heart jumping in her chest.

The little girl sitting upright on the bed behind Stella couldn't have been more than eighteen months old. Brown hair, the same hue as Stella's. Brown eyes. But something behind those eyes was older than it ought to have been.

Stella's breath was coming in shallow gasps.

Stars were flicking and worming around the periphery of her vision.

A memory. But Lola was just a baby.

"Lola, is that you?"

The toddler smiled.

"Of course I'm me, silly! What are the breaching rounds for?"

Stella groaned instead of speaking. Ripping off the gloves, she screwed her eyes tight against the vision. Pounded her forehead with her fists. Then opened her eyes again. The figure of the little girl had gone. Stella scrambled across the bed and ran her flat palm across the duvet. No dent. No warmth. She bent her head to the place where Lola-not-Lola had been sitting. No smell.

Nothing.

Now she wept. Great, wrenching sobs. Curling into a foetal position, she let the grief overwhelm her, once again, until, drained, she slept.

*

Figuring after his dance of death with the Salmonella virus Reg would be sympathetic to a plea of illness, Stella called him the next morning.

"Reg, it's Stella. I must have eaten some dodgy curry last night. I'm not coming in. Hope you can manage without me."

"Sorry to hear that, Stel. The old Montezuma's Revenge, eh? The old Aztec Two-step. Well, I've been there, my love, as you know. Take as much time as you need, and we don't need to involve those munchkins in occie health or HR either, do we? What happens in the exhibits room stays in the exhibits room, eh?"

"Right. And Reg?"

"What?

"Thanks."

Stella showered, dressed and ate breakfast of toast and coffee, then made more coffee and took it through to her own, private, incident room. She called up the list of five Bentley owners that Robin Brooke had given her. Barney Riordan's details were highlighted in yellow. She was due to meet him for lunch today at the Fulham ground. Shit! She'd arranged to leave with Daisy the exhibits room assistant at eleven from Paddington Green.

She picked up her phone.

Five minutes later, she'd agreed to a much better arrangement. Daisy was going to pick her up from Ulysses Road in her own car and drive them both to Craven Cottage on Stevenage Road.

"Now for the rest of you," she said to the list on her screen.

She dragged Riordan's details to the bottom of the list and then called the name at the top. The phone was answered at once.

"Hello?"

"Mark Easton?" Stella asked.

"Yes, this is he." The voice was cultured, deep, and bearing not even a hint of suspicion at this unidentified caller's intrusion into his morning.

"This is Detective Inspector St–" *No! Alias. Now. You already gave Riordan your name, which was a mistake.* "Stephanie Black, with the Metropolitan Police, Mr Easton. I need to ask you a few questions."

"I have a meeting in five minutes, Detective Inspector, so it will have to be quick, I'm afraid."

"I'll do my best, sir. At this stage a couple of questions will do. Can I ask, are you the registered owner of a Bentley painted in a special-order colour called *Viola del diavolo*?"

"Yes," a breathy note of suspicion had crept into his voice. "What of it?"

"Can you tell me where you were between the hours of three p.m. and seven p.m. on March sixth, 2009?"

"Not precisely. Not without my diary, which my PA manages for me. But I believe, if memory serves, I was in California for the whole of that month. San Francisco. Meeting investors. I'm a banker. I was working on an IPO for a tech start-up."

"IPO, sir?"

"Initial public offering. A privately held company sells shares to institutional investors, such as insurance companies, pension funds, banks, hedge funds and so on. Then they, in their turn—"

Stella cut him off.

"Did anyone else have access to the Bentley, sir? While you were in San Francisco?"

"Well, my wife did, technically. I mean, she could have driven it. The keys are at home, and she's on the insurance. But it's unlikely."

"Why is that?"

"Rebecca has her own car. An Alfa Romeo Spider. Little convertible thing. Bright red. She much prefers it to mine. Look, I'd be happy to answer further questions, inspector, but not now. I have to go to my meeting. I'll text you my PA's number. Talk to her."

The numbers for Singh and Godsby went to voicemail.

That left Sir Leonard Ramage.

CHAPTER TWENTY-FIVE
Is it Ever OK to Date a Suspect?

THE PHONE RANG seven times before being answered. Stella was out of patience.

"Come on, you fucker, answer your fucking–"

"Ramage."

Clipped. Brisk. Commanding. Used to being on control. Sixty-plus. Upper class. All this Stella picked up from two syllables delivered in less than a second. It flustered her and she almost gave him her real name as her mind blanked for a second.

"Uh, Mr Ramage, this is Detective Inspector Stephanie Black. I'm with the Metropolitan Police. I need to ask you a few questions."

"Oh, do you, Detective Inspector? Well, for a start, I'm not *Mister* Ramage."

"Sorry? I–"

"I *said*," he paused, "Ramage. As you would have heard, had you been listening closely. Those who wish to speak to me, or indeed question me, address me either as Judge Ramage, My Lord, or Sir Leonard."

Stella breathed in and out once, through her nose. Even though she hated herself for it, she couldn't stop her heart bumping uncomfortably in her chest. Going up against a judge, any judge, was nerve-wracking for a copper. But this one was a High Court judge. *Fuck! What if I'm wrong about him?*

"My apologies. Sir Leonard. May I ask you two questions?"

"Please do. It is your duty to ask questions, and mine to answer them. If I can."

"Do you own a Bentley painted in a special-order colour called *Viola del diavolo*?"

"Why do you ask?"

"Just routine, Sir Leonard."

"Don't try that with me Detective Inspector," he snapped. "I'm a High Court judge, not a spotty teenager with a pocketful of pills."

Stella had a split-second to make a decision. Put a potential suspect on notice she'd reopened the case or forget all about getting any more information out of the judge. She made her decision.

"We are investigating a hit and run incident from a year or so ago. We believe the car involved was painted in this particular shade of purple."

Ramage paused for two, maybe three seconds. A pause people take when they're deciding what to say. Stella had heard pauses like it before. Seen eyes rolling up as their owners sought inspiration in the painted ceilings of interview rooms or their own sitting rooms. Waited as they got their lies straight, or straight enough to say them out loud without blinking.

"Yes. I do own such a car. A rather fine Bentley Mulsanne, as it happens."

"And, if I may also ask you, Sir Leonard, where were you between the hours of three p.m. and seven p.m. on the sixth of March, 2009?"

Ramage laughed. A short, mirthless sound. Two percussive exclamations.

"Ha! Ha! Detective Inspector Black, was that your name? Are you asking me to provide an alibi?"

"Not at all. I am simply asking you if you can confirm your whereabouts between those times on that date."

"Of course I can't. It was over a year ago."

"Of course," Stella softened her own voice as the Judge hardened his. "It's quite understandable. And it was a long time ago. Look, I'm sure you must be very busy, cases and so on. I'll come to see you in your chambers."

"No," he said, silkily. "Don't come to my chambers. Come to my house. Do you have a pen?"

"Go ahead."

"It's 61, Egerton Crescent. Chelsea."

"Thank you, Sir Leonard. Shall we say nine o'clock this evening?"

"Bit late, isn't it?"

"The Met never sleeps. You should know that, Sir Leonard." The line went dead. Ramage had hung up. "Pompous old fart," she said.

She made a couple of notes on the document and was thinking about more coffee when her phone rang.

"DI Cole? It's Barney Riordan. The footballer?"

As opposed to Barney Riordan the bricklayer? Mind you, that's very becoming modesty for someone earning a few million quid a year for kicking a football about.

"Hello Mr Riordan. All set for our meeting?"

"That's what I'm phoning about. And please call me Barney. Mr Riordan's what they call my dad. Anyway, I can't make it. The manager is having us all on an extended medical right through lunch. Some new psycho-something or other he's bringing in. Supposed to make us more focused. So, like I said, I can't make lunch. Not today, anyway. Do you want to make it tomorrow?"

"I really would prefer to keep things moving as quickly as I can, Barney. Tomorrow isn't really an option, I'm afraid."

"Oh. OK." His voice suddenly lightened. He sounded excited, like a small boy. "I've got an idea! Oh, they're going to love this. Look, you know I said I had a charity dinner to go to tonight?"

"Yes."

"Come with me. You can be my 'plus one'."

"That wouldn't really be appropriate." *But it would be a massive coup.* "And you must have somebody who you'd rather take than a police officer. We've never even met."

"It's not like what they write in *Hello* and all them celebrity mags. I'm single. Those girls are basically groupies. I'm not seeing anyone. Plus, you're a detective, aren't you?"

"Yes. I am."

"That was my second choice at school. If I couldn't have been a footballer I wanted to be a copper, uh, a police officer, I mean. When I wasn't training, I used to love all them shows. *The Bill, Hill Street Blues, Murder One.* Hey, you could be like that female one off *Prime Suspect*. Helen Mirren, yeah?"

Stella smiled despite herself. He sounded so innocent.

"Fine. And thank you. I'd love to come." *Unless it turns out you killed my family, in which case I will gut you like a fish.* "Dress code?"

"Pardon?" He sounded worried all of a sudden.

"What's the dress code?"

"Oh, sorry. Thought you said arrest code. Had me worried there for a minute. Black tie. I guess that means a dress for you. Cocktail dress, probably."

"Thank you. Where and when?"

"It's the Café Royal. On Regent Street. Starts at seven."

"I'll meet you there."

"No need. Much better if we arrive together. I've got to keep up my image, haven't I? I'll pick you up at six fifteen."

Stella gave him her address then ended the call. She pursed her lips and frowned. *Didn't see that coming.* Then she slapped her forehead.

"Fuck! Daisy'll kill me."

Biting her lower lip, she twisted her wedding ring – a plain gold band – round and round. She called Daisy.

"Yes, boss? Everything OK? I've got my interview suit on and taken out my nose ring like you said."

Stella looked down at her wedding ring and the eternity ring on the next finger over: bands of rose and white gold with a single diamond set into the rose gold. For Lola. She straightened her back.

"I'm afraid we're not going. He's got a medical."

There was a second's pause and Stella could hear the young woman take a breath before answering. Could picture her, brow wrinkling in dismay. Then shaking her head.

"Oh, well. I guess I'll just have to ask him out then."

It was a pretty good attempt at masking her disappointment and Stella wanted to let her keep her dignity, even if keeping her lunch date with Barney Riordan had just been taken away from her. She decided on what to say before wondering if it were possible.

"Listen, don't be cross, but he's taking me to a ball tonight. Said it was the only time he could speak to me today. It starts at seven. Be outside the Café Royal, and I'll introduce you."

"Really? You'd do that for me?"

"Given you'll agree to be my tea and coffee slave for the rest of your career, it seems like a fair exchange."

That afternoon, Stella was waiting outside a stout wooden door at the Old Bailey. The door had four rectangular panels and a brass knob. Below the knob was an old-fashioned keyhole, surrounded by a battered brass escutcheon in the shape of a shield. It was dented and scratched but polished to a satiny sheen. In the centre of the upper portion of the door was a brass frame about ten centimetres by four, composed of two thin rails and a back-plate. Into it, someone, a clerk perhaps, had inserted a piece of beige card with the words 'Mr Justice Ramage' in elegant calligraphy.

Earlier, she'd rung round a few contacts in the barristers' chambers clustered around the law courts and discovered that The Honourable Mister Justice Sir Leonard Ramage – *See?* she'd thought. *You* are *a Mister!* – was hearing a case at the Old Bailey that day.

Heart thumping, feeling like a schoolgirl summoned to see the headmaster, she knocked twice, fast and loud, then twisted the doorknob and walked in. A middle-aged woman standing with a sheaf of papers in the centre of the room whirled around to face her. She was birdlike, thin, with stone-grey, collar-length hair held back by a black velvet Alice band. Her eyes were magnified by thick-lensed, gold-framed glasses. Her mouth dropped open, revealing small, off-white teeth.

"Excuse me! These are Sir Leonard's private chambers," she said, almost breathless at the sheer audacity of Stella's arriving unannounced.

"That's why I'm here. Is he in?"

The woman was gaping now, her mouth working like a landed fish, her eyes widened so that the grey irises appeared to float in the white.

"Is he in? Of course he's in! But you can't come in here. You'll have to leave, I'm afraid. Now."

The woman bustled towards Stella, who stopped her with an outstretched hand that held up her warrant card. The worn, black leather folder held the silver-and-blue force badge of the Met on the right, and Stella's official police ID on the left. She made sure her fingertips covered her name. She flipped it closed and pocketed it before the woman could get a closer look.

"Detective Inspector Stephanie Black. Is he through there?" She jerked her chin in the direction of a second door that led, presumably, to the judge's private office, or robing room.

Flustered, the woman was more compliant. "Well, yes. He is. But you really ought to have rung to make an appointment. You can't just go—"

But Stella did just go.

She pushed through the door.

Ramage sat behind a huge mahogany desk, inlaid with a sheet of dark red leather with a gold-tooled edge. He looked up at Stella. His eyes were so dark brown as to be almost black. He frowned, and the frown deepened as she flashed her ID again. Behind her, the PA hovered, trying to get round this intruder so she could protect her employer.

"I'm sorry, Judge," she said, her voice pleading. "She said she was a police officer, and, well, she was very persistent."

He smiled, though not at Stella.

"No matter, Shirley. I can deal with our guest. That will be all. He focused on Stella. "Detective Inspector Black, I presume."

"In one, Sir Leonard. I apologise for barging into your chambers, but I'm afraid matters have taken a turn that makes my coming to your house this evening impossible."

Now the judge did smile. But it was a grim, humourless expression, in which his canine teeth seemed to do most of the work.

"You have a great deal of confidence, Detective Inspector, to invade my place of work. You'd better have an extremely good reason."

"I think I do, Sir Leonard."

"Well then, you'd better take a seat and ask your questions. Do I need a lawyer? This place is crawling with them."

She shook her head. "Just routine enquiries, Sir Leonard, as I said on the phone. No need for a lawyer. You're not under caution. I'm not even going to take notes."

He smiled again. His eyes stayed clear and did not crinkle at the corners. Only his mouth moved, extending a fraction.

"Just helping the police with their enquiries," he purred.

"Exactly. Did you have a chance to ask your PA – Shirley, was it? – about your movements on the date I gave you?"

"Indeed I did." He moved to one side the paper he had been reading and withdrew a sheet of crisp, white, A4 printer paper from a folder. From her vantage point, Stella could see a single line of type. It looked like Times Roman. He took a pair of half-moon spectacles from the top pocket of his jacket and slid them onto his nose, peering down at the paper. "It says here I was having dinner. At my club."

"Which club would that be Sir Leonard?" *Jesus, if I have to say Sir Leonard one more time, I swear I'll start tugging my forelock. Must remember not to curtsey on the way out.*

"Black's. Ironically."

"Did you dine alone? Apart from the other members, I mean? Would there be someone who can corroborate your story?"

He looked up, staring at Stella over the lenses of his reading glasses, which made her feel as though she had been summoned to see a particularly fierce headmaster.

"Corroborate my story? My, my, Detective Inspector, are you sure I'm simply helping you with your enquiries?"

"I just have to follow routine, Sir Leonard. As I think you probably know. With your legal training."

"Just so. Well, for your *routine*, I was with someone. Someone you may have heard of. Detective Chief Superintendent Adam Collier. He's at Paddington Green. To which station did you say you were attached?"

He was watching her the way a lion watches an antelope as it stalks closer. Eyes zeroed in on her, muscles tensed. Ready to pounce.

"I didn't. But it's West End Central."

"Hmm. Well, I'm sure you can find a way to contact Adam. He'll *corroborate* my *story* for you. Now, if there's nothing else, I am trying a case, had you not determined that for yourself."

She stood. "No. There's nothing else. And thank you, Sir Leonard. You really have been most helpful." She turned to leave. Then stopped. Turned back as he was lowering his eyes to his paperwork again. "May I take that?"

"Take what?"

"That sheet of paper. With the details of the dinner on it?"

He sighed. "If you must, yes, take it. Then please leave."

*

Stella stepped out of the shower. It was half past five. Plenty of time for a girl to get to ready for a date with a professional footballer. *Oh, fuck, Stel! What the hell have we got ourselves into? There'll be press there, everything. Doesn't matter. He's a suspect.* She dried herself, scrubbing at her hair and pulling it through the bunched-up towel. Now: undies, then dress, then hair and makeup.

She owned precisely one cocktail dress. She took it off its silk-covered, padded hanger and laid it on the bed. It was almost black, but actually a deep, dark, green, like a mallard's neck. Richard used to call it her "Emily dress" after they saw an actress of the same name wearing one just like it to some awards event or other. It had been wheeled out for official dinners, hen nights and the very occasional legal party Richard had taken her to. She picked it up and held the stiff bodice up to her face.

Then she jerked it away again, tears pricking her eyes. It smelled of him. His aftershave. She remembered. They'd danced the last dance together at a ball organised by a barrister friend of his. What was her name? Caroline something? It was in aid of a children's charity her chambers sponsored. Stella had taken the piss out of him because he'd unaccountably drenched himself in the stuff. "Richard fancies Caroline, Richard fancies Caroline!" she'd chanted in the taxi, much to her husband's embarrassment and the driver's amusement. "Going to make a real impression on your ladylove tonight, aren't you? She'll swoon in your arms. Mind you, it'll probably be asphyxiation."

Shaking her head to rid herself of the memory, she selected her best underwear: matching black lace bra and knickers. Sheer black tights, too. Not stockings. Richard had loved them, used to plead with her to wear them. And she'd always given him the same answer. "You first!" She turned to the mirror to give herself an honest appraisal. *Still a little on the skinny side, Stel, but at least Bob and Charlie have come back.* She gave her boobs an experimental squeeze. Yes, enough cleavage to keep Mister Riordan interested.

With the dress safely wriggled up over her hips, she reached round to do the zip up. She managed all the way to the beginning of her shoulder blades before realising it had always been Richard's job to tug it home over the last four or five inches.

"Really?" she said, her voice loud in the empty bedroom. "I've got a loaded, untraceable, police-issue Glock in a shoe-box, but I can't get my bloody dress zipped?"

She sat on the bed. *Come on, Stel, it's just another challenge. Think.* She nodded, once, stood, and reversed the zip till she could step out of the dress. She hurried out of the bedroom for the stairs, almost skidding on the top step, unaccustomed to the slithery nylon of the tights. It took her five minutes of searching cupboards and the drawer of random odds and sods in the kitchen before she found what she was looking for: a ball of butcher's string. Thin, smooth, white and strong. She cut off a few feet. Upstairs, she looped it through the tab of the zip and then, as she pulled the dress up over her hips – *still a bit bony, Stel* – flipped the loose ends over her left shoulder. She wound them round her right fist, took up the slack, extended her arm towards the ceiling, and felt the two sides of the dress close around her. "Ta dah!" she whispered. "Now who's the practical one, darling?"

Hair and makeup in Stella's new world meant little more than a ponytail and a dab of moisturiser. She felt something more was needed for a black-tie charity ball at the Café Royal. It was odd, primping and preening for a man she might have to torture and kill, but then the world was a funny place. She did her hair in a tight plait at the nape of her neck, then pinned it up in a makeshift bun.

As she applied blusher, eyeliner, eyeshadow, mascara and lipstick, she watched herself in the mirror. The woman staring out at her – pouting, pressing her frosted pink lips together, opening her smudgy, smoky eyes wide – seemed to move of her own volition. Stella began to feel she was merely a spectator. As if the woman she was watching were the real human being getting ready to go out and Stella were merely a reflection. She suddenly felt cold, empty. The butterflies that had been swarming beneath the tight satin of her dress quietened, then disappeared altogether. The traffic noise from the road outside her open window faded. Her breath came in shallow gasps, then it, too, stopped. The face of the woman in the mirror smiled at her. Then it, she – *other-Stella* – spoke.

"If it's him, Stella, what are we going to do? I mean, we can't just abduct him from the hotel. There'll be about a million paparazzi outside."

Stella answered, mechanically. Fascinated by the other woman's poise.

"A back entrance? Through the kitchens?"

"Don't be stupid! Barney Riordan's a footballer. An athlete. He's twice your size. Come on, think."

"I'll say I feel sick. Ask him to take me home. He hasn't got a girlfriend, he told me. He'll come."

"Better. And you'll do it? If it's him."

A nod.

The woman smiled. Then she blew a kiss.

CHAPTER TWENTY-SIX
Charity

STELLA JUMPED, STARTLED by the doorbell. She misted her wrists and cleavage with perfume. She pushed her feet home into the high-heeled black suede shoes she'd bought to go with the dress and tottered downstairs to the front door, holding onto the bannister for dear life.

"Coming!" she yelled, then grabbed a small, black, sequinned clutch bag she'd pre-filled with credit card, tissues, emergency lippy, little helper, perfume, and door keys, and pulled the door open. Her bag promptly burst open, spilling its contents onto the floor.

"Fuck!" she said. Then, "Shit! Sorry. I mean, you look nice."

Barney Riordan stood on the threshold, his smile deciding whether it should stay in place or leave by a back door.

"Thanks," he said, grinning, "I think. Let me help you with your stuff."

He bent and handed a few things to Stella. She grabbed for the little helper before he could touch it.

Riordan had dark-brown eyes, blond hair cut short and brushed into a parting with some kind of gel, and a good smile. He'd gone for a kind of nineteen-forties look, like a hero in a film about wartime pilots. He was about five-eleven with wide shoulders and a flat stomach. Good posture, but then, you'd expect that from a professional athlete.

The dinner suit was clearly bespoke. Nothing fancy. No upturned lapels or contrasting buttons. But it fitted perfectly. His wide shoulders filled the midnight-blue, shawl-collared jacket, but didn't strain it like a bouncer's cheap monkey suit. He'd set it off with a crisp white shirt with a pleated front and black studs instead of buttons. The bowtie looked hand-tied. As he leaned forward to kiss her chastely on both cheeks, it caught the light from the lamp above his head and flashed indigo.

"You look nice too. Lovely," he said.

Outside, double-parked in the narrow street with its engine idling, was a deep, dark-purple saloon, its paintwork shimmering in the evening sunlight.

"Is that your Bentley?" Stella asked. "Of course it is! Duh!"

Riordan smiled. "Flying Spur. Not too flash, is it?"

She shrugged. "My usual ride's only got two wheels." She gestured at the black Triumph. "Anything with four is flash."

She sauntered around the car as if to admire it, and glanced down at the registration plate.

R104DAN

She experienced a sudden jolt of fear, then anger. *What if this is the car? The car that killed Richard? The car that killed him?* The churning in her stomach intensified. *What if it was the car that killed Lola? That burnt her to death, strapped into her little car seat?*

Her hand shook as she fastened the seat belt. The muffled click did nothing to reassure her as to her safety. If it turned out to be Riordan, she'd handcuff him to the steering wheel and sit a jerry can of petrol on his lap, then—

"Next stop, the Café Royal," Riordan said, breaking Stella's fantasy into little charred pieces.

He was a careful driver. As they motored silently south along Hampstead Road towards the Euston Road, Stella leant back in the seat, more of an armchair, really, and tried to relax. The interior of the car smelled of leather and Riordan's aftershave, a light, spicy fragrance that made her smile despite herself.

As they approached the huge east-west artery they needed to cross before heading into the centre of London, a small, grey car lurched out of a side street in front of them, just yards away.

Stella screamed.

Her hands flew out to clutch the dashboard.

Riordan swore and jammed on the brakes.

The little car weaved across the road in front of them and executed another signalless turn across the oncoming traffic. The driver appeared to be an elderly man, judging from the tweed cap, though it was impossible to be sure as the top of his head was barely level with the steering wheel.

The Bentley stopped, apparently without effort, though both Riordan and his trembling passenger were thrown forward hard enough for their seat belts to engage. Some sort of clever electronics must have been involved, because Stella felt herself pulled gently, but firmly, back into the embrace of her seat, rather than left to bounce around like a rag doll.

Riordan turned to Stella, once his own seat belt had released him.

"Are you all right? Sorry about that. Silly old sod could have killed us both."

Stella shook her head. "Fine. I'm fine. Let's just go, please."

Leaving the keys to the Bentley with a valet presumably employed especially for the occasion, Riordan escorted Stella across the pavement and towards the entrance of the Café Royal. A length of very new-looking red carpet had been laid from the kerb to the revolving doors, and someone had even strung twisted red-velvet ropes from brass poles along each edge. Thirty or forty people were clustered against the ropes, phones held aloft, some on selfie sticks, their owners facing away from the carpet the better to capture themselves in the same image as one of their idols. A group of paparazzi had bagged most of the front row and were firing their expensive-looking cameras every time a car arrived at the kerb to disgorge its occupants. Two dinner-suited security guys flanked the door, their eyes flicking left and right, mouths set in a professionally grim line. And there, front and centre to the left of the door, was Daisy.

"Barney, before we go in, can you do me a massive favour?" Stella asked.

"Sure, what do you want me to do?"

"See that girl there with the big round glasses, the pretty one with the fringe? Can you go and say hi? She was supposed to come with me today to interview you at your ground."

God love him, he was a generous soul, as well as a modest one. He smiled and ambled over towards Daisy, who looked as if she might faint before he reached her. Stella looked on, dazzled by the flashes from the cameras and bemused that anyone should want to photograph her in the first place. Barney was speaking to Daisy. Then he leaned in and kissed her on both cheeks before returning to Stella's side and escorting her inside.

"Thank you," she said over her shoulder, as she timed her entry into the revolving door.

The hem of her dress caught in the door, almost causing a 'wardrobe malfunction', as the paparazzi would no doubt call it, but Riordan shot a hand out and grabbed the edge to stop it turning before the final few degrees of rotation stripped the dress from her back.

Inside the foyer, bunches of sky-blue-and-white balloons bobbed at the ends of seven-foot silver ribbons tied to chunks of silver-grey granite on the floor. Knots of guests stood between two huge marble fireplaces, above each of which stood five huge glass vases filled with flowers that looked as though they had been picked in some exotic jungle earlier that day. The tall, lemon-yellow spires of tiny branching flowers glowed in the soft light emanating from hundreds of sky-blue or white candles.

A slim, beautiful waitress – deep brown skin, almond-shaped eyes and about nine feet tall, Stella judged – weaved through the thronging worthies and approached them. She carried a tray of champagne flutes.

"A drink, sir? Madam?" she asked in a south London accent that belied her supermodel looks.

"Have you got any sparkling water, please?" Riordan and Stella asked in unison.

The waitress nodded and smiled. "I'll be right back."

"I thought you footballers were all about the champagne and the high life," Stella said, taking a moment to reassess Riordan.

He smiled. "Some of us are. I don't drink."

"No?"

"No." Another smile.

She smiled back, a little more relaxed now. "Me neither."

The beautiful waitress returned with two flutes of sparkling water, each garnished with a slice of strawberry.

Stella sipped her water and looked around. The place was wall-to-wall penguin suits and the kind of dresses her mother would have called "too much of everything". The younger women had all apparently decided to enter a competition that was probably called "baps out for the paps". How else to explain the plunging necklines that threatened to depart east and west simultaneously? The hem lengths were just as bad. *Bad? Stella, when did you get so old and disapproving? When a girl leans forward to kiss someone and flashes her knickers at everyone behind her, that's when.* Some of the older women looked a little more elegant, although she could still see acres of crêpey flesh. Stella suppressed a shudder.

They moved through the crowd into the ballroom, a vast, glittering space in which every surface was painted, coated or plated in gold. The room had been decorated for the occasion with thousands more of the pale-blue-and-white ribbons, glued into the standard looped format that signified an anti-this or pro-that charity appeal.

Stella was asking Riordan more about his non-drinking – it was a fitness thing, apparently, though she wasn't entirely sure she believed him – when a hand tapped her on the right shoulder. A deep, male voice spoke. A voice with an Edinburgh accent.

"It's DI Cole, isn't it?"

She turned. Standing in front of her was a short man, wide through the shoulders and sporting a paunch. His immaculate dinner suit gave him a shape that was more solid than flabby. White hair cropped short and appraising eyes, crinkled with age, or experience or just a lot of laughing. His name was Gordon Wade. He was the Assistant Chief Constable for Lothian and Borders Police.

"Yes, sir. What are you doing here?"

He laughed. "We are allowed south of the border, you know. I didn't even get frisked in Carlisle."

Stella could feel herself getting hot. She strove to regain some kind of poise. "Sir, may I introduce Barney Riordan? Barney's—"

"Hello, Barney, how are you?"

The two men shook hands.

"Fine thanks, Gordon. How's Susan?"

"Och, mustn't grumble, that's what she always says to me. But it's her bloody highland spirit speaking. The pain comes and goes. We cope."

Stella blinked. "I'm sorry, sir, but do you two know each other, then?"

"We do. Barney and I are both patrons of the little outfit holding this shindig. Small world, eh? And as we're both off-duty, why don't you call me Gordon, then I can call you Stella, and it'll all feel a lot friendlier, eh?"

"Yes, of course. Certainly." A moment's pause. "Gordon."

He smiled again. "There, that wasn't so difficult, now was it? But now it's my turn to ask you a question." He took a sip of his champagne. "Mmm, bloody good stuff, though I'd rather a couple of fingers of Glenlivet and a drop of stream water. So, without wishing to sound rude, what's a nice girl like you doing at a bunfight like this? Especially being squired by young Mr Riordan here?"

Stella looked round at Riordan, but he seemed happy to listen.

"I'm looking into a cold case, sir— I mean, Gordon, and I needed to interview Barney and he was busy and we came here." Realising, as she finished, how lame this sounded, she continued, though she could feel the sides of the hole she was digging for herself getting steeper and steeper. "It's not a date, if that's what you're thinking."

"I assure you I wasn't. Or not until now, at any rate." He winked at her. "Your secret's safe with me Stella, though you might need to use the back door if you're to escape the attentions of the vultures out the front later on."

"Don't tease her, Gordon," Riordan said. "I think she's about as far out of her comfort zone as it's possible to get."

Wade touched Stella briefly on the shoulder. "Don't mind me, Stella. I'm an awful tease. But seriously, if you need any help on this cold case of yours.

Off the record, I mean. You know, someone to talk to. Well, after your work for me on that corruption case, I owe you one. Two or three, as a matter of fact."

She looked down for a second. An ally. Far away from London.

"Yes, Gordon. I would like that."

"Here, then," he said, and gave her a business card and winked again. "Take this. Break glass in case of emergency, eh? Any time. Now, if you'll excuse me, I need to go and rescue my wife, who seems to have fallen into the clutches of our major donors director."

Stella turned to Riordan, who was busy signing autographs.

"Barney, I need to talk to you about your car. It can't wait any longer, I'm afraid."

He smiled, shook hands with the final well-wisher and followed her away from the throng of donors, celebrities, charity staff and black-and-white-clad waitresses.

"I'm all yours," he said, when they'd reached the sanctuary of a Steinway grand piano that occupied an entire corner of the ballroom.

She put her empty flute down on the piano's mirror-polished lid.

"First of all, can you tell me, please, where you were on the sixth of May last year?"

"Yes," he answered straight away, surprising Stella.

"Go on, then."

"I was in Qatar. Playing a demonstration match for the sheikh, or the prince, or whoever's in charge there. He's a friend of our owner. It was his birthday. The whole team flew out for it. First class all the way, air conditioned stadium. Fuck knows how much it all cost. We all got half a million and a gold Rolex, just for a kickabout."

"And you're sure about the date?"

"Absolutely! Want to know why?"

"Why?"

"Because it's my birthday too. The sheikh found out, and he gave me a Ferrari as well. Bit over the top, but money doesn't mean the same to them as it does to us, does it?"

Resisting the impulse to ask him which 'us' he was talking about, Stella pressed on.

"Anyone have the keys to your Bentley while you were away?"

He shook his head. "Not a chance. Locked up tighter than a duck's arse with my other cars. Why are you asking all this, anyway? You never told me."

"Hit and run. We believe the man—"

"Or woman."

"Pardon?"

"You said, 'the man', but it could have been a woman, couldn't it?"

Stella remembered a case she'd worked on as a newly promoted detective sergeant. A woman had killed another woman in a hit and run. The victim had been the wife of a police officer; the perpetrator was married to an organised crime boss. The search for the driver had continued for six years. When they finally found her, she'd told them that by six p.m. on the day it happened, she was under the knife in the clinic of a Dutch plastic surgeon, having her face changed.

"Yes," she said. "It could have been a woman. We believe the person who committed this crime was driving a purple Bentley. The same shade as yours."

Riordan's eyes widened for a moment. Then he rubbed his knuckles over his chin, frowning.

"You're saying someone killed some people, and he was driving a car in *Viola del diavolo*?"

"Or she. And, yes, I am. A man and a baby girl." *My baby girl. Little Lola.*

Riordan frowned and wrinkled his nose, as if he'd tasted something bitter. "That's bang out of order, that is. That's not right. Look, it wasn't me, and it wasn't my car, all right? But this mate of mine, plays for Manchester United, right? He was really taking the piss out of me the other week. Says I've gone to all this trouble and I'm not even the only bloke in London with a Bentley in that colour. He texted me a photo he'd taken."

While Riordan was getting his phone out and scrolling through his photos, Stella kept very still. She could feel her pulse throbbing in her ears, as if she was deep underwater. Her palms felt sweaty and the tips of her fingers were tingling.

"Here it is!" Riordan said. "Look. Right there. He took it a couple of weeks ago."

It was a shot of the same car as she'd seen on the CCTV feed at Urban Oversight. There was the number plate. And there, clearly visible behind the wheel, was Sir Leonard Ramage.

"I've got you, you bastard," she whispered, so quietly that Riordan frowned and moved his head closer to Stella's.

"What did you say? Is that him?"

She looked at him, her eyes glistening in the light from the chandeliers. "Yes. It's him. Thank you, Barney. Thank you, so much. She'll get justice now."

"Who will? The little girl? Did you know her?"

Stella fought back her tears. Shook her head.

"She was someone else's daughter."

Halfway through her dinner – Thai-spiced tiger prawns, lemon sole, French beans – Stella's phone rang. Excusing herself, she took it out to the lobby. It was Vicky Riley.

"Vicky? Are you okay?"

Riley's voice was high-pitched, breathy. She was panicking.

"Oh, Stella, thank God! There's someone outside my house. I think he's trying to get in."

"Right. First of all, I want you to stay calm. You panic, you lose. Have you got anywhere in the house with a locking door?"

"Yes. My office. It's the back bedroom."

"Go there now. Lock yourself in. Do not speak to anyone who calls your name. No, wait!"

"What?" Riley's voice was still breathless, but she sounded like she could follow instructions.

"Get a weapon. A kitchen knife, a big torch, a fire iron. Then go. I'm coming as fast as I can."

She ran back to Riordan. "How do you fancy being a knight in shining armour?"

He put his knife and fork down and swallowed the lump of steak he was eating. "What's going on? You're all pale."

"I need to get to Hammersmith. Fast. That car of yours move, does it?"

He grinned.

They ran to the front door of the hotel, drawing wide-eyed glances from the people on their side of the ballroom, stopping just long enough to get the concierge to phone for the valet parker to bring the car round.

"Right, it's a terraced street just off the Goldhawk Road. You know how to get there?"

Riordan nodded, lips set now into a grim line. "More or less. Give me directions too. That way I won't fuck up."

CHAPTER TWENTY-SEVEN
Sending a Message

RAMAGE JABBED HIS knife at Adam Collier's face. He was scowling. While Stella and Barney were waiting for his car, the two PPM members were dining at an Italian restaurant just three hundred metres to the east, in Soho.

"I'm telling you, Adam, it's time you pulled your bloody finger out. I was confronted in my own robing rooms at the Old Bailey, for God's sake. My *sanctum sanctorum*! One minute I'm preparing to sentence some lowlife pimp procuring underage English girls for Russian oligarchs, the next I'm being interrogated by one of London's finest about my whereabouts for the night I dealt with Richard Drinkwater."

"What did she say her name was?"

"Black. DI Stephanie Black."

"Which station?"

"West End Central."

Collier pulled out his phone. "I'm calling Nick Ashley. He runs CID there."

Ramage sliced another piece of pink lamb, daubed it with mint sauce and pulled it off the fork between his teeth as he waited for Collier to dial. He watched, and waited. Collier waggled his head from side to side and mouthed, "Still ringing." Then he nodded.

"Nick, it's Adam Collier. How are you?"

Ramage wanted to grab the phone from Collier and ask the question himself. It took much self-control to sit, eating, while Collier bantered with his opposite number. Finally, he asked.

"Listen. Have you got a DI working there, goes by the name of Stephanie Black?"

Ramage scrutinised Collier's face for any sign of what his colleague was telling him, but it was still. Then a minute frown, just a momentary drawing together of those heavy, black brows.

"Well?" Ramage said, when Collier ended the call.

Collier shook his head. "No. There's nobody in his command called Stephanie Black."

"She had a warrant card. There's no way Shirley would have let her anywhere near me otherwise, however insistent she was."

"Did you see it?"

"Didn't ask. Quite honestly, Adam, when some wild-eyed harpy bursts into my private chambers, bearding me in my lair, as it were, and asking for alibis, I don't always think as straight as I should."

Ramage realised he'd made a mistake. Not asking for the officer's warrant card was a stupid error. Shirley would have to go.

Collier smiled. "We all make them from time to time, Leonard. Even you, the father of our chapel, as it were. What did she look like? Did she have an accent? Anything we could use to track her down?"

Ramage put his cutlery down and took a sip of his wine. Then another, larger, gulp. He shook his head, exasperated at his inability to remember anything useful. "Look, Adam, this is actually the second time I've been questioned by a police officer in the last forty-eight hours, and I can't say I care for it. She was a youngish, white woman. Brownish hair. Tied back, I think. Slightly built. One of those dreadful, lower-middle-class accents that's been improved by three years at some provincial university. That's all."

"You've just described about three-quarters of the female detectives working for the Met. There's nothing else?"

"No!" Ramage snapped. "As I said, I was surprised."

Suddenly, Collier's eyes popped open wide. He leaned back in his chair and smiled, looking at the ceiling. Back on Ramage again, he spoke.

"We're a couple of idiots, do you know that?"

"What the devil do you mean?"

"It's obvious. God, I'm getting too comfortable behind a desk. Who would have the most to gain by investigating you for Drinkwater's death?"

Ramage frowned. "Someone who wanted to shut Pro Patria Mori down?"

"No! His wife! It wasn't Stephanie Black. It was Stella Cole. Coal-black, do you see? And Stephanie-Stella. Amateurs always give themselves away when they choose aliases."

"I thought you said she was chained up in a filing office somewhere."

"I did. Obviously, she's decided to return herself to active duty. In fact, she's been poking into the case. She logged in to our autopsy files to look at the PM on her daughter."

A deep frown spread across Ramage's features. "I hate to say this, but I think it's time we convened the committee."

Collier swallowed his mouthful of veal. "What about our founding principles?"

Ramage leaned across the table, not fast, like a snake striking; more like a crocodile easing closer to its prey.

"I did my duty and removed a dangerous threat to our very existence. Now his wife is coming after me. She has to be dealt with. Before she goes any further. If you think I'm going to let myself be arrested, charged and brought to trial, Adam, you don't know me very well. Not very well at all."

Collier nodded. "Very well. I'll convene the committee for six tomorrow morning."

*

Cocooned by soft, quilted leather, deep carpet, and what she assumed were many square metres of sound insulation, Stella felt cut off from the traffic. The engine seemed far away, little more than a murmur from somewhere ahead of the vast raked windscreen. Yet her glance at the speedometer told her they were travelling at sixty miles per hour as they overtook a line of stationary cars and taxis.

"This is OK, right?" Barney muttered, eyes glued to the road as he swerved round the leading car in the queue and jumped a red traffic light.

"It's fine. You're assisting the police. Keep going. Don't stop for anyone."

Barney kept his foot down, leaving a succession of drivers blasting him with their horns.

"What if the police see me?"

"I *am* the police. Just get us there and let me do the worrying."

"You're the boss," he said, slamming on the brakes to avoid T-boning a supermarket truck with a giant box of strawberries printed on its side.

"Take the next right," she said suddenly.

"But that's a no entry!"

"It's wide enough. Take it."

Barney braked and spun the steering wheel through his hands as he hauled the car through a turn its manufacturers had never intended it to make. Tyres squealing in protest, engine now very audible as the automatic gearbox fought to manage the revs, the Bentley slewed round the corner into the one-way street, losing traction for a second and sending Stella's stomach flipping as the brick side of a department store rushed at her side window.

She flinched and squeezed her eyes shut, bracing for the impact, but the big car righted itself and, as she and Barney chorused a few oaths and blasphemies, raced for the other end of the street.

"Next left!" she ordered and was just starting to unjam her shoulders when a car turned into the road, blocking their path.

"Shit!" Barney shouted and wrenched the steering wheel hard over to the right.

The oncoming driver leaned on the horn and pulled as far over to his right as he could go.

The two cars passed within a hand's breadth of each other.

Stella looked sideways and saw a woman's face in the passenger-side window next to hers, pale in the street light, eyes wide, mouth frozen in a scream. The Bentley hit the kerb and crunched its transmission on the stone as it mounted the pavement, scraping the driver's side bodywork along a brick wall with a hideous metallic screech.

And then they were safe, pulling out into regular two-way traffic.

"Where now?" Barney asked, breathing fast.

"Second left then down to the end of the street."

Ninety seconds later, he pulled over into a residents-only parking space and both he and Stella swung their doors open and were out of the car.

"Follow me!" Stella said and ran back down the street to Vicky Riley's house.

"Knock and ring. Call through the letterbox. Make a noise," she ordered Barney. "Tell her who you are and say I'm going round the back. And if anyone comes near you, warn them off once then hit them."

Then she was gone, leaving the bewildered footballer hammering on the door and ringing the bell, before crouching to bellow his name through the letterbox.

The back of the house was protected by a six-foot wooden fence, overgrown with ivy. Stella took her shoes off and chucked them over the fence, then backed up a couple of steps, ran, and leapt, getting her hands onto the top edge of the fence and hauling herself over and into the back garden. As she dropped onto the soft earth of the flowerbed she felt the hem of her dress catch on something and heard a rip.

The lights were on in the kitchen and the room next to it, which appeared to be a sitting room. The picture window overlooking the garden was smashed. Just a few triangular shards of glass remained in the frame. Stella pulled her little helper from her handbag and gripped it tightly in her right hand. Her breath was coming in gasps, despite her fitness, more from adrenaline than exertion.

She looked at the kitchen door. The intruder could be in there. He could be armed. A knife, maybe even a pistol. *Fools rush in, Stel. Yes, they do. So do police officers.* She ran for the door, pushed the handle down and leapt through, swinging her head left and right, eyes probing the corners of the room. It was empty.

She went left, through the door that led to the living room. Nobody. Finally, with Barney's voice echoing down the hall as he called through the letterbox, she ran for the hallway, calling out as she took the stairs two at a time, ready to smack the little helper into any face that came towards her that didn't belong to Riley.

"Vicky? Vicky? It's Stella. Are you, OK?"

She reached the landing. It was narrow, with a dogleg halfway along marked by a flight of two steps. All four doors leading off it were closed. Panting, she put her hand on the brass doorknob of the closest door, twisted it and pushed through, little helper clamped in her fist.

A black-clad figure rushed at her from the shadows, arms outstretched.

CHAPTER TWENTY-EIGHT
Help Wanted

STELLA STEPPED BACK with her right leg, adopting the fighting stance taught her by Rocky. Soft through both knees to stay flexible and prevent her attacker using her own legs as levers. Weight borne equally left and right, up on the balls of her feet, ready to counterattack after her first feint. Her assailant threw herself at Stella, wrapping her arms tight around her middle.

"Oh, Stella, thank God you're here!"

Heart still thumping, Stella relaxed and returned the hug, little helper still clutched in her right fist. Riley seemed in no hurry to release her and so she stood, feeling the other woman's breath coming in fast gasps against her own ribcage. Finally, she prised herself free.

"There's nobody here, Vicky. It's OK. Come on, I've got reinforcements waiting at the front door."

Riley pulled the front door wide and then did a double take. Stella smiled, enjoying the fast-changing range of emotions taking turns to move Riley's features around.

"You're–" Riley managed, in the end.

"Vicky Riley, Barney Riordan," Stella said dryly.

"Hi Vicky," Riordan said, extending a hand. "Pleased to meet you."

Leaving the journalist and the footballer in the kitchen drinking coffee, Stella opened the door to the sitting room. At first, she didn't move; her training had been explicit on this point. You didn't contaminate a crime scene. Ever. The days of clueless plods marching through puddles of blood and smearing latent prints were, thankfully, a thing of the past.

Ah, what the hell, it's only a crime scene if there's going to be an investigation. *If there's going to be a* hunt, *it doesn't matter.* She stepped into the room. Splinters of glass were scattered on the pale green carpet like ice thrown across a frozen pond. Lying on one of its flat faces was a brick. Tied around the brick with string was a piece of ivory paper. Stella retrieved the brick and took it back to the kitchen, placing it dead-centre on the table between the three mugs of coffee Vicky had made.

"Present from your prowler," Stella said.

"That's old-school, that is," Barney said.

"How very post-modern," was Vicky's take.

Stella cut the string with her penknife and discarded it.

"Shouldn't you be, like, bagging that, or something?" Barney asked. "You know, for evidence."

She stopped, and turned to Barney. "Absolutely. Listen, Barney, you've been fantastic help, getting me here so quickly, but from here it's police business, as you said. This is going to take a while. You can get back to the ball and press the flesh a bit more. I'll be sure to mention you to my boss. You never know, there might be a commendation in it for you. Look good to be on the front page for a change, instead of the back. And we'll find a way to pay for your car to be fixed."

He frowned. "No need. I'll get it done on the insurance." Then he smiled. "If you're OK, then?"

"I am. And Barney," she said, putting out a hand to touch him on the arm as he was turning to go. "Thanks for inviting me. It was fun."

With Barney gone, Vicky looked at Stella, her gaze steady, unblinking. "You aren't investigating this, are you?"

Stella nodded. "I am. Just not through official channels." She unfolded the note and read out the short, printed message.

"Riley. You think you're doing good. But you're threatening justice. Beware.

Justice may retaliate. Find another story. Before you *become* the story."

"It's them, isn't it?" Vicky said. "Pro Patria Mori."

"Looks like it. You need to move out for a while. It isn't safe here. Not now they know this is your home." Vicky nodded. Glad that she wasn't dealing with a weepy, what-about-my-cats kind of victim, Stella gave her standard speech. "Do you have someone you could stay with? Someone they wouldn't connect with you?"

"My godmother. She lives in Wales. On a farm. She rears pigs. Gloucester Old Spots."

"OK, good. Pack a bag and leave now."

"I don't know if she's there. I'll have to ring."

"No! Don't ring. Don't use your phone at all. She's a farmer, she'll be in. They always are. If she isn't, find a hotel or a pub with rooms. And don't drive. They'll have your registration number. The ANPR cameras on the bridges will pick you up and then they'll have you again."

"The what?"

"Automatic–"

"Number plate recognition, OK, got it. So, the train, then?"

"Then a taxi. Get a disposable phone on the way if you can. Here's my number. Text me when you're safe."

*

At six thirty the following morning, Collier and four other senior members of Pro Patria Mori were sitting round his kitchen table. The others were Sir Leonard Ramage; Charlie Howarth QC; Debra Fieldsend, a Crown Prosecution Service lawyer; and Hester Ragib, a barrister.

"Ladies and gentlemen, we have a problem," Collier began. "Stella Cole, one of my officers, is pursuing leads that will, in all likilihood, take her to Leonard's role in the Drinkwater affair."

Howarth spoke next.

"Are you about to propose what I think you are, Adam? Because that goes against the grain, you know. Defending the police is one of our founding principles, you know that. It's who we are."

Ramage opened his mouth to speak, but Collier glanced at him, signalling with a minuscule shake of his right hand to stay quiet. For now.

"I'm fully aware of that, Charlie, since I *am* a police officer. But sometimes we need to forget the founding principles and concentrate on what's right in front of us."

"Which is a meddling detective trying to put one of PPM's members in handcuffs," Fieldsend said. "I'm with Adam on this. If Leonard had run down an innocent passer-by, or if you, Charlie, knocked down a yummy mummy out for a post-school-run jog, I'd say, 'You should have been more careful. Nobody is bigger than justice. Nobody is more important than PPM and the work we do'. But that's not the case here, is it? Leonard removed a very real and potentially devastating threat to our very existence. He deserves our support."

"Say he does," Howarth said, looking at Ramage, "and I accept what Debra says, Leonard. Offing a detective…"

"Inspector," Collier said.

"Offing a detective inspector isn't the same as delivering justice to some celebrity paedophile or a con artist charming old ladies out of their life savings."

"Au contraire, Charlie," Ramage said in a quiet, trembling voice, finally breaking his silence. His tanned skin was a pale, jaundiced yellow; all the blood appeared to have retreated from his face. "It is *exactly* the same. Drinkwater was poised to expose us. So, now, is his widow. We killed Drinkwater to silence him. We do the same to her."

"It'll take some thought, Leonard." This was Ragib.

"Then, with the greatest respect, Hester, might I suggest that we get our fucking thinking caps on?" Ramage's voice had risen to a harsh bark. "Because I am not going to go quietly into that good night that is our justice system, except as one who administers it. Needless to say, though, *were* I to find myself enmeshed in the arms of the law, long or otherwise, I cannot guarantee how long I'd be able to hold my tongue against what I'm sure would be expert interrogation."

"What are our options?" Fieldsend asked.

"She rides a motorbike," Collier said. "Sauce for the gander, etc."

"Too many variables," Ragib said. She took a sip of her coffee and placed the mug in the precise centre of the cork coaster. "She could be put into a coma then wake up a month later and blab to the doctors. We need something certain. Something fast, I think. Leonard?"

Ramage nodded his assent. "Yes. I don't know how far she's got, but I think it's fair to say she knows it was a car like mine, if not actually mine. And my alibi won't stand up to a solid examination, Adam, since you are it. Dare I say, three members of the same family being killed by hit and run drivers within a year of each other might raise a few eyebrows."

"Rape-murder," Collier said, wiping a croissant crumb off his cheek with a napkin. "Brutal. Messy. Unprovoked. Random." He looked at each of the others in turn, ending with his piercing eyes fixed on Ragib. "Certain."

"Who do we have who could do it?" Fieldsend asked.

"Something like that, I'd rather use a villain than a member. Too much DNA splashed about. We'll use him like we used Deacon. Get the job done, then dispose of him. And *that's* when we use a member. My attack dog, Leonard, remember her?"

Ramage smiled. "Drilled that little tart from a dozen streets away, and cleared up after herself."

"Exactly." Collier made a quick note on a sheet of notepaper, folded it into four and slipped it into his wallet. "Leave this one with me. I have someone in mind who'll jump at it."

*

Later that day, just after two in the afternoon, a car pulled into the visitor parking beside a low-level building in the Kent countryside, brick-built, with high, barred windows. Demarcating the perimeter was a double fence of galvanised steel stanchions, five metres high and three metres apart. Strung between the stanchions was 8mm chain-link fencing, several grades superior to the stuff municipal councils used to enclose playparks and housing estates. And adorning the tops of the stanchions, in a four-kilometre ring, were thousands upon thousands of loops of razor wire, glinting in the weak sunshine.

HMP Hemsleigh was a category A+ prison. Its inmates were deemed not just a threat to society or national security, but liable and in fact *likely* to reoffend within twenty-fours of escape. One man, in particular, was known throughout the prison. *Feared* throughout the prison. His name was Peter Moxey.

Moxey was fifty-three, though he looked much younger. His appearance was striking: pale, blue-white eyes like a husky's, deep-set each side of a sharp-ridged nose. High, protruding cheekbones, a pointed chin and a prominent Adam's apple. His face looked like a collection of blades. He was a wiry five-feet-ten in his stockinged feet, with corded muscles in his arms and legs and a flat stomach tautened into a solid sheet of muscle from thousand upon obsessive thousand of sit-ups. On his arrival a year earlier, having received a thirty-three-year sentence for sexually aggravated murder, the prison boss – not the governor, who tended to stay as far away from his charges as possible – decided to re-establish his right to rule.

*

Moxey was unpacking his few possessions in his cell when Dennis "Marley" DuCane, nicknamed for his passing facial resemblance to the dead reggae superstar, slipped silently through the open door and closed it behind him. That was all the only eye-witness to the event – a multiple rapist – was able to swear to in the subsequent police investigation.

The pathologist's report on DuCane made queasy reading. DuCane's muscular, fourteen-stone body bore evidence of multiple bite wounds, from which chunks of flesh had been removed. No biological material, barring blood – a great deal of blood – was discovered in Moxey's cell and it was assumed he had eaten what he had bitten free of DuCane's body. Both DuCane's tibias and fibulas were broken, as were his right humerus, his lower jaw, his cheekbones, the left-hand of which had been pushed back so hard it had popped the eye from its socket (the eye was also not discovered in the search) and the occipital bone at the back of his skull. His liver, spleen and both kidneys had been ruptured, "reduced to the status of a semi-liquid," according to the pathologist. Agonising though all of these injuries must have been, they were not the cause of death. That was reserved for a blow from a toothbrush (unsharpened), which had been pushed into the right eye so hard that it had shattered the thin bone of the socket and penetrated four inches into the frontal lobe of the brain.

*

A tall prison officer approached Moxey at a table in the recreation room, where he was reading a magazine. "Moxey, you've got a visitor," he said, keeping a respectful distance between himself and the prisoner. Moxey looked up from his reading, the fleshy brow ridge above his eyes dropping still further. "I never get visitors," he growled.

"Well, you've got one today. He said to tell you these exact words. 'I have something you will want to hear about. Something you desire more than anything else'."

Moxey stood, fast, causing the prison officer to step back too quickly and almost tumble over a chair behind him.

Five minutes later, Moxey was sitting at a small, red-topped table in the visiting area, his bare, muscular forearms resting on its cracked and worn surface. Both arms were tattooed with swastikas. In addition, the left bore a lifelike portrait of Al Pacino as Scarface, while the right was decorated with the words, "The devil makes work for idle hands" in a heavy, gothic script. He eyed the smooth-cheeked man opposite him.

"Who the fuck are you?" he asked.

In a low voice, the visitor spoke. "My name is Adam Collier. I represent some very powerful people. We'd like you to do something for us, and in return we can arrange for you to disappear from this place and start a new life somewhere else."

Moxey's eyes narrowed. He scowled. Then spoke.

"What people? What thing? Where else?"

"Take a look at this," Collier said, and he slid his warrant card across the table.

Moxey reached for the polished black leather folder with stubby fingers tipped with long yellow nails, slid it the rest of the way to his side of the table, and opened it. He studied it for a few moments, then closed it and pushed it back towards Collier.

"What are you, then, some club for bent coppers?"

Collier smiled, and shook his head. "At the moment, there is a person who's causing us a lot of trouble. She needs taking care of. We thought you might be interested in performing the task. Do what we ask, and I can guarantee you a swift exit from the UK to the destination of your choice, with a new identity and a new face, if you want one."

Moxey pushed his lips out and breathed in, deeply, through his sharp-edged nose.

"How do I know this isn't some kind of set-up?"

"No point. You're already inside, aren't you? You'll probably die in here."

"And when you say take care of, you mean what I think you mean, right?"

Collier nodded. "Do what you did to get sent to this place."

"How are you going to get me out of here? We can't exactly go out through the main gate holding hands, can we?"

"We'll arrange a transfer. We'll have our people in the van. We have a safe house in London. You'll stay there until the job's done, then we'll put you on a boat to France and after that, the world's your oyster."

"I haven't got any money. Can't do anything without cash in this world, can you?"

"A hundred thousand. On completion. In low-denomination, unmarked notes." Collier checked his watch. "What's it to be, Moxey? You're not the only person we're considering for this."

Moxey turned his head to look at the prison officer standing at ease by the white-painted door to the visiting room. Then back at Collier. He nodded. A single, terse bob of the head.

Collier stood. "I'll be seeing you in London. Goodbye, Moxey." Then he held out his hand. Moxey shook it, in a grip that made Collier wince.

*

The following day, Moxey was sitting on a leather sofa in a four-storey townhouse behind London's Harley Street. Dressed in jeans, a white T-shirt and a brand-new pair of Nike running shoes, he was drinking a quarter of a pint of cognac from a cut glass brandy balloon and listening as Collier briefed him.

"Her name is Stella Cole. She's a DI. Here's what she looks like, and here's her address." Collier pushed a photo and a sheet of A4 paper across the table towards Moxey. "She likes running. Follow her and do it somewhere out of the way if you can. And if you decide to have some fun with her first, just make sure she's secured. I don't want her rocking up at Paddington Green with you in handcuffs, all right?"

Moxey glanced down at the photo then back at Collier.

"Skinny little thing like her? Don't worry. I'd probably break her if I tried anything too exciting. I'll just do what needs doing and then, what? Back here?"

"No. Call the number on this phone." He handed over a cheap feature phone he'd bought in a local supermarket earlier that day. "We'll come and get you and start the process of getting you out of the country. When can you do it?"

"In a hurry, are we?" Moxey asked, a smirk sliding across his face like an eel. "I can do it tonight if you want."

*

With Moxey out of the house, working his way across London to Hammersmith in an old car they'd given him, Collier poured himself a tumbler of malt whisky that filled his nostrils with peaty fumes. He called Ramage,

"You should leave London for a few days. Just to be on the safe side," Collier said.

"Why? It's not as if she's going to attack me or anything."

"She suspects you were involved in her husband's death. We're sending someone after her. He'll succeed, I'm sure of it. But if he doesn't, well, I don't want her barging into your chambers with an arrest warrant or a posse of reporters, that's all."

"Who is it?"

Collier paused. "Best you don't know."

"Very well. My next case isn't scheduled to start until next week. I can go up to my place in Scotland."

Collier smiled. "Perfect. Do a bit of fishing. Catch up on your reading. I'll let you know when matters are resolved, and then we can resume our operations."

CHAPTER TWENTY-NINE
Moxey's Mojo

STELLA APPROACHED THE black-painted front door of Ramage's house in Egerton Crescent, London SW3. The road was equidistant between Knightsbridge and the King's Road in Chelsea, and, at ten in the morning, it was quiet. Anyone working had left long since, and anyone not working would by now have disappeared to their yoga class, shopping trip or brunch with similarly monied, at-leisure friends. Her heart was thudding in her chest as she leaned on the doorbell. From some distant part of the house, she could hear its chimes. While she waited for the appearance of the man she was certain had killed her daughter and husband, she fingered the trigger of the Glock. She'd loaded it that morning, and now it was snug in the bottom of her backpack, which she held by the nylon carrying strap.

Footsteps clacked on the flooring beyond the front door. *OK, Stel, as soon as he opens it, push him back hard, flat palm to the sternum, step through and heel the door closed. Don't take your eyes off him.* Gripping the butt of the Glock in her right hand, she readied herself. The door swung inwards. Stella tensed. Her breathing was shallow and she forced herself to inhale once, deeply. *No point passing out just as we have Ramage in our sights, eh, Stel?*

Every muscle felt hard and tight. She was ready to spring at her enemy.

Then she stopped.

The face with raised eyebrows staring at her from the doorway was female.

Plump. Soft skin. Lined, but not deeply – just age, not abuse of nicotine. The face spoke.

"Can I help you?"

Staring, Stella tried to recalibrate her behaviour to accommodate the housekeeper, or whatever species of domestic servant this person was.

"I'm looking for Sir Leonard."

"He's not here, I'm afraid," the woman said, crisply. "He's away at his house in Scotland."

"Oh. You wouldn't have the address, would you? I'm in the country briefly and wanted to say hello. I'm an old friend." The woman looked Stella up and down then, and she, Stella, became acutely aware of the disconnect between her 'old friends' story and the disparity in their ages. Ramage must be well into his sixties and she was early-thirties.

"Sir Leonard prefers to keep his address private. Journalists and so on. I'm sure you understand." The woman sniffed. "Being an old friend of his."

Stella forced her mouth into a smile that she felt sure the woman would detect as a fake. "Of course. No problem. I'll just give him a ring."

On the ride back to the station, Stella had to concentrate on the traffic while a thought ran round in her head like the rotating blue light on a marked car.

If he's in Scotland, in the middle of nowhere, maybe I need more firepower than a Glock.

As she leaned the bike onto its stand in the car park, other-Stella wandered over from a pool of shadow.

"Long guns are easy. No need for all that fannying around you went through to get that nine. We'll just buy a couple in bonnie Scotland. Oh, and good call on snagging those Hatton rounds, by the way. I've a feeling we'll need them."

Back in the exhibits room, Stella had barely stashed her bike gear and backpack under her desk when Frankie appeared at her elbow, leaning down, her white blouse straining across her chest and revealing a glimpse of nude-coloured bra through a gap in the buttons.

"Hi Stel."

"Hi Frankie." She found she was genuinely happy to see her former DS. "Nice top."

Frankie looked down and grimaced. "All my others are in the wash, aren't they? I shrank this one a bit, but it was this or my Wonder Woman T-shirt, so, you know, beggars can't be choosers. I've had to put up with half of CID staring at my tits all morning."

"Just stare at their cocks. Soon puts them off."

Frankie laughed. Then, "Everything OK?" she asked, clearly aiming for a casual tone, which her creased brow undercut.

Stella smiled. "Yeah. Tip-top. Listen, I need a favour. Just a little bit of cover for a few days."

Frankie stood straighter, taking her hands from her jeans pockets and hitching them up. "Anything." She leaned closer. "Legal," she continued in a whisper, before winking.

"I need to take a few days off. On a sick-note. I was about to come and find you, but as you're here, do you want to help me out?"

Frankie nodded. "What do you want me to do?"

"Not here. Let's talk in the ladies. Hold my arm first though, OK?"

Frankie did as she was asked and, once Stella had grabbed her backpack, they made their way along the corridor from the exhibits room to the toilets. Stella leaned on Frankie forcing her to use her other hand to support Stella. They made an odd couple, half-walking-half staggering along, and a passing detective asked if everything was OK.

"We're fine," Frankie said, with a tight smile.

Inside the sanctuary of the ladies' loo, Stella straightened. "Sorry about that."

"You want me to say I came to see you, you looked iffy, I took you to get some cold water, then you fainted and I drove you home."

"Smart girl."

"Where are you going?"

"Best you don't know. But I've found him, Frankie. I've found the bastard who killed Lola and Richard."

"Oh, boss. That's excellent. But you're not–?"

The question hung between them in the air. Stella could read the final few words as if they were painted there: –going to kill him, are you? *Oh, yes. I am going to kill him. Eventually.*

"Going to do anything stupid?" Stella asked. Frankie nodded, biting her lower lip. "No. I'm not going to do anything stupid. Just some intelligence-gathering before I go to The Model about it and get a warrant."

"Good," Frankie said. "Because I want to work for you again. When they let you back into CID and forget about this light duties crap."

"You will, Frankie, that's a promise. Now," Stella placed the back of her hand to her forehead and gripped the edge of a sink with the other. "Ooh, Frankie, I feel a bit poorly. I think I might be about to do a lady-faint and bang my head on the floor. I'll probably get concussion and have to stay off work for a bit."

"Don't you worry, boss. I shall take you home in my car and you can lie down. I am also a trained first-aider."

Frankie's instruction-video voice was too much, and Stella burst out laughing before suppressing it with a palm clamped over her mouth. She rolled her eyes.

"Come on, then," she gasped. "Take me home and give me some hot, sweet tea."

At Stella's front door, Frankie held her by both arms and looked straight at her.

"Promise me you're just going to arrest him. Bring him in. Please, boss." Frankie's voice had a pleading note to it. As if she knew her request was futile. "I'll back you up. Help you gather evidence. Do interviews. Whatever it takes."

Stella smiled.

"I promise. Now, off you go and catch some bad guys. I'm going for a lie-down."

Inside, she made a cup of coffee and sat at the kitchen table. She pulled Gordon Wade's business card from her purse.

The secretary's voice was businesslike, but softened by her Scottish accent.

"Assistant Chief Constable Wade's office."

"Hello. This is DI Stella Cole, from the Met. Is Gordon available, please?"

"Assistant Chief *Constable* Wade is in a meeting."

"I'm sure he is. Tell him I'm breaking the glass."

"I *beg* your pardon?"

You heard, you snotty-nosed bitch. "Please would you be so kind as to interrupt his meeting and inform Assistant Chief *Constable* Wade that DI Stella Cole from the Metropolitan Police is breaking the glass."

"Really! This is very irregular. What is this all about?"

Stella inhaled, then exhaled, letting the other woman wait, and listen to her breathing. When she was calm again, she spoke.

"This is all about your telling Gordon that Stella needs to speak to him. 'Call me any time of the day or night.' That's what Gordon told me when we met at his charity ball."

One … two … three … Stella could almost hear the cogs engaging and clicking in the secretary's brain: protect her master as she'd been trained, and risk angering him that she'd kept a friend in need away from him, or let a stranger past her guard and possibly have her master subjected to all manner of improprieties.

"Hold the line, please."

Stella waited, worrying at a hangnail on her left index finger.

Gordon Wade's voice was warm.

"DI Cole! Thank the Lord you called. Another minute of budget projections and I swear I'd have started shooting. Moira said you were breaking the glass, eh? What's the emergency?"

"I need to track someone down. He's in Scotland. If I gave you a name, would you be able to help me out? Maybe have someone do a little digging to find an address or something? Property records and so on?"

"Och, for a minute there I thought you were going to ask for something difficult. Yes, yes, of course. Fire away."

Stella drew in a sharp little breath and spoke before she could change her mind. Wade couldn't be part of PPM. The group had to be a London thing.

"Leonard Ramage."

"What? Wait a moment. D'ye mean *Sir* Leonard Ramage?"

"The High Court judge? Yes, sir. I do."

Wade dropped his voice. "Man's a fucking prick! Buys a big old place up near the Cairngorms and starts treating the locals like he's the Laird. Upset half the ghillies with his manners and pissed off the other half by diddling them out of their proper fees."

"You know where he lives, then?"

"Aye, I do. No need for any DS to be stuck in front of a computer screen. We might fight for independence from time to time, but Scotland's a small wee place. Some Englishman with a title comes sniffing around looking to play lords and ladies, pretty soon we all get to hear about it. Got a pen there?"

"Ready when you are."

"Craigmackhan. That's the name of the house. Big old Victorian stone thing with turrets. Looks like Dracula's castle. It's outside Blairgowrie, about half an hour north of Perth. Middle of bloody nowhere. Listen, DI Cole, or maybe I'd be better calling you Stella for now, as this is unofficial. You're not getting yourself involved in something you'll regret later, are you?"

"Absolutely not, sir. Just following up on something on my own time."

"Well keep your nose clean, that's all I'm saying. You're a big girl, and you know your law."

The next morning, Stella woke at 5.20.

After a cigarette on the deck and then a shower to clear the fog in her head, she packed for her trip to Scotland. Into a deep tan leather holdall on her bed went jeans, grey T-shirts, charcoal-grey hoodie, bra and knickers, socks, washbag, makeup, black ski mask, running shoes, a pair of rubber gloves, little helper, claw hammer, pliers, bolt cutters, three metres of blue polypropylene rope, needle-pointed awl, blowtorch, duct tape, cable ties, I.O. Shen cleaver and Maoui Deba cook's knife, 9mm hollow point ammunition, 12-gauge Hatton Rounds, Glock 17 semi-automatic pistol, and a piece of paper she'd spent part of the previous day filling in and stamping.

Her new birth certificate, passport and driving licence in the name of Jennifer Amy Stadden had all arrived the previous day and were bundled together with a thick, red rubber band and secure in a zipped compartment inside the holdall.

Finally, in went a padded envelope containing ten thousand pounds in cash that she'd withdrawn from her bank the previous day. The skinny woman behind the counter, looking undernourished inside her official uniform blouse and suit, had asked her what the money was for. None of your fucking business, was what Stella didn't say, knowing the law on money laundering and the banks' nervousness about aiding and abetting criminals, or worse, terrorists.

"New car," she'd said with a confiding smile. "Well, new to me. I'm going to try and get a deal by flashing cash in his face."

She'd been rewarded by a smile in return.

*

Outside, slumped behind the wheel of a beaten-up, twelve-year-old, silver Honda Accord parked twenty metres down the street, was Peter Moxey. He'd been staking out her house for the past thirty-six hours, watching her movements, planning his attack. He knew she went running in the evening, and the towpath looked like a good spot. The trouble was, it was far too popular with other runners, plus dog walkers, strolling couples on their way to the pub and lairy little shits trying to sell each other drugs.

He'd decided that if she didn't appear in her running gear by 7.00 a.m., he'd knock on the door and do her inside. Higher risk of contaminating the crime scene, but then the people he was working for would just make all that go away. In any case, he'd be out of the country and living high on the hog by the time the local plod started oinking around with their shiny, wet snouts. Stretching, and easing the cricks out of his cramped neck muscles, he peered along the street, using the rear-view mirror. Nobody about.

Maybe this would be his lucky day.

It was.

The front door opened, and out came the woman detective, like the little old lady in his Nan's Swiss weather clock. He'd loved that old thing. Used to spend hours watching it when he was staying with her, keeping out of the way of his father's hard hands and his mother's pawing ones. Loved how the two carved figures took turns to come out and say hello to skinny little Peter, depending on what was happening in the sky outside. Then Nan would make him his breakfast – eggs, usually, maybe a bit of bacon and fried bread – and send him off to school with a hug, careful to avoid squeezing his bruises.

He watched the detective scan the road, just like he had just done. Then she checked her watch and jogged off along the pavement, heading for the canal.

Moxey pulled the door-release catch towards him, adding a kick from his new leather boot to the Honda's stubborn driver's door. It gave with a creak and he straightened up. Not bothering to lock it, he strode off after the detective, his hands loose at his sides, arms swinging with simian ease. He was smiling.

*

Stella focused on her breathing, ignoring the rasp as the chill spring air seared her throat, patiently waiting for her heart and lungs to catch up with the new demands she'd placed on them. With each metre, as her cushioned Nikes rebounded from the pavement, she felt herself getting closer to that blissful state where the outside world faded, to be replaced by a contented sense of spaciousness, through which she could run for ever.

On some days, she would turn at random, letting her feet decide on the route, or perhaps being guided by the tiny shifts in weight and balance as she negotiated an obstacle in the road. Today, she wanted the familiarity and safety of ritual. There would be enough spontaneity later on. Her train was due to leave King's Cross at 10.43 a.m. She had time for her favourite forty-five-minute run: down to the towpath, along the canal for a couple of miles, then back through a park and a narrow strip of urban woodland that had somehow escaped the notice of the developers who'd largely concreted this part of northwest London.

She pounded along, through the early morning streets, heading for the river.

Down by the canal was her favourite place to run. The greenish water smelled of silt and the diesel leaking from the old wooden barges. With her feet landing lightly on the compacted earth where the tarmac had worn away near a tunnel under the railway, she let her mind drift to the work ahead, because...

... he'll whine at first.

Please, he'll beg. Please don't hurt me.

She'll remove the first finger with the bolt cutters.

No! This will be a scream, unnervingly high-pitched, although in her time as a cop she's learned that the noises men emit in extremis can be every bit as unsettling as those of women.

The blowtorch has a yellow flame. But when she twists the collar around the nozzle it colour-shifts to a vibrant turquoise with an invisible central cone fringed with violet. It roars quietly, though this harsh sound is drowned out by his wail of terror as the tip of the blue spear traces a boiling route across the skin of his chest. The flesh reddens, the skin blackens and bubbles, before cracking open. And the screams go on and on.

Stella works methodically. She has nowhere else to be, nothing else scheduled. She talks from time to time, reminding the man just why he is here, trussed and tied.

Because you killed them. Because you killed Richard. Because you killed Lola. Especially because you killed Lola.

His eyes are wide, popping, the whites visible all the way round his deep-brown irises.

The mouth works, but no sound comes out from between those cracked lips. She offers him the plastic bottle and he drinks, greedily, sucking at the threaded neck. Then he gags, and retches before vomiting the petrol back up and into his lap.

Stella moves the nozzle of the blowtorch down towards the mixture of saliva and petrol pooling around his exposed genitals. She...

... hears footsteps behind her.

CHAPTER THIRTY
One Down

HE WAS SMILING. That was the first thing Stella noticed about the man following her. It was a very unpleasant expression. It was the smile of a predator. It was a smile that said, "I'm higher up the food chain than you are." A smile that said its wearer took pleasure in inflicting great pain.

He looked fit and strong. He wasn't that much taller than her, but he had that look. The look hardened men of violence acquire or generate. Appraising eyes. Relaxed facial muscles. Lips uncompressed.

The next thing she noticed was the long knife he carried in his right hand.

By rights, she should have screamed and run. Briefly, she considered it. But Stella's screaming-and-running days were behind her. A long way behind her. As the man came closer – no more than ten metres now – she darted into the tunnel mouth she'd just passed. It stank of piss, the harshly alcoholic smell of high-octane blended British "wine" and the sweet lingering aroma of marijuana smoke.

His footsteps echoed from her position inside the brick-lined arch of the tunnel. They weren't picking up speed, though. He was confident. Stella looked around on the glass-strewn floor. Saw what she wanted and picked it up.

The light at the tunnel's arched entrance dimmed as the man turned left and entered. His arms hung loosely, not straight down but spread away from his torso. *Too much time with the free weights*, Stella thought. *That's going to slow you down, friend.* Time slowed down to a crawl as he came closer. Stella waited, balanced on the balls of her feet. Ready to practise.

The smile had changed to a grin. The knife was pointing at her throat. Then the man spoke.

"Powerful people want you dead, little missy. Rape-murder, they said. You're my meal ticket. Foxy Moxey's going to—"

Stella didn't wait to find out what Foxy Moxey was going to do to her. She got her retaliation in first, which the law was more than happy for citizens to do. Pre-emptive action, it was called. Basically, if you saw a man coming towards you with a bloody great butcher knife, you didn't have to wait until he stabbed you before fighting back. You could act with reasonable force to defend yourself. Stella knew her law, as every good DI did. However, the level of force she planned to use was more in the nature of being *un*reasonable.

Even in soft, air-sprung running shoes, her feet were vicious weapons, thanks to Rocky's teaching. She leapt forward, knee raised, and stamped with all her might on the side of Moxey's right knee with a full-throated yell of aggression. Screaming, he toppled over as his cruciate ligaments sheared with the sound of bubble-wrap crackling.

He slashed the knife at Stella's legs. The serrated blade *whished* past her left shin.

Stella swung her right hand out, so that the discarded Thunderbird bottle she held by its neck smashed against the slimy green Victorian brickwork.

Without pausing, she reversed the swing, swiping it down at Moxey's knife-hand with another battle-cry, knocking the weapon from his grasp and cutting through two fingers altogether, which spurted blood in jetting arcs from the tiny arteries she'd just severed.

He screamed again, struggling to get to his feet, swinging at Stella with his undamaged hand.

She stood, waiting, and as he straightened, she took her head back a little way then snapped it forward, ramming her forehead straight onto the point of his nose.

"Bitch!" he yelled – it came out *Bish!* – as the thin bones inside his nose smashed and blood jetted from his nostrils. He crumpled to his knees, screaming more obscenities at her.

The bottle was in motion again. Stella was stabbing it down at his face. Up and down the jagged crown of glass leapt, twice, straight towards his eyes. His bloodied mouth emitted a low moan.

"Oh, you cunt! Foxy Moxey don't take that from a bitch like you."

He was wiping at his eyes with both palms, trying to clear the blood sheeting across them from the circles of deep, jagged-edged wounds in his forehead and cheekbones. The finger-stumps were still bleeding profusely, though adrenaline had constricted the blood vessels, choking off the squirting.

That was when Stella bent, ducking under a roundhouse punch from the tautly muscled right arm, and retrieved the knife from the tunnel floor.

Dancing back from another swing, she moved behind Moxey and slashed the back of his right thigh, cutting deeply into his hamstring.

Another scream, gurgling with the blood he'd just swallowed.

As Moxey sank to the ground, she sat astride him and jabbed the knife underneath the point of his jaw. Reaching back she punched down hard into his groin, twice, riding him as he bucked and twisted with the pain.

A push of the knife sent the tip half an inch into the soft tissue between the wings of his jawbone. Blood pooled around the blade and trickled downwards past Moxey's ears.

"Answer me, or the rest goes in," Stella said, panting. "Who sent you?"

"Snow White and the Seven Dwarfs."

She pushed another inch of steel into the stubbled skin below Moxey's jaw. He ground his teeth together, but a groan still escaped from his pulled-back lips.

"Who?" she barked.

"Fuck you, bitch!" he said, though the tip of the knife protruding into his mouth below the root of his tongue made it sound like, *Huck oo, gish!*

She placed the wicked points of glass from the Thunderbird bottle against his staring eyes.

"They killed my husband, you know. And they killed my baby. They sent you to kill me too. But the story doesn't end that way."

She pushed down hard on the bottle, gripping it around the neck so tightly her knuckles turned bone-white as she twisted. Over Moxey's high-pitched scream, and the grating of glass on bone, she murmured to him:

"Tell them, I'm coming. I'm coming for all of them."

She levered herself off Moxey's writhing form and shook herself like a dog trying to dislodge a troublesome fly. Picked Moxey's bloodied head up by the ears and slammed it down onto the concrete, putting out the lights. She stripped the black running vest off, wiped her face and arms with it, and turned it inside out, which hid most of the blood. Then she walked back to the canal, tossed the bottle and the crimsoned knife into the middle of the turbid stream and ran off towards home.

"Clever of you not to kill him," other-Stella said while Stella showered. "No body, no forensics. He'll find a way to get patched up and disappear."

Stella shrugged as she washed the blood off her hands. "Doesn't matter either way. Stella Cole is already dead."

"Fair enough. Ready to adopt your *nom de guerre?*"

Stella dried herself and dressed. Jeans, hoodie, denim jacket and her bike boots.

From a shelf in her wardrobe she lifted down a carrier bag, which she emptied onto the bed. A blonde wig, coloured contact lenses in a tiny transparent plastic case and a tube of theatrical spirit gum tumbled out.

"Twenty minutes in front of the mirror and *voila*! I'm Jennifer Amy Stadden, born January fifth, 1978."

Dressed all in black, Stella cut an unobtrusive, if severe, figure at King's Cross Station. She paid cash for her ticket, queuing in line at a booth rather than using a machine. Twenty minutes after arriving, she slung her bag into the overhead rack and slumped down into her seat, facing backwards.

The wig itched, and she scratched at her scalp through the nylon mesh skullcap beneath the blonde hair. Her eyes were sore, and blinking only partially relieved the irritation. The girl in the tattoo shop where she'd bought the coloured contacts had recommended eye drops, "Murine, or something", and now, Stella was grateful for the advice. She fished out the bottle from her jacket pocket, tilted her head back and squeezed a few drops into each eye, dabbing away the surplus with a paper tissue.

As the engine hummed into life some dozens of metres ahead of her seat, she relaxed, just a little. Keeping her cap on, she plugged a pair of cheap earbuds into her phone and closed her eyes. The audiobook's narrator began reading to her – just like she and Richard used to read to Lola, even though they knew she couldn't understand – and she allowed his deep, northern voice to insinuate itself into her brain.

"Call me Ishmael–" he began.

At some point after showing the guard her ticket, she dozed off. Passengers got on, sat next to her, got off again, and Stella slept on. In her dreams, the members of Pro Patria Mori sat ranged around her like a medieval court, bewigged and masked with black porcelain faces that ended in sharp-pointed beaks.

"State your name," the tallest figure shouted at her from behind his mask.

"I have no name."

"What do they call you?"

"They call me lost."

"Lost?"

"Because I lost everything. You took them from me. You took her from me."

"We can't call you lost. State your name."

"My name? Call me Ishmael. I am coming for you."

A squat figure sitting to the first speaker's left interrupted. It spoke with a woman's voice. Well educated. Sarcastic. Cold.

"Really?" it drawled. "Let me remind you, it is you who is on trial here. Read her the charges."

The figure on Stella's extreme right spoke up from behind its mask. She noticed that the hands protruding from the sleeves of its snowy white robe were studded with thick, curling, black hairs.

"You are charged with being a bad mother. A disloyal wife. That you did wilfully and negligently endanger the lives of your baby daughter and husband. That you recklessly and with malice aforethought watched them die. Didn't you, Stella? You watched. And you enjoyed it."

"No!" she screamed, or tried to, although the noise that emerged from her

constricted throat was little more than a whimper. "I was on duty. I couldn't help."

Another of the masked figures piped up. "Don't interrupt! Us girls should know our place."

The central figure stood and pounded its taloned fist down on the wooden bench. It shouted at her.

"You failed them! You should have been there for them. Now they're burning still. Him and her."

"There was nothing I could do. Please! Let me explain. I loved them."

The figure shook its head. It turned to the right and waved a clawed hand at twelve blackened humanoid figures sitting crammed together inside the smoking ruin of a silver Fiat Mirafiori.

"Ladies and gentlemen of the jury, what is your verdict?"

Struggling to his feet, the jury foreman, smoke rising in greyish-green curls from the top of his split scalp, eyes criss-crossed by jagged red wounds, spoke:

"She did it. Guilty as sin, your honour. Foxy Moxey says so." Black scraps of charred flesh tumbled free from the outstretched index finger that jabbed at Stella.

"Well, well. It seems we have a conviction," the chief judge said, not bothering to conceal the satisfaction in his voice. "And as it's sweet and right to die for your country ..." He reached into a pocket and withdrew a square of blood-red silk, which he draped over his thinning silver hair so that one corner dangled between the eye slits of his beaked mask. "You will be taken from here to a place of execution, where we'll cut your fucking head off, douse you in petrol and set you alight for all the boys and girls to see."

Stella tried to speak, to remonstrate, but her lips were stuck together and she could feel the thin skin tearing as she fought to form the words. She stretched out her arms in supplication, but when she looked at them, they were the short, pudgy arms of a very young child. A toddler, really. Screaming soundlessly, she regarded them with horror as first the fingertips, then the soft, barely-lined palms, the wrists, forearms and upper arms scorched, split and smouldered into a dull orange glow before igniting with a soft pop like a distant balloon bursting.

Her strangled groan as she dragged herself out of the nightmare caused the elderly couple sitting opposite her to lean solicitously across the table.

"Are you all right, dear?" the woman asked, her papery skin mottled with beige liver spots. "You were talking in your sleep."

Stella swiped her sleeve across her face, which was wet with tears and sweat. She straightened herself in her seat.

"I'm fine, thank you. Just a bad dream. Really. No problem."

Still frowning, the woman sat back, although her husband was looking closely at Stella.

"Are you sure, you're OK?" he asked. "You said 'they killed her'. That was just before you woke up, wasn't it, Marjorie?"

He turned to his wife for confirmation. The woman nodded.

"I said I'm fine," Stella snapped. "Look, thanks for your concern, but let's leave it. Please."

She turned away and pressed her cheek to the cool glass of the carriage window, leaving the couple to their newspapers. *Probably think I'm an ungrateful cow, when all they were doing was trying to help.* She pulled her face away from the rain-streaked widow and turned to face the couple again.

"I'm sorry," she said, in a much softer voice. "I have nightmares. Bad ones sometimes."

"Army, are you, love?" the woman asked. "Only George and I read an article about how those poor boys and girls come back all knotted up inside. Psychologically, like. Didn't we, George? Like Doreen's Nick did last September."

The man nodded.

From Waverley Station in the centre of Edinburgh, Stella caught a cab to the city's outskirts then waited at the side of the road, thumb out. Perhaps because she was small, and not an obvious candidate for an article titled, "My Psycho Hitchhiker Tortured Me", she managed to find a ride in under twenty minutes. It was a car transporter heading north with eight hatchbacks in different shades of silver and grey.

Two hours later, the transporter huffed and grumbled to a stop on the edge of a small village called Calvine. Set back from the road was a stone-built, slate-roofed house. A slate sign screwed to the gatepost announced that the owners of 'Braemar' took in guests for B&B and that they had vacancies.

Thanking the driver, Stella retrieved her bag from behind her seat and walked up the path to the front door. The landlady was all smiles and waved to the truck driver as the huge vehicle pulled away.

Formalities dealt with, Stella found herself in a large bedroom furnished with a four-poster bed, a small desk with a hard kitchen chair tucked underneath, a cheap flatpack wardrobe in some sort of wood-grain finish, and a matching chest of drawers. The small en suite bathroom smelled strongly of lavender, and indeed, a bunch of dried stalks of the herb stood in a purple glass on a shelf above the sink. The towels, flannel, liquid soap and curtains were all in matching shades of purple.

After a long, scalding-hot shower, Stella wrapped a bath towel around herself and went back to the bedroom to unpack her gear. The juxtaposition of her underwear and the array of weaponry struck her as funny and a short laugh escaped her throat. Then it died.

"I'm coming for you, Ramage," she muttered, picking up the Glock and dropping the magazine out of the butt with a practised flick of the release catch. First putting on the nitrile gloves she'd packed, she inserted seventeen of the hollow point rounds into the magazine, enjoying the way the spring resisted the pressure of her thumb before swallowing each new brass-jacketed round. When the magazine was full, she slid it back and pressed hard until the catch engaged with a soft *clack*.

The Hatton rounds caught her eye. "No good without something to fire them from, Stel," a voice said from behind her right ear. She turned. In the wardrobe mirror she could see the other Stella. The cold-eyed one. The one with a sardonic smile on her red lips. "We passed a gun shop in the last town before this godforsaken place, did you notice?"

"Campbell's Gunsmiths," Stella said. "Halfway down the high street on the right-hand side. Tartan fascia, shotguns in the left display window, boots and jackets in the right."

"Very good!" other-Stella replied, stepping out of the mirror and raising her hands to offer a gentle round of applause.

"First stop in the morning," Stella said.

*

Back in London, Frankie O'Meara was having second thoughts. She was a good cop, and a good Catholic, and something about Stella's behaviour had frightened her more than she was initially willing to admit. Whatever anyone had done to Stella and her family, and God alone knew it was sinful as well as criminal, taking the law into your own hands was crossing a line. A big, fat line, marked with blue-and-white police incident tape that snapped in the wind. A line that flashed with bright blue lights and emitted the screech of sirens if you got within spitting distance.

She hesitated for just a second outside Adam Collier's office door, then straightened her back, hitched her trousers and knocked, smartly, three times.

"Come!" Collier called from beyond the varnished wood.

Frankie pushed open the door and went to stand in front of Collier's desk.

"Sorry to interrupt you, sir."

Looking up, Collier frowned. Then turned on his professional smile.

"Take a seat, Frankie. It looks as though there's something you need to get off your chest."

Frankie sat. "There is, sir. Something I really think you need to know about."

"And that would be?"

"Oh. Sorry, sir. It's Stel. I mean, DI Cole, sir." Frankie was aware she was babbling. She wasn't normally this easily flustered, but a night of broken sleep while she turned over her last conversation with Stella in her mind had frayed her nerves. She cleared her throat, touching the soft place between her collar bones where she knew a blush was creeping up towards her throat. "I think she's going to do something," she paused. *What, Frankie? Stupid? Dangerous? Career-limiting? What?* "I think she's going to do something that might not be the best course of action, sir," she finished. It even sounded lame to her as the words left her lips, which, annoyingly, had begun to tremble.

Collier leaned back in his chair, steepling his fingers and placing their tips under his chin. He pursed his lips.

"Is she going to join the Communist Party? Or buy a more powerful motorbike? Or start dating a witness? They would all, in my opinion, not be the best course of action for a serving police officer."

"No, sir. Of course not."

"Well, spit it out for goodness sake. I have work to do here." With a sweep of his hand he indicated a slew of papers that covered his desk. "As you can see."

"I think she's going to kill someone, sir!" Frankie blurted, feeling, as she did so, the hot blush storming up her neck.

Now she had Collier's attention. He leaned towards her across the desk. "Explain. Now. Quickly and clearly."

"She told me she'd found out who killed Richard and Lola, sir. Who really did it. Because Edwin Deacon was just the fall guy. I asked her if she was going to do anything stupid, and she said she was just gathering intelligence."

Collier's dark-brown eyes stayed locked onto hers. His face was expressionless.

"Did she tell you any names? Or how she'd tracked them down?"

"No, sir. She's not going to get into trouble over this, is she, sir? I mean, she's still grieving, obviously. Probably it's depression. She needs help, sir."

Collier frowned. "Let's save the amateur psychology for when we can talk to DI Cole again. You did the right thing, Frankie. Thank you. Now, if you'll excuse me, I have to make some calls. Urgently."

Relieved of her burden, Frankie heaved a great sigh, levered herself out of the chair and left the office.

*

Collier scrolled through his contacts and called a woman named Lucy Van Houten. She was a serving member of SCO19, and a decorated one at that. She was also an unofficial resource for Pro Patria Mori. It was she who had helped the group deal with the prostitute attempting to blackmail Leonard Ramage.

"Yes, sir?"

"I have another job for you."

"Of course, sir. Anything. When and where? Target identity?"

"Now. Scotland. A woman called Stella Cole. Though I suspect she's using the alias Stephanie Black."

"With respect, sir, Scotland's a big place. I need a location," she said.

"Of course, you do," he snapped. "I was coming to that." Then, realising her particular personality defect meant she neither understood other people's emotions, nor displayed a great deal of her own, he softened his tone. "Forgive me, Lucy. Under pressure here."

"That's perfectly OK, sir. I understand."

He doubted she did, but continued nonetheless.

"I want you to get yourself to a place north of Edinburgh. Today. It's a house called Craigmackhan, I'll text you GPS coordinates. It belongs to the man you saw with the prostitute the other day. You set up and wait. She's going to kill him. Once she's done it, you put her down, then leave the scene. Understand?"

"I understand, sir. I'll have to fly. What about my rifle?"

"You can't take a weapon with you, it will raise too many flags. There's a gun shop in the town nearest to the house, Pitlochry. Leonard, I mean the owner, took me there once. Get yourself whatever you need."

"Understood, sir. Will it be all right if I claim for it on expenses?"

Collier sighed. "Yes, of course. Keep all your receipts."

"I always do, sir, you know that."

"Oh, one other thing."

"Yes, sir?"

"She's a serving police officer. A DI. That going to be a problem?"

"Is she an opponent of our aims, sir?"

"Effectively, yes."

"Then, no it's not, sir. Not at all."

CHAPTER THIRTY-ONE
A Dead Child Buys Guns

AFTER A BREAKFAST of porridge with cream and a dash of Scotch over the top, followed by bacon, eggs, grilled tomatoes and some odd, but delicious, square potato pancakes, Stella thanked her landlady and walked into the centre of the village to find a taxi. Tucked away behind the village store was a single minicab office – James Duggan Taxi. Finding nobody behind the counter, Stella looked around, wondering whether she could use her ID to persuade some obliging local to ferry her into Pitlochry, but decided against it. As she turned to go, an elderly man came up beside her, walking a dachshund.

"Looking for Jim, were you, dear?"

"Yes, I need a cab." *As opposed to an airship. Idiot.*

"He'll be on a job. Probably the school run. He takes little Holly Baylis in every day. He'll be back in a wee while, I shouldn't wonder."

Stella thanked the old gent for his information and strode off, heading out of the village, intending to return in an hour.

An hour and fifteen minutes later, she returned to find the office manned by a young guy in a red, black and yellow tartan shirt and a cable-knit cardigan in thick, oatmeal-coloured wool.

Forty minutes after that, she stepped out onto the pavement in Pitlochry's high street, a few doors down from the gunsmith's. She turned away from Campbell's and sought out a smaller shop sandwiched between a pharmacy and a newsagent. She went in and bought what she needed, then walked back up the street.

She stopped, made one final, nervous, check that the document she'd stamped and signed at Paddington Green was there, folded in the inside top pocket of her jacket, then walked the final twenty yards and pushed through the door to the interior of Campbell's. A brass bell above the door jangled on its steel spring.

Inside, the shop smelled like the armoury at her station. Gun oil, steel, brass and a faint but unmistakable whiff of gunpowder. Overlaying the hard, machine-made smells was a softer, more organic aroma: leather polish. She wandered around, getting her bearings. A woman was pulling on a pair of shiny black, knee-high riding boots while a pretty brunette of seventeen or eighteen in a pleated skirt and a white blouse looked on. Two portly gentlemen in superbly tailored outdoor gear – plus fours and matching waistcoats and jackets in a pale, sage-green tweed – were laughing loudly with a young male shop assistant as they examined some fly fishing rods. A chocolate-and-white springer spaniel lying at their feet wore a matching tweed coat. It raised its head and sniffed at Stella's calf as she squeezed past the group.

To the left of the door was the area that really interested Stella. Behind a wood-framed counter, topped with an inset sheet of thick glass, was a wooden rack holding a couple of dozen long guns. Shotguns, rifles, even a handful of air guns on the far right of the rack. Under the glass, she could see boxes of shells, circular tins of lead pellets for the air guns, and a small selection of hunting and skinning knives, their steel blades gleaming dully in the light from the overhead pendant lamps. A stuffed and mounted stag's head regarded her morosely from a space between two of the shotguns, as if to say, "I only stepped out to get something to eat and now look at me." The thought made Stella smile.

A young man, maybe twenty-five, emerged from a doorway to the right of the counter. He was dressed in a sleeveless Fair Isle pullover in pinks, purples and browns, with a white shirt beneath, its sleeves bunched up against silver armbands like an old-time barman in a speakeasy. His eyes were a dark brown, almost black, and they were fringed with long, dark lashes.

"May I help you, madam?" he asked, in a soft burr, the smile on his thin lips widening.

Stella adopted a posh accent she'd recently heard in a cafe in Mayfair. Two women had been discussing their shopping woes. *I tell you*, one had said between delicate sips of her coffee, *Hermès was so stuffed with little Chinese girls spending Poppa Chan's money, one could hardly make oneself seen by the shop girl*. At the time, Stella had wanted to slap them silly, but now she was grateful for their unwitting assistance.

"Yes. I've been having some trouble with vermin. We're being simply overrun. I need a rifle. And a shotgun." She widened her eyes and ran her hands through the wig's long blonde hair. Making him notice it. Making him remember a posh blonde with dark-brown eyes.

At her words, his eyes popped open and he smiled broadly.

"Well, well, what are the odds?"

"What do you mean?"

"We have nobody but locals in here from one end of the year to the next and then, within the space of an hour, two English ladies come through our door looking to buy rifles."

Stella's mind began racing as she tried to assess what this could mean. A rat gnawed at her insides. *You're in trouble*, it hissed. *He's sent someone after you. Better be careful.*

"Goodness me. Well, I think I heard one of our neighbours talking about a shooting party. I dare say she was here for that."

"Oh, I'm sure you're right, madam." He was all smiles. "And this lady certainly knew her long guns. Very knowledgeable. Picked out a splendid rifle for herself without any help at all. Now, vermin, you said?"

"That's right," Stella said plastering what she hoped was a pleasant smile onto her face. "Deer mostly, eating my fruit trees. But the rabbits are absolutely pestilential too."

"Well, as you see, madam, we have a wide selection of shotguns. You can purchase them with a standard shotgun certificate. As to the rifle, you'll need–"

"A coterminous firearms certificate, yes, I know," Stella interrupted, letting the merest hint of impatience inflect her voice. "Here, you'll see everything's in order."

She flourished the certificate – genuine, not forged – at him. It was the product of fifteen minutes' work back in the records room at Paddington Green. It permitted Jennifer Amy Stadden to purchase shotguns, including those with high-capacity magazines – over three cartridges – and also one rifle in .308 calibre, one sound moderator, also for a .308, and up to a hundred .308 rounds at any given time.

He frowned, grooving three fine lines into his otherwise smooth forehead. "Issued in London, not here?"

"Yes. They are nationally applicable, you know." Her adopted persona was a woman used to getting her own way, but inwardly, Stella was fighting to calm an insistent tremor of anxiety that she feared would betray itself in a bead of sweat on her brow or top lip, or a tremor in her voice.

"Of course, madam. It's just that most of our customers have Scottish certificates."

"Well, that's very interesting, but as you know, you're still a part of the United Kingdom, for the moment at least, so perhaps we could continue?"

He folded the certificate up and handed in back to Stella.

"Of course, my apologies. And it's just as simple to write to the Metropolitan Police as our local force."

"Write?"

"To inform them of your purchases, madam."

"Surely that's all computerised nowadays?"

He laughed. "You'd think so, wouldn't you. But I'm afraid it's all a bit stuck in the pre-digital era. To be honest, you could be anyone, and as long as you have that piece of paper, you can walk out of here with whatever it says you can. All we do is write our letter within seven days of your leaving the shop."

By which time I'll be long gone. And after the Met call you to explain I died as a little girl, you're going to have a couple of detectives crawling all over your shop. They'll want CCTV, which I see you don't have, descriptions, the works. Sorry.

"So. Shall we look at some guns?" she said.

"The shotgun first, I think," he said. "Do you have a preference for style or make? We have the most popular brands out here and several others in our private handling room."

"Well, as I said, this is strictly a practical gun. My husband and I have our favourites for shoots, of course. He likes his Berettas, while I'm more of a Purdey girl. So, a semi-automatic. I'm not fussed about the maker, as long as the damned thing shoots straight."

The young man turned to survey the rack of guns behind him. To an inexperienced eye, which included Stella's, they looked virtually identical. Wooden stocks, blued or black steel barrels. Some with engraving on the breech, some with fine chequering on the cheek piece of the stock. He turned back.

"I think given your intended usage, there are two guns in particular that you might like. They're in our store room. Would you mind waiting for a few moments?"

Stella shook her head and made a show of pulling out her phone as he disappeared through the door leading away from the shop. He returned carrying in his left hand a long, flat, rectangular, cardboard carton, held closed by a thin, white plastic strap. This he leant against the rear wall. In his right, he held a shotgun, which he placed on the counter in front of Stella.

"Winchester SX3," he said. "Three-cartridge magazine and a nice compact gun suitable for a lady."

Stella let the opportunity for a put-down go by. Instead, she placed the gun's wooden stock against her shoulder and sighted along the black barrel.

"Easy to shorten it, Stel," other-Stella said from the far side of the counter. Take a hacksaw to the barrel and the stock, you could cut the best part of two feet off it."

"Only three shots," Stella said.

"True, madam, but reloading is a quick and simple affair," the young man said.

"Ask him about the other one."

"What's in the carton?" Stella asked, placing the SX3 on the counter.

"Let me show you."

Using scissors, he cut the strap and slid out from the carton a black plastic case. He flipped off the catches and opened it.

The weapon within was clearly a sister to the SX3, and from the same family as the smart, huntin', shootin' and fishin' weapons nestled together behind the counter. Equally clearly, it belonged to a different branch. Perhaps the one that drove too fast, drank too much and got into fights on Saturday nights. Its action was finished in a bright, metallic red and shouted where the other guns whispered. The stock was a plain satin black, some sort of plastic Stella supposed.

The shop assistant offered the gun to Stella. She took it and brought it up to her shoulder in a smooth movement, sighting along the long, black barrel at a light fixture on the far wall. She lowered it and turned it over in her hands. Pulled the cocking lever back and let it go with a loud *clack*.

"Nice gun," she said.

"Indeed, madam. This is the Winchester SX3 Raniero Testa. Twelve gauge, semi-automatic and with a twelve-round capacity magazine. It's that tube under the barrel."

"Reliable?" she said, musing that this young man seemed as obsessive about guns as Danny was.

"Oh, absolutely," he enthused, warming to his theme. "Obviously, with the Winchester name you can be sure it's developed to the very highest standards and tolerances, as is the SX3. It also holds the world record for rate of fire. I believe it stands at twelve rounds in under a second and a half. You'd be able to wipe out plenty of bunnies without reloading."

"Wouldn't work as a sawn-off," other-Stella said, pointing at the magazine tube.

"But twelve shots without reloading means I could do at least two doors," Stella murmured.

"I'm sorry?" the young man asked, frowning.

Without missing a beat, Stella lowered the gun and placed it on the counter.

"How much?"

"This particular gun is part of our pre-owned selection, madam. It's been thoroughly checked and we have our own seventeen-point verification checklist–"

"How much?"

"Nine hundred and ninety-five."

"I'll take it. Now, a rifle. What do you suggest?"

"For deer? Shooters will be debating the best calibre for deer hunting until we're all long in our graves, madam. Down south," – a momentary pause as if to hint that "south" was a synonym for "soft" – "for roe, a .247 might be enough. But for the full range of British species, especially the reds we have up here, I would recommend something in .308 calibre. We have a very nice Blaser R93 Luxus in stock. It comes as part of our Swarovski package."

"Very bling," Stella drawled.

"Oh, indeed," he said, allowing an indulgent smile to creep across his face. "No gemstones, I'm afraid, madam, but we supply it fitted with a Swarovski Z6i 2.5-15x56 telescopic sight and an A-TEC sound moderator."

The rifle, when it appeared, was fitted with a black webbing sling and a telescopic sight. It looked more conventional than the shotgun, with a polished stock made from a richly grained wood and a dull black, steel barrel tipped with the fat, black tube of the sound modifier. Stella raised it to her shoulder and looked through the scope. Imagined Ramage's head in the crosshairs. Breathed in, then out, waited, finger resting oh-so-gently on the trigger. *No, Judge Ramage. Nothing so clean for you, my boy. We're going to have plenty of time to discuss what's happening. Oh, yes. But this might come in handy if you've got protection with you.* The sounds of the shop faded, to be replaced by birdsong and the *shushing* of wind through trees. Stella was lying in a sniper's nest of soft bracken, knives in a backpack, Glock in the waistband of her jeans, shotgun lying next to her, loaded with the Hatton rounds.

"Madam?" It was the attentive young man, waiting for her verdict on the Blaser. "What do you think?"

Stella lowered the rifle and placed it parallel to the Winchester on the glass counter. Her head was hot under the wig. "How much?"

"The Blaser is five thousand, five hundred, madam." He paused.

"Although I'm sure, as you're buying two guns, we could offer you a better price."

"I'll take them both. And some ammunition." *Not that I need it for the shotgun. That is strictly for tactical entry and I brought my own for that. But let's not draw attention to ourselves.*

"May I suggest Lyalvale Express Pigeon Specials loaded with number six lead shot for the Winchester. It gives a good, humane kill without smashing the carcass." Stella nodded, smiling. She was thinking of smashed carcasses. "And for the Blaser? Let me see. If you were after foxes, I'd suggest Winchester ballistic tipped rounds, but soft points would be more appropriate for deer. Unless you like your venison minced." He coughed out a small laugh. Clearly, he'd made the same joke before. "We stock Federal Power-Shok in .308. One-fifty or one-eighty grain loads. They come in boxes of twenty."

"I think a hundred will be plenty for now. The one-eighties, please."

The young man smiled his pleasant smile again. "Will there be anything else, madam?"

Stella scratched absent-mindedly at the wig and shook her head.

"I think that's everything," she said.

Stella left the shop burdened by the two long guns in their cases: hard-shell, black ABS plastic for the Winchester; a soft green nylon for the Blaser. She also carried a plastic carrier bag bulging with ammunition and a second, even larger bag filled with camouflaged shooting jacket, trousers and cap. She'd paid cash for her purchases, which raised the young man's dark brown eyebrows a millimetre or two, and had refused his offer of membership of their loyalty scheme. *No sense leaving any more of a trail than we have to, eh, Stel?* At an army surplus shop on a side street, she paid more cash for a faded olive-green canvas kitbag capacious enough to hold her materiel.

Back at Braemar, she spread her purchases out on the pink Candlewick bedspread, stroking her fingertips along the polished wooden stock of the Blaser. She flicked the switch on the base of the tiny, white, plastic kettle – "*tea making facilities in all rooms*". While it chuntered and rumbled to the boil, she took out a few other items she'd bought in the town: a slim, aluminium vacuum flask, a dark-green backpack and some energy bars.

She loaded the long guns, wearing another pair of the nitrile gloves. Twelve Hatton rounds slid up into the magazine tube of the Winchester, each requiring slightly more effort as the long spring's increasing compression pushed back against her thumb. Four Federal soft-points clicked home into the Blaser's magazine insert.

While Stella made herself a mug of tea, other-Stella wandered over from the mirror to inspect the weapons.

"Overkill. I like it. You're going to take your time with him, though, aren't you?"

Stella looked over her shoulder. "What do you think?" she said, picking up the Maoui Deba and turning it this way and that, so its razor-sharp edge caught the light from the fringed lampshade overhead.

"How are you going to get to the judge's place from here?"

"Hire car."

"I thought you didn't like driving?"

"Needs must. Besides, I can always let you drive, can't I?"

"Fair enough. And we just won't mention to the nice lady at Avis that you died on April twentieth 1980, will we?" other-Stella said, running a red-varnished fingernail along the zip protecting the new identity documents. "Just one more thing."

"What?"

"The other woman. He said she was English. Knows her way around weapons. Bit of a coincidence, don't you think?"

Stella shrugged. "I'll just have to be careful, won't I?"

CHAPTER THIRTY-TWO
Ready, Aim …

THAT NIGHT, IN Craigmackhan's richly furnished master bedroom, Ramage was mired in the dream again.

He rolls up to the sliding steel doors of the body shop and kills the engine of his Bentley. A regular door has been cut into the massive shutters, and he pushes through, taking care to step high over the sill that tripped him the first time he brought the Bentley in for a service. A sharp edge rips the fabric of his scarlet legal robe and blood drips onto the floor.

Inside, the proprietor, a man he only knows as 'Big Sam', is working on the front axle of a 1951 Bentley Continental when Ramage steps through the door. His son, 'Little Sam', is hand polishing a brand-new model bearing the same name. A radio is playing in the background: Elvis Presley's "Burning Love."

Seeing his customer, the elder Blackbourn lays his wrench carefully on the floor beside the driver's side wheel of the big, gleaming limousine and straightens, easing his back with a few rolling stretches from side to side.

"Good morning, Judge Ramage, sir. Wasn't expecting to see you for a few months. Everything all right with the car?"

"Not as such, Sam. Had a bit of a prang yesterday. Sorted out the other driver, but now I'm left with a nasty scuff on my front offside wing."

"Well then, let's take a look. See what's what, eh?"

The two men step out, single-file, through the narrow door to the outside world. Ramage's robe continues to bleed, though Big Sam is diplomatic enough not to mention the smears and drips spoiling the immaculate floor of his garage.

Big Sam squats in front of the Bentley's front offside wing. He extends his right hand and then, as if inviting an animal to take his scent before advancing further, trails the backs of his fingers up and across the ruined metalwork.

The damage extends back from the headlight for forty centimetres or so. The dark purple paint has been cracked and scraped away, revealing weeping red flesh and shards of bone beneath. Scuffs of silver paint decorate the edges of the wound.

"Nasty," Big Sam says. He strokes the stubble on his chin and turns his gaze on the judge. "Hell of a prang to do that to a Bentley. Other chap all right, was he?"

"Parked car. I left my card. I came off worse, if you can believe it."

Big Sam stares at the dented wing for a few seconds. Pauses. Runs his blackened fingers through his thinning hair. "Job like that? Done properly. Going to have to take it back to the flesh and blend it in."

Ramage purses his lips and folds his arms, trying to avoid looking down where the blood is pooling around his feet. "Which I understand, Big Sam, believe me. But the timescale. Please."

"Setting the bone, sutures, debriding the dead flesh, prepping, base coat, two, maybe three top coats, clear coat … hand-polish. I'm thinking a week Friday. Priority job, obviously. Seeing as how it's you, Judge."

Ramage smiles. It is better than he'd been expecting. "A week Friday is fine, Big Sam. And your fee?"

Big Sam looks Ramage in the eye.

"Two million. Please."

Ramage smiles.

"Our usual arrangement will suffice, I hope," he says, opening his wallet and pulling out a sheaf of black-and-red banknotes with charred edges. "Ten thousand now and the balance on collection?"

Big Sam palms the notes and they disappear into the front pocket of his brown bib overalls.

"Always a pleasure, Judge. Oh," he says, eyes widening, as he looks into the rear of the car. "What do you want me to do about that?"

Ramage gazes past Big Sam's outstretched arm and pointing finger.

A baby sits in a child's car seat, strapped in and looking at him with slitted eyes of fearful intensity. It's a little girl to judge from the pale-pink ribbon tied in a bow on the top of her head.

"You killed my Daddy," she says in a dry, whispery croak that makes the hairs on the back of his neck stand on end. "You killed my Daddy. Then you burned me. I'm too hot. I can't sleep. I want a cuddle."

Black smoke curls from her lips as she speaks and when she coughs, a smoke-ring shoots from her rosebud mouth towards Ramage's face. She stretches her arms out towards him.

Not wanting to, but unable to resist, he reaches out to pick up the baby, noticing as he does so, that small orange flames flicker restlessly on her downy cheeks. But she screams, "You're hurting me!" before bursting into flames that leap the gap between them and ignite his hair.

Ramage awoke, screaming, and batting at his skull.

"Oh, God," he moaned. "How did we get to this?"

*

Stella arrived back at the B&B around noon the following day, behind the wheel of a rented silver Golf. She'd driven it carefully all the way back from Perth, never once exceeding, or even reaching, the speed limit. Even when the sweeping open road through the gorgeous landscape of lakes and yellow-and-purple moorland screamed at her, "open it up".

On the bike, it would have been a different story. She'd have cracked the throttle wide open and torn along the road, taking a racing line around every bend, getting her knee down and shrieking with the sheer unconfined joy of the machine's power and balance. But given her ambivalence about four-wheeled transport, and the fact that secured in the boot was an *intriguing* collection of firearms and other implements, she felt an encounter with the local traffic cops was best avoided.

Inside her room, she changed into the camouflaged shooting gear, packed, and went downstairs.

The landlady did a double-take as she took in Stella's hunting outfit.

"Off shooting, are you, dear?"

"Stalking, yes."

Stella settled the bill with cash, earning a smile.

"Well, good hunting and come again, won't you dear?" her landlady urged her as she left, pressing a hand-tied cellophane bag of homemade shortbread biscuits into her hand.

And then Stella left, pointing the Golf towards Craigmackhan.

Leaving the Golf parked at a picnic area off a narrow country road, Stella shouldered the kit bag and a backpack loaded with a groundsheet, a fleece, a flask of coffee and a dozen energy bars. She consulted her map, then began the two-mile walk through the woodland that bordered Craigmackhan. As she left the picnic area behind her, the birdsong and the soughing of the breeze in the tall fir trees grew louder. The combination of sounds had a calming effect on her nerves, which had been singing like wind through telegraph wires ever since she'd started the car that morning. Somewhere in the distance, she heard occasional deep booms coming in pairs. She'd seen on the map that the Ministry of Defence owned the land to the west of her position and assumed the booms were explosions.

A good day to be testing weaponry, she thought, shifting the weight of the kitbag. Yes, she could have slung the long guns over her shoulders and stuck the Glock in her belt. Hell, she could have wrapped a scarlet bandanna around her forehead and stuck the cleaver between her teeth. But a chance encounter with a couple of birdwatchers or hikers would, she felt, queer her pitch as an avenging angel. They'd smile politely then race for the road and be on the phone to the police in seconds. Mission over.

Pausing by a rotten log, she sat and lowered the heavy kitbag to the ground where it settled with a *scrunch* into the dry bracken. She unscrewed the flask of coffee and poured a cup, washing down a couple of energy bars with the hot, strong brew. The smell of the coffee overlaid a sweetish smell of rot wafting up from the decaying tree trunk. The sun chose that moment to come out, sending bright, golden rods of light splintering through the tree canopy, and mottling the bracken and leaf mould on the ground like a leopard's pelt. She inhaled deeply and rolled her shoulders, letting her head fall back on her neck and staring up through the leaves to the sky beyond.

"What if I just turned back? What if I just sold everything and disappeared?"

"No!" other-Stella snapped. "Not. Going. To happen. We've come this far and we're bloody well going to finish it."

The birds continued singing merrily as the two women discussed the mission. The wind strengthened, and the branches above her head swayed and snapped as gusts swirled through the wood.

Stella knew her ideas of vengeance were unlikely to bring her peace. After the accident, when she'd been living under the mistaken impression that Lola was still with her, she'd visited a grief counsellor. He'd been kind, and listened as she poured out the lurid fantasies of revenge that she was now in the process of enacting. He'd quoted some eastern mystic at her, something about holding onto anger being like gripping a hot coal and expecting it to burn the other person. It made sense. But at that moment, and ever since then, sense hadn't been high on Stella's list of priorities. The shock and grief when she realised she'd lost Lola as well as Richard had taken her last remaining shreds of rationality and burned them to a crisp.

In any case, Stella wasn't out for peace. After dealing with Ramage, she intended to find a quiet spot and join Richard and Lola. They'd be together again. Safe from harm. A family, just like all the other happy families. Mummy, Daddy and Lola. Safe for ever.

"Come on then!" a voice said, right into her ear. "Enough with the 'What iffing'. We're going to kill Ramage. Eventually. On your feet, DI Cole."

Other-Stella extended a hand and pulled Stella to her feet. Helped her lift the kitbag and settle it across her back.

"Thanks."

"Don't mention it."

Stella checked the map again and strode off eastwards, through a stand of Douglas firs and heading for Dracula's castle, chatting amiably to other-Stella about where she'd begin working on Ramage when she had him secured.

*

Lucy Van Houten was already in place. She'd arrived at Craigmackhan five hours earlier and was ensconced in a hide she'd constructed from bracken and fallen tree branches. She caressed the stock of her new rifle, a Sabatti STR chambered for 6.5mm Lapua rounds and equipped with a GECO 2.5-15X56 infrared telescopic sight. She'd brought neither food nor drink. She didn't feel she needed them.

*

Collier called Ramage, sure that by now his attack dog would be in place, watching and waiting.

"Ramage."

"Leonard, it's Adam. We've got a problem. A major problem. She's not dead."

What? You told me it would all be fine. That your man would succeed."

"I know. But somehow, she evaded him. I haven't heard a peep out of him either. Either she did him in and dumped him somewhere or he's gone to ground."

"Never mind that, Adam. Does this mean I have some homicidal detective coming after me?"

"I don't know. Possibly. I'm getting onto traffic next. Getting the ANPR cameras monitored for her bike. I doubt she'll have gone by road, but it's a start. I'll do what I can with rail and air but I have to be careful. She's a serving police officer. I can't go charging around setting up a manhunt without ringing the kinds of alarm bells I'd rather stayed silent."

Ramage sighed. "How did we get to this, Adam?"

"How did we get to what?"

"Murdering innocent civilians and their children, then planning to kill serving police officers?"

"You know how, Leonard. Don't start getting sentimental on me. Not now. The group comes first, never forget that."

"No, you're right, of course you are. Look, I have a couple of chaps up here who work for me. Part-time poachers, full-time ne'er-do-wells. They've helped me out with a couple of tricky situations in the past. I'll haul them up to the house and have them bring their guns. If she shows up here, I'll just have to take care of her myself. Then you can figure out a way to clear up the mess. And I'll repeat this for you, Adam, just in case you've forgotten: I am not going to sit around here waiting to be arrested by a rogue officer with a vigilante complex. And if I am, well, let's just say they'd better build a bigger dock at the Old Bailey, hmm?"

"Don't worry. It won't come to that. Not anywhere near."

*

Stella scraped out a nest in the crunchy, brown bracken on the hillside overlooking Ramage's house. Gordon Wade had been right. The thing was a monstrosity. Gothic windows, a tower, turrets, even a low, crenelated wall around the roof, giving the whole building the air of a fantasy fortress as imagined by a Victorian builder who'd read one too many penny dreadfuls about vampires in *Mitteleuropa*. The stone was dirty grey, mottled with scabs of white and yellow lichen. Ugly, white security bars had been fitted to the insides of the downstairs windows.

Through the Blaser's telescopic sight, she could see the purple Bentley sitting at the front of the house in a circle of pale-gold shingle. It looked as though someone had posed it there for an advertising campaign. She was considering shooting at it when a rough-edged engine note floated up towards her from the road on the other side of the house. She eased her finger away from the trigger and looked over the top of the scope. A Land Rover sporting a harlequin suit of petrol-blue, khaki and primer-red panels pulled round the side of the house and drew up next to the Bentley. Out jumped two men dressed in waxed jackets, corduroys and boots. One went round to the rear door and emerged a second or two later with a pair of what looked like shotguns. Long-barrelled weapons, at any rate. She put her eye back to the scope. Yes. Under-and-over shotguns just like those she'd ignored in Campbell's the day before.

As she watched, the front door – a heavy affair of oak with curved black straps of iron – opened, and out stepped Ramage. He was dressed in a pair of rose-pink trousers, an open-necked shirt and a mustard-coloured cardigan. Stella's breath caught in her throat and she could feel her blood rushing in her ears, the surf-sound swelling and receding in time with the throbbing behind her eyes and in the base of her throat. She sighted on his head, watching the way the cross hairs danced on his face, but they were bobbing up and down as her pulse throbbed in her chest. Besides, a clean kill was the last thing Ramage was going to get.

She observed the three men talking, then Ramage returned to the safety of the house, while his two guards broke open their guns, inserted cartridges into the barrels and then closed them with a double *crack* that reached Stella's ears a split second after she watched the barrels snap shut. The men walked in opposite directions, beginning a circuit of the house.

"How loyal are you to your master?" Stella asked aloud, as she settled herself more comfortably into her sniper nest. "Will I have to kill you too, or will you desert your post at the first sign of danger?"

"Let's find out, shall we?" other-Stella said, lying down beside her.

*

Three hundred yards to the west, embedded in an almost identical nest of vegetation, Lucy Van Houten kept watch on the house. She amused herself by sighting on each window on the side facing her in turn, imagining people appearing as if at a fairground shooting gallery, bobbling left to right, or snapping erect, like tin targets for her to knock down again.

When the two men arrived in their Land Rover, her heartbeat increased by just a fraction. She sighted on their foreheads, in turn, and considered blowing their heads apart like soft fruit, picturing the spray of pink in the air. But Adam had been clear. The detective kills the owner, then Lucy kills the detective. Adam would be angry if she disobeyed his orders. He might not give her any more assignments. She didn't think she could bear that.

*

While Stella waited for the men to reappear at the front of the house, she closed her eyes and let her mind drift back to her six-month rotation with the

Metropolitan Police's firearms squad. Being fast-tracked didn't simply mean a series of promotions and cushy duties. She'd walked the beat with a forty-two-year-old sergeant named Jack Hempstead while he instructed her on the various forms of villainy he'd encountered in his eighteen years of pavement pounding. She'd looked on as private crime scene cleaning firms scraped blood and body parts off floors, walls and, on one memorable night, ceilings. She'd donned waders and elbow-length, red rubber gauntlets and waded through a sewer searching for a shooter that the mid-level drug dealer they'd been chasing had chucked down a drain. So, all in all, she felt she'd earned her place on the fast track and could take the good-natured jibes of her colleagues as she was promoted, first to detective sergeant and then detective inspector at the tender age of twenty-six.

Back then, when she was doing the rounds of all the major commands, armed police were SO19. Since then, the command had undergone another couple of the Met's endless name changes, emerging as SC&O19. Everyone in the job thought the ampersand was fussy and just called it SCO19.

Her firearms instructor was ex-army, like a lot of the firearms officers themselves, although by no means all of them. He'd patiently guided her through the loading, operation and care of handguns, rifles and shotguns. His words on shooting rifles came back to her now, floating down through the intervening years like gun smoke on the outdoor range.

"Breathing's key. In all the way, let it out as you squeeze the trigger to first pressure, wait a single heartbeat, then squeeze off the round."

Stella waited, trying to calm her thoughts and with them, her heart rate, which was still fluttery and fast. Other-Stella lay down next to her and placed a calming hand in between her shoulder blades.

"You heard what he said, Stel," she said. "Breathe. Nice and easy."

While Stella focused on breathing, other-Stella pulled a pair of compact binoculars from her pocket and brought them up to her eyes.

"They're coming back, look."

Stella raised the rifle and looked down at the gravelled circle through the scope. The two guards, or whoever they were – Pro Patria Mori muscle, presumably – were walking towards each other, shotguns resting over their left arms, right hands on the trigger guards. They stopped a foot or two apart and exchanged a few words. Then one leant his gun against the side of the Land Rover and fished a packet of cigarettes and a lighter from his jacket pocket.

"What a kind chap," other-Stella said, "offering his mate a fag. Now would be a good time if you felt like testing their loyalty, you know."

The two men stood close together, blowing clouds of steel-grey smoke into the air above their heads. Talking and laughing.

Stella worked the smooth, straight-pull bolt to chamber a round. She wound the webbing sling around her left hand and adjusted her grip on the wooden fore-end so that the webbing held her arm tight with an enjoyable tension. Using her right thumb, she released the safety catch with a soft click and brought her right eye to the rear end of the scope.

Through the optically perfect lenses, the man appeared to be within arm's reach. She traversed the cross hairs down from his head, through his chest and his stomach, to his right thigh. He was sturdily built, at least fifteen stone, and the broad expanse of sand-coloured corduroy made a reasonable target. *Sorry, mate. But it'll only be a flesh wound. Not like the kind your boss and his friends have been dishing out.*

She began.

Breathe in, all the way.

She checked her aim. The cross hairs were rock-steady.

Let it out, nice and smooth.

She let her index finger curl round the trigger as she held the cross hairs steady on his leg.

Tighten the pressure.

She squeezed the trigger until she felt it resist, ever so slightly: first pressure.

Wait for a beat.

Her heart sent another charge of blood coursing through her arteries.

Fire.

CHAPTER THIRTY-THREE
Fire!

THE REPORT OF the rifle as the bullet hurtled from the muzzle was loud, despite the sound moderator, and the recoil bumped the rubber heel pad hard against Stella's shoulder. A sharp whiff of burnt, smokeless powder caught in her nostrils and made her blink.

*

Deep inside Lucy Van Houten's skull, her limbic system, that primitive organ responsible for modulating risk and reward behaviours, squirted a shot of dopamine into her brain. The neurotransmitter flashed through her system, making her feel good in a way she could never put into words. Gunshots always did that to her, and once, as a teenaged girl, she had actually experienced an orgasm as she shot a new rifle.

She knew her moment was approaching and began checking over her weapon.

*

One hundred yards away from Stella's sniper nest, the soft-point bullet penetrated the man's corduroy trousers, the skin of his leg, the thick layer of creamy yellow fat beneath, the silvery fascia enveloping his quadriceps, and finally the solid meat beyond.

Before he knew what was happening to him, the partial copper jacket that shrouded all but the tip of the bullet peeled back into jagged petals. The force of impact compressed the lead, which spread out in front of the copper petals, quadrupling its original surface area and tumbling through the soft tissue before stopping dead against the femur.

The man fell sideways, his mouth stretched open in an 'O', his eyes wide with pain and fear. Stella heard his cries, though the fractional time delay between his mouth moving and the sound waves reaching her ear drums lent them a comical air as she watched through the scope. The trouser leg was turning from beige to red as he lay, writhing, on the ground, hands clamped over the wound.

"Not turning red very fast, though, Stel. You missed the femoral artery, whether you meant to or not," other-Stella observed.

His associate was scrambling to help him whilst looking frantically all around for the shooter attacking them. He drew a piece of fabric from his pocket – it looked like a handkerchief – and pressed it against the entry wound, bringing another scream from the wounded man.

Ramage appeared at the front door. Seeing the pair of guards, he ran over, which was, in the circumstances, an unwise move, and stood over them. The second man and he exchanged a few words. Then Ramage pointed at him, shouting. The man replied, waving his hand wildly in Stella's direction, then pointing down at his friend and then at the Land Rover. Stella couldn't hear the words themselves, but their meaning was clear enough.

I paid you. You're staying.

Not enough. We're going.

*

Lucy watched with mild interest as the three men argued. It had been a good shot, and she was impressed by the other woman's marksmanship. She recognised the silver-haired man now, and wondered whether the detective would kill him now or go in close to do it personally.

*

Ramage laid a restraining hand on the unwounded man's right arm as he was bending to help his friend. He shook it free and pushed Ramage hard in the chest, sending him staggering back. Ramage turned and ran back into the house. Moments later, the men were inside the Land Rover and it was slewing around on the gravel, its rough-treaded tyres gouging four dark-brown curves through to the earth beneath, before roaring off back the way it had come and, Stella assumed, to hospital. The cover story would be easy enough to imagine. A stray bullet from a hunter while they were hiking.

Stella pulled the bolt back to eject the brass casing. It leapt from the action with a metallic *ping*. She'd worked enough crime scenes, read enough ballistics reports, hell, she'd read enough thrillers, to know that professionals never left their brass behind. She followed the twinkling, golden, metal cylinder as it flipped into the bracken, but as she moved to start searching for it, other-Stella offered her a piece of advice.

"Leave it. It doesn't matter. The gun's registered to a dead kid from the seventies. The brass won't tell them anything."

"Fair enough. Let's get down there."

*

Ramage had probably locked and bolted the heavy front door from the inside. Stella knew she would have done exactly same, faced with the imminent arrival of an armed intruder. Wanting to be as unencumbered as possible, she laid the Blaser in the bracken, bent some dry stalks over it, then walked down to the house with the shotgun in her hand.

The front door had two locks about a foot apart. One, a standard five-lever mortice, the other a more expensive Ingersoll. Tough for an opportunist thief to deal with, not so much for a determined police officer armed with a door-breaching shotgun.

She aimed at the Ingersoll first, keeping the Winchester's muzzle a couple of inches back from the steel, and pulled the trigger. *Bang.* The recoil wasn't too bad. Just a hard shove into her right shoulder. Then the mortice. *Bang.* Then she loosed off four more of the Hatton rounds to take out the hinges and any frame bolts locking the door into the frame.

Bang.

Bang.

Bang.

Bang.

The semi-automatic action worked sweetly, propelling a new round into the chamber with each shot fired. Maybe five seconds had elapsed. Not exactly world record-breaking, but it did the job. Each of the Hatton rounds blew a six-inch diameter hole in the timber, showering Stella with chips of burnt wood that smelled of bonfires.

She leaned back and kicked the door at waist height. The massive slab of oak fell away from her, slamming onto a stone-tiled hallway with a crash, softened only marginally by the fast-escaping cushion of air pushed down and away by the two square metres of oak planking.

"Ramage!" she yelled, stepping over the fallen door and onto the hall's polished herringbone parquet floor.

No reply, but then she hadn't really been expecting one.

"Sir Leonard?" she called again, this time in a singsong voice as if they were engaged in an adults-only game of hide-and-seek. One where the loser was likely to end up with his brains splattered over the ceiling. "Remember me? It's Stephanie Black here. Only I'm back to Stella Cole now. Well, technically I'm Jennifer Stadden, but it's me anyway. You murdered my family. With your car. Now I've come for you."

Striding around the ground floor, she pushed the doors of each room she came to with the muzzle of the Winchester. They were opulently furnished with huge, deep-red Turkish carpets on which stood sideboards, bookcases and chairs carved from richly figured woods in shades of dark chocolate-brown, a dark red that could only be mahogany, and golden honey. Buttoned leather sofas in cherry-red and bottle-green faced each other in front of huge stone fireplaces filled with dry logs, or, in one room, a vast arrangement of dried flowers including great swags of the local purple heather. Standing like a forgotten sentry at the foot of the stairs was a suit of armour complete with seven-foot-long pikestaff.

The house smelled of furniture polish, a strong, sickly perfume; she wondered how Ramage could bear it. After completing a search of the ground floor, she concluded he must have run for the top floor. Hell, there might even be an attic. The stairway beckoned. It rose from the centre of the hall, directly opposite the now-ruined front door. The architect had designed it so that it appeared to rise, unsupported, to the first floor. There were no cupboards behind it, just a couple of narrow wooden columns.

First, she adjusted the Glock; it was digging into the flesh at the small of her back. Gripping the Winchester in one hand, she began to climb, pausing on each step as she scanned the upper hallway, which ran in a square above the hall below. The stairs were well made – silent – so it was easy to listen for movement on the next floor. Then, on her seventh step, the tread beneath her foot emitted a loud squeak. She flinched and swore. She waited longer this time but heard nothing, and continued.

At the top of the stairs, she pulled out the Glock. Leaning the Winchester against a bureau for a second or two, she racked the pistol's slide then continued, one weapon in each hand in the gloom at the end of the hall. Her breathing was fast and shallow and she was tensed, ready to shoot if Ramage should show so much as a whisker in the crack of a bedroom door. She wasn't scared. The feeling was more of a heightened sense of readiness, a lioness closing in on a kill.

She stopped at the first door on the right. Stuck the Glock into her waistband, at the front this time. Twisted the brass knob while standing to one side so her body was protected from any outbound fire by the wall. No shot came, so she plucked the Glock out and, holding it level with her eyeline, pushed the door open with her foot.

Still nothing, so she went in at a crouch, pistol aimed upwards, shotgun at a matching angle. The room was a bedroom. Not the master bedroom, to judge by the plainly dressed double bed and serviceable but unmemorable wooden furniture standing around the edge of the room. Stella scanned the four walls. No more doors, no en suite bathroom where a cornered householder might be waiting with a weapon of his own.

She retreated and walked on another eight feet to a second door. She repeated the process with the knob and the tactical entry. Another guest bedroom. Another *empty* guest bedroom.

At the third door, she sighed and reached for the knob. Another brass sphere, this one engraved with three concentric circles around its waist.

Already imagining the empty room beyond, Stella twisted and pushed the ball of cold metal, shifting her weight forward as she did so to make a fast entry into the room beyond the door.

Her forehead banged into the unmoving door with a soft *clonk*.

The door was locked.

She backed up, stuck the Glock away and raised the Winchester to her hip, pointing it at the lock.

"Are you in there, Ramage?" she shouted. "Is this your hidey-hole?"

The Winchester roared.

The Hatton round punched a fist-sized hole in the door's midline that took out the lock.

Silver-grey smoke curled out of the shotgun's muzzle. The air was full of the sharp smell of gunpowder, mixed with the sweet, sawdust smell of freshly exposed wood. But of Ramage there was no sign. No fusillade of shots peppering the inside of the door. No screams for mercy. No breaking glass as he jumped through the first-floor window.

Faster than the previous time, Stella blasted away at the hinges and corresponding sites high and low on the lock side of the door. Her ears rang with the explosions, and her nose itched as the tang of the burnt propellant irritated its soft lining.

This door fell inwards on its own with a deep *whuff* onto a thick jade-green and rose-pink Chinese carpet.

And there
(you)
he
(murdered)
stood
(my family.)

In the centre of the carpet, clutching a shotgun and fumbling two shells into the barrels, was the man who had destroyed Stella Cole's family, and with them, her sanity.

A faint whisper made her pause for a second. *Are we the same as them now, Stella?* She shook her head. "They made me like this," she whispered.

She brought the Glock up and shot him in the right bicep.

Blood spurted out of the wound as the hollow point slammed home.

Ramage screamed and dropped the shotgun, clamping his left hand over his injured arm.

"That worked well. Let's do the other arm as well," other-Stella said with a smile. "And forget about the cases. You loaded it with gloves on, didn't you?"

The flat crack of the Glock smacked out again and Ramage's other arm sprayed blood back against the wall. He was retreating now, eyes wide with pain and shock. His white shirt sleeves were soaking with blood, but there didn't seem to be any actual *fountains* of blood, so the brachial arteries were obviously intact. That was good, because Stella didn't feel like giving this … this *creature* first aid.

*

Lucy had been waiting patiently for some time now. She'd listened to the shotgun blasting away at the front door and then an internal door. Felt herself becoming aroused at the thought of what was about to happen.

She watched through the scope as the detective aimed the Glock at the silver-haired man. Slowed her breathing. And centred the cross-hairs on the woman's left temple, just as she had with the tart.

The woman fired twice. Not a double-tap. Too slow. Probably one to the body and a coup de grâce to the head.

Lucy readied herself for her own shot.

*

Ramage's back made contact with the dark wooden panelling behind him and he stood, legs trembling, his arms limp at his sides, blood dripping from his fingertips and pooling on the carpet.

"You can't just kill me," he said, panting as the adrenaline constricted his chest muscles. "You're a police officer. You'll go to jail. Kiss your job goodbye, and your police pension too."

"You're a High Court judge. It didn't stop you, did it?" Stella retorted, pointing the Glock's smoking muzzle at his face.

"That was an accident!" he squealed.

"Then why didn't you report it? Why did you set up that half-wit Edwin Deacon to take the fall for you?"

"I was frightened," he blurted through bloodless lips. "The media would have had a field day. You know what those jackals are like."

"Yes. I do. In fact, I'm friends with one of them. Someone sent her a nasty message, wrapped round a brick. That wouldn't have been one of your little chums, would it? One of your," *here it comes, Stel, get your comic timing right,* "Pro Patria Mori friends, warning her off?"

Ramage's face had already taken on a deathly pallor, but she could have sworn it paled still further. He blinked rapidly.

"Wh-what do you mean, Pro Pat–"

"Oh, for fuck's sake, *Sir* Leonard. Don't insult my intelligence. I know about your little crew of vigilantes. How do you think the media'll like *that* story?"

*

Lucy took up first pressure on the trigger.

*

"Fine," he said and she saw him try to raise his arms in a placatory gesture. His palms opened up, but the arms swung uselessly at his sides and he yelped with pain. Blood dripped more freely off his fingertips onto the carpet. "But then, if you know what we do, what we stand for, surely you can understand that we're doing good. We're actually helping you."

Stella heard a *snap* inside her head, an electric shock in her brain. She shot him again, this time in the right knee. The brass cartridge case bounced off a Tiffany shade on a table lamp – *plink* – and skittered away underneath a nearby roll-top desk.

Ramage screamed again and collapsed sideways, banging his head on the corner of the desk as he went down. He ended up in an untidy heap, slumped sideways and folded at the waist, with his neck bent where his head rested against the side of the desk. His trouser leg had exploded outwards at the knee when the hollow point round hit the patella, smashing it and the ligaments and joint beyond. Fresh blood blossomed through the ridges of the fabric, turning the colour from rose to an angry red that, were it a sunrise, would herald the worst kind of day for shepherds.

*

Lucy kept both eyes open, despite the scope. She was enjoying managing the images of the two differently-sized women. The tiny one in her left eye and the large one, so close Lucy could reach out and touch her, in the right.

*

A triangular cut had opened on Ramage's right temple. It was bleeding freely: a delta of scarlet streams running down his cheek, along his jawbone, over his neck and into the collar of his shirt.

"Such a lot of claret, Stel. Careful. We don't want him bleeding out before we're done with him, do we?"

Stella turned to other-Stella. "He won't bleed out. They're bad, but they're not going to kill him."

Ramage gaped. "Who are you talking to?"

"Me? Nobody."

"But you, you were just talking to somebody. Are you wired up, is that it?"

Stella bestowed a pitying smile on Ramage, much as one would if speaking to a particularly stupid child.

"This isn't official business, Sir Leonard. I didn't do all of this just to arrest you, you stupid prick. Have you forgotten? You killed my husband. You murdered him. And my poor baby too. Lola, her name was. Did you even know that? She was five months old when you killed her. Do you know how she died?"

*

"Any moment now," Lucy whispered, squeezing the trigger a little more with each passing second.

*

Ramage shook his head. He did know, though. How could he not have known? He'd read the papers. He'd even arranged to read the pathologist's report, though it had started the nightmares where the burnt and bleeding baby clamoured for him to hold her, and his fingers popped through the crackling, blackened flesh like so much bubble wrap.

"I think he does," other-Stella said. "I think he knows *exactly* how she died."

"So do I," Stella said. She turned to Ramage whose eyelids were fluttering. "She was strapped into her car seat. The petrol tank ignited. Richard died instantly. But my Lola … you burned her alive!"

*

Now. Lucy squeezed off the shot. The rifle jerked back into her shoulder, and the explosion echoed off the stone wall of the house with a double *crack*.

*

Stella lunged violently towards Ramage and shoved the barrel of the Glock hard against his mouth, splitting his lower lip and smashing a couple of his lower incisors. "She burnt to death, you fuck!" she screamed into his face.

At the same moment in time, Lucy Van Houten's .308 calibre, copper-jacketed Winchester round burst through the window, showering Stella's back with fragments of glass. The space where her head had been was penetrated by the copper-jacketed bullet, which flashed through the Stella-shaped absence and buried itself in the wall opposite.

Aware of, yet unable to process, the explosion of sound and stinging specks of shattered glass, Stella continued across the short gap between her and Ramage and hit him hard across the side of the head with the Glock. Ramage's head lolled forward as consciousness deserted him.

Now she turned. Now she registered the broken window, and the twinkling fragments of glass and scraps of lead on the carpet.

The other Englishwoman! She must be here. A PPM shooter sent to silence me.

Stella used thick cable ties to bind Ramage's wrists together around a pipe beneath a huge cast-iron radiator.

"Stay there," she whispered. "I'm not done with you yet."

*

"Shit!" Lucy Van Houten said. "I missed. I never miss."

She stood and brushed the leaves and bracken fragments off her tactical outfit, then started walking towards the house.

CHAPTER THIRTY-FOUR
Hunter/Hunted

STELLA DROPPED TO her belly and crawled away from Ramage. She kept her hands off the glass-strewn carpet, using her elbows, knees and feet to propel herself to the doorway. Once she reached the fallen door, she got to her hands and knees, covered the last six feet in a second or two and was out into the hallway. She darted along to the neighbouring room and went in. It was a guestroom, though clearly unused for many years, as the furniture was covered with sheets, giving the room an air of being occupied by ghosts. The floor-length, plum-coloured velvet curtains were drawn. She crossed the room in a handful of long strides, knelt by the window, and inched back the right-hand curtain from the side, rather than the centre.

Peering out through the narrow slit she'd created, she saw the shooter approaching the house. It was a woman, five-six maybe, and stocky. Blonde hair tucked under a black baseball cap with POLICE stencilled across the front in white. *Fuck, Stel. They've sent the Cowboys and Indians after us.*

"Let's not jump to conclusions," other-Stella said. "It looks like a single cowboy. Oh wait, it's a cowgirl. Not very pretty is she?"

The face under the baseball cap was pale, even under the shadow cast by the long peak. *Slabby* was the word that sprang into Stella's mind. The details weren't clear, but she could see wide, flat cheeks and a thick nose. Mouth a straight, lipless line. She was wearing full tactical gear that bulked her frame out still further. And in her right hand, she carried a long gun with a telescopic sight. It looked very like the Blaser Stella had left behind in the woods. But she was swinging it by her side as she walked, and her gait was relaxed, almost as if she were a weekend guest admiring Craigmackhan's grounds.

She thinks she hit me!

"Looks like it. Which means we have the element of surprise," other-Stella mused from beside her. "We could just wait by the front door and do her as she comes in."

"No!" Stella said sharply. "Not a cop."

"She tried to kill you."

"I don't care. She's probably under orders from PPM."

Stella drew the curtain back into place, sat cross-legged on the floor and stared upwards, racing to find the best option. Or the least worst option.

Go outside and confront her.

"She's a trained markswoman with a rifle. A long-range gun. You're a lucky shot with a Glock and a shotgun loaded with breaching rounds. Two short-range guns. No cover, no advantage to you. She'll kill you from fifty yards out, no bother."

Stay here and wait for her.

"Better. Now her gun is less useful compared to yours. And you have the element of surprise. She thinks you're dead, remember."

Stella jumped to her feet. She had a plan. Wait here in the room next door, then come up behind the SCO19 woman when she checks for bodies, force her to disarm, then cuff or cable-tie her and continue with Ramage as before.

Pulse throbbing uncomfortably in her throat, Stella crouched beside the bed and checked the magazine of the Glock. She had no idea how many times she'd fired. *Plenty of bullets left – good.* With the magazine out, she racked the slide to eject the live round in the chamber and worked it a couple of times more. *Smooth as silk. Also good.* She slotted the ejected round into the top of the magazine and reassembled the gun. The Winchester was less useful, she knew. Plus, as she totted up the shots fired, six at the front door, then five for Ramage's hidey-hole, she realised it only contained one round. She considered dumping it on the bed, but other-Stella wasn't happy.

"Keep it. It's still firepower. And it looks threatening too."

Stella waited.

She started as she heard heavy boots crunch on the gravel below the window.

Just as she was readying herself to move, a faint cry came from the other bedroom. A man's voice. Ramage's voice.

"Help!"

Shit! He's coming round.

This changed everything. He could warn the cop.

In a flash, Stella saw salvation.

Grabbing the Winchester, she sprinted from the room and ran down the stairs, taking them three at a time, stumbling at the bottom and almost sprawling to the floor.

From above she heard Ramage's voice, stronger this time.

"Help me! I'm up here. Please. For the love of God, somebody help me!"

Grabbing the newel post, she swerved round the final curving flourish of the handrail and skidded to a stop beneath the staircase. Checking her weapons, she looked back, trying to breathe silently even as her lungs screamed for more oxygen. She couldn't see the front door; she was completely hidden by the wide wooden treads. She looked up. On their underside, the treads were sanded and polished but left unpainted. The reddish-brown timber looked recently waxed: it glowed with a dull sheen.

The crunching of boots grew louder, and in a few seconds, Stella heard the sound of their heavy-cleated soles walk across the fallen front door and stop on the flagstones.

A quartet of hard metallic sounds grouped into two closely-spaced pairs came next. *Click-clack, clack-click.* A rifle bolt being worked back and forth.

Then the footsteps approached the foot of the stairs.

Ramage called again.

"Up here! Help! She's armed. Be careful. Oh, thank God!"

Slowly, Stella knelt on one knee, raised the Winchester to her shoulder, and placed the muzzle against the underside of the seventh tread. She curled her finger around the trigger, and waited.

The shooter began to ascend. Stella listened to the heavy steps.

Clump.

Clump.

Clump.

"Such tight, solid joints, eh, Stel?" other-Stella whispered.

Clump.

Clump.

"Tighten that finger."

Clump.

Creak.

Stella pulled the trigger.

In the confined space beneath the stairs, the roar as the Winchester discharged its final Hatton round was deafening.

Through the fog of gun smoke, Stella looked up. The final Hatton round had blasted a four-inch circle through the seventh tread.

With particles of burnt propellant stinging her nose she scrambled out.

As she did, the other cop's screams suddenly became audible through the ringing in her ears.

The woman was lying on her back at the bottom of the stairs. Stella ran to her, stopping to pick up the rifle and sling it out through the front door.

The woman was white-faced with shock and struggling to reach her right foot.

Or what was left of it.

The front portion of the right boot was missing altogether. Emerging from the remaining black leather were shreds and tatters of flesh, with broken and splintered bones poking through the mess. A lot of blood too, but Stella knew there were no major arteries down there. This was a serious injury, but not fatal.

"On your front!" she said.

The woman's eyes were rolling in her skull like a cow about to be slaughtered. "You shot my foot off!"

"Yes, I did. And I could have killed you. Like you tried to do me. Turn over or I'll shoot you where you lie."

The woman complied, grunting with the effort and the agony she must undoubtedly be feeling.

Stella pulled the handcuffs free from the woman's belt and cuffed her wrists behind her back. Then she rolled her over again onto her back.

"Don't move," she commanded her. She ran to the tall window to the left of the front door and ripped away the twisted silk tie-back from the curtain. She returned to the supine form of the injured cop and wound the cord around her calf before yanking it tight and tying it off. "Right," she said. "You're not going to bleed out. Tell me. Who sent you?"

"Fuck you!"

"*Not* very polite," other-Stella said. "We'll give her a little encouragement."

Stella prodded the woman's ruined foot with the tip of her index finger, eliciting a scream. She asked the same question again.

"I said, tell me who sent you. Do it now or I'll shoot the other one off."

The woman looked up at her, eyes screwed into slits as she fought what must be agonising pain.

"And I said, fuck ..." A groan. "You."

"We'd better get on with it then," other-Stella said. "You could do her with her own rifle. That would be ironic."

"No! She's a cop. I'm not going down that road."

Other-Stella shrugged. "Suit yourself. What are you going to do, then?"

Stella didn't answer. Instead, she ripped open the Velcro of the woman's jacket and began searching for ID, a wallet, a phone, a notebook – anything that could give her a clue as to what was happening.

She found the first two in seconds.

She opened the ID.

"Lucy Van Houten. Metropolitan Police, SC&O19." She looked down at the woman, who appeared to be sliding in and out of consciousness. "Bit far from home, aren't you?"

The woman hissed through clamped teeth but said nothing.

Stella opened the wallet. It was a roll-fold of tough, black nylon, closed with more Velcro. Ignoring the notes and credit cards, she riffled through the bits of paper. They were mostly receipts, including one from Campbell's in Pitlochry, but then she saw a folded piece of shiny paper with colour print. It looked like something torn from a magazine. She unfolded the square. It was covered on one side with black type, from an article about diversity in London policing. She recognised the formatting – it was from *The Job*, the Met's own magazine. When she turned it over, she gasped. Smiling out at her in full dress uniform was Adam Collier, his white teeth bright in the badly lit photo. Scrawled in the white border, in rounded handwriting, were two words:

Lucy Collier.

"School-girl crush, do you think?" said that sardonic voice in her ear. "Looks like Collier's got his own private little death squad."

"No! It doesn't have to mean that. OK, she's got the hots for The Model. She wouldn't be the first."

"Come on, Stel! Do you really believe that a Met firearms officer just happened to be up here on holiday when she decided to stake out Ramage's house and attempt to murder you? A Met firearms officer who's clearly in love with the SIO from Richard's case? Who is your boss. Who sent you down to the exhibits room to rot. Remember what they taught us at Hendon? There's no such thing as coincidence."

"It's not proof. Not definitive. I can't deal with this now."

Stella shook her head then swivelled Van Houten around and dragged her over to the stair case. She unlocked the handcuffs, threaded the freed hands between two of the balusters and then cuffed them again.

The wound was still bleeding, but the blood was pooling, not pumping. Stella looked around and spotted a leather ottoman in a corner of the room. She pulled the squat, red, padded cylinder over and lifted the right leg, placing the calf down on the buttoned top.

"You'll survive," she said, with a sigh. "There'll be blue lights converging on this place well before you need an undertaker."

She stood and climbed the stairs, avoiding the ruined seventh step.

CHAPTER THIRTY-FIVE
Ramage

INERT HUMAN FORMS are notoriously hard to manoeuvre. Stella had had plenty of experience. The occasional drunk, back when she was pounding the beat with Jack Hempstead as a wet-behind-the-ears detective-in-training, albeit one with a first-class honours degree in psychology from the University of Bath. Victims of muggings, ditto. And then, the kind of victims who stayed inert. Once the CSIs had done their job and collected their evidence and the pathologist had had a good look and a poke around, sticking her thermometer where no decent citizen would want it stuck, Stella had been assigned to help lift the dead into sturdy black plastic body bags and then lift them onto stretchers.

When she reached the bedroom where she'd left Ramage, she realised she was going to have to do it again. His cries for help having had no effect on his situation, he'd clearly run out of energy. His head lolled forward onto his chest, and when she checked for a pulse, which she found, he didn't twitch. Dragging Ramage out of the makeshift panic room, down the stairs and onto the drive took all her strength. She cut the cable ties binding him. Then she hooked her hands under his armpits and locked her fingers together over his breastbone. Pushing up from her knees and leaning back, she hauled his deadweight up, then began the hard work.

Halfway down the stairs, Ramage's left heel caught on the broken step. Stella swore and jerked him backwards to free his shoe from the splintered timber, then bumped him the remaining six steps to the ground floor.

Halfway to the front door, she heard Van Houten groan.

"You won't get away with it. We'll find you."

Stella lowered the judge to the floor and walked back to the cuffed firearms officer.

"Who'll find me? You and Adam Collier? You know he's married, don't you? And I don't think he'd see much to get excited about in you, by the way. Have you seen his wife? Slim and brunette, that's Adam's type."

The woman's face twisted, her teeth baring in a snarl, but whether it was of rage or pain, Stella couldn't tell.

"You're dead," she whispered.

"No. But *he* will be, very soon," Stella said, jerking her thumb over her shoulder.

Almost falling backwards on the gravel, Stella kept her balance and dumped Ramage by the rear wing of the Bentley. Her lip curled upwards in a feral snarl of hatred and disgust, partly from the wet iron smell of the blood, but mostly because she couldn't bear to touch him. The catastrophic knee wound had left a five-inch wide smear of blood along the polished herringbone parquet floor and a pool when she'd stopped to talk to Van Houten. The ruined biceps had soaked her own sleeves with the judge's blood. The rifle she'd taken from Van Houten lay with its barrel poking into a large rosebush growing out of the gravel. She decided to leave it there for the local cops to find. Van Houten would have some explaining to do when they found the bullet in the wall of Ramage's guest room.

On the way out, she'd noticed a key cupboard screwed to the wall by the front door above a circular wooden table with a few letters on it, waiting to be posted. She went there now and opened the dinky double doors. Hanging dead-centre was a chunky black-plastic-and-chrome key fob. It bore a chrome winged 'B'. She plucked it from the L-shaped brass hook and returned to the car, thumbing the door-unlock button as she went.

The door was surprisingly easy to pull open. Clever engineering, she supposed.

"Well, we can't have – what did that helpful sales guy at Bentley HQ call them, 'enthusiasts of the marque', was it? – struggling with a hundredweight of steel and glass and all those shopping bags, now can we?"

She turned to other-Stella. "Could you maybe give me a hand with him, instead of just standing there looking all self-satisfied. Please?"

After much grunting, pushing, shoving and twisting of recalcitrant limbs, Stella stood back, wiping the sweat from her forehead with a bloody sleeve. Ramage was sitting – *all right, lolling* – in the rear passenger-side seat. She folded his arms across his chest, leaned over him, and pulled the seat belt out and around his arms and torso, securing it in the latch with another of those damned muted clicks. An extra-long, black plastic cable tie secured his wrists together. For good measure, she reached down into her rucksack, retrieved the bolt cutters and crimped the chromed seatbelt latch with a crunching sound that suggested it would never release the judge.

The bullet wounds looked messy close up. The blood was still wet on Ramage's clothing, suggesting that even if she'd missed clipping an artery, the hollow point rounds had damaged plenty of blood vessels beyond repair.

She backed out, seized with a sudden desire to wound the huge car. She pulled out the awl from her rucksack and wandered round the Bentley, dragging its sharp point up and down its glassy flanks, and over the bonnet and boot, raking off chips of paint with a metallic squeal. They stuck to her hand like fish scales.

While she waited for Ramage to regain consciousness, Stella toyed with the pliers and the pair of razor sharp I.O. Shen knives she'd brought with her. He was powerless now and hers to do with what she wished. But the idea of torturing him had lost much of its savour.

Ten minutes later, Ramage's eyelids fluttered, then opened, revealing those dark-brown eyes that had looked at her so scornfully the day she'd tackled him in his private chambers at the Old Bailey. Stella enjoyed seeing them widen and stretch as they registered the sight of her sitting cross-legged on the gravel by the open passenger door. She watched as he took in the rifle and shotgun at her feet, the Glock in her lap and the knives she held loosely in her hands.

He wriggled inside the grip of the seatbelt then groaned, squeezing his eyes shut against the pain he must have felt as the webbing belt tightened against his ruined arm muscles. His face was pale, the lips colourless.

"Where's your phone, Sir Leonard?" Stella asked.

"My what? Phone? Why?" he muttered.

"Is it in your trouser pocket?"

His eyes flicked down to his right hip pocket. "Why should I tell you?"

She jumped to her feet, causing Ramage to flinch, and poked the point of the Maoui Deba into the corduroy above his ruined right knee. In a single flowing movement, she slid the blade up towards his hip, slitting the fabric as if it were wet tissue paper. As the pocket peeled back, a phone tumbled free and fell onto the seat beside him.

Stella pouted as she took in the lock-screen. "Oh, Sir Leonard, you coded it. Well, a quick scan at the grease marks on the glass and I'll soon work out which numbers to play with."

He smirked. It was probably involuntary, but Stella caught the expression all the same.

She paused. "You didn't code it?" She touched the tip of her nose. Then she looked at the phone again. "But someone as sensible as you, as *security conscious* as you, wouldn't leave his phone unprotected, would he? That would be silly. So, it must be biometrically protected. What did you use? Retinas. Will I have to twirl my little friend here round and round in your eye sockets to remove your eyes, then?" Again, that involuntary twitch of the lips. "Ah! No, just a simple fingerprint for you, Sir Leonard. Well," she said briskly, putting down the knife and picking up the bolt cutters, "we'd better get to work, then."

He flinched and struggled against the seat belt, but that was the full extent his bonds would allow his fight-or-flight reflex to carry him.

Stella readied the bolt cutters, gently sliding their short, hard, sharp jaws down to the base of Ramage's right index finger, ignoring his pleading.

CHAPTER THIRTY-SIX
A Mother's Love

RAMAGE'S SCREAM BOUNCED off the stone front of his house.

With the lifeless digit grasped between her own thumb and forefinger, Stella dabbed its tip onto the surface of the phone.

"Success!" she said, bestowing a wide smile on Ramage, who was moaning with pain. "At least we won't have to take any more off. Now, let's see. First, let's disable the security, then we'll find your contacts. Where are they?" She tapped and scrolled, *hmm*-ing as she did so, her eyes scanning the screen for a set of initials. "Aha! That wasn't very difficult. You must have been feeling very confident when you created this little group."

The screen displayed a group called PPM. Stella tapped the 'notes' tab and a set of names and numbers appeared. Her eyes flicked up and down the screen. Then her mouth tightened. Adam Collier's name was blaring at her from the screen as if written in bright, flaming capital letters eight feet tall.

"Told you so," other-Stella said.

"They'll come for you, you know," Ramage said in a hoarse voice, though still finding the energy from somewhere to sneer at Stella. "Kill me and I guarantee it. If you let me go, I'll see no harm comes to you. I can do that, you know. I have the authority. I promise."

"It's a tempting offer, Stel" other-Stella said, with a wink. "Let this bastard go and he *promises* to see we live out our lives in peace."

"You're right! We *should* let him go. Oh, wait. No, we shouldn't." Stella scowled at Ramage. "Here's the thing, Judge. I actually don't care whether your friends come for me or not. Maybe I'll invite them myself and sit at an upstairs window with the rifle. Pick them off as they arrive."

Ramage tried again, his voice thickened by pain and raspy as he dragged air into his lungs.

"Listen to me, Stella, isn't it? Your career is over. Your life doesn't have to be. Let me go, and I'll give you enough cash to disappear. There's a safe in my office, where you found me. I've gold, cash, stock certificates and my wife's jewellery in there. It's yours. All of it. Please. I'll give you an hour's start. A day's start."

He was shaking violently now, whether from shock, blood loss or stark naked terror, Stella neither knew nor cared. She felt calm and at peace. No nerves. No fear. She hefted the cleaver in her right hand.

"What did you think about on your drive home?" she asked.

"My what?"

"Your drive home. After you left my husband's body and my baby daughter burning in the car. What did you think about?"

"I don't know what I was thinking about," he wheezed. "How can I remember? You shot me, you crazy bitch. I feel sick. I feel faint. You have to let me go."

He struggled against the seatbelt, but only succeeded in tightening the last few inches of slack against the inertia reel mechanism. He was panting, and the colour had drained from his face after returning, briefly, during the off-kilter conversation.

Stella leaned down and slapped him with her free hand.

"Don't faint on me, Judge. If you do, I'll kill you where you sit."

Ramage shook his head. Stella could see him making an effort to focus, although his eyes were sliding to one side every few seconds.

"Not long to go now, Stel," other-Stella said.

She reached down and slit the cable tie with the cleaver. Ramage pulled his arms free from the seat belt, yelping with pain from the bullet wounds in his upper arms. He lunged for the seatbelt latch and thumbed the square red button repeatedly, tugging on the seatbelt as he did so. Nothing happened, and he swore as he noticed the ruined mechanism that trapped the belt's steel tab in the latch.

Stella watched him, then she spoke. At least, she heard herself speak. But the voice didn't sound like hers. It was colder, harder. It was more like other-Stella.

"Take these."

She proffered the pliers she'd retrieved from the rucksack while Ramage struggled with the seatbelt. He looked first at the pliers with their red and yellow rubber grips, then the latch, then up at Stella.

"They're no good for this. You smashed it."

"They're not for the latch."

"Then what *are* they for? What are you going to do?"

"Me? Nothing. But you are. I want you to pull one of your front teeth out. Do it and I'll let you go."

Ramage's face suddenly suffused with blood, turning his pale cheeks a dark cherry red. "You're out of your mind! I won't do it."

Then he screamed as Stella smashed the cleaver down onto his left knee. It stuck in the complex web of tendons, ligaments and bones surrounding the joint, handle upwards, as if a careless butcher had abandoned a cutting job and wandered away from his block.

She took a couple of paces back and picked up the empty Winchester. Turning, she pointed the muzzle at Ramage's stomach.

"It's loaded with Hatton rounds, Judge. They're what we use to blow the hinges off doors when we're busting drug dealers and burglars. There won't be a great deal of your midsection left if I pull the trigger. But you might survive for a few minutes before you bleed to death. Or the shock might kill you, I suppose. You won't make a very pretty corpse, is what I'm trying to tell you. And getting there will be extremely painful. I once found a guy in the back room of a club who'd taken a round from a sawn-off in the guts. God, he was making a racket. But then, he had a hole in his stomach you could reach through without touching the sides, so I supposed he was well within his rights. So, what's it to be? DIY dentistry or a hollow feeling inside? I'll give you three seconds. One, two—"

"No!" Ramage screamed. "Give me the pliers."

"I beg your pardon?"

"I said, give me the pliers."

"Give me the pliers–?"

Ramage was crying now. "Please, you sadistic bitch, give me the fucking pliers. I'll do it, then let me out and you can go. Take the money, whatever you want from me. Just let me live."

Stella held the pliers out again, handles towards Ramage. She could see two right hands wrapped round the red-and-yellow grips. "Fine. An eye for an eye and a tooth for a tooth. Do it, and I'll let you go. I promise."

He extended a shaking hand and took them from Stella using his thumb and three remaining fingers. His eyes were pleading but she just stared back into them.

Inch by inch, Ramage lifted the pliers, his mutilated arms shaking with the effort as other muscles compensated for his ruined biceps, and let the jaws close around an upper incisor. Stella watched his knuckles whiten as he squeezed the grips to lock the jaws around the tooth.

Ramage closed his other hand over his right fist, clenched his eyes shut, took a breath and yanked downwards. A broken scream erupted from his throat as he wrenched the gleaming white tooth from the gum. Bright red blood spurted from the wound, sheeting over the broken lower teeth, his lower lip and his chin.

His hands fell to his lap, still gripping the pliers.

Finally, he looked up at Stella, his eyes sparkling with tears.

"There. I did it. Now let me go." His words were mushy as his mouth struggled to form the correct shapes.

CHAPTER THIRTY-SEVEN
Stella's Final Shot

STELLA SPOKE CALMLY and quietly.

"No. I don't think I can let you go. Lola would never forgive me."

"But you said it, that you'd let me go. You promised."

Leaning down towards him and pushing her face up close to his, she whispered. "I lied." Then she stood back up. "I hope you're hurting, *Sir* Leonard. I hope you're in so much pain you can't think straight. But before I leave you, I just want you to know that you won't even have the satisfaction that your work is going to continue. PPM is finished. I'll expose you – sorry, *them* – in the media. You'll be a footnote on some crappy Wikipedia page about domestic terrorism."

He seemed stunned. Then his lips began working again. His voice was broken and low.

"Stella, listen to me, please. We both believed in the law. In justice. We both saw it fail. And we both crossed a line." His missing tooth, and the blood, were making his tongue struggle to form the words without lisping. "You know, we're not so different, you and I. We both want justice."

The effort seemed to exhaust him, or else shock was kicking in. His head flopped back against the seat and his eyes were staring at the roof lining.

"Oh, but we are different, Judge. You see, you want justice. But me?" She closed her eyes for a second, and watched a flickering movie play in her head: a mother and daughter laughing together on a see-saw; a first day at school in a smart new uniform; a nervous boyfriend arriving to take the girl on a date; a beautiful young woman in cap and gown holding a scroll and mugging for the camera; a sweat-reddened new mother holding a newborn baby to her breast, smiling a tired but blissed-out smile. The image faded to black. Then orange. Stella opened her eyes. "Me? I want vengeance."

She used the Maoui Deba to cut a strip of material from the front of Ramage's shirt, not troubling to avoid the pallid skin beneath, then stood back and slammed the heavy door.

She opened the driver's door and pressed the switch that unlocked the petrol filler cap. She'd noticed its position during the drive with Riordan from the Café Royal to Vicky Riley's house. *Jesus, that seems so long ago.* Moments later, she was clicking the trigger on the blowtorch, having left the strip of Ramage's shirt twisted into a makeshift fuse and stuffed down the filler pipe towards the petrol tank. The tank was full, and she'd watched the fabric darken as fuel climbed up through the thin cotton.

She held the blue flame to the end of the shirt fabric. It caught instantly, and a soft yellow flame blossomed, then began creeping upwards towards the circular aperture of the filler pipe.

Stella retreated at a jog, the rucksack and the shotgun bouncing on her back, the Glock in a side pocket of her jacket.

Twenty yards from the car, she turned and stopped. She was exhausted. Not just physically, but mentally. Other-Stella seemed unaffected and was in control now.

"Good girl," she said. "Now we can watch him die."

Stella watched the flames disappear into the filler pipe.

Began counting.

Got to three.

Whoomp! The petrol tank exploded, bursting the rear bodywork of the big purple car and showering burning fuel in a circle around its rear. She could see Ramage inside the car, thrashing from side to side. His mouth was open wide and even at this distance she could see the gap where he'd pulled out the incisor.

Then Lola was by her side. She was pointing at Ramage.

"The bad man is burning, Mummy," she said.

"I know, darling."

"No, Mummy. The bad man is BURNING. Like I was."

Stella stared at Ramage's twisted expression through the glass. His mouth was wide open and the pleading expression in his eyes was that of a man beyond lying, beyond killing... beyond vengeance.

"Oh, Jesus!" She clapped her hand to her mouth to stifle a scream.

She looked down.

Pulled the Glock.

And marched back towards the car.

The fire was burning strongly now, and she couldn't get closer than ten feet. But it was close enough.

She levelled the pistol.

Aimed it.

And shot The Honourable Mister Justice Sir Leonard Ramage between the eyes.

She turned and ran, tears running through the greasy soot stains that had turned her face corpse-grey.

Lola was waiting for her.

She nodded solemn approval at her mother.

The blaze intensified, and it appeared that the interior had ignited too. The windows darkened as black fumes – *melting plastic?* – coated their inside surfaces.

Stella stayed and watched as the heat reached the point that the air inside the tyres expanded and burst them with four loud bangs. The air was rich with the acrid smell of burning rubber and plastic, and scorched leather and metal.

That expensive purple paint was blistering and charring now, and Stella could see patches of steel appearing like bone beneath burning skin. She flinched from another, harsher *boom* that battered the air as the oil in the engine and the sump boiled, then vaporised, the dramatic increase in internal pressure exploding the engine. A silvery piston blew out through the side of the car, whickering past Stella's head with a breathy whine before bouncing off the trunk of a pine tree behind her.

The blaze contained a great many colours Stella had not been expecting: turquoise, bright lemon-yellow and even an unearthly green as if ghosts had risen up and taken control of the burning car and its dead occupant.

She felt a small hand search out and hold her own. She squeezed back without looking down, knowing what was coming

Then the flames roared out from the engine bay, and when they had died down and the car was a charred hulk sitting on its rims and all Stella could hear was the plinking and popping as metal components cracked and split in the heat, her hand was empty. Lola was gone.

Stella turned away.

"It's done," she said and sat on the ground.

"*He's* done," other-Stella said. "But there are others."

"Yes. There are others. On his phone."

"We should be going. I can hear sirens."

It was true. The wails of emergency vehicles were drifting up from the main road. Hardly surprising, given the height of the column of black smoke rising above the burnt-out car. Even if Ramage's closest neighbours were a mile away, someone would have noticed the smoke signal and called the fire brigade.

Stella packed her gear, slung the shotgun over her back and trotted away towards the trees to collect the Blaser.

She'd always imagined that this would be the end. *Her* end. Deal with Ramage and then find somewhere quiet where she could join Richard and Lola. But having seen what was in the phone, she knew it wasn't the right time. She had work to do. A lot more work to do.

EPILOGUE

THE blonde waiting in line at the ferry terminal looked relaxed as she listened to the radio and waited for the column of cars to begin moving. Given that the boot of her car held three firearms and a sizeable quantity of ammunition, all of which had been acquired illegally, this was something of an achievement. She was listening to the radio. The BBC news had just revealed that Sir Leonard Ramage, a High Court judge, had been found dead at his home in Scotland after a house fire. According to the police, there had been no suspicious circumstances. She'd smiled wryly at that. She turned to the woman sitting next to her.

"A wounded police markswoman and a burnt-out Bentley with the judge inside it was unsuspicious?"

"Damage limitation," other-Stella said, looking straight ahead. "Collier must've pulled in some massive favour from the local plods. Anyway, it doesn't matter. When we come back for him, we can ask him how he managed it."

Stella turned her head at a *tap-tap* on the side window. She buzzed it down.

"Hi, there," said a middle-aged guy in an orange hi-vis jacket.

"Hi there," she said, smiling up at him. "Ticket?"

"Yes please. Just yourself travelling today?"

Stella looked to her left.

"Yes. Just me."

He checked her ticket, handed it back and smiled. "OK, Miss Stadden. Have a good trip."

GLOSSARY

A* – top grade at A-level, equivalent to US A+

A-level – exam taken in a single subject e.g. biology at the end of British secondary school education at age 18

arsey – pugnacious, argumentative, especially with authority e.g. police

banging up – sending to prison

bobbies – British uniformed police officers

boffins – scientists, technical specialists

bollocks – literally, testicles; slang expression of disgust meaning, "Oh, shit!", "rubbish"

brief – British lawyer equivalent to a US attorney, especially a trial lawyer (barrister in British legal system)

cut-and-shut – illegal practice of making one car by welding together two undamaged halves of other cars

diddling – cheating (someone out of something)

dip – pickpocket

DC – detective constable (lowest rank of detective in British police forces)

DCI – detective chief inspector

DCS – detective chief superintendent

DI – detective inspector

DIY – do-it-yourself (in the UK reserved mainly for household jobs like putting up shelves, minor electrical or plumbing jobs)

dodgy – unreliable (of people or things), not completely legal

DS – detective sergeant

DVLA – Driver and Vehicle Licensing Agency

fag – cigarette

FATACC – FAtal Traffic ACCcident

fence – someone who buys and sells stolen goods, to perform that activity

filched – stole (sneakily rather than brazenly)

FLO – family liaison officer, police officer whose job it is to comfort families of victims of crime and keep them informed of developments in the case

FMO – force medical officer

GCSE – general certificate of education, single-subject exam taken at age 16 in British secondary schools

ghosted – moved from one prison to another with no notice

ghillie – (Scottish) man or boy who helps people on a hunting, fishing or deer stalking expedition

git – horrible person

Hendon – short for Hendon Police College, Metropolitan Police Service's main training centre hob – cooktop or stovetop

holdall – carryall

home counties – the counties surrounding London: Surrey, Kent, Essex, Middlesex, Hertfordshire, Buckinghamshire, Berkshire, Sussex; as an adjective applied to accent, it means upscale/privileged

IPCC – Independent Police Complaints Commission, body responsible for overseeing the police complaints system in England and Wales

J20 – a fruit-flavoured, juice and water soft drink available in British pubs and bars

kit – equipment, to provide equipment e.g. "kit you out"

kosher – trustworthy

lairy – loud, aggressive, excitable

loadout – a soldier's personal array of weapons and equipment

M&S – Marks & Spencer, British department store

Met – The Metropolitan Police Service

muppet – stupid or dimwitted person

nicked – stolen

numpty – stupid or dimwitted person

occie health – Occupational Health, police department responsible for monitoring, protecting health of officers

PACE – Police and Criminal Evidence Act 1984, legislation governing conduct of police officers in England and Wales

pissed – drunk

plods – uniformed police officers

Portakabins – brand name for portable or mobile buildings

posh – upscale (in case of newspapers, "serious" broadsheets as opposed to tabloids)

ructions – trouble, complaints, shit hitting fan

SC&O – Specialist Crime & Operations, unit within the Metropolitan Police Service responsible for dealing with all serious crime in London

SC&O19 – specialist firearms command

screw – prison officer

SIO – senior investigating officer

Special Brew – super-strength lager (9% alcohol by volume) brewed by Carlsberg, AKA "tramp juice"

tags – simple graffiti, usually a set of initials or a nickname

toe-rag – despicable or worthless person

topped – killed

tweaking – obsessive repetition of simple act like scratching face, common to methamphetamine addicts

UDT – unarmed defence (or defensive) tactics

villains – criminals

witness nobbling – threatening or blackmailing witnesses of crimes into not testifying

WPC – woman police constable

Stella Cole will return in *Hit Back Harder*.

Andy Maslen

Andy Maslen was born in Nottingham, in the UK, home of legendary bowman Robin Hood. Andy once won a medal for archery, although he has never been locked up by the sheriff.

He has worked in a record shop, as a barman, as a door-to-door DIY products salesman and a cook in an Italian restaurant. He eventually landed a job in marketing, writing mailshots to sell business management reports. He spent ten years in the corporate world before launching a business writing agency, Sunfish, where he writes for clients including The Economist, Christie's and World Vision.

As well as the Stella Cole and Gabriel Wolfe thrillers, Andy has published five works of non-fiction, on copywriting and freelancing, with Marshall Cavendish and Kogan Page. They are all available online and in bookshops.

He lives in Wiltshire with his wife, two sons and a whippet named Merlin.

Want to know more?

To get two free books and exclusive news and offers, join Andy Maslen's Readers' Group at www.andymaslen.com.

Email Andy at andy@andymaslen.com

Follow and tweet him at @Andy_Maslen

Like his page "Andy Maslen Author" on Facebook.

<<<<>>>>

Printed in Great Britain
by Amazon